NIGHT ANGELS

Snake Pass, the Peak District: the car of Gemma Wishart, a young researcher in Russian languages, is discovered, abandoned; the driver has vanished without trace. In Hull, a woman is found battered to death in a hotel bathroom; the only clue to her identity is a card bearing the name of an escort agency notorious for its suspected trafficking in Eastern European prostitutes.

For Detective Inspector Lynne Jordan, the missing academic and the murder victim have a tenuous connection. Jordan is in charge of a police operation to stamp out the illegal trade in human flesh and Wishart was helping her with transcripts of an interview with one such woman, who has subsequently turned up dead in the Humber Estuary. But it's possible there is another, even darker, force at work, and when two more bodies turn up, Lynne is forced to conclude there may be a serial killer on the loose.

COLLINS
CRIME

NIGHT ANGELS

Danuta Reah

HarperCollins*Publishers*

Collins Crime
An imprint of HarperCollins*Publishers*
77–85 Fulham Palace Road, London W6 8JB

The Collins Crime website address is:
www.**fire**and**water**.com/crime

First published in Great Britain
in 2001 by Collins Crime

1 3 5 7 9 10 8 6 4 2

A catalogue record for this book
is available from the British Library

ISBN 0 00 711627 6

Set in Meridien and Bodoni
Typeset by Rowland Phototypesetting Ltd
Bury St Edmunds, Suffolk

Printed and bound in Great Britain by
Clays Ltd, St Ives plc

With many thanks to the people who helped me when I was writing this book. I would particularly like to thank Superintendent Steve Hicks for his advice about police procedure; Professor Malcolm Coulthard for his advice about forensic linguistics; Dr Peter French for his advice about forensic phonology; and to those people who gave me information about the lives of refugees and asylum seekers.

I would also like to thank the people who read this manuscript for me while I was working on it, particularly Sue and Penny, the e-mail writers' group; Teresa for her advice, support and encouragement; Julia for her editorial advice, and Anne.

for Alex

1

It had been a game at first. The dark BMW had pulled out of the car park behind her and followed her along the main road back into the centre of Manchester. 'Bloated plutocrat,' she'd muttered, using the epithet she'd heard Luke use when he saw someone in possession of some consumer item that he, in truth, coveted. The BMW had followed her back on to the motorway, and the driver hadn't, to her surprise, used the capacity of his car to vanish once the three lanes opened up in front of him. Or at least, she kept seeing its dark sleekness, sometimes in front, sometimes behind, but never far away. She began to look in her mirror more closely, trying to see the driver to see if it was the same car each time. The windows were tinted – pretentious git. Another Lukeism. She got the impression of fair hair – blond? white? She couldn't tell.

The light was starting to fade as she left Manchester, and by the time she got to Glossop, along the straight road, past the high stone walls, past the shops, it was dark. She slowed down as she came to the square. The street had been busy when she'd driven through that morning, the pavements full of people ducking in and out of the shops, jaywalking with that infuriating insouciance that seemed to imply it was her responsibility to get out of their way, heads turned away from her as though, having seen her, she was no longer their concern, eyes watching out for the cars and lorries coming in the other direction.

She had hated the morning drive. The worst had been the congested city centre, where she had got lost travelling too fast to read the signs, missing her lane, harassed and flustered by the horns of drivers who knew where they were going and were determined to cut the newcomer ruthlessly out of the pack.

Then, the journey back had been something to look forward to. The meeting would be over, and she would be on her way home. The roads would be quiet, and after the hassle of the city driving, she'd have the quiet of the countryside, the drive across Snake Pass and the bleak height of Coldharbour Moor, the winding road down between Kinder Scout and Bleaklow, past Doctor's Gate and then to the gentler wooded slopes past Ladybower, across the emptiness of the moors that always seemed to prolong the journey more than she expected, then the outskirts of Sheffield and she could relax.

The drive back through Manchester had been quieter, the motorway busy, but no longer crowded with impatient cars that hung on her bumper and threatened in her mirror. The long urban sprawl past Ashton and Stalybridge was almost peaceful, almost monotonous. Except . . .

She thought she'd left the BMW when she'd come off the motorway and followed the A57 signs towards Glossop. She was starting to relax, to realize that the day was over, it had gone well, she had done well, everyone would be pleased, when it was there again, a couple of cars in front. The light had gone now, and the streetlamps were lit. It was hard to make out the details, but it looked like the same car.

What was she worrying about? That someone else was following the route that she was? Loads of people must be. It was just that this was a distinctive car. *And it's kept pace with you all the way from Manchester.* It may not even be the same car. How many dark-coloured BMWs were there on the roads? *And how many did you see this morning?*

She was at the turn now, where the road signs to Sheffield directed you towards the Woodhead Pass. She ignored the sign and turned right towards Glossop and the A57, towards the lonely, narrow road so aptly named the Snake, the road that crossed the Pennines from the south-west of Sheffield.

2

After Glossop, she would be travelling through countryside until she reached the city. She seemed to have lost the BMW at last.

Now, as she slowed approaching the square, she would have been glad of some signs of life. It was drizzling, the water obscuring her windscreen. She turned on the wipers that scraped and clunked. She needed to replace the blades. The closed shops were dark and unwelcoming. A takeaway shone yellow light on to the pavement, but it looked deserted. There must be people in the pubs, but the rain was keeping them off the streets. The empty pavements reminded her of long winter nights to come, the gleam of the wet flagstones made her shiver.

She peered through the darkness, looking for a phone box. She'd half promised to go round to Luke's when she got back. She needed to contact him, let him know she was running late and probably wouldn't make it. Now the tension of city driving didn't seem so bad. It was the dark night on the tops, the lonely drive through that bleak landscape and then the long, winding road back towards Sheffield that disturbed her. Suddenly, she hated the prospect of driving across the hills on a winter's night, though these days, the winters were rarely cold enough to close the high roads. She could remember drives from her childhood, crossing the Pennines with her father, driving between high banks of snow, trusting the route the plough had pushed through the drifts.

There. She knew there were phone boxes in the square. She pulled up on to the cobbles, and hurried across, cursing as her foot slipped into a puddle and her shoe filled up with icy water. Limping, feeling her toes start to chafe, she pulled open the door of the booth and fished around in her purse for some change. As she listened to the ringing phone, she checked her watch. Seven-thirty, at least another hour before she would be home, then a large gin, no, a whisky mac, a vice Luke had introduced her to at Christmas, then into a hot, foamy bath, and then bed. She could almost taste the slight burn of ginger on her lips.

The phone was still ringing, then she heard the click, and

Luke's voice: 'Leave a message and I might get back to you.' The answering machine. She felt a stab of – what? – anger? with him for not being there when she needed to talk to him. *That's not fair!* She heard the beep, and said quickly, 'Hello, I'm in Glossop. It's about half past. I got held up so I'm going straight home. I'll be there in about an hour.' She waited to see if he would pick the receiver up – sometimes he waited to see who was calling – but there was no reply. 'See you tomorrow,' she said, her voice sounding small and rather bleak.

She hadn't really needed to talk to him, she told herself as she ran back to the car. The thing was to leave the message. Except she'd relied on talking to him, just to have that couple of minutes' communication before she began the climb on to the dark tops to face that lonely journey across Snake Pass. She put the key in the ignition, then stopped. A cigarette. She'd have a cigarette. She was still stressed after a hard day. It would make sense to take five minutes to relax before the next stage of her drive. In fact – she looked round quickly, but the road was still empty – in fact she could do better than that. She fished around in her bag for the little pouch, for the small roll-up Luke had given her the previous evening. Had she brought it? *Yes!*

She sat quietly, breathing in the smoke, holding it in her lungs and slowly releasing it. She felt herself relax and her dread of the lonely drive receded. Her head began to feel pleasantly giddy, and the light from the streetlamps shattered and danced in the falling rain. Enough. She had a drive ahead of her. She adjusted her seat and fastened the belt. She fiddled with the mirror before she realized that she was just postponing the inevitable. Her anxiety had turned to somnolence, and she would happily have stayed where she was, enjoying the cocooned silence of the car. The sooner she started, the better.

She turned the key in the ignition, and put the car into gear. She glanced in the mirror, let the clutch in and moved off. A car pulled out behind her and followed her along the road. She wasn't the only person heading over the Snake that night. Car lights behind her would be some comfort, make her feel less as though the world had ended and she was the last survivor of some catastrophe. But as they travelled along the last straight before the road began its climb, the car behind pulled out and overtook her smoothly and effortlessly. *Bloated plutocrat.* She watched with detachment as the tail-lights disappeared, the afterlight dancing in the darkness ahead. She was more stoned than she'd realized. She'd better be careful.

She shivered and turned up the heater. The air roared and blew, bringing the smell of the engine into the car. Her feet were hot, but the rest of her was chilled by the cold air that seeped in through the loose-fitting windows and the rattling door.

She was climbing up the hill outside Glossop now. The road curved to the right past a house that glowed a warm light on to the road, then turned left, rock on one side, a drop on the other. The climb was long and steep, and she changed down to third, then second. The engine roared. There were white wisps in the air in front of her, and suddenly she was into a bank of fog, her lights reflecting in a white glare. She slowed down, peering ahead, wiping the windscreen futilely, trying to see. Then it was clear again, the lights shining on to the wet road, illuminating the rocks, the moorland grass, a sheep tucked into a lee of stone. She was nearly at the top, and the road flattened out. There was just wilderness round her now, flat peat and grassy tussocks and bog. Her headlights reflected on water, sullen pools in the dark ground. Soon, the road would start dropping down, past Doctor's Gate, between Bleaklow and Kinder Scout, down between the thick trees, and on through the empty night.

She was in a half-daze as the road disappeared under the wheels. *Home soon, home soon.* It was a soothing mantra in her head. She thought about Luke and wondered if she should phone him when she got back. It had been good these past few months. She was going to miss him . . . Lights were dancing and drifting in the darkness and she watched them

5

with incurious interest. The car swerved, and she jerked back to concentration. The smoke had been a bad idea. Grimly, she wound down the window, flinching as the rain spattered on her face and arm. Lights ahead? She remembered the car that had passed her as she drove out of Glossop. *Bloated plutocrat* . . . She tried to get a picture of it in her mind. Dark, it had been dark . . .

Without warning, her engine cut out. What the . . . ? She pumped the accelerator. Nothing. She looked at the petrol gauge. Still half full. She'd topped it up that morning. The car rolled forward, slowing. She pulled into the side of the road as the car rolled to a halt. How . . . ? Her headlights shone on to falling rain and blackness. She was cold. Her fingers were clumsy as she fumbled for the key in the ignition. The starting motor whined, but the engine was dead. She tried again, and saw the headlights begin to fade. Quickly, she turned them off. The battery was old. She should have turned them off at once.

She sat there, staring into the darkness, hearing the rain hitting the roof and doors. The wind had a thin, whistling sound. Then she saw the lights ahead. Suddenly, out of the darkness, two lights coming towards her. Like a car, only . . . Reversing lights, a car was reversing towards her, fast. A big car, a dark car? She turned the key in the ignition again, and again as the whine of the starting motor faded to nothing.

The engine was dead.

2

Sheffield, Friday, 7.30 a.m.

It was a cold morning. The rain of the night before had frozen on the ground, leaving the pavements shiny and treacherous underfoot. Puddles were patterns of white frost where the ice had shattered. The sky was clear as the sun came up.

Roz shivered as she got out of the car and the cold caught her. She saw her breath cloud in the air. The car park was deserted this early in the day, and she was able to park directly in front of the Arts Tower. She craned her neck to look up the height of the building. On windy days, when the clouds were moving, she would sometimes stand like this and watch until it looked as though the building was racing across the sky and the clouds were still. She pulled her briefcase off the back seat and locked the car door.

She checked her watch. Seven-thirty. Plenty of time. She ran the arrangements for the meeting through her mind. Roz was the senior research assistant for the Law and Language Group, a small, recently established team in the university, headed by Joanna Grey. When Roz had come to Sheffield a year ago, she had joined the linguistics department, hoping to pursue her research into interviewing techniques. Joanna, ambitious and dynamic, had encouraged her to develop her skills in computer modelling and analysis of language and had then guided her into the field of forensic linguistics, an expanding area that looked at all aspects of language in its legal context.

As she settled in to the new department, Roz had realized that Joanna was carefully building a team. Roz had done her early research into the subtexts of interviews, the meanings that lay below the surface of candidates' responses in these situations, and Gemma Wishart, a recent Joanna appointee, specialized in the English of Eastern European speakers.

Joanna had staged her coup with care. She had got the support of her current Head of Department, Peter Cauldwell, for two grant applications, one to analyse police interview tapes with a view to designing training material and software, and the other to develop systems of analysis that would identify the regional and national origins of asylum seekers. At the same time, she had pursued her aim to set up an independent research group with the various boards and committees within the university who were, at this time, all for the idea of self-funding groups.

Once she had got her money, Joanna had made her bid for freedom and set up the Law and Language Group as an independent research team. She had a year to prove that the group could be an income-generating unit. The grant money kept them afloat, and they also kept up the routine legal work that had come Joanna's way for years: the document analysis, the analysis of witness statements, the retrieval of documents from computers, work with audio and video tape.

Today's meeting was the first of a series with the people who could, if they withdrew their support, put an end to the project tomorrow. Everything had to run with the smoothness, efficiency and effectiveness of a well-written piece of programming. These were the money people. They didn't want to know about philosophies of pure research, or the abstractions that the true research scientist could chase for months and years. They wanted to know that Joanna and her team could deliver.

Joanna's timetable had run into an unavoidable snarl-up. She had had a meeting the day before, and was relying on Roz to get everything organized. 'I'll be in well before nine,' she'd said, before she left. 'I'll pick Gemma up on my way in. Just make sure everything's set up.' Roz could feel the slight adrenaline tension of responsibility as she pushed through the main doors. The porter greeted her as the doors closed behind her. 'Morning, Dr Bishop.'

She nodded, a bit abstracted. 'Morning, Dave.' The familiar smell of the university closed round her. She usually climbed the stairs to her department – her concession to keeping fit – but this morning she was wearing her meeting gear, and her shoes weren't designed for stair-climbing. She ignored the lift and stepped on to the platform of the endlessly moving paternoster elevator, drawn by its regular clunk, clunk. She was carried up past the blank wall between the ground floor and the mezzanine, the floor numbers appearing on the wall above her head, gliding past her and opening up on to the lobbies which then sank away under her feet as she was carried higher and higher.

She stepped off the moving platform as it reached her floor, timing her exit with the expertise of one familiar with its regular use. The department was silent apart from the distant whirr of a floor polisher as the cleaners wound up their early-morning routine. The corridors were dark, their shadowed length interrupted by swing doors. She unlocked the door of her office, dumped her bag and got out the folder of material that she and Joanna had prepared for the meeting. She sorted out her notes for the presentation, read through them and ran the details of the morning through her mind, making sure that she had covered everything. Success, as Joanna kept telling her, was not just a matter of showing the right action and the right figures; it was a matter of presenting yourself as a success. This was why Joanna's suit came from Mulberry; this was why she had dipped into her own pocket to buy the porcelain coffee cups, the good coffee.

Roz looked at her watch. Nearly eight o'clock. She needed to check the meeting room, make sure that Luke had done his bit and all the equipment was set up and working, and she needed to make sure that coffee had been ordered and would arrive on time. She locked the door of her office behind her, her mind running through and through the things she needed to do. The corridor where they were based ran round the lift shaft and the stairwell. It was empty, the lights dim and the office doors locked. She paused as she left her own office, looking at the sign on the door: DR ROSALIND BISHOP, RESEARCH ASSISTANT. Next door, Joanna's office: DR JOANNA GREY, HEAD OF DIVISION. Then the double doors with the exit to the stairway before the turn. Joanna had been very clear about the arrangement of the rooms. She and Roz next door to each other on one arm of the L, forming what she called her executive corridor, establishing, she explained, just that important physical distance between the two of them and Gemma, their post-doctoral research officer, Luke, the technician, and the new research assistants, whoever they may be. Roz had regretted that loyalty to Joanna had stopped her from passing that one on to Luke. He would have enjoyed it.

Someone was on the corridor ahead of her, walking away from her, but the lights were off and it was too dark to make out any detail. It was too tall for Joanna. Whoever it was disappeared round the corner towards Gemma's room. She pushed the second set of doors open. Either her eyes were playing tricks and it was Joanna – or possibly Gemma, she amended – or else it was someone who shouldn't be in the section at this time.

The corridor was empty by the time she was round the corner. Whoever it was must have gone round the next corner heading back towards the lifts. She shrugged, dismissing the matter. She was standing outside the door of Gemma's room now. She looked at the piece of paper tacked on to the wood: DR GEMMA WISHART. She frowned. Gemma's contract ran for a full year. What would it cost the department to keep its signs up to date? Though there were the new research assistants coming, and Joanna had plans to put one of them in the same room as Gemma. Perhaps she planned anonymous labelling for the door – RESEARCH ASSISTANTS. She went on down the corridor.

Next to Gemma's room was the meeting room. Roz unlocked the door and looked in. Everything was set up. The blinds were angled to keep the morning sun off the screen, the tables were together with the right number of chairs – a small detail but it was the details that Joanna would have her eye on, that gave the sense of efficiency she wanted the group to project – and the overhead projector stood ready by Joanna's chair at the head of the table. She pressed the switch and a square of light appeared dead centre on the screen. Luke must have stayed late last night and set the room up.

She checked her watch again. It was nearly ten past eight. Joanna should have been in by now. They'd agreed to get together before the meeting and go over some of the main points. She was outside the computer room now, the end of Joanna's domain. Roz always called the computer room 'Luke's room', because it was where he was based – where he had been based before he'd been transferred to Joanna's newly formed group – and where he was usually to be found. There wasn't space for a separate technicians' room. Joanna wasn't happy with the proprietorial attitude Luke took towards this space. She had talked to Roz about her plans to base the new research assistants in here for some of the time, to take away his exclusivity. Luke was the only member of the team Joanna hadn't chosen herself and she made no secret of the fact that she didn't like him, and wouldn't be sorry if he left. 'I want people with first-class minds,' she had said to Roz once. Luke, with his 2.1, apparently didn't come into this category, no matter how good a software engineer he was. Joanna had her blind spots.

She pushed the door open, and the fragrance of coffee drifted into the corridor. Luke was there, sitting at one of the machines, his chair pushed back, his foot up on the rungs of another, a mug in his hand. He hit a button on the keyboard as she came through the door, and the screen darkened. Then he swivelled round in his chair. 'Roz,' he said. His voice was neutral. She and Luke were wary with each other these days.

'Hi. Thanks for getting everything set up.' For all his insouciance, Luke was efficient.

He didn't respond to that, but just said, 'You want to run through the slides?'

'Are they all set up like we had them yesterday?' He

nodded and put his mug down on the desk. He was wearing jeans and trainers. That was going to go down a bomb with Joanna. She wondered if he ever thought about compromising, just a bit, to keep Joanna happy. 'Just show me the first one, the one we changed.'

He tapped instructions into the machine, and she looked at the slide showing the group's income projections for the first two years. It looked impressive now that the European money that Joanna had managed to get against all the odds was highlighted. It *was* impressive. 'That's great,' she said.

Luke was still looking at the screen. 'We need a group logo,' he said.

Roz gave him a quick look. Luke had no time for concepts like corporate identity, mission statements, quality procedures, the kind of management speak that Joanna was so keen on. His face was expressionless. She matched his air of bland imperturbability. 'Yes,' she said. 'Yes, perhaps you could design one.'

Luke's mouth twitched as she caught his eye, and then they were both laughing. 'Thanks, Luke,' she said again, meaning it. She knew that everything for the meeting would work without a hitch. He'd have made sure. 'I'll see you later.' She checked her watch as she headed back towards Joanna's room to see if she had arrived yet.

Eight forty-five. Joanna should definitely be here. She began to feel worried. It wasn't like Joanna to be late, especially not for something as important as this meeting. She felt the tension in her stomach and made herself relax. She headed back along the corridor, through the swing doors. She paused by Gemma's door, then unlocked it and looked in. It was empty, the desk clinically neat, the in- and out-trays empty. A pattern drifted across the monitor. The screensaver. The computer had been left on. It should have been switched off. Joanna would go spare if she saw it. Anyone could get access to Gemma's data with the machine on and unattended like that. She shut it down and looked at her watch again. It was eight-fifty. She and Joanna were supposed to get together at nine and run through the agenda, checking for last-minute hitches. Peter Cauldwell would be looking out for a chance to put the knife in. The meeting started at nine-thirty. She felt an unaccustomed panic grip her.

Damn! She took a couple of deep breaths. She ignored the sinking feeling in her stomach, and pulled her mind back from rehearsing disasters. There was no point in worrying about something going wrong, because nothing would go wrong. Joanna would be here. If there were any problems, she would have let Roz know. Repeating this as a kind of mantra, she made herself relax.

The air sparkled with frost. Out beyond the university, out to the west of the city, the Peak District was bathed in the light of the winter sun. Along the top of Stanage Edge, grey millstone grit against the dark peat and the dead bracken, ice glinted, making the ground treacherous. Ladybirds were suspended in the ice, red and black, a frozen glimpse of summer. The road cut across the edge, went past the dams at Ladybower and Derwent, and began the climb to the pass over the hills. The heights of Kinder Scout and Bleaklow looked almost mellow in the light, their deceptive tops inviting the casual walker to wander just that bit too far, just that bit too high.

The traffic was slow on the road to the Snake Pass. It was an uneasy combination of business traffic coming from the west side of Sheffield and leisure travellers who wanted to meander, enjoy the scenery, park and sometimes walk. As the road climbed higher, the traffic became lighter as the landscape became more bleak, the hills more threatening. Walkers who had come to climb Bleaklow from Doctor's Gate noticed a car pulled off the road into the culvert. An old Fiesta, red, rather battered. Maybe it belonged to an enthusiastic walker, out on the tops early.

Hull, Friday, 8.00 a.m.
The clouds were low and dark, with the threat of rain or snow. The traffic was heavier now, as the rush hour began to build up. The Blenheim Hotel was at the cheaper end of

the market, one of a row of Edwardian terraces, converted from residential use years ago. The hotel was a Tardis, small and narrow on the outside, endless and labyrinthine inside. Every door led to another door. Every staircase led to another staircase. The corridors got no daylight, and the lighting was dim. This may have been accidental, or it may have been for reasons of economy, but it was fortuitous. The dim lighting concealed, to a certain degree, the worn, stained carpet, the places on the walls where the paint was cracked or dirty, where the paper was starting to peel.

The cleaner was already at work as the last visitors were finishing breakfast in the downstairs room that doubled as a bar. The smell of beer and cigarettes greeted the breakfasters as they came down the narrow flight of stairs from the entrance hall, following the signs that said 'dining room'. The stairs were too narrow to be a regular flight, were probably the remainder of the back stairs from the days when the hotel had been a private house, from the days when the area had been prosperous, residential and middle class.

Some of the breakfasters had undoubtedly spent the evening before in this room, leaning against the bar or fighting their way through the crowds, and the smell of the beer triggered queasy memories.

Rows of individual cereal packets stood on the bar, with jugs of very orange orange juice. The waitress came to the table and took the orders that arrived in the form of pink bacon, flabby on the plate with a slightly rancid smell, translucent eggs, sausages that oozed as the knife went in. The smell of frying temporarily overlaid the smell of beer and tobacco.

Mary's husband had phoned in. She'd been in an accident the night before. 'Been drinking, I shouldn't wonder,' Mrs Fry had said to Anna. 'You'll have to manage on your own for this morning.' Her voice was impatient. Anna always managed. She was young, and when you needed work the way she needed work, you managed. Mrs Fry knew that. So now Anna was working on her own, and already the old witch was hassling her, saying she wasn't fast enough, the

14

rooms weren't going to be done in time, she'd have to speed up. She muttered Mrs Fry's litany to herself – 'Haven't you got any further, Anna? Hurry it up, Anna!' – as she worked her way along the passage. She was at the second back stair-case now. There were three rooms in this part of the hotel – a different part from the one containing the bar and res-taurant. This was at the back of the house and opened on to a garden, more a yard, where the bins were stored, where a few shrubs fought against the litter that was thrown down from the alley that ran behind the terrace. She picked up the cylinder cleaner and carried it down the narrow stairs, knocking it against the walls as she went. There was always the sour smell of damp down here, faint but unmistakable.

The first room was a shambles. Anna screwed her face up. The damp was overlain by a smell of stale alcohol and cigarettes, sweat and old perfume. An empty bottle – whisky – was on the floor by the wastebasket, and a glass with a cigarette end dissolving in the bottom was on the floor by the bed. The ashtray was full. There was a used condom on the bedside table. She pulled new gloves out of the pocket of her overalls. She brought her own gloves these days. Mrs Fry always said, 'Oh yes,' when Anna said that she needed new gloves, but somehow the supplies were never replen-ished often enough. She switched on the bathroom light. Better to know the worst.

She dumped the used sheets and towels on to the floor of the corridor. She couldn't get the laundry cart down the narrow stairs. She would have to gather the pile up in her arms and carry it. She looked at the towels and made a grimace of distaste. The second room was better. Its damp smell was overlaid with the smell of soap and toothpaste. The bed was disordered, as though the occupant had leapt up in haste, scattering the sheets and thin quilt. There was talcum powder on the carpet, and the print of a bare foot. But the bathroom was respectable, the toilet flushed, the bath mat damp, the towels neatly folded on the rail.

She checked her watch. She had nearly caught up. The rooms were supposed to be done by ten, or Mrs Fry would

15

have something, a lot to say about it. She wouldn't get rid of Anna though. Anna had managed to keep this job for five months. She didn't complain to anyone about minimum wages. She was reliable. She'd never had a day off in the time she'd worked for the hotel. She was never late. She kept out of the way of the guests. She always finished her work and she always did it properly. People never complained about the rooms that Anna had cleaned.

Down here in the basement, she could have a cigarette. She could have a break. The extractor fan in the windowless bathroom was roaring away. She reached into the pocket of her overalls and took out her cigarettes and lighter. Five cigarettes a day. Her ration. She lit up, leaning against the bathroom wall, blowing the smoke towards the fan. She hated the smell of smoke.

The last room in the basement was cramped and uncomfortable. She pushed past the closed bathroom door, stumbling on something, and ran her eye over the room. The wardrobe was small, crammed against the narrow back wall next to the French windows that opened on to the yard. The window nets were damp with condensation and stuck to the glass. The dressing table was against the long wall opposite the bed. The gap was so narrow, Anna had to turn sideways to squeeze between them. The room was ... She looked round. The bed appeared unused, but there were clothes thrown across it – a woman's jacket and skirt. A shoe lay in front of the French windows. The other shoe was in the narrow entrance way. She'd trodden on it on her way in. The occupant must not have checked out yet.

Anna stripped the bed and dumped the pile of clean linen in the middle of the mattress. Unused or not, the beds had to be changed. She picked up the shoes and put them in the bottom of the wardrobe, put the skirt and jacket on a hanger. Maybe this occupant was one of the rare visitors who stayed for more than one night. The room was cold, unlike the stuffy dampness of the other basement rooms. A line of cold seemed to run down her back, and a draught blew around her ankles. She buttoned her cardigan up round her neck.

16

The vacuum cleaner was plugged in from the corridor. She switched it on, but the poor suction told her the bag would have to be changed. More time. She dumped the full bag in her cleaning tray and, with the speed of familiarity, fitted a new one and gave the small expanse of carpet a thorough clean. She ran her cloth over the skirting boards and over the surfaces of the dressing table and the small bedside table. The ashtray was unused, and the tea tray untouched. Something sticky smeared under her cloth, leaving a brown stain. She rubbed it clean. She felt dissatisfied with the room, as though she'd forgotten something important. She looked at the nets sticking to the window, and decided to wipe the condensation off. It might get rid of that ... *that was it!* – that slight taint in the air that made the room feel unclean. For a moment, she thought she smelt burning. A sense of unease, a sickness, began to stir in her stomach.

The window moved as she wiped it, and she realized that it was open slightly. Someone had opened the French windows and left them ajar. That was why it was so cold in here. Why would someone do that? Running away rather than pay the bill? And leave a good suit and a pair of shoes? Someone who wanted fresh air? And leave the room so insecure? She shook her head, puzzled. If there was one thing she'd learnt as a hotel cleaner, it was that you couldn't explain the way people behaved away from home. She pulled the windows shut, slamming them to lock the bar. The smell was probably coming from the bins in the yard. It would go now that the windows were closed.

Just the bathroom to do now. Anna had left the bathroom until last. She looked at the white painted door off the narrow entrance lobby to the room. It was shut tight. Guests usually left the bathroom door open, the steam drifting out into the room with the smell of soap and shampoo, or less pleasant smells; towels carelessly dumped on beds, on carpets, on chairs. She put her fingers on the door handle. She didn't want to open that door. *Stupid fancies!* She pressed the handle down and pushed. The door stayed shut. She frowned.

17

Locked? Now she came to listen, there was a trickling sound and the sound of water running in the pipes. She knocked. Silence. Surely, if there was someone in the bathroom, they would have come into the room and told her to leave the cleaning until the room was free. She checked her watch. She had lost all the time she had gained earlier. She was running late again. Mrs Fry would be down shortly to find out what she was doing. The thought galvanized her, and she pressed the handle down harder and pushed against the door. This door stuck sometimes, she remembered now. But there was a feeling of sick anticipation in her stomach. Something in her mind was trying to make her turn away. *Don't look! Forget!*

The door resisted for a moment then flew open. She was suddenly in the bathroom, in the hot, steamy air, and the smell was there, heavy like the smell in the meat market at home. Sour. Cloying. Unclean.

The drip, drip of the water as she creeps through the bushes. The smell of burning is still in the air, but it is a smell of old burning. Ashes, the remains of a fire. Fires mean warmth and parties and music and voices. Voices! She stops, listens. Silence, just the dripping of the water. But coming through the smell of burning is something else, heavy, sweet, rotten.

She can see the house, now. It's just outside the village, on the edge of the trees. The burning must come from the village, of course, not from her house. She peers through the leaves. She listens for the sound of her mother calling to the children, or her father laughing with the men as they took a break. They'll all be worried. She's been gone, what, two nights? Three nights? 'I'm back . . .' she whispers, looking through the leaves at the shell of her house, at the bundle lying half in and half out of the door, tiny on the ground, with the sole of a shoe pointing towards the bushes where she is hiding. The rain must have put the fire out. She can see the water dripping from the eaves and the remains of the roof.

Her foot squashed in something and she looked down, recoiling instinctively, mechanically wiping her foot on the carpet. The floor was wet. Something dripped on to her neck and she jumped, turning round. Condensation was dripping from the ceiling, and the walls glistened. A steady trickling sound came from the bath as though the shower was running, just a bit, turned down very low. The shower curtain was pulled across, pink and translucent. The water ran and trickled, gurgling in the pipes, making the plughole of the basin echo.

Someone was in the shower. That was her first thought. Someone in the shower who ran the water in a slow dribble, someone who ignored the sound of movement, the vacuum, the banging and knocking attendant on cleaning. Someone . . . *The broken door in front of her now. Through there, mother, father, the table where they all sit to eat and talk and the little ones running around and the smell of* . . . Sour, rotten.

Slowly, she put out her hand and pulled the curtain back.

She thought it would be her mother.

The woman – it was a woman, she could still tell that – was slumped in the bath. She looked . . . broken, like a toy that had been dropped and crushed. Her face – *Krisha* . . . ? – her face, *like Krisha's doll, they'd trodden on Krisha's doll and the doll's face was distorted and smashed, the eye sockets and eyes not quite aligned, the mouth cracked into a feral grin. Krisha's doll!* Water dripped from the woman's hair as it trickled from the shower. *Ribbons. It's like* . . . Her first thought was that there should have been more blood. Then her legs felt weak and she was cold all over. Her mouth was full of saliva and she was dizzy. She couldn't stop herself. Her knees thumped on to the floor. She felt the wetness on the floor seeping through her stockings on to her legs. Her hands slipped on the side of the bath, trying to keep her from falling down into it. *Don't let it touch me!*

She pulled herself to her feet, turned on the basin tap full blast, splashing water on to her hands and face, on to the floor again and again and then again, trying to make the place clean, restore order, do her job. She pulled the towel off the rack, felt wetness on her hands, let it fall to the floor. There was something floating in the toilet. She flushed it, and again, and again. Her eyes jumped frantically from towel rail, to basin, to tooth glasses, to the bath . . . *No!* She stared at the floor, concentrated on the pattern of cracks on the tiles.

There was something on the floor between the lavatory pan and the bath. A piece of paper, no, a card, like a business card, stuck to the wet floor, something that could have fallen out of the pocket of someone sitting there, sitting next to the bath, maybe talking to the person who was having a shower, who was . . . *the sound of the water as she creeps through the bushes* . . . There was a stench of burning in her nostrils. Her stomach heaved. Litter on the floor. Mechanically, she reached down, picked up the card and looked at it.

Then she was back in the bedroom, her legs shaking, holding on to the door, the walls, anything to help her get out of there. She had to find someone, she had to get help, she had to . . . had to . . .

She had to think.

She opened the vacuum cleaner and took out the bag she'd put in before she'd cleaned the room. The old bag was full to bursting, but she managed to get it back in without tearing it or spilling too much of the contents. She refolded the new bag and pushed it down into her overall pockets. Her hands were shaking. She scooped up the bedding and the towels and carried them to where the laundry basket was waiting at the top of the basement stairs. She listened. The distant sound of traffic. Footsteps along the corridor overhead. Quick. She had to be quick.

She pulled out some of the bedding and shoved her load down into the bottom of the basket. She piled the dirty linen on top, keeping back a set of sheets and towels. Back down the stairs. She dumped the linen on to the floor where the sheets she had moved had been minutes before. *Shut the door or leave it open?* Her bag and coat were in the back kitchen. She dithered for a moment, then stepped back into the room, closing the door behind her. She went over to the French windows and pushed down the bar. She wouldn't be able to close it behind her. Then she was in the yard, past the bins, along the road to the next yard, past another set of bins to the back door. She pushed it open. No one. She grabbed her coat and her shopping bag, and, not waiting to change into her outdoor shoes, hurried down the road towards the bus stop. She flagged down the first bus that came along, and didn't relax until it was around the corner and heading along the main road.

The woman's face formed itself in her mind. And Krisha's doll, smashed on the floor. *Soldiers' toys*. The air seemed to smell of old burning. *Got to run, got to run.*

3

Despite its importance, Roz found the meeting tedious. She was interested in the research side of their work, and though the funding was crucial, she didn't share Joanna's taste for the politics and the dealing that the money side generated. She suppressed a yawn and glanced across at Luke, who was leaning back in his chair, his eyes veiled, occasionally jotting something on the notepad in front of him. He looked distracted as well. Roz watched Joanna do her stuff, outlining the financial and the research projections for the team, putting forward her staffing proposals, neatly turning away from anything that strayed into areas where the picture was less rosy. Joanna was good. She was better than good. No one, watching her now, would believe the state of tension she had been in before the meeting started. She had arrived at five to nine, held up because she had been round to pick Gemma up – something they had agreed on Wednesday, apparently, so that Gemma could brief Joanna on the outcome of her trip to Manchester before the main meeting started. Only Gemma hadn't answered her door, and Joanna had wasted time trying to rouse her before she had concluded that Gemma must not be there.

Roz frowned. It wasn't like Gemma to be unreliable. What was worse, she hadn't phoned but had sent an e-mail some time the previous evening. Joanna had found it when she checked her mail before the meeting to see if any last-minute changes or apologies had arrived.

Please accept my apologies for tomorrow's meeting. The car has broken down and I will have to stay in Manchester tonight. I will contact you as soon as I get back to Sheffield.

Gemma

Joanna had gone thermonuclear. Then she had put it all away for later consideration and taken Roz briskly through the meeting strategies.

Roz let the voice of the representative from the university grants committee fade into a background drone as she studied the other delegates. There was Peter Cauldwell, Joanna's nominal line manager, who was watching her with a sceptical smile. Whatever Joanna proposed, Cauldwell would oppose. He and Joanna had clashed too many times in the past to be a good team now. One of Joanna's more urgent plans was to take her group out of Cauldwell's sphere of influence as soon as she could. There was the grants committee representative. He was the one who could stop Joanna now, today, if she failed to convince him. There was the representative from the Academic Board, whose support was crucial in these early stages, and there was a representative from the vice-chancellor's office. As Luke had said the other day, 'All the university brass out to watch Grey nail Cauldwell's scrotum to the table.' She caught his eye across the table, and felt a childish impulse to laugh.

Peter Cauldwell was speaking now, his voice that of modulated reason as he explained why Joanna's plan for autonomy for the Law and Language Group was a waste of time and of valuable resources. 'There are small departments all over the country who pick up the forensic work,' he said. 'And there are a few private firms. We're an academic institution. We need to use this money' – the grant money Joanna had managed to get for the group – 'to build on the research we've carried out so far. I've no desire to end our forensic work, but I think we can accommodate it within our existing structures.'

Joanna smiled, and Roz again caught Luke's eye. Under

the guise of shifting his position, he ran his finger across his throat. Joanna began running her presentation slides, talking briefly to each one as she did so, demonstrating the amount of money and support she had managed to attract in the last six months. Her charts had been put together so that the income Cauldwell's group attracted overall was also shown, apparently incidental to the figures that Joanna wanted the meeting to study. Her small team had, according to the chart she was using, attracted more grant-based and commercial funding than Cauldwell's much larger team had managed in a year. Roz knew that these figures didn't show the true picture. Peter Cauldwell's group had been involved with a long-term project that was coming to an end, and the new grants that were coming in were either not yet available or were quietly sidelined into different compartments to ensure that the staffing and equipment budgets were properly supported. Cauldwell, like all good heads of department, was a genius at stretching the funding he got to the maximum. But on paper, his figures looked bad, and Joanna knew it.

By one, it was all over. Roz, headed back towards her office, was waylaid by Joanna who was looking pleased. As she had every right to, Roz thought. Joanna's main problem now was likely to be a knife in the back. She remembered Cauldwell's sour face. He wasn't going to forgive Joanna – forgive any of them – soon.

'It went well. I think I've put paid to Cauldwell's hash,' Joanna said cheerfully. 'We'll get our extra staffing now, or I'll know why.' She looked into the distance, calculating. 'We'll need more space. This is just the start.' Her eyes focused sharply on Roz. 'What about Gemma?' she said.

Roz was used to Joanna's abrupt subject switches. She wondered why Joanna should expect her to know any more about Gemma's absence than Joanna herself did. 'I've no idea,' she said. 'Luke might know something.'

Joanna maintained her intense stare. Roz, used to this quirk, waited for Joanna to formulate her response. 'Luke?'

Roz sighed. Surely Joanna must at least be aware that *some* kind of relationship existed between Luke and Gemma.

Gemma, academically brilliant, was quiet and self-contained away from her computer and her books. She had come to Sheffield after a spell at a Russian university, and Roz sometimes got the feeling that Gemma – for all she produced work of a high standard – was not committed to what she was doing, had ambitions in other directions. And then she had taken up with Luke.

Though she tried not to, Roz had minded. She and Luke had been friends from the time Roz had first arrived in Sheffield a year ago. They were both unattached, both – apparently – avoiding serious commitment. They had a shared taste in clubbing, in dancing, in music. Luke could be reckless, fuelling his tendency to wild behaviour with bouts of drinking, and his occasional nihilism appealed to something in her. It had been a friendship she valued. And then a few months ago, under the influence of a bit too much music, a bit too much wine, they'd spent a night together, an intimacy that they had always avoided, never talked about, and one she had shied away from afterwards. There had been an awkwardness between them after that. Roz's promotion to Joanna's second-in-command had put a further strain on the friendship, and once he became involved with Gemma it had dwindled to almost nothing.

Joanna was still looking at her blankly. Roz shook her head. 'I'll see if Luke knows any more,' she said. Joanna thought about this in silence, then moved on to discuss outstanding projects. Something flickered in Roz's mind, and she made a note to go and check Gemma's schedule. There was something . . . She shelved it and listened to Joanna as she wound up.

'. . . and then there's the report for the appeal court, and that's it.' She checked her watch. 'Peter Cauldwell wants to see me.' She raised an eyebrow at Roz in unspoken comment. 'I'm meeting him in half an hour.'

Reports! That was what had flashed into Roz's mind. Gemma's analysis of that tape they'd got from the Hull Police. Gemma had said that she was going to phone her report through today, but she'd wanted to discuss something with

25

Roz first. Roz frowned. She couldn't think what kind of problem Gemma might have had with it. It had seemed a fairly straightforward request, though the tape itself had been . . . odd. The report would probably be on Gemma's desk. She could check it to see if there were any obvious problems, then phone it through herself. Gemma could finish off the hard copy and get it in the post over the weekend. If the report wasn't there . . . Then Joanna would have to know.

Luke, or Gemma's report? The report had priority. She turned back down the corridor to Gemma's room and switched on the computer. She knew the password – she and Gemma often needed access to each other's files. She scrolled through the list of documents: acoustic profiles; fundamental frequency analysis of . . . There it was: draftreport hull. Roz opened the file and went over the details, reminding herself of what exactly Gemma had been doing. The tape from Hull was a police interview with a woman who was possibly Eastern European. It had been sent to Gemma to try to ascertain the geographic origins of the woman more closely.

Roz flicked through the correspondence. The officer who had contacted Gemma was a Detective Inspector Lynne Jordan. The request that came with the tape was clear. DI Jordan wanted to know where the woman, who was clearly not a native speaker of English, came from. There was very little information about the tape itself.

Roz had listened to the tape with Gemma, and had found the words, which were halting and difficult to decipher, disturbing. She wondered what had happened to the woman whose voice was on the tape, why DI Jordan was not able to ask her directly where she came from. Was she pretending to come from somewhere else, an EU country, something that would allow her to stay in the UK? Had she run away? Had she already been deported? Had she died?

He [they?] hit . . . I say no, he [they?] make, he . . .

Not Roz's business. She hit the print button and skimmed through Gemma's draft report on the screen. When the report had printed, she read it in more detail. It was typical

26

Gemma; very thorough, very clear, and, as far as Roz could see, complete. Maybe Gemma had sorted the problem out, whatever it was. She wondered what Gemma had wanted to discuss with her. She tapped the report against her chin, thinking. Wednesday afternoon, late, Gemma had come to Roz's room to say that she had to go to Manchester in Joanna's place the following day. 'Joanna's only just told me. She said you'd fill me in on the details.' She'd looked annoyed. She'd dropped her bag, fumbling for her notes, then the pen she was trying to uncap had flown out of her hand across the room.

Roz had explained about the meeting. 'I think Joanna will want you to pick this one up,' she said. 'It's your area.' The Manchester team were partners in the grant bid for the analysis of the English of asylum seekers.

'I'd have preferred a bit more notice,' Gemma said, with some justification, Roz had to admit. 'I've got that report to do. I told Detective Inspector Jordan that I'd be putting it in the post tomorrow.'

'Phone your findings through. You can put the report in the post so she'll get it on Monday. She'll get the information she wants on Friday, that's the main thing. Is it finished, the analysis?'

'Yes. I've done what she wanted. It's just . . . There was something I wanted to . . .' She checked her watch. 'Oh, God, look at the time. I'll have to go. I'll run it past you on Friday. It'll keep.' Looking happier, Gemma had left.

Whatever it was that had been worrying her, Roz could find no trace of it. Gemma had identified the woman as a Russian speaker, with language features that suggested she came from East Siberia. She had pages of analysis to support her findings. Roz flicked through them. Everything looked fine. She printed out the transcript of the tape and looked at that. Three of the lines were marked with an asterisk: 25, 127, 204. That was the only sign of something not completed, and there was nothing to show what had made Gemma mark those lines.

With the feeling that her legitimate investigation was now

turning into snooping, Roz flicked through Gemma's diary to see if she had a to-do list that might clear things up. Nothing. Aware that she was now looking at things she had no business to look at, Roz dumped the report on her desk and went to find Luke.

The door to his room was pushed to. Roz opened it and went in. An audio tape was playing, a crackle of background noise, tape hiss and, buried under it all, voices. Luke was standing by one of the computers, looking at the screen display. An acoustic profile appeared on the screen. Luke highlighted a section. He didn't look up, but said, 'Coffee's in the pot.' He usually had coffee on the go to feed his caffeine habit, and Roz – and Gemma – came to Luke's room, rather than the coffee bar or, worse still, the machine. He was locked in a war of attrition with Joanna, who liked clear lines of demarcation – coffee in coffee lounges, books in libraries, work done at desks.

Roz looked over his shoulder at the screen. 'What's that?' she said. He seemed distracted.

'It's that surveillance thing from Manchester. They want this tape cleaning up. If they'd get some decent equipment it'd save them a fortune,' he said. He was sampling the background noise to remove it from the tape; a simple job now there was software that could handle the whole process. He pressed a button on the keyboard, and the tape played. This time, the voices were free of the obscuring noise, but they were distorted, wavering and echoey. He hit another key, and the screen cleared. He turned round and looked at her.

'Have you got the results from our last run with the software?' she said. Luke was working with her on her analysis of the police interview tapes.

'I got those on Wednesday. Don't you ever listen?' He hit a key and the screen in front of him went blank. He looked across at her now. 'So. Roz. No coffee, then?'

'I'll have some while I'm here.' She took a cup down from the shelf and filled it. The coffee was thick and black. 'You?' He shook his head, leaning back against the desk, waiting to see what she wanted. 'Gemma,' she said. 'Joanna was really pissed off. Have you heard anything?'

'Like what?' He seemed slightly defensive, the way he always was with her, these days. For a moment, she thought he wasn't going to say anything else, then he added, 'She was going to come across to mine last night, after she got back, if she wasn't too tired. She said she might phone, but she didn't.' He shrugged.

'Oh.' Roz didn't know what to think. She told him about the e-mail.

'That's shit,' he said.

Roz was irritated. Joanna seemed to be holding her responsible for Gemma's absence, and now Luke was being obstructive and difficult. 'Come off it, Luke,' she said. 'It's there in the mail. All I'm asking is, has she been in touch with you? And you're saying that she hasn't. That's all I wanted to know.'

He ignored her, and stared into space, his hands in the pockets of his jeans. 'That's shit,' he said again. There was a slight frown on his face now. 'What time was the mail?'

'I don't know. Last night, I think.'

'Why would she stay over in Manchester? It doesn't make sense.'

Roz was surprised. She hadn't really thought about it. She'd been annoyed that Gemma hadn't phoned in the first place, and then hadn't had the courtesy to follow the message up with a phone call this morning, but had assumed that she was tied up with the rigmarole of garages, repairs and all the rest of the hassle that came with a broken-down car. 'How do you mean?' she said.

'Why didn't she get a train back? She knew the meeting was important.'

Roz thought about it. It still didn't seem a matter to spend much time on. It was a bit odd, but Gemma would explain when she got back. 'Maybe she couldn't get to the station,' she said.

'That's what I mean. If she couldn't get to a station, she must have been on her way back when the car broke down.

29

She wouldn't have been able to find a hotel either. She's got AA. They'd have got her home if the car was too bad to fix at once. If she was still in Manchester, why go to all the expense of a hotel? Get a train, come in for the meeting, go back later and pick the car up. Simple.'

When she thought about it like that, it was odd. 'I think . . .' she said, when the door flew open and Joanna was there. She looked at them, and Roz could see the picture it formed in Joanna's mind, she and Luke leaning against the desks, drinking coffee, chatting. She felt guilty, and she felt irritated with herself for feeling like that. She suppressed the instinct to put her cup down and start explaining. 'Problem?' she asked. Joanna was frowning.

Joanna's face cleared as she looked at Roz. 'No,' she said. Then she turned her gaze on Luke. 'The Barnsley analysis. I said I needed the report today.' *And you're wasting time drinking coffee and gossiping.*

Luke held her gaze for a minute, then as the silence began to get awkward and Roz could feel the tension in herself, a desire to start talking to break it, he said, 'It's on your desk. I put it there last night.' He smiled. 'After you'd gone,' he said.

Joanna's pause was barely perceptible. 'Don't just dump things on my desk, Luke. Put them in my in-tray.' She cast a critical eye over the coffee pot, the cups, the clutter on the desks. Roz glanced quickly at Luke, and was surprised to see a gleam of laughter in his eyes.

Joanna had obviously decided to quit while she was ahead, and turned her attention to Roz. 'I'm going to see Cauldwell now,' she said. Suddenly she looked pleased. 'I should be free in about half an hour. We need to talk about the new staffing. I'd like to get started on that this weekend.'

Roz checked her watch. 'I'm lecturing in five minutes,' she said. 'I'll come along to your room after. Three?' That would give her time to get something to eat.

Joanna gave this some thought. 'Two-thirty,' she said. 'We've got a lot to get through.'

So much for lunch. Luke had turned back to the computer.

Ignoring his grin, Roz said, 'OK,' and followed Joanna out of the room. She realized, as she pulled out her file of lecture notes, that they hadn't resolved anything about Gemma.

Roz's undergraduate lectures were always popular. She offered them as a small part of the linguistics module that the English Literature undergraduates had to follow in their first and second years. Anything with the word *forensic* in aroused the curiosity of the students, and Roz tried to fill the lecture with interesting examples of the way the theory they had been struggling with could be applied. Though a lot of their work was to do with the individual features of the human voice that made each one distinctive, possibly unique, she focused on the less technical areas of the work of the Law and Language Group, work dealing with threatening letters, contested statements and confessions. High-profile cases, the ones that had a bit of glamour.

She told them about a recent case where the recorded keystrokes on a word processor showed that an apparent suicide note was most unlikely to have been written by the dead woman – an experienced user of word processors. 'Whoever wrote that note didn't know how to use the machine – they used the "enter" key the way you'd use carriage return on a typewriter. And there's other information recorded on a computer that people don't know about: dates and times that can tell you if a document is what it claims to be. On the other hand, you can't say which actual machine a document was written on, whereas each typewriter had its own idiosyncrasies.'

She showed them a signed witness statement where extra lines had been interposed to make the witness incriminate himself, and the ways in which analysis had identified the different authorship. The students were quiet, attentive.

But as she talked, her mind was not really on the familiar lecture. She made her usual jokes, put examples up on the screen, answered questions, all on autopilot as she thought about Gemma and about what Luke had said. He was right. Of course Gemma would have come back, unless it was so late there were no trains. And that was ridiculous, because those meetings never went on after about four. Maybe she'd stayed for something to eat, maybe planned a wander round, gone sightseeing down Canal Street . . . But it didn't seem very likely. Not Gemma. That reminded her of the call she had to make to DI Jordan over in Hull.

She thought about the voice on the tape, the woman whose spoken English was rudimentary, single words, a few phrases, unclear with tape hiss and the background noise of a hospital, footsteps, metal clashing on metal, voices in an incoherent babble. And the woman's voice, quiet and unin-flected, which made the things she said more shocking, more disturbing. '*He* [or was it they?] *hit*, she kept saying, and, '*He beat up* . . .' and a phrase which Gemma, who knew Russian had translated as, *I don't know how to say it*, and *home*, and *he kill me*, and *go*, and other words, *men all days* and *I say no, he* [they?] *make* and *hurt*. And here the unnaturally calm voice had wobbled as though the woman was swallowing tears. She remembered the impersonal terms in Gemma's report that turned the words into patterns of sound, the sentences into structures divorced from meaning. She remembered Gemma's face as they listened to the tape together, puzzled and alert, and she wondered again what it was that had been worrying her.

Hull, Friday afternoon
The call had come through at eleven-thirty. By midday, the scene was secure and the investigating team was moving into place. A young woman, dead in the bathroom of one of the cheap hotels on the road out of the centre, to the east of the city. The first – and easiest – assumption was that the woman had been a prostitute who had fallen foul of her client. The Blenheim was a known haunt of the local prostitutes. She had been severely beaten – her face was smashed beyond recognition – and there was evidence of other injuries on her body. By one, John Gage, the pathologist had finished his work at the scene. 'You can move her now, unless there's anything you need to do before she goes,' he said, wincing

slightly as he stood up from where he had been kneeling by the bath.

Detective Chief Inspector Roy Farnham stood in the doorway, his hands carefully in his pockets. The photographer had finished, and the Scene of Crime team had moved through the small bathroom, bagging evidence for removal. 'What have you got?'

Gage looked up, still pulling faces as he worked his stiff legs. 'I'm too old for crawling around on bathroom floors,' he said. 'Hello, Roy, didn't see you there. Well, she's been dead for a few hours, but I'll need to get her on the table before I can be more specific than that. Cause? I don't know yet. There's ligature marks round her neck. She's got head injuries that could have been fatal, but she's taken one hell of a beating. Whoever it was – he's a nasty piece of work.'

Farnham wasn't going to argue with that. But Gage hadn't answered the question he needed answering. 'Is it another one?' he said.

Gage shot him a quick look. 'I'm not guessing anything before the PM, Roy. The others – there were no ligature marks.' He looked down at the body. One of the investigating team was leaning over the bath now, carefully cutting through the rope that bound the woman's wrists to the heavy mixer taps. 'I'll get her printed, and get the stuff to the lab as fast as I can. You're not going to get an ID from her face.'

Farnham looked, and looked away. 'Can't you patch it up a bit?'

Gage shrugged. 'After a fashion. You'll be better IDing off the prints. Or you might get something off her watch – it's engraved.'

Farnham looked round the cramped room, and pushed at the wall behind the bed. It was thin – a partition. 'The other rooms down here were occupied last night. Someone must have heard something.'

Gage looked doubtful. 'She may not have been killed here. There isn't enough blood. It's possible the running water washed it away, but . . . You'll need to get into that drain.'

Roy Farnham contemplated the prospect of trying to find

a murder scene and felt depressed. One of the SOCOs came over to him. 'Sir?'

Farnham looked at what the man was showing him. It was a card in a clear evidence bag, like a business card, that had been dropped on the floor of the bedroom. In one corner there was a silhouette: a woman kneeling with her hands crossed behind her head. The lettering was fine italic, *Angel Escorts*, with a phone number. At the bottom of the card it said, *International escorts. Our pleasure is to give you pleasure.* 'OK,' he said. He made a note to get on to Vice, see what they knew about this Angel Escorts place.

The photographer had finished. Farnham nodded to Gage. 'All right,' the pathologist said to his waiting assistants. 'Get her out of there.'

Farnham watched as they moved the woman's body carefully, sliding plastic sheeting underneath her to prevent the bloodstained water from dripping on to the floor. He looked inside the bath as they lifted her. Gage was right. There was very little blood, just a diluted wash that left a dark tidemark as it moved with the disturbance of the water. It was possible the killer had cleaned up after himself, got rid of the blood and debris from the death. The room was awash with water. Farnham needed the people who'd been in the other rooms that Thursday night, to see if they'd heard sounds of a fight, the sound of water running late, anything that would help locate what had happened.

Once the body had been removed, he found it easier to work. It became a job, a problem-solving task. With the woman still there, it was more personal, involving anger and disgust at the things that human beings were capable of doing. He wondered why they did it, women who sold themselves to strangers. It had to be more than money, for the women who walked the streets or who went to hotel rooms with men who ordered them over the phone, the way they ordered pizza brought to their door. So many of them ended up dead – from drugs, from violence, from self-harm. This was the third one within the last two months, and there were disturbing parallels between the deaths. His superiors weren't convinced there was a link, but Farnham had a bad feeling.

He wondered what the story was of the woman in the bath. She had looked so small and broken.

The priest was only sixty, but he often felt like an old man. He had spent his life in inner-city parishes, a life that had been properly devoted to poverty, chastity and obedience. He had seen a steady decline in the power and influence of the church that had been his life from his earliest memories. And now he was tired.

He walked slowly down the aisle, the words of the canonical offices in his mind, the ritual of the prayers working like an automaton on his tongue, but always real, always meaningful as he whispered them into the hushed silence, into the still, close air of the sacred, of the transcendence that was God.

Holy, holy, holy, Lord God of hosts . . . Sometimes the words came back to him in the old Latin – long gone, and for good reasons – the old Latin that he remembered well and sometimes missed. *Sanctus, sanctus, sanctus* . . . The church was silent and empty. It was carved out of the stone, reaching up into the high vaulting of the roof spaces, where light diffused through the lacework of the windows, dappling the colours from the stained glass against the stonework of the pillars. The flags on the floor were worn smooth with the feet of worshippers, penitents, communicants. Now, the feet of occasional tourists wore away the names cut into the memorial stones.

He read the familiar descriptions as he walked. *Libera me!* Deliver me, O Lord! The plea was still legible, but the name had vanished from the permanence of the stone decades ago. *Requiescat in pace*. Rest in peace. The statues waited in niches and on plinths with banks of candleholders in front of them. There were boxes for offerings, and candles that could be lit in memoriam, for a soul gone before, as a plea for mercy and forgiveness for the souls of dead sinners. The holders were empty, unused, the metal tarnished now. He could remember when each saint had its row upon row of devotional candles burning steadily in the shadows, scenting the air with the smell of burning wax.

His curiosity was taking him to the farthest corner of the church, where the side aisle met the transept. In an obscure niche, a statue stood, some forgotten saint, cowled and tonsured. The statue may have been painted once, but now it was grey stone, caught in the moment of stepping forward, one hand raised in blessing, or in threat. The eyes, smooth and blind, watched from the shadows.

The priest paused in his slow procession. Though the bank of candleholders here was smaller, he had noticed recently that some of the sconces, always the same ones, held candles recently burnt down. His hand touched a blackened wick lightly, and it crumbled away. But it was warm, and the metal around two of the sconces was encrusted with wax that had dripped over weeks and months. Under the third candle, the wax deposits were less, as though this one were less used than the other two. No one cleaned the darker corners of the church. The candle sconces were used so seldom that no one thought to check. He sighed for the days when cleaning the church was in itself an act of worship. But someone had come here to place a light in the darkness, a light to ask for mercy or forgiveness, a light to shine on the road of the dead, a light to ask for their souls to be remembered.

4

Hull, Friday

The woman had been found three weeks ago in the mud of
the Humber Estuary as the tide went out. The cause of her
death wasn't clear. There were marks of recent violence on
her body, healing bruises that suggested she had been the
victim of intermittent, casual abuse. Witnesses had seen her
walking late at night near the bridge, her distinctive coat
standing out in the frosty dark. People who plan to jump
will often stand for a while contemplating the means of their
oblivion. Detective Inspector Lynne Jordan wondered what
had drawn the woman to the restless, surging Humber. But
her interest wasn't in the death of this woman, it was in her
life.

Lynne Jordan was after contraband – but not the usual
alcohol, tobacco and drugs that made their way past the
barriers intended to prevent their import. The contraband
she was looking for was more tragic and far more problem-
atic. Social and political upheavals have their cost. The naïve
optimism of the West may celebrate the death of an 'evil
empire' but the East has a clearer view. A curse. *May you live
in interesting times.* The communities of Eastern Europe were
being torn apart by the forces of change that brought wealth,
corruption, poverty, war and death in their wake. The contraband that Lynne was looking for was some of the human
flotsam from that upheaval.

Lynne's job was to monitor her patch for women who
had been brought into the country illegally, or who were
overstaying their visas, and working as prostitutes. It had

been a problem in London, in Manchester, in Glasgow – women brought to the country and then prostituted to endless numbers of men six, seven days a week.

The trade was spreading. Escort agencies around the country now offered 'a selection of international girls'. The women were effectively kept in debt bondage. A woman's travel documents, if she had any, were confiscated. From her earnings – only a fraction of the price the pimp charged for her services – she had to pay the charge for being brought into the UK, and had to pay high prices for accommodation and expenses. They tended to be kept in flats, enslaved by debt and fear, not allowed out without a minder. They were young, some of them were very young – a team in the north of England had found eleven-year-old girls on one of the premises they raided – and most of them were too frightened of the British authorities to seek help even if they could escape. Hull presented Lynne with an interesting problem. It was a large city, a major port, but it didn't have an immigrant community as such, in which the women could hide or be hidden. Or it hadn't until the dispersal programmes had started to move asylum seekers out of the crowded centres of the south-east and to dump them on to the stretched provision of the northern cities: Liverpool, Manchester, Sheffield, Newcastle, Hull.

The support organizations that had been hastily set up were either circumspect or hostile in response to Lynne's queries. 'Not my responsibility,' Michael Balit, the Volunteer Co-ordinator who worked with the council and some of the refugee organizations, told her. 'I don't have time to spend looking for exotic dancers or nannies trying to boost their income.' He caught Lynne's eye. 'Look, prostitutes can take care of themselves. It's a police matter. Your business. Let me know what's going on. Keep me informed. I'll pass on anything relevant that comes my way. Now, if you'll excuse me . . .'

The woman had been very young. She had been found in the old docks area in a distressed state, and had been brought to the casualty department of the Infirmary by one of the workers from a refugee support group. The hospital had called the police, but the woman's English was limited and she was in shock so very little of her story was clear. Lynne had listened to the tape an astute officer had thought to make while they were talking to her at the hospital. Though she had seemed willing and eager to talk to them, something had frightened her, and she had run away. One of the officers, a young woman herself, had said to Lynne, 'She was OK with us. With me. But she seemed a bit . . .' she made a gesture at her head to indicate mental confusion. 'She kept talking about cats. The medic who examined her said he thought she might have been raped, so we were going softly, softly. But she was in distress, so I went to get the nurse again, and when I got back, she'd gone.' The officer described the woman as – almost – oriental, with the rounded face and high cheekbones of the east. Her hair was raven black, and under the blue of death her skin was sallow. The security cameras had picked her up leaving the hospital alone. She had paused at the entrance, looking round, allowing the camera to catch her picture, hunched into the coat the support worker had given her when he drove her to the hospital. That was the last they had seen of her until her body had been found by a walker, in the mud of the estuary in a frenzy of ravenous gulls.

And the gulls and the tearing tides had done their work. The woman's face was gone. All that was left of her was the battered body, the raven black hair, the coat, its Christmas red an ominous and incongruous marker of the last place she had stood, abandoned on the bridge – and the interview. The Senior Investigating Officer on the case, Roy Farnham, had sent it through to Lynne with a request for any information that she might have to help him. 'We don't even know, yet, if we're dealing with a murder,' he'd told Lynne when she spoke to him. The post-mortem findings had been inconclusive, the cause of death undetermined, but the dead woman had been in the early stages of pregnancy.

The little Lynne knew about the dead woman was assumption. Her nationality – she spoke Russian – and, possibly, her name. She said twice on the tape something that sounded like 'Katya', but the tape quality was poor. The material on the tape suggested that she had been working as a prostitute, but so far Lynne had found nothing that would give her any more information on the woman.

Unless her inquiry on the tape came to anything. A couple of months ago, she'd attended a seminar on developments in analytical techniques – these seminars were held regularly, and Lynne found it useful to keep up to date with what technological tools were available to help her. She'd remembered the seminar as soon as the Katya tape came into her hands. A woman from one of the South Yorkshire universities was touting for trade. She had talked about the ways in which apparently incomprehensible tapes could be cleaned of background noise and restored, the ways in which the actual machine a tape had been recorded on could be identified, and – here Lynne had paid close attention – how the nationality of a speaker could be determined by the way they spoke English. The woman had been talking in particular about establishing the regional and national origins of asylum seekers, but Lynne could see immediate applications to her own work.

The woman hadn't particularly impressed her at first. She'd seemed a bit intimidated by the scepticism of the officers present, a scepticism that was honed on long experience of botch-ups, courtroom fiascos and 'experts' who flatly contradicted each other using identical material. But Lynne had rather warmed to her when she was recounting the success they'd had in convicting an obscene phone caller from a message he'd been unwise enough to leave on an answer-phone. 'And you tracked him down from that?' one of the group had asked.

'Oh no,' the woman had replied. 'We helped to convict him on that. I think it was the phone number he left that tracked him down.' She'd looked up from her notes at that point, and her eyes had glinted with laughter. Lynne had made a note of her name – Wishart, Gemma Wishart. She'd sent the Katya tape to her as soon as she'd got it from Farnham with high hopes that at least they could find out where the woman came from.

Which reminded her, the report was supposed to be in today. She checked the post in her in-tray but there was no sign of it. She phoned Wishart's direct line, but she got a secretary who told her that Wishart wasn't available. Lynne identified herself and asked about the report. 'I'll see if I can find someone to talk to you,' the secretary said, her voice sounding uncertain, and left Lynne to drum her fingers on hold before someone finally took her call.

'This is Dr Bishop,' a voice said. 'I'm sorry to keep you waiting. I'm a colleague of Gemma Wishart's.' She started talking about a car breakdown and Lynne had to cut her off. 'I'm sorry,' the Bishop woman said again. 'We've been held up by Gemma's – Dr Wishart's – absence. I can give you the details of the report now, if you want.' Lynne made notes as the other woman spoke. Katya, according to Wishart's report, was from East Siberia.

'How certain is she?' Lynne's geography was rusty, but she had a feeling that 'East Siberia' covered an area that was considerably larger than the British Isles. 'Can she be more specific?' If they could pinpoint the area more closely, they might be able to identify Katya, assuming her family or friends had reported her missing.

'You'll need to talk to Gemma if you have any specific queries, but . . .' There was the sound of pages turning. 'She says, "The accent is consistent with the area of north-east Siberia."' She rattled out some technical detail about *vowels* and *devoicing* and *intonation*. Lynne made minimal responses as she thought about it. There didn't seem to be anywhere to go with the information. She thanked the woman, cutting her off in the middle of something about acoustic profiles, and rang off on the promise that the full report would be in the post that day.

She put the Katya file to one side. She could think about it again when the report came through – Monday now, probably. It was irritating. Academics tended to operate on a different timescale from other people.

It was nearly a month since 'Katya's' death. There was very little chance of getting a line on the woman's real identity. When the pathologist's final report came through, her death might be formally recognized as a suicide, and she and her unborn child would lie in an unmarked grave in a foreign country. *Some corner of a foreign field that is forever . . . where?* In the absence of any obvious cause of death, in the absence of any identification, there was very little that the investigating officers could do.

Sheffield, Friday evening
It was dark by the time Roz got home. She lived on the east side of the city, away from the expensive residential suburbs. Pitsmoor had trees and quiet roads, rows of terraces and big, detached houses. Burngreave Cemetery, the small park and a recreation ground provided green spaces among the shops and houses and roads. But the area was run-down. Shop fronts were boarded up. Low property values meant that landlords left their rentals to decay. As the streets became more unkempt, graffiti started to appear on walls and bus stops. The signs of regeneration struggling in the city centre had made no impact here.

Pitsmoor suited her with its varied and varying community. And she had fallen in love with the house from the moment she saw it. She loved the square bays of the double front, the high hedge of privet and bramble and rambling roses, the stone lions that guarded the steps, the wide entrance hall and wooden stairway, the huge, flagged kitchen with the old range, the labyrinth of conservatory and outhouses that led from the back of the house to the double garage that reminded her that Pitsmoor had once been a place where the wealthy, or moderately wealthy, of the city lived. She even found the house next door an asset; a house like the one she lived in, but one that had stood empty for too long and had been vandalized into dereliction.

Everyone had said Roz was crazy when she bought the house. She'd been in Sheffield for three months, and knew she was going to stay for a while. 'Not Pitsmoor!' they'd said, and 'Wait until you've had a chance to look round.' But the house had reminded Roz of the house where she had lived with Nathan, and Pitsmoor had reminded her, just a bit, of the place she had left. She was happy.

She stood at her back door now, looking at the derelict house. A tree was growing out of the oriel window, and fringes of ivy and dead grasses hung over the eaves. On summer evenings, she could sit in the yard and watch the pigeons flying in and out of the holes in the roof where the slates had been removed by weather, time and local children. She shivered. It was getting cold. The moon was nearly risen now, and she had things to do. She went back inside.

She put bread under the grill to toast, and opened some beans. She wasn't in a mood to cook. She ate a spoonful of beans out of the tin while she was waiting, leaning against the side of the cooker, her eye on the bread to catch it in that moment of transition from pale brown to charcoal. She wondered if Gemma was going to phone her, or if she should try and make contact herself. She remembered the tape that Gemma had been working on. The recorded voice had sounded emotionless, probably because the woman was concentrating hard on finding the right words. But she knew . . . *Shit!* The toast! She turned off the gas. The toast was just about retrievable. She tipped the beans into a pan and put it on the hob, dumped a plate on the table and took the toast over to the sink to scrape off the burnt bits.

She sat at the kitchen table to eat, staring at the window that had become a square of darkness. Friday night, and here she was alone in her house, eating tepid beans on toast, planning an evening's work, and happy, *contented*, to be doing that. It seemed such a short time ago that she had been a student, and Friday night would have meant clubbing, hitting the town with her friends, going to parties, having fun. Maybe she'd tried to recapture that time with Luke.

Then there had been her time with Nathan. Friday night still meant the weekend, still meant special times, but it was time that they wanted to spend together or sometimes with friends . . . And then there had been the isolation of his illness. Their friends had tried, but a lot of them had disembarked. They hadn't been able to cope, and in the end, nor had she. She twisted her wedding ring round her finger. 'You find out who your true friends are,' her mother had said philosophically.

And now, she was a successful research academic, well on her way up the ladder, and Friday night was just another evening – an evening without the immediate demands of the next day's work, so one that could be used to catch up with longer term projects. Her book, for example; unimaginatively titled *An Introduction to Forensic Phonology*. She picked a couple of stray beans off her plate. She could try and get that tricky fifth chapter sorted out. She licked the tomato sauce off her fingers, washed her plate and the pan and left them to drain, then collected her briefcase and went into the downstairs room where she usually worked.

Privet pressed against the bay window, shutting out the light. The room was cool and cavernous, a huge mirror illuminating its shadows. The mirror had been left in the house by the previous owner. It was old, the gilt chipped, the glass slightly distorted and marked. The reflected room looked drowned, softened in the dim light. Roz stood at the far end of the table and saw her face a white blur in the shadows. Her gold-rimmed spectacles reflected the light and obscured her eyes. She took them off. She didn't really need them. She untied her hair, and let it fall round her shoulders. The imperfections in the glass made the light waver like a candle flame, made her reflection look as though she was swimming through deep water, pale face and fair hair floating in the brown shadows. Rosalind. *If there be truth in sight, you are my Rosalind*. Nathan used to say that to her, Mozart on the tiny cassette player that was all they could afford, the gas fire combating the draughts from the ill-fitting windows and rattling doors of their flat. *You are my Rosalind*.

Work, she had work to do. She turned on the desk light, its pool of illumination dispelling the shadows in the mirror. She had brought one of the laptops from work, more powerful than her own machine. She wanted to try out some new

44

software that Luke had recommended, as well as work on the book. She switched the machine on, and sorted through her disks while she waited for it to boot up. She realized, as she looked at the files on the machine, that this wasn't the laptop she usually brought home, it was the new one, the one that Gemma had been using. She'd thought that Gemma had taken it to Manchester. She must have taken the older one. Maybe she hadn't wanted the responsibility of the more expensive machine. Roz tried to imagine what Joanna would say if it got stolen or damaged, and decided that Gemma had made the right decision. That made her uneasy about the security in her own house. Break-ins were not unusual in Pitsmoor. They weren't unusual anywhere these days. Gemma had lost her sound system just a couple of weeks ago when her flat had been burgled. Roz decided she'd lock the laptop in the cellar head before she went to bed.

Gemma. Ever since her conversation with Luke ... Gemma should have been in touch at some time during the day, or she should have phoned this evening to let someone know she was safely back. Joanna would want to know how the Manchester meeting had gone. Maybe Gemma had been in touch with Joanna, bearded Grendel – Luke's occasional name for her – in her lair. Roz wondered if she should phone. But Joanna was going out this evening; she'd mentioned it to Roz on her way out. 'Must rush. I'm going to the concert tonight.' Joanna probably wouldn't welcome the intrusion, especially not if she'd already been reminded about Gemma's delinquency by a phone call.

Luke. Luke would have heard. She tried his number, but she got the answering machine. He must be out. She held the phone against her ear, thinking. Then she tried Gemma's number, without much hope. Nothing. She was seeing Joanna tomorrow evening. She'd find out then. She pushed the problem out of her mind, and turned to the computer. Gradually, the work absorbed her, and the problem of Gemma retreated to the back of her mind. The hours passed, unnoticed, as she sat there in the dark, in the pool of yellow light, the words scrolling up and up the screen.

Lynne Jordan sat in Roy Farnham's office, wondering if she was pissed off at the delay, or pleased that she had actually been called in. On the whole, she decided that she was pleased. There had been no overt hostility to her arrival. It was more that a lack of interest meant that things she should be notified of, things that were clearly or possibly within her area of responsibility were just not passed on to her. Michael Balit's attitude was not uncommon. Prostitutes were prostitutes, the argument seemed to go. Sometimes they got killed. Illegal immigrants were illegal immigrants. Sometimes they got killed as well. Lynne could remember a conversation at a dinner party, where the wife of a colleague had held forth with indignation about a young man who had tried to smuggle himself into the country riding on the roof of a Eurostar and had electrocuted himself. 'He's occupying a bed in intensive care,' the woman, a nurse, had said. 'Someone else could be using that bed. It makes me so angry.' Lynne had wondered what, exactly, the woman thought should have been done with the injured man, but didn't ask. The answer would probably have depressed her.

Farnham was afraid they had a prostitute killer on their patch, a street cleaner, or a man who wanted to kill women and found that prostitutes made the easiest prey. And if the previous two were illegal immigrants, women in the situation that Lynne was just starting to monitor, how much easier would they have been to catch and kill? 'How many have there been?' she said.

'That's the problem,' Farnham said. 'Until this one – it's inconclusive. There's the woman from the estuary, the one you're trying to identify . . .' *Katya*, Lynne supplied mentally, '. . . and there was something up the coast at Ravenscar.' Lynne listened as he ran through the details. The body of a woman had been found just over two months earlier on the shingle below the plummeting cliffs of Ravenscar in the incoming tide. Lynne looked at the report and the photographs. The woman had been small, five foot three, and thin. She had a tattoo on her left wrist, a spider in a web that formed a lacy bracelet round a wrist that should have been chubby with disappearing puppy fat, and she had needle marks on her arms and on her thighs – the tattoos of the heroin user. The pathologist had put her age at around seventeen. Her body had been washed clean by the sea, leaving her with weed tangled in her hair and round her legs. She had been battered by the pounding tides. Her skull had been shattered, leaving the face distorted, the mouth smashed. It was still possible to map young features on to the wreckage that remained, which was more disturbing than if it had been smashed to a pulp. She had been found early one Sunday morning by a walker who had made his way down the precipitous path to watch the sea.

There was no identification, but the dental work suggested she was Russian. 'Russian, no record of her arrival. They think she was working as a prostitute. That's too many parallels,' Farnham said. 'Have you heard anything on the street?'

Lynne hadn't. 'I'll ask around,' she said.

'The women usually know something about what's going on,' he said. 'And you're looking for an identification on the Humber Estuary woman? Any progress?'

'I'm trying to narrow down her place of origin,' Lynne said. 'She might have been reported missing.' She explained about the tape and Gemma Wishart's now overdue report.

'OK,' he said. 'Keep me posted.' He looked down for a moment. 'We might have another one,' he said. He told her about the woman found in the hotel the previous day. Another faceless woman. 'But we've got a cause of death. This one was strangled. We got the call around midday Friday.'

'Do you know when she was killed?' *You*, not *we*. Lynne was always careful with her language. She wasn't on the murder team, she didn't want anyone to think she was poaching on their turf.

'Thursday night some time.'

'And they didn't find her until lunch-time? How come?'

Farnham shook his head. 'It's a mess,' he conceded. 'The

47

manager, a woman called Celia Fry, went on a hunt for a missing cleaner. According to Fry, they were short-staffed Friday morning. The cleaner started doing the rooms. Later on, Fry comes down to find her because the upstairs rooms aren't done, and she finds the vacuum in the middle of the passage and the linen basket out, and no sign of the cleaner. She's a bit pissed off about this and she starts looking round, and that's when she finds the Sleeping Beauty in the bathtub.'

'And the cleaner?'

'No sign of her. That's where I thought you might be able to help us.' He looked across at her. 'There's nothing on the books for her and the manager is trying to pretend she doesn't exist. Casual worker, student, stuff like that. I think she's wishing she'd kept her mouth shut in the first place.'

'You think she might be someone who's working illegally?' Cleaning was a largely unregulated area. 'I'll need more information.'

'I told her to expect full checks on all the systems and all the accounting within the next week. Did wonders for her memory.' He grinned, and checked through the folder. 'Name of Anna Krleza. Age about twenty. Five foot two, three. Shoulder-length dark hair. According to Fry, she's only been working in the hotel for a week or two. She was supposed to be bringing in her national insurance and P45 any day. Fry says she was getting suspicious about the delay.' He raised a sceptical eyebrow at Lynne. 'I'm looking for her. But you're the one with the contacts.' He pulled another file across his desk. 'Do you know anything about a firm called Angel Escorts?'

'You think she was killed by a client?' He didn't respond, but waited for her to answer his question. 'I don't know any escort firm called Angel, not operating around this area. But a lot of the agencies operate online these days. Basically, they claim to act as contacts agents – the girls give their details and the agency passes them on to clients.' She shrugged. The sex-for-sale sites on the internet were blatantly brokering prostitution, but they were hard to track down, the ones who operated from cyber-space, and the ones that had a more terrestrial reality kept themselves within the law by careful wording, or sufficiently within it not to attract scarce police resources.

'Mm.' He was noncommittal.

Lynne pushed. 'Why do you think she was on the game?' she said.

'I don't,' he said. 'But I think she might have been. The Blenheim's a bit of a giveaway. And she was wearing some specialist gear – one of those corset things, laced. Bondage stuff. And the room wasn't booked out to a woman. It was a man, single booking, made that evening by phone. A sales rep, apparently.' He checked his notes again. 'Name of Rafael. That's with an "f", not a "ph".' He read the question in Lynne's face. 'No luck yet. He scribbled something in the hotel register. We've got someone looking at it, but I don't think it says anything. The phone number doesn't exist, and he didn't give a car registration. He booked in as normal, paid his bill – they do that if they want to get off first thing – and that's all anyone saw of him.' He rubbed between his eyebrows with his thumb and index finger. 'Anyway, the name – Angel Escorts, Rafael . . .' He looked at Lynne. 'There's an archangel called Rafael.' Lynne knew. She was surprised that he did. 'Client's joke or killer's joke? Or are they the same person?' He frowned. 'We found this card.' He pushed it across to Lynne. She looked at it. *International women.* That was why Farnham thought she might know it. She kept her eyes on the card, letting her mind wander over the possibilities as she listened to him. No address. No URL. Just a phone number.

'The phone's a pay-as-you-go,' Farnham said, anticipating her question. 'We're waiting to get some location information on it – at least find out where it's been used. Nothing so far. We need an ID.'

She was about to ask how far they'd got with that, when he pushed a photograph across the table to her. She looked at it, looked away then looked more closely. 'Christ.'

Farnham nodded. 'He beat the shit out of her.' Lynne

49

looked at the photographs, at the woman's destroyed face. The body was small and slender; the hair, which had been brushed back from the ruined face, hung in loose curls. Lynne tried to imagine the features that had been obliterated, and the faces of dead women from her past flickered in her mind. And more recently. Anonymous, dead women. The woman at Ravenscar, Katya, and now ... she heard Farnham's voice in her mind. *The Sleeping Beauty.*

Sheffield
Saturday evening found Roz at the entrance to the block containing Joanna's flat. The building was low – three stories – and set back from the road. The front overlooked the park and the back looked on to a wooded hillside. It formed an enclave of rural seclusion in the centre of the city. Roz sometimes wondered how Joanna afforded to live here on an academic salary. She rang Joanna's bell, and gave her name as the intercom crackled incomprehensibly at her. She straightened her shoulders and pushed the door open. She found Joanna's parties a bit of an ordeal, and she wasn't sure why she had been invited to this one. She'd queried this with Luke as she left work on Friday. 'You'll be the cabaret,' he'd said, without looking up from his screen. 'Take your fancy knickers.'

Thanks a bunch, Luke! She was at Joanna's door now, and Joanna welcomed her with the social kiss she never used with Roz at other times. She took the wine that Roz had brought with a quick glance at the label. Bringing wine was probably a *faux pas*, Roz reflected as she and Joanna exchanged meaningless social pleasantries. Joanna was wearing a black dress of impeccable elegance and looked beautiful. Roz told her so, and for a moment a look of genuine pleasure appeared on her face. 'We're in here,' she said, ushering Roz into the lounge. Roz envied Joanna this room with its huge windows that filled the whole of the far wall. She had spent an afternoon here before Christmas when the Arts Tower was closed, going through some spreadsheets in preparation for the finance meeting, watching the winter sunset turn the clouds grey and brilliant red, the sun an orange fire through the trees.

She felt the cloudy softness of the carpet under her feet as she crossed the room, nodding to one or two familiar faces as she followed Joanna to where a small group was admiring one of the paintings. Joanna performed the introductions quickly. There was Mark Bell who Roz knew by sight; an influential member of the grants committee, one of the new breed of industry-based academics. 'And this is Petra, Mark's wife,' Joanna went on. 'I don't think you've met Jim, Jim Broadbent. Jim's with Ashworth Lawrence.' One of the biggest legal firms in South Yorkshire. Roz had recognized the name – another man with influence in both the legal and academic worlds. She found herself wondering if Joanna had any friends who were just that – friends. Presumably, Roz's role tonight was to sell the Law and Language Group to these people whose influence stretched beyond the confines of the university.

'And you may have met Sean Lewis,' Joanna was saying. 'He completed his doctorate at MIT. He's with Martin Lomax's team.' The computer department. 'Sean, this is Rosalind Bishop.'

Roz found herself looking into the appreciative eyes of a very young man. 'I don't think we've met,' she said.

He smiled. 'I'm sure we haven't.'

Joanna pressed a glass of wine into her hand and Roz, tasting its almost astringent coolness, decided that her bottle of supermarket Chardonnay had certainly been a gaffe. She looked at Sean Lewis, wondering why Joanna had made a point of introducing them. 'MIT,' she said. 'That's an impressive alma mater.' Massachusetts Institute of Technology. She wondered what someone with a doctorate from that institution was doing in Sheffield.

He seemed to pick up her unspoken question. 'It's where it's all happening,' he said, 'but it's a bit one-sided. Great if you're a total geek – they're all like, "Work, work." I'm more, "Get a life." There's a lot of places I haven't been yet. They don't understand that over there.' He shrugged.

Roz nodded, amused. She had spent most of her early working life focused on getting her toe-hold and pulling herself up the ladder. So had most of her contemporaries. It had seemed, then, possible to put other things on hold. She found Sean's attitude refreshing.

They talked for a bit longer, then she did her duty and circulated, talking about the politics of the health trust with Jim Broadbent, and the importance of PR with someone she knew she knew, but whose name she couldn't remember. Then the groups reformed and she relaxed for a moment as she listened to the swirl of chat around her; something about hospital funding on her left, something about the current state of theatre in Sheffield to her right, something about the plight of the universities and the role of research in modern technological societies from a group in front of her. Roz listened to them talking about the new Home Office regulations, about the hidebound administration of the university, before Joanna took them through to where food was laid out.

The dining room was a minimalist contrast to the soft comfort of the lounge, with a polished beech floor, and a table that gleamed with crystal and candlelight. Roz looked at the impressive buffet and wondered again where Joanna found the time to do all the things she did.

Joanna came towards her with the young man, Sean Lewis, in tow, and Roz wondered what she was up to. Whatever. It was just for an evening, and Sean was attractive and entertaining company. Their talk was impersonal, work-based, but there was a subtext that Roz was aware of inherent in the way he stood slightly closer than necessary, the way that when their eyes met he maintained the contact, the way he stood forming a barrier between Roz and the rest of the room. *You've pulled, Bishop.* Luke's voice, in her mind. It made her want to smile, but she kept her face serious.

Sean seemed genuinely interested in her thoughts about the Law and Language Group, and talked quite knowledgeably about it. He understood her interest in the research side of the group's work. 'It's the technology and the software every time,' he said. 'Take the grants, develop the prototypes and then get out there, market them yourself.' He thought they were wasting their time with the criminal work. 'Pissing about with tapes,' he said dismissively.

Roz was suddenly alert. This young man was clearly a high-flier. His field was computing and software. He seemed well travelled, talking about America, Europe, the Far East. Attending one of Joanna's parties was hardly the way he would choose to spend an evening. He looked as if he would be more at home in one of the notorious Sheffield clubs. She wondered what the attraction was.

She could see Joanna glancing across at them, a speculative gleam in her eye. She understood, now, why Joanna was so interested in Sean Lewis and why she wanted him and Roz to get on. If Joanna could pull it off, he would make a perfect replacement for Luke. It wasn't as far-fetched as it seemed. Joanna had talked about enhancing the post, giving the software researcher control of the European grant work. He wanted to travel. He could still pursue his own interests – in fact, a link with a successful research group would be an asset. He smiled at her and helped himself to a piece of asparagus off her plate. Making a pact with the devil? She wondered if she should be using a long spoon.

5

The phone woke Roz at seven. She swore and pulled her head under the blankets. Let the answering machine take it. She was due a lie-in. She hadn't got back from Joanna's until after two, and she'd been woken up again in the small hours by a gang of youths, fighting and shouting in the road out-side. Now she just wanted to sleep. Who'd phone her at this time, anyway? Her mother? Not even Paula would phone at this time on a Sunday. Then the voice on the machine penetrated, and she sat up, grabbing for the phone. '. . . your lazy arse out of bed, Bishop . . .'

It was the old Luke, the friend who had never had any compunction about rousting her out of bed in pursuit of some enterprise that had caught his fancy. 'It's the middle of the night, Luke! For Christ's sake!' Then she remembered Friday. 'What's wrong?'

'I'm round at Gemma's,' he said. 'There's . . .' Suddenly his voice sounded uncertain, the new Luke, slightly wary, slightly withdrawn. 'I'm not quite sure. Maybe I shouldn't have called you.'

'Oh, come on, Luke. I'm really going to go back to sleep now, aren't I? What's wrong? Is Gemma ill? Is that why she didn't come in yesterday?'

'Gemma's not back,' he said, after a pause.

'Luke . . .' She felt an uneasy sensation in her stomach. 'Has she been in touch? Anything?'

'Nothing. But . . .' Again the un-Luke-like uncertainty.

'Don't you think we should call someone – the hospital?

54

Maybe she had an accident.' Or was she being melodramatic?

'I did that bit yesterday. I told you that car shit didn't make sense. There wasn't anything. But then there wouldn't be.'

'Why? What did they say?' There must be something, or he wouldn't have phoned. 'I'll come round, shall I? To Gemma's?'

'I don't know . . .' That uncertainty again. She tried to remember any time, in the year she had known him, when Luke had asked her for help.

'I'm coming round,' she said.

There was a moment's silence. 'OK. See what you think.' He hung up.

Roz looked out of the window, trying to assess the weather. She didn't bother with curtains. Her bedroom looked out on to the derelict house, the oriel window visible from where she was lying. She rolled out of bed on to the floor. It was the getting-up technique she'd adopted in her teens, when the act of getting out of bed had seemed impossible to achieve. Her fatigue had retreated, but she knew she would feel it later. *Getting old* . . . The shower pulled her further awake. She put on jeans and a warm jumper, stuck a croissant under the grill and switched the kettle on. Fifteen minutes later, the half-eaten croissant in her hand, she was reversing the car out of her gate.

Gemma rented a flat in Hillsborough. Roz had picked her up there once or twice, but had never been inside, she realized, as she pulled up outside the small terrace, behind Luke's bike, a Vincent Black Shadow that he devoted more time and care to than he devoted to himself. 'Brings out the geek in me,' he'd admitted once to Roz. He must have been looking out for her, because he opened the door as she came through the gate.

She followed him into the house. The entrance hall and stairway were common territory, and had the dark, uncared-for look that areas of transit often have. Gemma's flat was on the ground floor, her door to the left of the entry. Roz looked round as she went in. It was – presumably – pretty much like any of the furnished flats on offer in an area that had a large transient population. Gemma had draped the chairs with pale throws, and painted the walls a light, neutral colour, as though she had tried to make the room non-intrusive, a background to her presence. Here and there were patches of colour – the green of a plant, a peacock blue table lamp, a brilliant tapestry on one wall, cushions embroidered in scarlet. Roz was drawn to the tapestry. It seemed to glow with life in the stark room. She looked more closely, admiring the brilliant colours and the intricate weaving of the threads.

Luke came up behind her. 'Gemma got that when she was in Dudinka,' he said. Gemma had spent three years in Russia, mostly at the Siberian university of Novosibirsk when she was studying for her PhD. 'They gave it to her when she left. She's going to go back there, when her research money runs out here.' Roz was surprised. She'd thought that Gemma planned an academic career in Britain – or America.

Luke turned away from the tapestry. 'Through here,' he said. He led her through a small kitchen – more of a lobby than a kitchen – to the bedroom, which was at the back of the house. It was smaller than the front room, and was sparsely furnished with a bed, a small chest of drawers, and an empty hanging rail by the chimney breast. Under the window was Gemma's desk, with her computer. The screensaver wove intricate patterns in ever-changing colours. Luke went over to it. 'Look,' he said. He clicked the mouse to open the documents window, and then jerked his head to bring Roz over. She looked at the screen. The documents window was open, but there was nothing there, no files or folders, just empty space: 0 objects. 0 bytes.

Roz looked at it, and looked at Luke. He shrugged a shoulder. 'Last time I saw this, Tuesday night, that would have been, she had loads of stuff on here,' he said.

'Maybe she wiped it – for space,' Roz said. 'Maybe it's all saved on disks.'

Luke pulled open the desk drawer. 'She keeps her back-up stuff here,' he said. The drawer was empty. 'Anyway, Gem keeps all her stuff on her hard disk. She says it's easier to keep track of. And she has back-up disks for everything.' He folded his arms and looked at her, leaning against the desk, waiting.

Roz wondered what he wanted her to do. She wondered what she should do. Gemma had gone to Manchester on Thursday and attended a meeting. She had definitely been there – Joanna had checked on Friday. She was due back on Thursday evening. Luke had said that he expected her to phone – or half expected her to phone. She was certainly expected in the department on Friday morning. The meeting had been the main focus of Joanna's attention for the past month. Gemma had sent an e-mail with a lame excuse. She hadn't come back, and she had apparently wiped her document files from her hard disk before she went. Luke was still watching her from by the desk, waiting to see where her thoughts took her. 'The police?' she said.

'I did that as well,' he said. 'Yesterday.'

'And?' It was like pulling teeth.

'They weren't that interested. They took details, but they didn't see any reason to worry. Gemma does go off sometimes, weekends. Said to leave it until Monday. They thought I was overreacting, thought we must have had a row. Lovers' tiff.' He said it lightly enough, and she wondered why he was worried, if Gemma was in the habit of taking unplanned trips. There didn't seem much point in asking him. He wouldn't talk to her these days. 'I just thought there was something wrong. Thing is, I hadn't been round here then.'

'What do you mean?'

He jerked his head impatiently. 'Just look round you, Roz.'

She looked, and the implications of the empty hanging rail hit her. She went over to the chest and opened the drawers. They were empty. 'All her stuff's gone,' she said. That meant that wherever Gemma had gone, she'd planned it, but the sense of unease stayed with her.

'First prize for observation, Bishop.' Luke had turned back to the computer and was moving the cursor across the screen.

'Look, *did* you two have any kind of, you know . . . ?'

'Any kind of what, Roz?'

'Any kind of row, or disagreement or *something* that would have upset her. You know what I mean, Luke.'

His expression didn't change. 'If I knew of a reason for her being away, I wouldn't be looking.'

So that's a 'no', then. 'If Gemma deleted those files, should you be planning a raid on them?' she said. She was beginning to understand that Gemma must have personal reasons for going away and that Luke knew more than he was telling her. She wasn't prepared to be the patsy in whatever complicated game he and Gemma were playing. He smiled at her and waited. *You haven't thought it through, Bishop.* 'You've already looked,' she said.

'It's no problem getting deleted files back,' he said. 'But . . . someone's taken a bit of trouble here – all I'm getting is gibberish.'

So Gemma had done more that just issue a delete instruction. 'Can't you get them back at all?'

'If I . . . I don't know. Probably not. Not from something like this.' He frowned, looking into space, thinking. 'I don't think Gemma could have done it. She could have wiped her hard disk, no problem. She knows how to do that . . .' Roz reflected that she herself had managed to achieve just that, once, without either meaning to or knowing exactly what she'd done. 'But she'd have needed a bit more for this.'

Roz thought about it. She wondered how she would tackle the problem if she wanted to take stuff off her hard disk in such a way that it was permanently removed. You couldn't work in her field without knowing how easily such files could be retrieved. If she wanted to do it, she'd probably ask Luke. But if she didn't want Luke to know . . . She thought she might have been able to come up with some kind of a solution. She just wouldn't be 100 per cent confident that the files would be permanently deleted. And that, presumably, wouldn't be too difficult to find out. 'Gemma could have done it,' she said.

Luke shrugged. He clearly thought she was wrong. He shut the machine down and stood up. 'I'm going into the department,' he said. 'I'm going to look on her PC there.'

The Arts Tower was quiet on a Sunday. Students were using the library, and people were riding the paternoster – a university never really closes down – but the milling crowds of weekdays, of lecture and seminar days, weren't there. They rode up in the paternoster in silence. N floor was deserted, the lights out, the corridors dim and empty. Luke led the way to Gemma's room and used his master key to open it. Roz looked round. Everything was as neat and ordered as it had been on Friday. She remembered being in here, looking for Gemma's draft report. She realized the significance of that as Luke switched the computer on, and felt a relief she couldn't quite account for. 'It's OK,' she said. 'I'd forgotten. I looked up one of Gemma's files on Friday. There was a report she had to get in. Everything's there. Or at least the files I was looking for were there. I . . .' Her voice trailed off as she looked over Luke's shoulder. The computer was flashing a message at them, white letters on a black screen: *error, error, error.*

Luke looked at her. 'It may have been here on Friday,' he said, 'but it isn't now. It's been wiped.'

Roz pushed her hair back from her face and shook her head. 'I can't think of anywhere else to look,' she said. Whoever had wiped Gemma's machine, they'd done a thorough job. The painstaking removal of files from her home computer would have taken a bit of time. Here, the hard disk had been reformatted. Everything was gone.

Roz and Luke had gone through the desk and the filing cabinets in Gemma's room, checked the shelves, the window sill, the pockets of the lab coat that hung on the back of the door. Roz wondered why it was there. She'd never seen Gemma wear it. They were looking for Gemma's back-up disks. Luke straightened up from the filing cabinet, and for a moment, his face was unguarded. He looked anxious, confused, and there were lines of tension around his mouth and eyes. He saw she was watching him, and made an attempt at a smile. 'What's the point in wiping the computer and leaving the back-ups?' he said. 'They're not here.'

'Whoever did it might not have known . . .' Roz was still hoping the back-up disks that Gemma should have kept would turn up. Maybe they'd missed something. She turned back to the desk.

'They aren't here, Roz. Stop wasting time.' He shoved his hands into the pockets of his jeans, and looked round the room, his face angry now. 'I told her we needed an automatic back-up system.'

'Who?' Roz pushed the desk drawer shut. He was right. There was nothing here. They'd looked everywhere. She pushed her glasses back up her nose, then, irritated by them, she took them off.

'Grey. I told Grey.' He ran his hand through his hair and moved restlessly round the small room. Roz pulled open the top drawer of the filing cabinet. She didn't want to admit he was right.

'You think Gemma did this? Came back yesterday and wiped everything off her machine?'

He reached past her and slammed the filing cabinet drawer shut. 'How the fuck should I know?'

The anger in his tone froze her. She knew that Luke could be volatile, but she'd never seen that sudden rage in him before. She stepped back, moving away from the filing cabinet, wanting to put some distance between them. She tried another question, tried to keep her voice normal. 'Why the blitz job on the hard disk here? Why did . . . whoever . . . wipe the whole disk, and just do the files on the other machine?'

He didn't look at her, kept his hand on the filing cabinet. 'I don't know, Roz.' His voice was tightly controlled. 'Work it out for yourself.'

She looked at his rigid stance. Suddenly, it was like stepping back two years and seeing Nathan's confusion transform into fury. Then, the only thing to do had been to get out of the way, fast. Until the night she hadn't made it. She had been woken up by the sound of him moving round the house, the confused stumbling, and had got up as she had done before. And he had been there at the top of the stairs, his face twisted with anger and panic. She could still see his face, his arm drawn back. Then his fist had slammed into the side of her head, her hand had grabbed at the banister rail in a futile attempt to save herself in the frozen moment of her fall before the pain and the fear hit.

She couldn't deal with Luke like this. 'I'll be in my room,' she said, after a moment.

He didn't look at her. 'OK.'

She walked along the empty corridor past the stairwell, her footsteps echoing on the lino. A security light was a red glow on the ceiling, and light from the lobby cast a faint gleam at the end of the corridor. Roz went towards her room, trying to think the situation through. Her mind was dividing down two paths: one, the main one, was concern for Gemma, a feeling of queasy uncertainty that told her something was wrong. Luke said he'd been in touch with the police, and that they hadn't been concerned, but that was before the discovery of the missing files. Or would the police say that showed Gemma had meant to leave, that she had wiped all her files because . . . because what? Because she had something to hide?

That was the second strand of Roz's concern. If Gemma had gone deliberately, the implications for the group could be serious. Roz closed the door of her room, and leant against it. The silence closed round her. She needed some time to think, and, she realized, she needed to contact Joanna. Joanna had to know. She dialled Joanna's number, but got the answering service. She hung up. She'd better plan what she was going to say. She pushed a pile of papers out of the way to reach her notepad and a pen. The papers were her Monday's to-do pile. The various tasks snagged her mind, and she leafed through the stuff as she tried to work out what, exactly, to say to Joanna.

That reminded her about the draft report for DI Jordan. Gemma needed to complete it and send it off. But Gemma wouldn't be there. Suddenly, she was sure of that. Whatever had happened, Gemma would not be back soon, maybe not at all. Roz would have to check that report, phone the rather brusque DI Jordan and explain why it was being delayed for another day. She remembered Joanna's ebullience on Friday. She dreaded telling her.

A disk that had been concealed in the pile of papers slipped out and fell to the floor. She frowned as she picked it up. She was very careful not to leave disks lying around, careful to keep them filed and classified where they could be found as soon as they were wanted. She must have been distracted on Friday. She picked it up to see what it was. No label. That was odd. She never, *never*, put anything on a disk without labelling it. It must be someone else's, but who would leave this in her office?

Then she remembered Gemma in her room on Wednesday, fumbling nervously and dropping her bag on to the desk. It must have fallen out of the bag, and Gemma hadn't noticed. She picked up the phone to call Gemma's extension, tell Luke what she'd found, but then she put it down. Better see what she'd got first. Gemma must have been planning to take the disk with her. She put it into her machine, ran it through the virus scan, and opened it.

There were three files: JPG files, pictures. The file names weren't very helpful – AE1, AE2, AE3. Roz was disappointed. She didn't want pictures, she wanted some of Gemma's work files. She double-clicked on one and watched the picture form on the screen.

At first, her mind wouldn't process the image. Then she was . . . what? Shocked? Embarrassed? Amused? No wonder Gemma kept these in her bag, not lying around the department. It was a picture of a woman – of Gemma – naked, sitting on a patterned quilt with her knees drawn up and her arms resting on them. She was looking over the top of her arms, straight at the camera. Her eyes gleamed with suppressed laughter. Her legs, below the drawn-up knees, were parted, exposing her to the camera's eye.

She opened the next file, not knowing if she should, or if she wanted to. Gemma, standing this time, her wrists held above her with a rope that was stretched painfully tight, pulling her up so that she was standing on tiptoe. Her eyes looked directly out of the screen, challenging and inviting. The third file showed Gemma on a bed with her hands tied again and again pulled above her head. Her knees were bent and her legs were splayed. She was wearing a basque that was laced so tightly it bit into the flesh. The background was dark and shadowy. Roz sat in silence. She didn't know what to do. She didn't understand why the pictures were stored on the disk. Why would Gemma be carrying them around in her bag? Who did she plan to show them to?

Hands touched her shoulders and she jumped. She swung round, and Luke was behind her. Her heart hammered in her throat and for a moment she felt sick. 'Luke! *Shit!* You scared the life out of me!' She tried to catch her breath.

'What have you got there, Roz?' His voice was quiet and even. He didn't apologize for startling her.

'It's . . .' Her voice sounded artificial, and before she could think what to say, his hand was on the mouse and he ran through the other files. Neither of them spoke for a moment. Then he closed them and took the disk out of the drive.

'Gemma's, I think,' he said.

'Luke . . .' She didn't know what to say.

'It's OK.' His voice was carefully empty of expression. 'We took those a couple of months ago. They were just photographs.'

That was true. They were just photographs. But Roz felt angry with Luke. She wished she hadn't seen them – or wished, at least, that it hadn't been him who had taken them. Gemma had put them on a disk and was taking them somewhere. Why? She looked at Luke, who was holding the disk between his thumb and forefinger, his eyes narrowed in thought.

'It's none of my business,' she said. She could hear her voice sounding cold. 'I thought . . .' What? What had she thought? That the files would contain some explanation for Gemma's disappearance?

He met her eyes. He seemed distracted, as though he was thinking about something else. 'No, no problem.' His voice was detached, that flash of anger in his office gone as fast as it had come. He raised his eyebrows at her. 'Well, you know something you didn't know before.'

She knew that she didn't know Luke as well as she had thought. She felt as though she didn't know him at all.

Snake Pass, Sunday morning

As Sunday dawned over the Pennines, it became a fine winter's day. The sky was cloudless blue and the air was still. The temperature had dropped, and the ground glittered with frost. It was a day to bring the walkers out, and Keith Strong had decided to get ahead of the rush and make an early start. He knew the Peak well – he worked as a part-time ranger, keeping an eye on visitors to the park, offering a helping hand, getting walkers out of difficulty, taking part in rescues when things went drastically wrong. In the Peak, rescues usually meant someone had been stupid – tried to walk the path up Mam Tor, the shivering mountain, in high-heeled sandals (really, he'd seen it), gone on the tops in bad weather without the right equipment, gone climbing on the edges without safety gear. Today, he wasn't working; he was out just to enjoy the countryside. His mate, Tony, was driving over to Manchester first thing, and Keith had persuaded him to go via the Snake and drop Keith off at Doctor's Gate. He planned to take the path up Devil's Dyke, following the route of the Pennine Way, and walk across to the Flouch Inn. It was a long walk and a hard one, but the weather was right, and he needed a day out. It would do Candy good as well.

Tony dropped him on the straight stretch of road before Doctor's Gate. 'I'm not stopping on that bend,' he said. Keith raised his hand in thanks as Tony drove off, shouldered his rucksack and set off up the hill towards the culvert. He kept Candy on the lead for the road bit. She was obedient – all his dogs were well trained – but she was young, and she was excited and full of energy. It wasn't worth the risk. She pulled at the lead and he spoke firmly to her, but he let her pull again as the hill got steeper. It made carrying his rucksack up that incline just a bit easier. As soon as they reached the culvert and crossed the road, he let Candy off the lead and she ran ahead up the dyke, sniffing eagerly, dancing with enjoyment. Keith reflected, not for the first time, that it was much easier to make a dog happy than a woman.

He let Candy explore. There were sheep, and at this time of year they could be in lamb, but Candy knew better than to chase them. He sat down on a rock to tighten the laces on his boots and put on his gaiters. Frost or not, it could be muddy up on the tops. He noticed the car with the half awareness of distraction – he was planning his route – and then with annoyance. Its red intruded on the landscape, and, anyway, it shouldn't have been there. He thought that people who couldn't manage to make their way here without a car should walk somewhere else. He knew he was being inconsistent, and that irritated him more.

He thought that the car was parked a bit oddly. He called Candy back, and she came bounding down the path with a piece of heather root in her mouth which she laid at his feet, looking at him expectantly. 'Leave!' he said, as he walked towards the car. It was pulled right in, close to the rocks. Getting it in there must have damaged it – Keith couldn't see any way that careless parking would have brought it so far in. He checked the front and back. The number plates had been removed. Right. It was probably stolen, then. Joyriders? It seemed unlikely they'd go to the trouble of half hiding a car up here. Maybe it had been used in a burglary, a get-away car or something. The idea quite appealed to him.

Candy was exploring, her heather root forgotten. She was round the passenger side, sniffing at the wheel, her tail up and her ears perked with interest. Then she froze, her ears forward, her eyes intent. Her tail was down now, cautious, as she lowered herself in stalking mode and peered under the car. She was making little whining noises in her throat. Keith got hold of her collar and hauled her back. 'Daft dog. You'll get covered in oil under there.' Candy looked up at him, and moved round to the other side of the car, still low to the ground, still cautious. Keith followed her, interested now. She moved slowly up to the driver's door, her nose testing the air, the whines turning to low growls. She pressed her nose against dark stains that had splashed the sill. She scratched at the door, whimpering.

The driver's door was hard to reach because the car was parked up against the rock. Keith tried the handle, and the door opened a short way. A smell like – he couldn't quite find the comparison – like a city alleyway, like a . . . It was the smell of sweat and the geriatric ward, the ward where his mother had died, the smell of ammonia and decay. The smell made him step back and Candy jumped straight in, and began burrowing in the foot-well. Keith grabbed the thick hair on her hindquarters and hauled her out. She squealed. There were dark stains round her muzzle. It was hard to see the inside of the car, but they looked like the same dark stains that were on the dashboard and on the steering wheel, with smudges on the seat and, now he came to look, on the windows. It reminded him of the thick, black mud from the bogs and stagnant pools of Coldharbour Moor up on the tops. Had someone fallen in, come back to the car to clean up and change?

He went back round to the passenger side and tried that door. It opened. He snapped a command at Candy who was trying to get past him again into the car, and looked round the interior. The glove compartment was hanging open and empty. There was nothing in the car itself. He touched the driver's seat. It was damp. He checked the boot. It was locked. He shut the car door and scratched his head. He'd better call in, report this to someone. But the hills on either side were blocking the signal to his phone. He'd need to walk right up the path before he was high enough above the rock faces and the steep sides of the dyke, and the signal came back. He set off, whistling for Candy to follow. She raced past him, leaping over the rocks, stopping to look back at him, her mouth open and her tongue hanging out. It was half an hour before he reached the top, breathing hard after the steep climb, feeling his boots heavy with the dark peaty mud that clung to them. Candy was worrying a stick now, her energy undiminished.

He checked his map and took a compass bearing, more to

keep his hand in than because he needed to. A kestrel circled in the sky above him. Then he headed off across the hills with Candy bounding ahead, detouring off the path into the heather, disappearing from view and waiting for him to catch up. It was a beautiful day for a walk.

Hull, Monday
Anna put her bag down on the floor, keeping it carefully between her feet. She could feel the eyes of the cloakroom attendant on her. Should she say something to the woman to account for her dishevelled appearance, or should she just act as though nothing was wrong? Her heavily accented English tended to produce a hostile response. *Get back to where you came from!* She ran water over her hands, and squeezed liquid soap on to her handkerchief. She needed to clean herself up. She needed privacy. She needed a cubicle. There was a queue, and she shuffled forward, keeping her head down. No one would be looking for her here. No one would be looking for her at all. It was a coincidence, just an accident, just . . .

A cistern flushed, and she jumped. She could feel the sick coldness coming over her. If she passed out here, someone would call the police and then . . . Before anyone could move, she pushed ahead and went into the vacant cubicle, pushing past the woman who was coming out. She could hear a muttering behind her: 'Excuse me! Who does . . . ?' 'There's a queue . . . !' She bolted the door behind her and sank down on to the seat, her bag under her feet, and put her head down until the cold dizziness passed. She was tired. She was so tired. And she was hungry. *Get away, get away, get away*. But it wasn't that easy. She didn't know where to go. She had no money, she had no papers. She had, *had* to get the stuff from her room. She couldn't leave it, not now, not after all the work and all the time and all the planning.

She felt as though her head was floating and the things she was hearing came from a distance. She had spent the last three nights walking around the city centre – *Keep moving, keep moving* – huddling herself up on park benches during the day; dozing off, feeling the treacherous warmth creeping through her, waking with a jerk as she began to slump off the seat. While she still had money in her purse, she had ridden on the buses, on the top deck because she didn't want to be seen from the street, drifting into a doze as the true warmth began to bring the feeling back to her face and feet and hands, and jerking awake, aware, suddenly, that she was alone, and footsteps were coming up the stairs.

'. . . in there? I said, Are you . . .' She jolted upright in a wash of cold. The door was rattling. For a moment, she couldn't understand what the voice was saying. She was shivering and she couldn't control it. She took a deep breath. *Calm, calm.* 'Fine,' she said, relieved that her voice came out steady. 'Just, a little sick. In my stomach.'

She could hear voices, footsteps. She couldn't work out what they were saying. She wiped the damp, soapy rag over her face, rubbed hard until her face felt clean. She untied her scarf and pulled her hair firmly back, then she tied it again, tightly. There was no mirror in here. The action made her feel a little better. She picked up her bag, and opened the cubicle door. She could feel the eyes of the queuing women on her, and could see the cloakroom attendant watching her again. She managed a smile. 'Thank you,' she said. 'Just a little sick . . .'

The woman ignored her. Anna could hear the voices as the door closed behind her: '. . . back to where they . . .' She was walking through the furniture department now, and there were mirrors on the walls, and free-standing mirrors, and mirrors on dressing tables and wardrobe doors. She could see a woman in a crumpled jacket and stained trousers with her hair jumbled up under a scarf, a bag bulging under her arm. She stopped and turned round. The woman was there behind her, and in front of her as she moved faster down the aisles, and the woman twisted and turned and followed her until she came up against some railings and there was nowhere to go.

'Can I help you?' The young man wore a suit. His mouth was pulled down and his nostrils flared slightly. *Yes! Help me,*

Anna wanted to say, then she realized that he didn't see her. She was just garbage, a nuisance, something to be disposed of. She could smell her clothes, a sour, unwashed smell. Suddenly, her eyes were full of tears, and she battled them down. He wasn't looking at her now; he was looking round, looking for someone to help him.

'I wanted the way out.' Anna's voice was just a whisper. He put his hand out to steer her in the right direction, then withdrew it. He pointed instead, and she saw that the top of the escalator was just opposite where she was standing; the rails were a balustrade protecting the top of the stairwell. She felt her way round the edge, afraid she might fall, not trusting her eyes to find the way for her. 'Thank you,' she said quietly.

He followed her, and watched her on to the escalator. She saw him talking to a man in a peaked cap with epaulettes on his shirt who followed her as she went down one, two, three floors, and there was the way out in front of her. The cap and the epaulettes made her legs shake as she walked until she reached the safety of the street.

She was going to have to go back to her room.

6

Hull, Monday

The Sleeping Beauty investigation intrigued Lynne. She had no intention of stepping on to ground that belonged to others, but Roy Farnham had invited her opinions and expertise, and now he was going to get them. She enjoyed the challenge. Her work was demanding, often stressful, frequently distressing, but, above all, it was interesting, and no matter how stressful the cases, she managed to keep herself, the essential Lynne, separated from the things she saw and the things she had to do. She sometimes thought that was her main skill as a police officer. Maybe it was the same skill that made a good concentration camp guard, she didn't know.

She pulled the files out of her in-tray, and spread the contents across her desk. Two women: Katya, in the mud of the Humber Estuary, and the nameless woman on the rocks at Ravenscar. Was Farnham right in thinking that there might be a connection between these two deaths, and between these and the Sleeping Beauty?

She read through the reports, slowly and carefully, making notes as a point struck her. Everything pointed to Katya having committed suicide, but . . . She had been seen walking in the direction of the Humber Bridge a few hours after running away from the hospital. One sighting was inconclusive – a driver coming out of Hull on the A63 had seen 'a woman in a red coat' walking by the side of the road. But the other witness had given more detail. He'd mentioned the woman's dark hair and the heavy metal buttons on the coat.

Her body had been found three days later. The pathologist had been inconclusive about the length of time she had been dead. He thought probably not more than forty-eight hours. 'Water, mud, it makes it difficult, Inspector,' he'd said when she had asked him if he could clarify the rather vague conclusions of his report. 'A private guess?' Lynne had asked, but he had refused to commit himself. The cause of death was also inconclusive. There was nothing to show that she had drowned, so the crucial question – had she been dead before she entered the water? – was unanswered.

'They don't realize,' the pathologist had said, tiredly. 'Jumping into water from a height, they might as well jump on to concrete.' The head injuries were probably, but not conclusively, post-mortem. 'You get post-mortem bleeding in head injuries when a body is in the water,' he said. 'And the gulls took the soft tissue. There wasn't much to work on. I can't be definitive in this case. Sorry. It's possible we're looking at vagal inhibition here – that she went into cardiac arrest as soon as she entered the water. The shock of cold water can do it.' He shook his head again. 'Let's see what the lab tests show.'

Lynne looked through the next file, the anonymous woman who had been found at Ravenscar. As with Katya, the cause of this girl's death was undetermined, but there was a bit more information here. She had probably died no more than fifteen hours before she was found, and circumstance suggested that she had probably died within a time period between early evening and midnight. The blow that had shattered the bones of her skull would probably have been fatal, but that blow had been post-mortem. Other, ante-mortem, injuries were not sufficiently severe to have caused death, the most recent being some bruising that had not broken the skin. The pathologist had speculated that they could be looking at an accidental death here, something that had happened in the course of sex that had got a bit rough – a bondage game that had got out of hand, something like that.

Lynne looked at the laboratory reports. There was some

alcohol in the woman's bloodstream, but no other drugs. She had clearly been a user if the track marks were anything to go by, but she hadn't used within the forty-eight hours preceding her death. She'd eaten shortly before she died – there was bread in her stomach.

She thought. Three women, possibly prostitutes, two of them dead from an unknown cause or causes, all anonymous, and all with severe damage to the face, sufficient to obliterate the features. All dumped in water – a good way to destroy forensic evidence – and all killed somewhere other than where their bodies had been found. She could understand Farnham's concern, but she could also understand his circumspection. She had been involved in a high-profile investigation a couple of years before, where a man had been stalking and killing women in South Yorkshire. She knew it was easy to start crying 'serial killer' on the basis of very slight connections.

Farnham had given her a photocopy of the business card found on the floor of the hotel bedroom. Angel Escorts. It wasn't an agency she had come across locally, which suggested that it wasn't one of the places operating under the cover of a massage parlour or sauna. A lot of escort services were internet-based these days. If the Beauty had worked for one of these agencies, then her picture would be on their website. Lynne was equally sure that once they realized what had happened, she would vanish from the site as if she had never been there.

It might be too late already. The Beauty had died on Thursday night or Friday morning. It was now Monday – plenty of time for a website to be cleaned up or even removed completely. She logged on, checked her e-mail – all rubbish which she deleted without reading – and then started searching. There was an abundance of sites offering escorts. Some were subscription sites that you had to pay to enter. She ignored those for the moment. If Angel was a straightforward escort agency, then they presumably wouldn't deter potential clients by charging them. They'd want them to browse.

'Angel' was a popular name. She found several listed. She

made a note of contact numbers, and went on looking. She was hoping for a site with pictures, a site where you could hire a woman online; presumably, a local woman. None of the Angel Escorts she'd found mentioned the east coast. She narrowed her search to the local area. Now, the number of possible sites was much smaller. There were three she'd looked at already, and a site that said simply Escort Services Links. OK, she'd try that.

The screen went black – a porn site cliché. Then there was the warning that the site contained adult material. Lynne pressed the 'enter' button, and the name, Angel Escorts, appeared in pulsating red. Pictures began to form with strategically placed lettering to encourage the browser to go further into the site. A tiny picture of a woman fellating an anonymous penis. *She's young, free and willing!* Another picture: a young face, fair hair, pigtails. Her blouse was open, exposing her breasts. *Fresh teens!* Lynne wondered what kinds of clients might greet a woman who had advertised on this site. *100% free live anal video feed!* Lynne looked for the link to the escorts. *Meet our girls.* OK. She clicked on the button.

Ten small photographs of women appeared – Lily, Jasmine, Rose, Jemima, Suzy . . . The pictures provided links that allowed a customer to browse further and inspect the attractions of the merchandise. Four of the women were clearly eastern – Korean? Lynne wondered. Filipina? They looked seductively and submissively at the camera. Lynne clicked on a couple of the pictures to get an idea of how the site operated. The sequence of pictures for each woman was almost identical. Shots in skimpy clothes and underwear, standard nude shots, the general range typical of glamour photography. There was a brief text in which the woman expressed her willingness to be a warm and talented companion for an hour or a night. *I am toned and flexible. Tell me your most secret fantasies and I will make them come true.* She was reminded of girlie mags, but the difference between these and top-shelf magazines was that you could, should you choose, buy one of these women for a short time. A man could lift her down from the top shelf and play with her, though he'd need a good income to do it regularly. She wondered how much of the money the women actually managed to keep. She knew from the work she'd been doing recently that the men who bought these women had a taste for, or a yearning for, an elusive exotica, a dehumanized sex toy. They saw these women as fair game for their more . . . outlandish . . . tastes. But – Lily and Suzy and Rose . . . It was a pseudo-exotica. Fish and chips in Spain. Pie and peas in Tenerife.

The dead woman was Caucasian and white. There were four who fitted the bill. Their initial photographs were too small to give her the detail she wanted, so she checked through each one. The pictures appeared and vanished on the screen, a procession of exposed breasts, offered buttocks, pouting mouths. She paused on one, Jasmine, and then on another, Terri, who looked like possibilities, but in each case the build was wrong.

She moved on to the next one. Jemima. Jemima had dark brown hair and a slight build, like the Sleeping Beauty. Her initial picture had been a bit different, everyday, a woman in jeans and a tight T-shirt, smiling at the camera. The picture reminded Lynne of someone. She looked fresh and outdoors and innocent. But it made the contrast all the more effective. The other pictures of Jemima were unusual and striking. They were all nude shots, but the standard poses had become studies in light and shadow, the chiaroscuro creating a dra-matic, almost sinister effect. There was one where 'Jemima' was looking into the lens with her knees tucked up under her chin. She could have been unaware of the extent she had exposed herself to the camera – the pose was almost casual – but the rather mischievous glint in her eye said otherwise. It was an engaging picture.

There was that sense of familiarity again. Lynne frowned, trying to pin it down, but it was elusive. She needed a clearer view of the woman's face, something she could show to people who might know. She moved on to the next picture, and stopped. Here, Jemima lay on the same bed, on her back. Her legs were bent, the knees spread. Her hands were above her head, the wrists crossed. Lynne tried to magnify the top of the picture, but it was too dark. She couldn't tell if the wrists were tied to the headboard, or if the woman was gripping it, but her arms looked taut. Her face looked relaxed and inviting. She was wearing a white basque and stockings.

Lynne took the crime-scene photograph out of the folder she'd brought back with her. The woman's body was positioned with the hands tied above her head, wrists crossed. Her legs were drawn up, the knees pushed to either side of the narrow bath. The garment she was wearing, twisted and stained though it was, was a white basque. The hair, which was thick and glossy in the photograph, was dull and wet. The face was a smashed and bloody palimpsest. But the slim arms, the small breasts, the narrow waist, they were the same.

There was a knock on her door, and without waiting for a response from her, the person outside pushed the door open and came in. It was one of the men on Farnham's team, one of his DCs, she couldn't remember the name.

'Don't just walk in,' she said briskly.

'Sorry, ma'am.' She saw him clock the computer screen. She could read his face. *Nice work if you can get it.* 'DCI Farnham sent these across.' The rest of the crime-scene photographs. So Roy Farnham was serious about working with her.

She indicated her in-tray. He put the files down and was about to go when she summoned him back and pointed at the screen. That sense of familiarity . . . she didn't want to waste her energy on trying to remember, and then, weeks or months later, see a singer or a soap star with a passing resemblance to 'Jemima'. 'Who does that remind you of?' she said. She could see him running several possible responses through his head. Probably a – what, twenty-year-old? – young man wasn't the best person to ask, not with a picture like that. She sighed and moved the screen back to Jemima in her jeans and T-shirt.

Now, he was looking properly. He shook his head and looked at her expectantly. 'No one,' he said, waiting for the answer.

'OK. Thank you . . .'

'Stanwell,' he said. 'Des Stanwell. Ma'am.' He looked at the picture again. 'She looks like some kind of posh student type, something like that. Not . . . You know.'

She knew. 'Thank you, Des.' She waited as he shut the door behind him. She needed prints of these pictures, but she wasn't linked up to a colour printer. She started downloading the Jemima pages, drumming her fingers with impatience at the sluggish way the files came through. As she waited, she remembered that she hadn't checked her post. She flicked through it, and noticed with annoyance that the promised report on the Katya tapes had still not arrived. She waited for the download to finish, and picked up the phone.

Sheffield, Monday, 8.30 a.m.

Low pressure settled over the city and Monday began for Roz in uniform dullness, the sky a still, opaque grey. She drove to work through the rush-hour queues, feeling a lethargy creeping into her spirit. Nathan had always hated days like this. 'Why would anyone bother with getting up? Come on, Roz, phone in. Tell them you're sick. Come back to bed.' Why was she thinking about Nathan? As she edged her way into the lines of traffic, as she stopped and started in the queues, she tried to think of other things. The day ahead of her presented a range of distractions. *Gemma*. There were tutorials Gemma was supposed to run that would need covering or cancelling. There was her work programme. Roz would need to go through all of Gemma's outstanding work and see where . . . Except that she couldn't. All her files and all her back-ups were gone. And then there was Roz's own work. She had to complete the next stage of the research proposals by the end of the week. She had a seminar at twelve. She had an appointment with the PhD student she was supervising who was her preferred candidate for one of the research posts Joanna was planning . . . And Gemma. She banged her fist against the steering wheel in frustration, jumping when the horn sounded. She smiled apology to the driver ahead, and made herself concentrate. She felt like turning the car round and heading back along the almost empty carriageway away from the city centre. *Very constructive, Roz!* Days like this happened. She just needed to prioritize.

The traffic was so bad that she was later than she'd intended, and there was no space in the car park. She had to waste time weaving in and out of the side streets looking for somewhere to leave the car without getting a ticket or, worse still, getting clamped or towed away. The steps into the Arts Tower were alive with students when she finally arrived from the parking space she'd found a good five minutes' walk away, and the entrance was blocked with queues for the lifts and the paternoster. Roz pushed her way through the crowds, nodded a good morning as she passed the porters' lodge, and took the doors to the stairs. A climb of thirteen floors was a good way for someone with a basically sedentary job to keep fit. Her routine was automatic. Walk up the first five, run up the next five, and walk the last three so that she wouldn't arrive red faced and sweating.

As the doors to the stairwell closed behind her, she was in silence. The stairs were concrete and breezeblock, the steps covered in grey-flecked lino, the light the flat glare of fluorescent tubes. There was no daylight. She concentrated on her climb, feeling her energy start to come back after the initial fatigue. It was claustrophobic on the stairs, with just the high closed-in stone and the steps above and below her. For a moment, it was almost as if she was alone in the building, then she heard a door above her open and bang shut, and the sound of feet moving fast. The echo on the stairs was confusing, making it impossible to tell until the last minute if someone was climbing up or coming down.

There was a sudden rush and a young man shot round the corner, bounded past her jumping the stairs three at a time and vanished round the landing below her. His 'Sorry!' seemed to hang in the air after he was gone. Students. Youth. Roz was mildly amused by the display of energy and heedlessness. It shook her out of her weather-induced depression.

She'd lost count of her floors. She checked the number on the landing and began her jog up the next five, feeling slow and cumbersome in comparison to the lithe young man.

She arrived on N floor not too out of breath and allowed herself a moment of satisfaction that lasted until she came through the door of her office and found Joanna waiting for her. Roz glanced at the clock as Joanna said, 'I expected you in earlier today.'

It was only ten past nine, but it was the worst day she could have chosen to be late. 'Parking,' she explained. 'Is there any news about Gemma?'

Joanna's face was set. 'This arrived, just this morning. Posted in Sheffield on Saturday.' She was holding a letter, pleating the paper between her fingers. 'You'd better read it.'

Roz looked at Joanna, and took the letter. It was written on official university stationery and dated Friday:

Dear Dr Grey

Personal circumstances make it impossible for me to continue with the Law and Language Group. Please accept my resignation effective from today's date. I apologize for not giving you full notice of my intentions.
Yours sincerely

Gemma Wishart

Roz was thrown into confusion. She remembered the discussions they'd had the week before, Gemma's concern that she might be late with her report for DI Jordan, her assessment plans for her students, her research schedule. She couldn't believe that Gemma had been planning, then, to leave her job, suddenly and without warning. She clearly hadn't discussed it with Luke, or he wouldn't have been stirring up the police and the hospitals. She remembered his words on Sunday: 'She's going to go back there, when her research money runs out here.' He and Gemma had talked about the future, but he hadn't known about this. What had happened? What kind of trouble was Gemma in? *Personal circumstances* . . .

'Aren't you worried?' she said. 'About Gemma?' Gemma was Joanna's protégée. Joanna had spoken to Roz often enough about the brilliant future she thought that Gemma could achieve.

Joanna frowned, staring into space. 'Gemma's been planning to leave for a while,' she said. So Gemma had discussed this with Joanna as well as with Luke. It was just Roz she had kept in the dark. 'She's put in several applications for funding to go back to Novosibirsk,' Joanna went on. 'I don't want to lose her, but I supported her. The university there is excellent, and if that's the direction Gemma wants her research to take, then she will be better off there.' There was a faint line between her eyes. 'I didn't expect her to do it like this,' she said. There was silence for a moment, then Joanna gave herself a shake. 'I don't have time for this now. We have the situation here to deal with. I had that Jordan woman on the phone half an hour ago, asking about her report. I can't find it.'

Roz remembered the report. She'd promised to put it in the post on Friday, and she'd forgotten. 'I'll deal with that,' she said with evasive diplomacy.

Joanna nodded. 'I want to go through Gemma's desk and her filing cabinet as well,' she said. 'I need to know exactly what's missing.'

Hull, Monday
Lynne went over the statements that Farnham's team had taken after Katya's body had been found. Katya had been taken to the casualty department by someone called Matthew Pearse, a volunteer worker at a refugee support centre down near the old docks. Lynne read through his statement. She had understood that Katya had been found on the street, but now she came to read Pearse's statement, she realized that Katya had actually come to the support centre seeking help. Pearse had seen the condition she was in and had taken her to the Infirmary. It had been the obvious decision, and

the sensible decision, but, with hindsight, the wrong one.

Lynne needed to talk to Pearse. The statement gave an address in the Orchard Park area of Hull, but no phone number. She didn't want to trail all the way across the city and find him out. Maybe she could track him down at this support centre. She needed to know when he was likely to be there. OK, the Volunteer Co-ordinator, Michael Balit, should be able to help her there.

Balit was his usual, unhelpful self. 'Matthew Pearse?' he said. 'What do you want with him?' It would have been easy to pull rank on him, tell him to co-operate as she was in the process of an investigation, but she knew that Farnham wanted to keep things low-key for the moment. The Michael Balits of this world existed to give her practice in the skills of patience. She reminded him of the Katya incident, and indicated that her inquiry was part of an 'i'-dotting and 't'-crossing piece of bureaucracy. 'We just need to close our file on the case,' she said with vague mendacity.

He accepted this at face value. The place where Pearse worked was called the Welfare Advice Centre, he told her. 'We don't use the word "refugee",' he said. 'For obvious reasons.' There had been a series of racially motivated attacks on people since the dispersal system had sent groups to Hull, stretching the social services to the limit. 'So the voluntary sector had to step in,' Balit said. The advice centre was based in the old docks area, part that was still awaiting gentrification. 'We've taken over one of the derelict buildings down there,' Balit said. 'It used to be a shop. We were using it to store donated furniture. We still do, but we cleared out some office space, put a translator in place and set up.' So he clearly could get things moving when he had to. Perhaps he just didn't see that Lynne's work was his problem.

'Matthew Pearse?' she said.

'Well, Matthew's a volunteer outreach worker. He's disabled, can't work full-time. But he's had a lot of experience in immigrant communities – we don't have that kind of experience in Hull – so he's been giving us a lot of help at the centre.'

80

And now she was looking at the latest addition to the refugee support network. The old shop was down a side street, beside one of the empty warehouses that were awaiting demolition or redevelopment. It had a boarded front and a look of abandonment in its sagging pipes and leaking guttering. But the door was well kept, the locks efficient and the notice on the door, typed in several scripts, looked recent. *Welfare Advice Centre. 8.30–5.30 daily. Out of hours, ring night bell.* She wondered if they had any information about this place back at the station, and she took out her phone. But the signal was weak – the area was low and she was surrounded by high buildings. She could check later.

The Centre reminded Lynne of the corner shop where her grandmother used to take her to buy sweets when Lynne went to stay. Just for a moment, she had a vivid picture of her grandmother's front room, the textured wallpaper that had a mottled, sandy pattern, the tiled fire surround, the picture on the chimney breast – some gilded religious theme with clouds and halos and wings. How many years ago? Twenty-five or more. For a moment, she felt old. The shop near her grandmother's had been the last survivor of a shopping parade that had been demolished now. There had been a window display, she remembered that, with plastic bananas, vivid yellow that somehow looked dusty and faded, with tins and packets that had lost their new brightness. The shop itself seemed dark in Lynne's memory, the customers old like her grandmother. She had never liked that shop, with its dingy and run-down interior. She had liked supermarkets with their wide aisles and bright lights.

The Welfare Advice Centre had the same air of slow decay. The door gave a faint *ting* as she pushed it open, and for a moment she expected to find herself in the dark shop from her childhood, and hear Mrs Rogers' voice saying, 'Have you come for your sweeties then, flower?' But this door opened on to a small room, the old shop with the counter adapted to a makeshift reception desk and chairs round the wall. The room was empty, but a door behind the counter opened and a woman in a shalwar kameez came through and looked at

Lynne warily. Lynne showed her identification and said, 'I'm looking for Matthew Pearse.'

The woman looked closely at the card Lynne was holding up. After she had studied it, she shot Lynne a closed look, jerked her head and said, 'Come,' indicating the door behind her. Her English was heavily accented.

Lynne followed her and found herself in a small office that was cramped with just a desk, a filing cabinet, some shelves and a couple of chairs. There was no one else there. The shelves contained some books, in a script that Lynne couldn't read. Arabic? There were also boxes of leaflets that Lynne, without asking, looked at. They were mostly to do with welfare rights and health care, particularly relating to children: *Immunization; Feeding your toddler; Housing Benefit; Family Credit.* Welfare, as the notice on the door said. Tacked on to the wall behind the desk was a typewritten list of addresses and phone numbers, with handwritten additions. The woman watched her in silence. Lynne held out her hand. 'Detective Inspector Jordan,' she said.

The woman hesitated then touched the proffered hand. 'Nasim Rafiq,' she said, after a moment. Then, 'Matthew Pearse is not here. But soon.' Pearse would be back soon. OK, Lynne could wait. She smiled at the other woman, and got a hesitant smile in return.

'Mrs Rafiq.' Lynne wondered how good the woman's English was. Good enough, presumably, to work here. 'I wonder if you could tell me something about this centre, about the work you do.'

Rafiq looked at Lynne in silence for a while, then indicated the leaflets. 'Welfare advice,' she said.

This was presumably not irony, but a genuine attempt to explain. 'Who do you offer advice to, Mrs Rafiq?'

'Refugee,' the other woman said, after another pause for thought. 'They come from ... other places? From government?'

A centre that was offering help to refugees sent north through the dispersal system. This matched the pattern Michael Balit had described to her – a patchwork of voluntary organizations, often run by members of the refugee communities themselves, often poorly trained and ill-equipped, trying to fill the gap. This was the kind of place she might find useful. She looked round the room. There was a door, presumably leading to the rest of the building. 'May I look round?' she said.

Rafiq seemed unsurprised by the request, and stood up. She locked the door leading through to the front, and took Lynne into the back room, gesturing for her to look at anything she wanted to. This room was virtually unfurnished. There was a settee pushed against one wall, and a chair with wooden arms, the upholstery sagging underneath the seat. A small Calor Gas heater was pushed against another wall, and the faint, sweet smell of the gas permeated the air. Beyond the room was a corridor leading to the stairs and a cubbyhole of a kitchen. Another door led to a dank back yard that was overshadowed by the high wall of the warehouse.

Lynne looked at the stairs and then at Nasim Rafiq. 'We store,' Rafiq said in response to Lynne's look. 'Go –' she gestured permission to Lynne. Lynne took the opportunity to check the upstairs rooms, which seemed, as Rafiq had said, to be used for storage. There were stacks of boxes, the dust suggesting they had been there for a while. Lynne pulled up a cardboard flap of one, and found it was full of clothes, woollens. Some rather shabby furniture was piled up and pushed against the walls. Lynne came down the stairs wiping her hands on her skirt. They felt grubby. Rafiq saw, and gestured towards the small sink in the kitchen. Lynne washed her hands and dried them on the immaculate towel that the other woman gave her.

'Thank you, Mrs Rafiq,' Lynne said. 'I'm interested in the welfare services for refugees. You're very quiet here today.'

Rafiq made a weighing gesture with her hands. 'Is quiet, is busy,' she said. *It varies*, Lynne interpreted. The woman's spoken English didn't seem to be very good, but she had few problems understanding Lynne.

They went back to the small office, and Lynne took out

the still from the security video that showed Katya leaving the hospital. It was a back view; the face was in profile and blurred, but it showed the dark hair, and gave an impression of her features. She put it on the desk and saw the woman lean forward in interest.

The door from the shop opened suddenly, and a man came into the room, carrying a pile of boxes. Lynne noticed that he moved awkwardly. He stopped as he saw her. Lynne smiled and offered her hand. 'Mr Pearse?' she said. He put the boxes down on the desk and shook her proffered hand, looking at Nasim for guidance. It was hard to judge how old he was. His hair was white, and he had the slight stoop of age, but his face looked younger.

His eyes fell on the photograph, and he stepped forward. 'Have you . . . Do you know . . . ?' He had a slight stammer. Michael Balit had said he was disabled.

'Is police,' Nasim Rafiq said quickly. She kept her eyes on Pearse's face.

'Mr Pearse,' Lynne said, 'I understand you found this woman and took her to the hospital.'

He looked confused for a moment. 'No. I mean, yes . . . that is . . .' Lynne waited while he disentangled his sentence. 'I took her to the hospital,' he said. 'She found us.' Lynne was aware of Nasim Rafiq hovering protectively by his side. 'I made a statement,' he added.

'Is there somewhere we can talk?' she said. After a moment's hesitation, he nodded and led her through to the back room she'd seen earlier. Lynne was aware of Nasim Rafiq's eyes on her as the door closed. She sat on the chair, and adopted a relaxed, friendly pose – *You can help me here* – as she took him through his previous statement. It always helped her to listen to the spoken voice, observe the face of the witness. He had very little to add to what she already knew. He worked as a volunteer for the Welfare Advice Centre, he explained to Lynne. 'There's just the two of us at the moment,' he said. 'We aren't properly set up yet. But word gets around, so we're starting to get busy. It varies.' He had trouble with his voice, a slight stutter that made him speak slowly and carefully, making his words sound hesitant. 'It's been used as storage for clothes and furniture,' he said. 'But now we're getting the asylum seekers coming up here. They need a lot of support while . . .' He struggled with his stammer.

'While their claims are checked?' Lynne said. He looked at her. 'Into genuine and fraudulent,' she explained.

'I don't make that distinction.' His eyes were dark and direct. His disability, a slight curvature of the spine, had made him seem diffident and self-effacing, an effect enhanced by his speech impediment, but his manner was quiet and assured. 'Poverty can be just as bad as political oppression. I'd do the same if I were young. Or if I had children.'

It was a sidetrack, but an interesting one. Here was a man who was sympathetic to the refugees, and who had contacts. Was this why Katya had come here? 'Tell me about the woman who came to the welfare centre, Mr Pearse.'

He composed himself, and moved his lips once or twice, trying to find the words. 'She came on . . . I can't remember the date. I can check it.' He paused, expecting a response, but Lynne said nothing. 'She had very little English, but she had been hurt. Someone had beaten her quite badly, I think.' The effort to control his stammer kept his voice level, but there was anger on his face.

'Why did she come to you?' Lynne wondered if this place was known as one where people might help and ask no questions.

Pearse shook his head. 'I don't know. By the time I thought to ask . . . I took her to the hospital.'

She nodded to him to go on. 'I dropped her at the entrance and told her where to go. I said I would come in when I'd parked the car. I don't know if she understood me. I watched her go in, then I went to park.' He gave Lynne a faint smile. 'That took some time. And I phoned Nasim to let her know what I was doing. It took me a while to find the pay phone. They'd taken her in by the time I got back. I waited. I went for a walk. My back gets painful sitting in those chairs. And I was just returning when I saw her. She came out of the hospital and started walking towards the car park. Then she waved to someone.' He caught Lynne's look. 'I couldn't see anyone, not from where I was. By the time I'd got there, she'd gone.'

'Did you get the impression she'd seen someone she knew?' Lynne said.

He hesitated. 'I think so, yes.'

'So what did you do then, Mr Pearse?' If he'd just got someone . . . 'Did you contact anyone about her? Talk to the hospital staff?'

'I knew the hospital had called the police,' he said. 'I saw them go in. I thought that was why she'd run away.' He looked at his hands, then looked back at Lynne. 'I thought at the time she had been working as a prostitute,' he said. 'I didn't want to get her into trouble, God help me. I thought I'd persuaded her to come back to the centre – after she'd been to the hospital, I mean.' He looked sad.

This was, more or less, what he'd said in his original statement. He'd gone back to the centre, where he'd found Nasim dealing with an influx of people. 'We were open late that night,' he explained. 'There'd been some new arrivals. I thought it was lucky, at the time.' They'd worked together to clear it, then he'd taken Nasim home. 'It isn't safe for her on public transport at night,' he said.

Nasim Rafiq had little to add. She had seen the woman when she first came to the centre, and had seen Matthew later when he came back from the hospital. Lynne confirmed her original statement, noticing Rafiq's fingers picking at the fringes of her scarf. Her nails were bitten down. Lynne kept to the details of the statement, maintained her air of relaxation. Rafiq saw her to the door of the advice centre, giving Lynne that same rather hesitant smile.

Lynne drummed her fingers on the steering wheel in thought as she waited at a red light. She had the information she wanted – there didn't seem to be anything that had been missed in the first statements – but she needed to talk to Nasim Rafiq again. She wanted to know where the woman's nervous watchfulness came from, why she had tried to warn

86

Matthew Pearse before he spoke to her. It would be worth her while paying Mrs Rafiq another visit.

Sheffield, Monday

Luke was working when Roz tapped at the door of the computer room later that morning and tentatively pushed it open. He was hunched forward staring at pictures on his monitor. 'Coffee?' she said, recognizing in her voice the hushed tones used to address the wounded and the sick. She cleared her throat and said it again. 'Coffee?'

Luke banged his hand down on the keyboard. 'Shit!' He sounded tense and angry. He switched the monitor off.

Roz wasn't going to tiptoe around him. 'Is that a yes or a no?' she said, checking the coffee pot. Luke's silence was eloquent of unexpressed anger. She ignored it, and poured two cups, rinsed the pot out and put fresh coffee in the machine. She put a cup down beside him and sat in the chair next to him.

'Thanks.' It was grudging, but at least he was talking to her.

'Joanna said you've been on to the hospital and the police again.'

'All a waste of time, it seems.' He swivelled round in his chair to look at her. 'Something's wrong.' He ran his hand through his hair. 'Look, Roz, it's . . .' She waited, but he shook his head. 'Nothing . . . It just doesn't feel right. The only thing Grey's worried about is her group. And you . . .' He sounded tired.

'Listen,' she said, 'I talked to Joanna earlier. She knows that Gemma's been applying for grants to get back to Russia. She's been helping her.' She couldn't tell from his face whether this was news to him or not. 'Joanna's worried. It's just that she can cope with worrying about grants and things, and she can't cope with worrying about people.'

Luke shrugged. 'So that's all right then,' he said.

'Oh, for . . .' Roz took a deep breath and finished her coffee. Losing her temper with Luke wasn't going to help. She wanted to tell him that she was sure everything would be fine in the end, but she could remember in the aftermath of Nathan's illness, friends' well-meaning insistence that it would all be OK, it would all work out, Nathan would recover. 'How do you know?' She'd snapped at one woman. 'I just know,' the woman had said. 'I can feel it.' Roz hadn't wanted spurious consolation from people who claimed some kind of hotline to providence, she wanted it from the experts, and they were no longer offering it. Any attempt of that sort to offer support to Luke would be patronizing and naïve. In the end, there was work. 'Have you had any luck with retrieving her files?'

He gestured at the machine he'd been working on. 'Nothing. Fragments. I can't see any way . . .'

She looked more closely at him. His face was drawn. He needed a shave, and his restlessness and the glitter in his eyes suggested to her that he'd taken something to keep him awake. 'Luke, how long have you been working on it? Did you get any sleep last night?'

'Oh, for shit's sake, Roz! Stop fussing.' But his tone was more normal now, more like the Luke that she knew. He smiled at her, and if she hadn't known him so well, she would have thought the smile was genuine. 'Go and look after your boss. She's got her grants to worry about.'

Roz made a face at him. *You don't fool me, Hagan.* She finished her coffee and stood up. 'Let's get lunch at the Broomgrove,' she said. Then wished she hadn't said it. Lunch at the pub was one of the things they used to do, when they were closer, before they'd messed it up, before his relationship with Gemma.

But he didn't seem to notice, just nodded and said, 'OK. Let me know when you're ready,' and turned back to his screen.

Hull, Monday evening
The bar was almost empty. There were just a few drinkers, marking the end of the working day, scattered here and there among the tables. Lynne Jordan sipped her coffee and shuddered. Stewed. It must have been standing on the hotpl-

ate for most of the afternoon. She wondered if she could be bothered to ask for another cup, freshly made. London and Leeds had spoiled her. She had got used to decent coffee on tap, interesting cafés and snack bars, places that were prosperous and thriving. Hull was developing, but it was a city that had lost its main source of wealth, and had yet to replace it.

She checked her watch. One of her contacts, Marie, had arranged to meet her here. Marie was a prostitute who worked the streets around the old docks area. She used to work for escort agencies, safer work than soliciting on the streets, but like many women who ventured into prostitution, she was slipping down the hierarchy of escort, call girl, streetwalker. Lynne checked her watch again. Marie was about fifteen minutes late now. Not a lot, given the rather vague sense of time she had shown on their previous meetings, but Lynne had expected Marie to be on time for this meeting. Lynne had managed to hold back a soliciting charge – one that threatened to prove one too many and land Marie with a prison sentence. Marie owed her, and Lynne could still let the charge go through.

She opened the small folder she had been carrying around all afternoon. It contained photographs taken from the Angel website, photographs of the Sleeping Beauty, the jeans and T-shirt picture that young Des Stanwell had identified as a 'posh student type', and the face from the shot that had been mirrored in the positioning of the body. She had spent the afternoon asking a few questions about Angel Escorts, trying to see if anyone recognized 'Jemima' from the photographs.

But no one could help her, either with the Sleeping Beauty or with Angel Escorts. She wasn't surprised that the immigrant support groups had no information, but she had had hopes that she might get something from the local prostitutes. Lynne had managed to form reasonable relationships with some of them. They now accepted that she wasn't interested in moving them on or arresting them, and treated her as one of the minor hazards of a life that teemed with more serious hazards, but they had been evasive and unhelpful.

Lynne wondered if they were frightened, and hoped that Marie, in a more secure environment, might be willing to talk.

Marie arrived ten minutes later, looking anxiously round the bar before she joined Lynne. Though this pub had been her suggested rendezvous, she seemed uncertain and insecure beneath a superficially confident exterior. 'I can't stay,' she said, as soon as she sat down.

Lynne offered her a drink; she refused and lit a cigarette. She didn't offer one to Lynne. 'Not when I'm working,' she said. Her pale blonde hair was piled on top of her head, and her make-up, though skilfully applied, was heavy. Lynne wondered how old she was. She admitted to thirty, but she looked at least ten years older than that.

She looked at the first photograph of Jemima. 'Never seen her,' she said dismissively. But that didn't mean much. Marie worked on the street. What was happening on the streets was, to a certain extent, open and known. If Jemima had been one of the women brought into the country illegally, then she may well have been kept under strict control, except that control had broken down somewhere.

Lynne waited a moment to see if she would say something else, but Marie remained silent. She moved on. 'These women I'm looking for,' she said, 'the ones that have been brought in, are there any on the streets? Have you seen many working?'

Marie shrugged. 'There's a few,' she said cautiously. She met Lynne's eyes briefly then looked down. 'They'll do anything,' she said. 'It's like the druggies, don't give a monkey's, just want the cash.' *What can I do?* She needed to make a living.

'Do you know any of them?' Lynne said. 'Do you know who's working them?'

Marie shook her head. 'I keep right away from it,' she said. 'I'm not daft.'

Marie probably knew more than she was saying, but Lynne didn't want to push her too far at this stage. 'I'm trying to track down one of the agencies,' she said. 'It's one that works online.' Marie drew on her cigarette, listening.

'It's called Angel,' Lynne said. 'Angel Escorts.'

Marie looked quickly round the room. Lynne took out a copy of the business card and pushed it across the table. Marie didn't look at the card. She looked at her watch and then across the table at Lynne. 'I've got to go,' she said abruptly, standing up. 'I told you I couldn't stay.'

'Marie,' Lynne said. 'Angel Escorts?'

'Never heard of them,' Marie said. She was pulling on her coat as she spoke.

'Marie –' Lynne said.

'I'll ask around,' Marie said.

'Do that,' Lynne said. Her eyes met Marie's, reminding her that the charge still hung over her.

Marie pulled her collar close round her in a nervous gesture. 'I will,' she said, backing away from the table. 'I'll call you.' She usually would, once her funds began running low. Lynne watched Marie leave and tried her coffee again. It wasn't just bitter, it was cold now. She took it back to the bar and, after some discussion with the young woman serving there, got another, freshly made cup. She was just turning away from the bar when she almost collided with a man who was coming through the door bringing a waft of icy air in with him. It was Roy Farnham. He stopped when he saw her. 'Lynne – I didn't know . . .'

'I've just been . . .'

They both broke the silence together, and then started laughing as they got into the 'After you' 'No, after you' that such situations engendered. He came across to the table she had been sitting at. 'Are you on your own?' he said.

She told him about her meeting with Marie, and he looked interested. 'Anything?'

'I don't know.' Lynne needed to think that one through.

'You were right about the Angel website,' he said after a moment. 'I had a look at it this morning. The Jemima pages have vanished.'

'I downloaded them,' Lynne said. 'Any luck with the ISP? Or the phone number?'

'I'm working on the ISP,' he said. 'No luck yet. The phone is a pay-as-you-go. We can't get a name or an address. I'm on to the company. I want the records for that number, see what kind of activity there is on it. We may be able to get a location from that.' He thought for a minute. 'How are you getting on?'

Lynne ran through her afternoon, aware as she was speaking that she had very little for him. 'No one recognized her,' she finished, 'but I've got some more people to talk to.' She pulled the photograph of Jemima out of her bag. 'I wish I could remember who she reminds me of,' she said.

Farnham looked at it. 'Doesn't ring any bells with me,' he said.

Lynne told him about her interview with Matthew Pearse and with Nasim Rafiq. 'You think she might know something?' he said.

Lynne wasn't sure. 'She might just have been nervous. But I think I'll go back, just in case.'

He picked up the menu on the table, and looked at it. 'I came in here for something to eat. I missed lunch. Do you want anything?'

It was one of the hazards of the job – meals missed, food eaten in a hurry, on the hoof. It could lead to a diet high in convenience food, takeaways, quick, unhealthy snacks. She looked at the menu without enthusiasm. It was a standard pub-chain menu – pseudo European and eastern food, or various deep-fried offerings and chips. She knew what the salads would be like: a plate piled high with tasteless lettuce, dressing in a plastic sachet like shampoo or shower gel. She made a quick decision. 'I'm starving, but not for this stuff. Let's go to the Italian down the road.' A bog-standard pasta house, but better than what the pub had to offer.

He shot her a quick glance then looked at the menu again. 'Sounds OK to me,' he said. He finished his drink, and they headed for the door. Lynne shivered as the chill of the street caught her after the warmth of the pub.

There were just a few early evening diners at the restaurant, and music was playing quietly. As the waiter hurried over to light the candle on their table, Lynne wondered if she had made a mistake. She smiled apologetically at Farnham. 'The food is much better here,' she said. 'But it'll probably take longer.'

'That's OK.' He seemed quite relaxed. 'I'm in no rush.' He was studying the menu. 'If we're doing this, let's do it properly. Want some wine?'

Lynne felt her guard dropping as they drank the first glass. She was still unsure if this was wise, but he was good company, easy to talk to, and, she had to admit it, attractive. They drifted away from work for a while as they tested the ground between them. They began to talk about the difficulties of maintaining a personal life if you were committed to the job. He was divorced, he told her. 'Got married young when I was starting out,' he said. 'She couldn't stand the pace. We never saw each other. It just died on its feet.'

'Children?' Lynne said.

'One. A boy.' He didn't seem to want to elaborate, so she didn't pursue it. 'You?'

She shook her head. 'No marriage, no kids.' There didn't seem to be anything else to say. The waiter brought their food over, and Farnham steered the conversation back to work as they ate. 'No one recognized her?' he said, going back to what they had been talking about in the pub.

'Not so far,' Lynne said. 'I've more or less run out of people to ask.' The photograph was on the table between them. As Lynne looked at Jemima's face, the Katya tape drifted into her mind again. *Some kind of posh student type . . .* Those eyes . . . She had a sudden picture of a woman talking at a seminar, making a joke about an obscene phone caller who'd left an answer-phone message with his phone number, looking up quickly from her notes. A rather diffident woman, shy, but with a quiet sense of fun. Of course! That was who Jemima reminded her of: Gemma Wishart, the forensic linguistics expert. Just another of the odd connections her job threw up. She was glad to have that nagging familiarity sorted out, even though it didn't help.

But the similarity, now she came to look more closely,

was marked ... That was ridiculous! Gemma Wishart was in Sheffield, working on the Katya tape. Except ... she remembered the phone call on Friday. Gemma Wishart's report had not arrived as promised, the woman she had spoken to had sounded flustered and uncertain, and Wishart herself had not been available, either then or when Lynne had phoned a second time. She tried to picture the face of the young woman she'd met at the seminar, but now the face of 'Jemima' interposed itself, and she couldn't tell if her memory was reliable or if she was seeing something that didn't really exist. She was going crazy. It *had* to be a coincidence.

She blinked, and became aware of Farnham looking at her expectantly. 'I'm sorry. I've just realized who it is that Jemima reminds me of.' She looked at the picture again. 'I hope this is all a coincidence,' she said.

Anna waited until the light was starting to go. It had been an overcast day, and by four, the dull shadows of evening were lying across the city and a mist was starting to obscure the buildings and shop fronts. The streetlights loomed through the damp fog as Anna walked the emptying streets. She had planned to spend the day moving from one city-centre shop to another, using their warmth to protect her from the cold before she faced another shelterless night. She had hoped that she might find a quiet place to sit down, maybe doze for a few minutes, but after the morning's encounter, she didn't dare. Suppose the stores had warned each other, suppose they had called the police? She was too nervous to stop or to loiter, and the confusion of hunger and exhaustion had begun to catch up with her.

She had to do something. She had to decide before she became too weak to do or to decide anything. By midday, the hunger had been acute and she'd felt light-headed, the world around her appearing both brighter and less substantial as she trekked across the cobbled pavements back towards the docks. She had to get something to eat. She could feel a cold sweat starting to break out down her back.

94

If she collapsed in the street, they'd take her to hospital, and then ... Her eyes had scanned the passers-by, trying to decide who might be friendly, who might be sympathetic – but not too friendly, not too sympathetic. Her bedraggled appearance would make what she wanted clear.

She had tried approaching one woman, her 'Please ...' coming out as a cracked whisper that the woman didn't hear. She'd tried again, a bit louder, 'Please ...' But the woman walked past, staring at the ground. It had been easier after the first time, but the people she approached ignored her, or veered past her, or crossed the road if they looked ahead and saw her. She was making herself noticeable. She had huddled herself deeper into her coat as the cold seeped in. A woman was walking past her. Anna tried again. 'Please ... ?'

The woman had looked at her. 'I'm sorry,' she said. 'I didn't see you.' She was fumbling in her purse, not quite meeting Anna's eye. She had pushed a coin towards Anna who was frozen for a moment and then took it.

'Thank you ...' But the woman had already walked away. She looked at what the woman had given her. A two-pound coin. She could buy ... something that was hot and filling, something cheap and plentiful. She needed to eat, get her strength up. There was a van selling chips down near the market. She had bought a bag and slipped down a side street to huddle over their warmth as she ate them. Some youths had pushed past her, knocking her against the wall. 'Gyppo!' one of them had shouted. She froze. 'Gyppo!' and a burst of raucous laughter as they vanished round the corner.

She had felt better after she had eaten, more able to think. She had spent the rest of the money on a bag of broken biscuits in the market, and a cup of tea. She needed to plan. She would have to walk back to the house where her room was; she couldn't afford the bus fare. It would take her about half an hour, a daunting prospect in the cold, in her present state. Then she could wait until it was quiet, and slip in. She would collect her stuff, her papers, maybe some clothes. If it was quiet, if there wasn't anyone around, maybe she could have a wash. She wouldn't be able to put anything in the meter so the water would be cold, but at least she would be clean. Once she had got her papers, she could get away.

Now it was dark enough, and the obscuring fog would help. Maybe no one was watching for her, maybe no one knew she was there. But she couldn't be sure. *Angel!* Eighteen months ago. 'I always collect,' he'd told her. 'Don't try and cheat me.' But Anna had. She had run away. Her mother had helped her, had spoken to her in the voice that Anna could still hear, *Anna-kin, Anna, you must go before it's too late.* She had watched and waited for her chance, had been as quiet and as good as he wanted her to be, done anything he had asked her to do. And all the time she had thought, *Tomorrow. Tomorrow I will be gone. Or the next day. Soon.*

Six months ago. The room had been dark, just the light from the table lamp making a pool of yellow by the bed. Angel had brought the man himself. 'He's my special friend, Anna,' he'd said, smiling, and running his hand down her face in a gesture that was half caress, half threat. Anna had tried not to see the man's face, his eyes that were already appraising her in her silk and lace. He had smelt of alcohol and some kind of sweet chemical that only partly masked the smell of sweat, of excitement. Angel had given her a long look, a look she couldn't quite decipher. She felt her stomach clench with apprehension. There was something wrong. And then he went, and for the first time she felt as though some protection had been taken away from her.

She suppressed her fear. Angel protected her. She was valuable. 'My investments always pay. Remember that. You'll be all right with me.' She smiled her smile, bright and inviting, hearing Angel's voice giving her his approval. 'That's right, sweetheart.' She retreated behind the mask and let the mechanical doll take over. But the alcohol the man had drunk gave him problems, and his anger at this had inflamed his cruelty, or maybe he had just wanted an excuse to do the things he wanted but didn't dare admit he wanted. Anna knew the stimulus of cruelty. Her mother, her sisters, even the little one, had died in a frenzy of excitement driven by the knife, the fist and the flame. Anna had seen the bodies.

The man had pinched her nipple until she couldn't stop herself from crying out, had sunk his teeth into the delicate skin high up on the inside of her thigh. She couldn't understand why someone didn't come in and stop him. She struggled, and called out. He knelt on her, pinning her legs with his weight. He put his hand round her throat and squeezed. She could feel her breath start to cut off, feel the pressure building up in her head. 'Angel owes me,' he said. 'So you'll do what I say, bitch.' He smiled at her and relaxed the hand round her neck. She could see the sweat shining on his face. 'You love it really, don't you, you dirty gyppo cunt.' He jammed his fingers inside her and she clenched her teeth against the pain. 'Don't you?' Her stomach heaved. 'Don't you? Don't you?' Each time he asked, he rammed his fingers in harder.

'Yes!' She shut her eyes, trying to make her mind switch off, trying to make the doll take over so that she wouldn't feel what was happening to her, wouldn't be there while he did . . . whatever else he was going to do.

She thought about her mother. *Anna . . . before it's too late!* Her mother had fought for her life, for her children's lives. Her mother hadn't submitted and sent her mind scuttling away to some hiding place where nothing mattered. The man was muttering angrily now, 'Dirty bitch, dirty . . .' a litany of abuse that was inflaming him more and more. Angel had said he would take care of her, but she was already torn and bruised. What use would Angel have for her? Angel was letting him do this to her. The man was pulling her on to her knees, putting his hands round her neck again, freeing her arms. It was now. If she got it wrong, if she made him so angry that he killed her, maybe the first blow would bring oblivion. Maybe that would be better. She reached out and gripped the table lamp, knowing there was slack on the flex, pulling at it to make sure it wasn't caught up. *Now!* Her first swing barely touched him, the awkward angle making it impossible to get any force behind her arm, but he pulled back in shock and amazement. His face was beginning to change from incredulity to anger as she swung it again and caught him on the side of the head. The drink had made his reflexes slow, and he lost his balance and fell to the floor. And now, her mother was watching over her. He hit his head on the side of the table as he fell, and stayed crouched on the floor, his hands against his head, making a strange moaning sound.

She was off the bed in an instant. She had no clothes apart from the lingerie that Angel had her wear when she was working. The drunken man's clothes were draped over a chair. He had put them there carefully, folding them as he took them off, as she had smiled at him, the way Angel told her to. She pulled on his sweatshirt, letting it hang loose like a dress. It was enough. The summer night was warm. She didn't have time to waste. She hesitated, then reached into the pocket of the jacket draped over the chair. Her fingers closed round a fat wallet and she shoved it inside the shirt. She resisted the impulse to look at the man on the floor again. He was still making that moaning sound. Someone would realize what had happened, someone would come. She called her mother's face into her mind, and smashed the base of the lamp against the window. The glass shattered. She could hear the sound of running feet as she swung her leg over the sill. She was three stories up. *Mama, help me now!* She strained sideways, her fingers touching the drainpipe as she slipped. The web of pipe-work on the back wall slowed her fall into a scrabbling descent and she landed on the ground with no more than a few grazes.

Water splashed on to her head from an overflow, and she staggered to her feet . . . *the drip drip of the water* . . . and away into the night.

She had run away from Angel. She had cheated him. She had hurt, maybe killed his friend and stolen his money.

There was no one to help her. She was on her own.

7

Sheffield, Monday evening

As she closed her front door behind her, Roz welcomed the
sense of peace. The day had been a mixture of frustration
and tedium, of tasks started that were impossible to complete,
and of nagging, unfocused anxieties. At lunch, Luke had
determinedly kept away from the subject of Gemma, talking
instead of the software they were developing to analyse the
interview data, of the latest gossip in the department about
the Joanna/Peter Cauldwell feud.

This led on to a discussion about where the group was
going – casual, work-related chat. On any other occasion, it
would have been a pleasant and relaxing half-hour, very
typical of the times that she and Luke used to spend together
shortly after she came to Sheffield, when she was finding
her feet in her research post.

But that had been an oasis of calm in the middle of an
increasingly frenetic day. She made herself coffee and wandered into the study to stand and stare into the depths of the
mirror. It was dark outside, and only the reflected moonlight
illuminated the room. It had been a bad day, one that had
brought out the worst in Joanna, her normal smooth efficiency turned into a hectoring panic as she tried to deal with
a situation she couldn't understand.

Then there had been the report. When Joanna had greeted
her with the news of DI Jordan's phone call, Roz had confidently said that Gemma's report could be sent at once, something that had mollified Joanna a bit. 'You should have sent
it off on Friday,' she said. 'It was obvious that Gemma wasn't

planning to come in to finish it.' It hadn't been obvious at all, but Roz had left it, knowing that Joanna needed something to be angry about, something that didn't matter, something that she could deal with. 'And there's another Manchester meeting next Monday,' Joanna went on. 'I can't go. You'll have to attend that. You'd better contact someone and get them to send you the minutes.'

Roz had managed to get herself up to date with the Manchester meeting, but she hadn't been able to give much thought to the report until she came back from lunch, and when she had gone to Gemma's room to find it, the report wasn't there. She'd checked the filing cabinet, the desk drawers, the window sills, even the floor and the back of the filing cabinet. It wasn't there. And then she felt a dawning unease. She could remember reading it on the screen, but had she printed it out? She'd been distracted with the meeting, with the annoyance of Gemma's non-appearance, and her mind had been on her lecture as well.

She tried to take herself back to Friday morning. She'd found the file on Gemma's machine. Then she'd read the report, yes ... while it was printing out. She *had* printed it. Then she'd gone to find Luke – but she'd put the report on her desk, along with the transcript and Gemma's notes. That was it. There had been a pile of papers on her desk, things for dealing with today. She must have misfiled the report, got it mixed up with her own stuff.

She'd gone systematically through all her files, knowing how easily a few sheets of paper could disappear – but it wasn't there. And she hadn't told Joanna. She'd chickened out. She told herself that it might have got mixed up with papers she'd brought home. Now she not only had to tell Joanna that the report was missing, she had to tell her that she had concealed the fact for a whole day. If the report wasn't available, then DI Jordan should have been informed at once. It was just something else that would make the group look unprofessional.

She was tempted to phone Luke and unburden herself to him, but that wasn't fair. He had Gemma's sudden departure to cope with, and, in his position, it was better if he were well insulated from Joanna's wrath. Joanna had already decided, or tried to decide, that it was Luke's fault the back-up systems weren't in place. Roz had jumped on that one quickly, and Joanna had grudgingly accepted responsibility. But Roz knew Joanna's mental picture of Luke would now include someone who hadn't been sufficiently forceful about the importance of an automatic back-up system.

She wondered what to do. After the day she'd had, the thought of working on her book was depressing. She toyed with the idea of phoning someone and going out, but that didn't appeal either. She wandered into the kitchen and picked up the paper that she'd dumped on the kitchen table. Nothing on television tonight. She thought about going to see a film, and hunted round for the local entertainment guide half-heartedly.

She decided to phone someone, see if anyone had any plans for the evening that could include her. Lorna. Lorna was a teacher at a local comprehensive and would have tales of woe that would put Roz's bad day into its proper perspective. She'd phone Lorna. But when she got to the hall table where the phone was, she saw that the message light was blinking – three messages. The first one was Joanna, from nine o'clock this morning, asking her where she was. The second one was silence and the sound of the receiver being hung up, and the third one was from her mother. Paula's bright, answering-machine voice er'd and rambled through the message. '. . . and anyway, it seems ages since we've talked, Roz. Phone me.' Roz sighed. It was true, she hadn't talked to her mother for several weeks. She hesitated for a moment, then picked up the phone and rang the number.

Paula Frost was delighted. 'Roz! How lovely. Now don't apologize, I know how busy you are.' She chatted on, filling Roz in on the details of what she and Robert, Roz's stepfather had been doing, what various acquaintances – people who no longer had any part in Roz's life – had been doing, and her own involvement with local politics. Roz reciprocated with news – somewhat edited – from work, talk about her future career plans, the possibility of a visit. She was relaxing now, hoping she was going to get away with it, when she heard a new note coming into her mother's voice.

'Listen, Roz, it's lovely to talk to you, but there was something important I wanted to say.'

Roz stiffened. 'Oh yes?'

'Oh, listen to you, Roz!' Her mother said impatiently. 'We haven't talked for weeks, and when we do talk, you rattle on about work, work, work. And as soon as you think I'm going to talk about anything else, you're on the defensive.'

'I'm not.' Roz felt wrong-footed.

'Yes you are. Now listen. I saw Graham Highgrove last week.' Graham was her mother's solicitor. 'He's very concerned about your situation. About the legal implications.' Paula's recent tactics had been to place her own concerns in the mouths of others, in an effort to get Roz to listen to her. 'He thinks you should get a divorce. That would stop that terrible drain on your finances. Darling, I know that you . . .'

'No, you don't. I'm sorry, Mum, but I'm not going to talk about it.' Roz pressed her forehead against the wall. Why, *why* did she have to have this conversation with Paula once every few months or so? Why couldn't her mother accept the decisions she had made?

'What good are you doing Nathan by hanging on?' Paula's voice was reasonable. 'It isn't as if . . .'

It isn't as if you ever saw him. 'I said I don't want to talk about it.' Roz took a deep breath. 'Please listen to me. *I don't want to talk about it.*'

She heard her mother sigh. 'Robert and I are very worried,' she said. Roz doubted that her easy-going golf-playing stepfather gave the matter much thought. He seemed to think that she could look after herself.

'I can't help that.' Roz cut the topic short. 'Now is there anything else?' They spent another minute or two mending fences, and then Paula rang off, leaving Roz with the shards of the evening scattered around her. She wandered back into her study and shifted the books and papers round on the table she used as a desk. The mirror threw a dark reflection back.

She didn't want to think about it, but it wouldn't go away. Paula was right. Why was she hanging on to a marriage that had died – that had been destroyed – years ago? *For better, for worse, in sickness and in health, the good times and the bad times.* Partly, it was a safeguard, for Nathan. As his wife, she still had a say. But mostly, it was a promise that the very young Roz had made to the very young Nathan. Would she have expected him to keep the faith? Twenty-one-year-old Roz would have done. Thirty-year-old Roz did not.

Twenty-one. She had been twenty-one to Nathan's twenty-six when they had married. They had gone to the Register Office, she and Nathan, with two friends as witnesses, and made their vows as privately as they could. *I do solemnly declare* . . . She could still see Nathan's face, serious for once, his fair hair tidy, his eyes looking into hers . . . *That I know of no reason* . . .

Hull, Monday evening
The house was at the end of a side street, backing on to derelict industrial land. The houses were tall, three stories, with elegant patterns in the brickwork at odds with the neglected paintwork and rotting timbers. The traffic from the main road, out of the city to the east coast, made a constant background roar. They'd given Anna the address at the Welfare Advice Centre when she had found her way there two days after she had run away from Angel. 'It's not much,' Matthew, one of the volunteer workers, had told her, his voice stumbling over his words. 'But no one will ask you any questions. As long as you can pay them.'

'I have money,' she'd told him. She could see from his face that he knew how she'd earned it. He'd looked sad, and that sadness made her feel she could trust him. She'd wanted to talk to him, to tell him what had happened. But of course she couldn't. She couldn't tell anyone.

The room wasn't much, but it was enough. She'd handed over the first week's rent to the landlord, who had not appeared again, just sent people to collect the money each week. 'If you're late, you're out,' he'd told her. She'd known what she wanted to do with the money she'd got from the drunken man. It hadn't been enough for the papers she needed, but she'd been able to save, because Matthew had told her about places where she might find work, casual work, early-morning work, evening work. She'd chosen places she thought that Angel wouldn't go. Places she had thought were safe.

She hovered uncertainly at the corner, common sense telling her that no one would be watching the house, not day and night. It was four days since she had been there, she wasn't worth a constant watch. But someone might have been told, 'If she comes back . . . this number . . . at once . . . worth your while . . .' She would need to be quick, but she didn't need to be afraid now, not right now.

Her heart was beating in her throat as she walked down the street, keeping in the shadows. If he saw her, the watcher, let it be as late as possible, to give her a chance to be in, out and away.

She could see the house now, the last one on the street. There was a light in the downstairs front, she could see it through the chinks in the cloth that was hung in front of the window. A young man lived in that room, a young man who kept erratic hours, going out late at night, coming home in the early hours of the morning. There were no other lights.

If the young man was in his room, he would be playing music. That would help, would obscure the sounds of Anna opening the door and climbing the stairs. She craned her neck, looking up towards the top of the house, the dormer window where she had her attic room. She almost expected to see a light up there, a flickering, moving light . . . But the window was a dark square, the skeleton rail of the old fire escape silhouetted against the night sky. She moved closer. There was a streetlight just in front of the house. She couldn't avoid it. She kept her head down and stepped into the circle of light. A sudden movement to her right made her jump and look up. A cat ran along the wall. She hunched her shoulders, hurrying through the gate. The cloth over the window trembled slightly as she ran silently up the steps.

She had her key in her hand, and was inside with the door shut behind her before she had time to think. Then she stood for a moment, catching her breath, listening. Silence. Not even the music that the young man always played. Just the distant drone of the traffic. The stairs in front of her were dark. She wanted to run away, but she knew if she did that, she wouldn't come back here again. She pressed the switch on the wall, and a dim light came on above her. She moved cautiously now, on to the first landing. The light went out and the staircase was in darkness. She listened. Nothing. A creak. A whispering sound in the pipes. Her eyes strained into the shadows until she saw shapes and patterns moving. She pushed the switch again, poised to leap down the stairs, to run. The empty corridor lay in front her.

She moved on to the next flight, the curved flight that led to the attic rooms. She pressed her shoulders against the wall as she slid up the stairs, trying to see to the top, to see round the corner. The light went out. Her breath was coming in gasps and she stumbled as she reached the top of the stairs. It was black night on the tiny landing, and she had lost her bearings. She reached her hands out for the switch, feeling the wall, the slight give of the paper. Something cold and hard made her recoil. The pipes. The wall vanished, and she stumbled forward, her hands hitting against a door with a solid thud. She froze.

Now the silence had a waiting feel. She couldn't find the switch, couldn't find her door. *Run, run,* a voice was saying in her head. She had to get the papers. She had paid all her money for them, the papers that would let her stay, let her get money, let her work. Her hands blundered against the second attic door, and suddenly she knew where she was. Her hand found the switch and pressed it, and she was on her familiar small landing. She listened again.

Footsteps downstairs. A door opened and shut. Silence. She waited, listening. Nothing. The last hurdle. She slid her key into the door, and pushed it open, closing it silently behind her. The moon shone through the window, casting a square of light on to the floor and the shadow of the wooden cat on the sill that was like the one Anna used to have at home. It was the only thing, the only non-essential thing, she had used her wages to buy. She didn't dare turn the light on, so she waited for her eyes to adjust to the dark.

Slowly, the familiar shapes of the room formed in front of her. The bed in the moonlight, the chair over by the wall, the wardrobe that leaned slightly on the uneven floor. Its door was hanging open. She listened again. Silence. No one could come up the attic stairs without her hearing the characteristic creak. Her ears were open and alert for it. She pulled the chair in front of the wardrobe and stood on it, reaching up on to the top for the box where she had hidden the papers. Her hands felt behind the ornate front, skimmed across the dusty surface. Nothing. Frantically, she felt round, felt each corner, ran her hands across the wall behind the heavy cupboard. Her eyes, growing more accustomed to the dark, could see now. Nothing. The box was gone.

She jumped off the chair and knelt down, feeling under the wardrobe with her hands, telling herself that the box had fallen off, was lying on the floor. It wasn't there. There was nowhere else to look. That was all she had: the bed, the wardrobe, the chair. She looked in the wardrobe, and saw, noticing it for the first time, the disorder. Her things, her toothbrush, her soap, all her personal things, were scattered across the bottom and spilling out on to the floor. Her clothes, the few that she had, were thrown on the bed where someone had pulled them out.

She sat on the bed, cold with shock. The passport with the visa, the papers that would allow her to move on, to work, to live, the papers she'd spent the rest of the money on, the papers she'd waited six months for, were gone. She covered her face with her hands. There was nothing else to do. She wanted to stop, to give up, to lie down and sleep. *Anna . . . Anna . . . before it's too late . . .*

She braced herself and looked round. She found two carrier bags, and stuffed her remaining possessions inside. Her movements were slow and clumsy. She stood for a moment, still listening, but the sense of urgency had gone. She heard a door below her, the front door she thought, slam.

The moonlight had moved and was shining on to the bed and up the wall. She could see the pattern of the window, the shadow shape that was the wooden cat on the sill. She would have to take the cat with her. She couldn't leave that behind. The air seemed thick and heavy now, the pipes knocked and whispered, and something breathed in the darkness behind her.

There was a metallic sound, the clunk of something knocking against iron. Something moved across the shadow on the bed, obliterating the shape of the cat and she watched with the frozen immobility of shock as the shadow formed, the shadow of someone on the fire escape, outside the window, hands feeling around the frame.

Sheffield

Roz knew better than to look at the photographs. They weren't preserved in an album, or tucked safely in frames, just stowed away in a box that she kept on a shelf. Since she had left Bristol, she had put them away, put them out of her mind, got on with her life. It was pointless to brood over memorabilia. She avoided the camera these days, except for the unavoidable occasions: her passport, her university card, once at a departmental celebration, her face half turned away as she realized the camera was on her, once at a friend's wedding, a stiff and formal smile on her face. But the box of photographs had nagged at her eye, and in the end she had succumbed. Now they were spread out on the table in front of her, making a story she no longer thought about, no longer told herself. There, from twelve years ago, Roz and a group of undergraduate friends struck elegant, Jane Austen poses, a Bath terrace in the background. Another showed a group on an anti-nuclear protest – Roz could see herself in the middle, determined, banner waving. Chernobyl, just a couple of years before, had galvanized her anti-nuclear politics.

And here, two people, Roz and Nathan, at the students'

union bar. They had their arms round each other and were holding their glasses up to the camera. Another one, this time just Nathan, a photograph that had always been one of her favourites. He was smiling at the camera, the laughter lines already by his eyes, turning on what she always thought of as his *aw shucks* charm.

She remembered how she used to see him in the bar, her first year at university, with one girl or another, never the same one, or with a group: one of those people who naturally drew your eye. She'd talked to him a time or two, found him friendly and fun. He was a post-graduate working for his doctorate, teaching part-time, and she'd been slightly intimidated by his status.

She remembered the party when he'd sought her out and they'd spent the night walking the streets of Bristol hand in hand, talking into the small hours, coming back to her lodgings as the sun was rising; he'd broken a flower off a shrub, a piece of forsythia, and tucked it in her hair. She'd kept that flower for years.

She remembered the time when they'd first spent the night together. He'd forgotten about his students the next morning, and they'd run to the university in guilty panic to be met by the irate secretary. She'd watched him charm the woman into smiles and forgiveness. 'You're shameless,' she'd told him as they walked towards the library. He'd grinned at her. 'Works, though,' he'd said, his smile, and the way he'd run his fingers lightly up her arm, a reminder of the night before. *If there be truth in sight . . . Oh, Nathan.*

And now she was paying the price for a moment of sentimental nostalgia. She could feel the tears running down her face and groped round for a tissue. She mopped her eyes and blew her nose. The photographs were the past. They should stay sealed in their box and forgotten. She had more immediate things to think about.

It was raining. She could hear it spattering against the window, drumming on the ground. She drew the curtains against the night and looked at her watch. It was almost nine. Maybe she should just write the evening off. She could have a glass of wine – but in her present mood, alcohol would be dangerous. She could have a bath and an early night, except she wasn't tired. She was standing in frustrated indecision when she heard the knock at the door.

It was late for people to be dropping in, and she opened it on the chain. Luke was on the doorstep, hunched inside his jacket, his hair dripping. She pushed the door shut and released the chain. He came in, shaking the wet off himself as best he could. 'Who were you expecting, Bishop?' he said irritably. 'Hannibal Lecter?' She saw, with exasperation, that he was wearing jeans and a light jacket. He looked as if he was soaked to the skin. He was shivering.

'Christ, Luke,' she said. 'What are you doing?' She steered him into the kitchen and stood him in front of the range. 'Here.' She passed him a towel and watched him as he rubbed his dripping hair.

He made a face that was somewhere between a grimace and a smile, fished in the pocket of his jacket and brought out a bottle of wine. 'It seemed like a good idea at the time,' he said. 'I put the bike round the back of the house. Is that OK? There's something I wanted to talk to you about. And I needed some company.' He frowned slightly as he looked at her. 'You look as if you could do with some yourself.'

Her nose and eyes would still be red from crying, she thought with resignation. She smiled at Luke and realized that her eyes were filling again. She sniffed and groped futilely in her pockets for a tissue.

'Here,' he said helpfully, offering his sleeve, and then they were both laughing, and though there was an edge of hysteria to her laughter, Roz felt better.

'I'm sorry,' she said, using the towel to wipe her nose and eyes. 'Wine is the best idea. Come through where it's comfortable.' She took him into the study, scooped the photographs off the table into the box, and crammed the box on to a shelf. She looked round for a corkscrew.

Luke sat at the table. 'I'll soak your armchairs,' he explained. He picked something up. 'This your husband?' he said.

She turned round. He was looking at a photograph that she must have missed in her sweep. It was just a snap, her and Nathan on Clifton Downs near the Avon Gorge, one of their favourite walking places. 'Yes,' she said, turning away from him. The mirror gleamed above the table.

'You've never talked about him, Roz.' She didn't look at him. 'There was a time when you should have talked to me about him, you know that.' She still couldn't say anything. 'You've been apart from him for more than two years. It happens, Roz. People get ill, they grow old, they die. In the end, you have to move on.'

She stood in the centre of the room, watching herself in the deep mirror, like a portrait from centuries before, watching out of the darkness, lost in the shadows while the words whispered around her. *If there be truth in sight . . . my Rosalind.* She thought of the thread of memory you reach for each morning as you wake from sleep. She thought about that thread breaking, leaving you cast off, circling round in an eternal now. *There is no truth in sight, Nathan. Not any more.*

Nathan's illness had been sudden, severe, life-threatening. One day he had been well, the next day, pale, uncharacteristically irritable, complaining of fatigue and headaches. She had joked with him about hangovers and people who wanted to get out of going on holiday. That night, he had been taken into hospital, sunk into the coma that held him for four long days and nights. 'It's a virus,' the neurologist had told her. 'It's affecting his brain.' Then he'd murmured something about 'bilateral involvement', and left her listening to the hiss of the ventilator, holding Nathan's unresponsive hand. They thought he might die. They thought he would die.

Then there were the signs of recovery, the morning when he squeezed her hand, the eye movement in response to voices and questions, the signs of returning consciousness that told her that she and Nathan had been lucky, that they had been challenged, lived through it, faced it down and survived. She had slept that night for the first time in almost a fortnight, slept until the midday sun had woken her, and felt a surge of new-born energy run right through her. Then there had been the few frustrating days of slow progress as Nathan, confused with drugs and illness, began the long crawl to recovery.

She could remember the day she phoned the hospital, and the ward sister, one who had shared her vigils with her, told her that Nathan was awake, was talking. Nathan awake, Nathan back. She had pulled her clothes on anyhow in her hurry to get there, and then stopped to look in the mirror, brush her hair, as if they were meeting again after a separation.

She remembered walking into the hospital ward, and seeing him there, pale and tired, in his dressing gown, but in a chair, awake, and the wash of relief when she realized that what they had told her was right and could be trusted. 'He's pulling through, Mrs Bishop, I think we're winning.' And just twelve days before, they had been planning a holiday, a trip to Amsterdam, a celebration of Nathan's new job and her PhD. He stood up when he saw her, pale and shaky, but there, awake, aware, his face lighting up with the same relief she felt. 'Roz!' He put his arms round her. 'God, it's been so long! I'm so glad . . .' and his voice had broken. So long. It had seemed like an eternity, those four days while his life hung in the balance, the slow creep of time as he moved towards recovery. Over his shoulder, she saw the ward sister standing in the doorway looking at her. They hadn't been expecting her just yet.

Nathan was talking again. 'I've been ill, I've been, god, it's been awful, but I'm feeling much better. Roz, I've missed you. It's so good to see you again. Where have you been?'

There was something wrong, something she couldn't quite put her finger on. She heard the nurse behind her. 'Hello, Nathan, who's this?'

And there was that tone in her voice that Roz recognized, the tone of talking to a child – and she looked at Nathan and saw him frown with bewilderment. It was a stupid question. This nurse knew exactly who Roz was.

'This is my wife,' he said. 'Roz.'

The nurse smiled at Roz and said, 'Would you like a drink? I've got some tea in . . .'

'I'll get a coffee,' Roz said quickly. She looked at Nathan. 'Do you want some?' He was looking at her as though something was puzzling him, and she went to the machine with a sense of escaping from a situation that she didn't understand. She saw the sister waiting outside the office as she came back with the flimsy cup that was slopping scalding coffee over her fingertips. She didn't want a nurse-and-relative confab that excluded Nathan. She had hated standing by his bed while the medics talked about him to her. She hated Nathan being 'he' and 'the patient' and 'your husband', when he was there in the bed, and his eyes were open, but blank and empty, and for a time a machine breathed for him – she could still hear, even today, the regular hiss of the machine as it kept Nathan's unresponsive lungs working. Nathan wasn't 'he' or 'the patient' or 'your husband'. He was 'you' and 'Nathan', and he was her love.

She veered round the nurse's, 'Oh, Mrs Bishop, Roz –' and carried her coffee triumphantly to Nathan. 'I'm back,' she said.

He was looking out of the window, and he turned round at her voice, his expression of bewilderment changing into one of surprise and relief. 'Roz! I'm so glad . . . God, it's been so long!' He stood up again, the weakness in his legs apparent in the way he staggered slightly. He looked over her shoulder and she could see that same expression of confusion on his face. She turned her head, and saw the nurse hurrying towards them. His eyes went to the window again, and he looked out, frowning slightly. Then he looked round the room, his face puzzled and lost. When his eyes came back to Roz, that same surprise and relief spread across his face. 'Roz! You're back! It's been ages . . .'

The coffee cup dropped from her hand and the hot liquid splashed down the front of her dress.

'It's called Korsakov's Syndrome,' she said. 'Memory loss.' Luke started to say something and she said quickly, 'I don't mean that he couldn't remember who he was or that kind of thing. I mean he *lost his memory.* It's as if his life began and ended in the last two minutes. The whole world just collapses into blankness behind him, all the time. It's like . . .' She saw incomprehension on his face, and struggled to explain what she had seen and had barely been able to grasp herself.

She remembered how she hadn't been able to understand, at first, what they were telling her. She'd taken Nathan home, briefly, and watched him tumble through the frenzied abyss of panic, an abyss that would be renewed again and again as he went through the litany: 'I've been ill, Roz, it's been so long . . .' He had lost the thread that anchored him to the world, lost the narrative that was Nathan. There had been hope in those early days. 'There is a real chance of improvement,' the neurologist had told her. But Nathan had been one of the unlucky ones. He'd had a series of fits that had wiped more and more of his story from his mind. In a matter of weeks, he had lost their marriage, their relationship, even their friendship. His memory stopped about a year before they had met.

The sky had clouded over, and now there was no light for the mirror to reflect. She was just a shape in the darkness. 'I hang on to my marriage because it's the only useful thing I can do. Except there isn't anything useful I can do. I just . . .'

Luke's silhouette obscured the mirror as he stood up. '. . . do penance,' he said.

'Maybe.' Her eyes were growing accustomed to the dark now, and she could see him dimly, leaning against the table in front of her, his hands in his pockets. 'Maybe I need to.'

He put his arms round her for a moment, rubbing the back of her head. 'Don't talk to me about penance, Bishop,' he said. 'I'm Irish and a Catholic. Used to be a Catholic,' he amended. 'Penance and guilt. I'm good at those.' He released her and reached into the other pocket of his damp jacket and pulled out a bottle of whisky. 'Here's another good catholic remedy,' he said.

Hull, Monday evening
It was raining now, a fine, wetting drizzle that made the ground more slippery and added the discomfort of wet to the cold. A wind was starting up, driving the rain into people's faces, making the night an unpleasant time to be out. Those who had a choice huddled in their cars in the traffic queues, watching the wipers *chunk, chunk* against the windscreen, or hurried to close their front doors behind them and shut themselves away from the inhospitable night.

Anna didn't care if she was seen, didn't care who heard her coming, didn't care about the rain that had soaked her to the skin. She just wanted to find the one person she knew she could trust. She had fallen on the stairs as she threw herself out of the attic room, had picked herself up and been down the second flight and out of the door before she noticed the stabbing pain in her back. She had run, hearing feet clanging on the iron steps of the fire escape, hearing them hit the pavement behind her, a voice shouting as she reached the end of the street. And as she turned the corner, as if her mother was still watching over her, a taxi for hire went past. She waved it down and fell on to the seat. She gave the driver a landmark close to the docks, and hunched over in her seat, catching her breath, feeling the stabbing pains in her back as she breathed and a dull ache in her ankle where she had landed awkwardly.

She had taken the risk and she had nothing to show for it. Her papers had gone. She had left the bags she had packed in the panic of her flight. She needed somewhere safe, somewhere she could sleep – even for just one night – and know that she was with someone who cared about her. She didn't want to put him in danger, she didn't want him to take any risks, but now there was nowhere else. There was just the welfare centre. It had been five months, maybe longer, since she had been there, but she could still remember Matthew's kindness, and the sadness in his eyes.

The taxi was slowing for a red light. She could see the driver's face in the mirror. He was looking at her, and his eyes looked doubtful. They were still some way from the centre, but they had left her pursuer behind. She eased herself along the seat, and as the driver slowed to a stop at the light, she had the door open and was out before he realized what she was doing. The pain in her ankle almost stopped her, but she forced herself away down the first dark street, confident that the small amount she owed him wouldn't make chasing her worth his while. She would be just another thief, just another *gyppo*, just another one on the take. She began to walk, limping now that her ankle had stiffened up.

It was after ten by the time she reached the centre. A sliver of light showed through where the boarding on the window had cracked, but otherwise, the shop looked deserted. The piece of paper was still on the door, black printed on blue, protected by a plastic cover. *Welfare Advice Centre. 8.30–5.30. Out of hours, ring night bell.*

She had hoped he would be there. It had always been him before. She didn't recognize the woman who let her in. The woman said something to Anna in a language she didn't recognize, the syllables sounding harsh and stabbing. The gestures she made as she hurried Anna through the door into the small office seemed brusque and impatient, but her face was kind, and she brought Anna a hot drink, sweet tea made with boiled milk.

The tea was syrupy and comforting. The woman pointed at herself and said, 'Nasim.' Anna managed a smile and offered her own name. The warmth from the heater was reaching through her and her eyes felt heavy. She was creeping through the bushes, hearing the sound of water dripping, dripping. *There was a smell of burning in the air . . .*

Nasim made a reproving noise and caught the cup as it began to spill on to Anna's lap. She pushed the cup back into Anna's hands, and held them round it for a moment, then made fierce gestures towards Anna, indicating that she should drink. Anna smiled weakly and put the cup to her lips again. She heard footsteps and the door at the back of the counter opened. She tensed and then, when she saw the man who edged his way into the room, felt herself relax, truly relax for the first time since Friday morning. He smiled apologetically and then stopped as his eyes focused on Anna, and he came round the counter with a look of welcome, and of concern. His lips moved silently for a moment, then he said, 'Anna.' She hadn't dared hope that he would still be here. She was aware of Nasim hovering, looking as though she wanted to speak.

'Matthew.' Anna smiled, and she saw him gesture Nasim away. He sat down in the chair next to her, careful of her space. He moved awkwardly, a slight twist to his spine making one shoulder higher than the other. 'Born with it,' he'd said with a shrug when Anna had asked. She remembered Krisha, the special shoe she'd had to wear on her twisted foot. Krisha had been born with it, too. Just for a second, she saw a bundle on the ground, the sole of a small foot pointing towards the bushes. She shuddered, and his face registered concern.

He struggled with the words for a moment, then said, 'What happened?' He looked older. There was more grey in his hair, and his eyes looked tired. She put out her hand, and he took it. They sat there together in the cold, damp room with the smell of Calor Gas in the air. He'd wait, she knew, until she was ready to talk. Her eyes wanted to close.

'There's no one in the back just now,' he said. 'Come through there.'

She got up and followed him through the other door. Beyond the office was another, slightly larger room with a two-seater settee and an armchair. The room was cold, but there was a fire and he lit it, clicking the ignition button twice impatiently when it failed to light the first time. She sank down on to the settee, on the edge, wrapping her arms around herself against the cold. 'It'll soon warm up,' he said. 'There's no one using this room tonight.' He took the blanket that was draped over the back of the settee and wrapped it round her shoulders. She was aware again that her clothes smelt, that she smelt. She wanted to talk to him, but she could feel the first warmth creeping through her, feel the icy numbness of her feet start to give way to sensation, feel sleep creeping through her like a mist that clouded her mind and made her eyes shut and her head droop forwards. Sleep.

She was pulled briefly back to wakefulness as she felt him tuck the blanket more closely around her, and her mother smiled down at her. *Anna.* She dropped into the first proper sleep she had had since her flight from the hotel on Friday morning.

It was evening, and a mist was coming off the river, making the streetlights glow in a halo of white and mingling with the misty breath of people hurrying through the streets. Girls walked in groups in the icy air – tiny skirts, cropped tops, bare skin and Mediterranean clothes in the winter evening. The priest waited at the back of the church. Two worshippers knelt in the pews, almost indistinguishable in the shadows. The light was fading, the colours in the high vaulting darkening to grey as the night came.

Holy Mass tomorrow. He had said the Mass every day since his ordination, attended Mass every day since he was a child. He couldn't remember a time when it hadn't been a central part of his life, and now, as seemed to happen as people got older, the words from his childhood came back – sometimes more easily than the words he said today. *Introibo ad altare Dei. Ad Deum qui laetificat juventutum meam.*

The Latin Mass: 'I will go to the altar of God. To God, the joy of my youth.' The stained glass was dark and waiting. The stone walls and the pillars of the nave rose into shadows. The sanctuary light was a red glow above the altar, and behind it, on the tabernacle, a cross gleamed faintly, the candlelight catching the crucified figure, the stretched limbs and the drooping head. 'I am poured out like water . . .'

Confetior Deo omnipotenti, beatae Mariae semper Virgini . . . 'I confess to Almighty God . . . to Blessed Mary, ever a virgin . . .' The shadow of the rood screen lay across the aisle, the crucifix massive on the crossbar, the two attendant figures gazing up in meek acceptance. Behind the rood screen, the high altar was dark. When he was a child, he would watch the priest standing with his back to the congregation, raising the chalice, the Precious Blood, and the altar bell would ring three times. The consecration, the transformation of the bread and wine into the body and blood, the moment of sacrifice.

He switched out the lights, leaving the church in darkness. He was about to pull the doors closed behind him, when he saw the light in the shadows. He paused, then walked back down the central aisle, towards the place where the side aisle met the transept. Whoever lit the candles had been there that evening. They were only half-burned down, small, steady gleams in the empty church. The blind eyes of the saint stared ahead. The priest looked around. The rows of pews vanished under the pillars, the aisles were dark and silent. He wondered which of the worshippers who had come to the church that evening had lit the candles. He wondered what help that small light in the darkness could give.

8

Tuesday morning

Roz had a headache. She seemed to wake up from nothing, and felt a moment of confusion, then she remembered the night before, sitting across the table from Luke, talking, the mirror on the wall reflecting the dim floor-light. It was like the old days. She remembered pouring more whisky into her glass, putting on a CD and, later, dancing round the room watching the walls spin past her. She remembered giggling helplessly at some slip of the tongue she'd made, something stupid about knives that had taken her fancy and sent her collapsing into her chair as the sheer brilliance of it struck her again. In short, she remembered getting drunk. And now she had a headache.

The sky had cleared in the night and the first January sun reflected through a gap in the curtains and cut into her eyes. She was lying on her bed, the quilt half off her, wrapped in her dressing gown – that was right, she could vaguely remember taking a shower. And she could remember someone supporting her along the corridor as she rambled her way through an analysis of her situation and her future, with the true self-centredness of the drunk. She was cold. She tried to pull the quilt back over her, but something heavy pinned it down. She opened her eyes and turned her head very slowly. Luke was beside her on the bed, on top of the quilt. He looked strangely vulnerable lying there, his face resting on his hand, the other hand tangled in her hair, which had spread across the pillow.

She freed herself, trying not to disturb him. His hand was

icy cold. He was still wearing the jeans and T-shirt that had been soaked through the night before. His shoes and jacket were on the floor. She sat up, holding her head, her face screwed up against the pain.

Then she heard it again and realized what had woken her. Knocking at the door. Now she realized she had been conscious of it as she rose out of sleep. It was loud, urgent. 'All right, all right!' She was aware of Luke stirring as she rolled out of bed and staggered into her slippers. She ran her fingers through her hair. She'd probably blocked someone in. She'd left her car in the road the night before. Someone had parked half across her gateway and she couldn't be bothered to manoeuvre round it. 'Coming,' she called.

She had to hunt round for the keys, and then the bolts stuck, but eventually she got the door open. Her house was slightly above the road. The steps wound down to the path, the stone lions on either side. She saw the police car first, and then the two men on her doorstep. She blinked. One of the men held something up for her to look at. 'DS Anderson,' he said. 'Hull Police. Are you Mrs Rosalind Bishop?'

'Doctor,' she said automatically. Her mind wouldn't function. She felt thick-headed and slow. Hull?

'Mrs Bishop, Dr Bishop, I'm looking for Luke Hagan . . .'

'Luke . . . ?' Seeing his eyes move to look behind her, she turned to see Luke coming down the stairs doing up his belt, looking half asleep, the way she had been just a moment ago.

'Roz,' he began, 'did . . .' Then he saw the men on the doorstep.

'Luke Hagan?' The man who'd introduced himself as DS Anderson stepped forward. Luke stared at him blankly and nodded. Anderson looked at Roz and said, 'Can we come in?' It wasn't a question. Roz stood back from the door and the two men came in to the hallway. 'Mr Hagan, DS Anderson, Hull Police.' He showed Luke his identification. Luke barely glanced at it. 'I'm afraid that I have some bad news for you.' He paused for a moment, watching Luke's reaction closely.

Luke looked back at him. His face was white. 'Gemma,' he said.

Anderson nodded. 'She was found in Hull. It's bad news,' he said again. Roz moved towards Luke, her breath catching in her throat. She wanted the man to stop speaking, now. 'I'm sorry to tell you that Gemma Wishart is dead.' His voice was flat and formal. He was still watching Luke closely.

Roz found that she could only focus on the moment. She watched Luke grip the banister and sink down to sit on the stars, his head slumping forward. She crouched beside him, holding his hand that was still icy cold. 'Luke,' she said. She remembered her own drunken self-pity of the night before and felt ashamed. Luke must have been anticipating just this outcome, because he seemed like someone hearing something he knew but didn't want to believe. She looked up at the two officers who were still standing there. 'What happened?' she said. 'Was there an accident? When was she . . . ?'

They ignored her questions, and the one who hadn't spoken yet said, 'Mr Hagan, we need to talk to you. We'd like you to come back with us.'

Slowly, Luke sat up. His face was deathly white, but he looked calm. 'I'll get my stuff,' he said. Roz tried to follow him up the stairs, but he said sharply, 'Leave it, Roz.'

Her head spinning, she looked back at the police officers. They weren't in uniform and for the first time the significance of this hit her. They were detectives, investigating officers. This was a criminal investigation. *Gemma!* Her mind, sluggish from the alcohol, made more connections. They wanted to talk to Luke. They'd come here to collect him. She looked at DS Anderson. 'How did you know Luke was here?'

For a moment, she thought that he wasn't going to answer, then he said, 'Someone at his address told us that Mr Hagan came here last night.'

Roz tried to think past her headache to formulate her next question, but she heard Luke's footsteps on the stairs and he came down fully dressed. She wanted to touch him, to give him that reassurance, but she felt inhibited under the eyes of the two officers, and somehow he seemed distant and unapproachable. He looked back at her as he went out of the door. 'I'll pick the bike up later,' he said.

Blank with shock, she went into the kitchen and, like an automaton, switched on the kettle, put bread under the grill. She went through to the study, where the air was stale with the smell of whisky. She looked at the depleted bottle. They'd drunk a lot last night. And then . . . but her mind was clearing now. She could remember that they had talked about penance and guilt, sitting at the table, fuelling the debate with whisky. Later, as he was guiding her erratic progress along the corridor to bed, she'd elaborated this into a desire to work for some unidentified deserving poor, a maudlin wish to make some kind of sacrifice of her life. 'I've got to put something back,' she'd kept insisting.

Luke had pulled the quilt over her and sat on the bed beside her. 'You think the Third World has a crying need for a forensic linguist?' he'd said, stroking her hair, sounding amused. 'Shut up and go to sleep, Bishop. You're pissed.'

The smoke alarm brought her back to the present, its penetrating beeps cutting into her headache like a knife. The bread had caught fire under the grill. She smothered the flames and threw the back door open, trying to clear the smoke and shut the alarm off. Gemma was dead. She wondered how she was going to tell Joanna what had happened.

She sat at the table crumbling the burnt toast between her fingers and staring blankly at the wall. It was after nine. Gemma was dead. She pulled herself to her feet and went to the phone. She needed to contact Joanna. She phoned Joanna's extension, but got Alice Carr, the departmental secretary, Peter Cauldwell's confidante and ally. 'I'm afraid there's no one available from your group, Roz,' Alice had said. 'Dr Grey is tied up with the police. Isn't it terrible?'

She should have realized. Of course, one of the first places the police would go would be Gemma's work. 'It must have been such a shock to you, Roz, to have the police on your doorstep first thing.' Alice's tone was sympathetic, but the message was clear. *I know you spent the night with Luke Hagan.* Roz didn't have the energy to feel angry that the departmental grapevine had got hold of that piece of gossip. Presumably, the police would have come to the same conclusion. There was nothing she could say to Alice to dispel the image that hung in the air: Gemma lying dead and she and Luke . . .

She left a message with Alice, one that would undoubtedly get to Peter Cauldwell before it got to Joanna, then she drove into town to the police headquarters, where two detectives grilled her for what seemed like hours. They wanted to know about Luke. They wanted to know about his relationship with Gemma, about Gemma's social life, about rifts between the pair. She didn't know. She couldn't tell them.

They wanted to know about her relationship with Luke. She told them as honestly as she could, but she couldn't tell what they made of it. She didn't tell them that she and Luke had been lovers. That had just been a mistake. It wasn't something they needed to know. She told them about the Friday meeting, about Gemma's e-mail and about the data vanishing from the computers. As she told them, it seemed to build up into a sinister picture, but at the time – she tried to explain it to them – it had only seemed strange, puzzling. 'I thought Gemma had done it,' she told them.

They wanted to know if Luke could have wiped the data from Gemma's computers. She shrugged her shoulders. Of course he could have done. A lot of people could. She told them about the report and the transcript, and the fact that the copies she had printed out seemed to have vanished. She didn't tell them about the photographs. She would have done, she told herself, if they'd asked her something that led that way, but they didn't. It wasn't her business. She should never have seen those. She should never have had that information. That was the way she rationalized it. She left, feeling like a hospital patient who has been given the all-clear from some dread disease, but feeling no relief because she hadn't mentioned one symptom that surely, surely didn't count . . .

It wasn't until she was at work, sitting at her desk, that it began to come into focus. She felt cold, and put her hand on the radiator. It was on. The coldness seemed to be coming from inside her.

The worst of the hangover had faded. Her headache had retreated under a hefty dose of Paracetamol and, though her stomach felt uneasy, the feeling of nausea had gone. She was starting to feel hungry. It seemed wrong to feel hungry, somehow. She thought about Luke on his way to Hull, in the interview room, facing hostile, intrusive questions. Would he lose his temper? She remembered her own indignation at the questions she'd been asked.

What's your relationship with Luke, Roz?

Best to tell us about it, Roz.

Does he often spend the night with you?

And Gemma was dead. She tried to feel sadness, regret, but all she could feel was a kind of blank shock. Gemma, with the whole world in front of her if she wanted to take it; bright, talented, young. But how young could Gemma have been if she was days, maybe hours away from her death?

She listened to the sound of footsteps in the corridor outside. She hadn't spoken to Joanna since she came in. She might be in her office now, and she would want to know what little Roz could tell her. She went to Joanna's room and knocked on the door. She could hear Joanna speaking as she went in, and she saw that Peter Cauldwell was there, sitting in the chair opposite Joanna. '. . . confidential material that should be handled properly,' she was saying.

Cauldwell looked at Joanna solemnly. 'Joanna, this is a murder investigation. We must not only be seen to co-operate, we should *want* to co-operate. The police will be sensitive to any problems about confidentiality. It's very possible, I'm afraid to say, that there is a link. This loss of data . . .' Cauldwell looked pleased. 'You really should have brought this to my attention as soon as you knew about it.'

Roz felt tired. She heard Luke's voice in her head, 'All the university brass out to watch Grey nail Cauldwell's scrotum to the table.' Peter Cauldwell was out to get his revenge. 'I don't think there are any confidential documents left,' she

124

said. Her voice sounded flat in her own ears. 'Does it matter?'

Cauldwell looked round. 'Roz,' he said. 'This is a terrible business.'

Joanna stood up. 'I'll talk to you later,' she said to Cauldwell. He began to object, but Joanna said sharply, 'This is neither the time nor the place, Peter,' and Roz was aware of Joanna's eyes flickering towards her. Cauldwell nodded and left the room. Joanna sighed and sat down. 'Do you want to tell me about it?' she said. 'Do you want some coffee?'

Roz slumped into the chair opposite Joanna. 'No coffee,' she said. She told Joanna about the morning visit, that Luke was *helping the police with their inquiries*. As she spoke, she could hear it all making a horrible kind of sense. Joanna had been worrying that she had employed a woman who'd made off with the confidential material the group held, and details of potentially valuable software they were developing. Now she must be worrying that she had employed the man who killed her.

Joanna sat in silence for a moment when Roz had finished. 'I can't believe that when I spoke to Gemma about the meeting, it was the last time I was ever going to see her. There was so much . . . the whole world.' She pinched the bridge of her nose between her thumb and forefinger, and took some deep breaths. She looked confused for a moment, then her eye fell on the papers on the desk in front of her. 'Perhaps we ought to look at these,' she said, with uncharacteristic tentativeness. 'The new round of grant applications . . .'

Roz remembered what she had said to Luke: 'She can cope with worrying about grants and things, and she can't cope with worrying about people.'

'Luke hasn't been arrested,' she said.

Joanna stood up. 'I know,' she said, 'but there's been something about Luke since Friday – and don't tell me that's hindsight,' she added. Roz, who had been about to say something, stopped. Joanna was a quick – and shrewd – judge of people. And she was right. There had been something wrong with Luke. Joanna's office door hadn't shut properly, and now it swung open as a man walked past with Gemma's

125

computer in his arms. Roz looked at Joanna, seeing the glint of anger in her eyes.

'I know they've taken Luke in for questioning, Joanna,' she said. 'But they would. He was Gemma's boyfriend.' She found that hard to say. 'He was the one making the fuss about her going missing. They have to question him.' As she spoke, Roz felt herself relax. Of course they would want to question Luke. How could they not?

Joanna's face remained tense for a moment, then she relaxed. 'I know,' she conceded. She closed her eyes. 'I just . . . I need something to do. I can't think about it, not now. It's not a good atmosphere for work in here. It's not a good atmosphere for anything. I'm going to work at home today. If I were you, I'd do the same, Roz.'

Roz didn't need to think about it. 'No, I'll stay here. Keep an eye on things.'

Joanna looked relieved. 'Thank you,' she said, the genuine gratitude on her face reminding Roz of the woman who had befriended her and supported her when she first applied for a transfer to Sheffield. Roz picked up the grant application forms. 'I'll make a start on these,' she said.

But when she got back to her room, she sat and stared out of the window at the grey winter sky and rain that was starting to spatter against the glass. The police must think that Luke had killed Gemma. Or that it was possible. It was something that her mind didn't want to face, and she had to force herself to consider it. She thought of Luke as she had known him before Gemma came into their lives. His laconic irony had been a good foil for her seriousness. He'd stopped her from burning out in her first months as a research assistant, getting her to prioritize, to resist unreasonable pressure from her students: 'They're trying it on, Bishop. They know you're on a temporary contract. Look, this department needs a researcher, not a teacher. Focus.'

He'd taught her to have fun again. Like her, he was prone to depressions and periods of dark brooding. They were good at lifting each other out of these lows with viciously competitive games of squash, dancing at insalubrious clubs, wild drives down the motorway on his bike. And he'd never asked her about Nathan, had respected Roz's abrupt explanation, 'My husband is seriously ill,' as the *Keep off* sign that it was.

She remembered the first time she'd met him. She had just arrived in Sheffield to take up her contract, still reeling from the sudden and unexpected changes in her life. She felt like someone who had been sailing downstream on a calm and sunny stretch of river, and then found herself in the rapids, a storm lashing down and an ominous roar of water in the darkness ahead. At the time, she really hadn't cared much whether she researched into the sound systems of the English language or worked a till in a supermarket.

She'd been familiarizing herself with some software, and was trying to install a program she'd used in her earlier research. The machine was playing up and she couldn't get the program to run, but she wasn't really concentrating, just staring out of the window wondering what she was going to do, not now, not immediately, but in the next months and years.

'Are you doing that on purpose?' A man was standing behind her, looking at her screen. She jumped, and swivelled round in her chair, angry that someone had interrupted her, angry at being surprised. 'I'm only asking,' he said, 'because I have to account for this equipment, and when they want to know what's happened to this one, I'd like to be able to give them chapter and verse.' His tone was one of mild inquiry. 'I'd hazard a guess,' he went on, 'that the program you're loading was written for a different operating system, and what it is currently doing is overwriting the hard disk on that machine.' He gave her a cheerful grin. 'Doesn't always work, but it's infallible when you don't want it to.'

She stared at him. For a moment . . . his smile, gentle and self-deprecating – it was so much like Nathan's smile. But there, the similarity ended. His voice had a slight lilt to it that suggested Ireland in his background. His hair was dark where Nathan's was fair, his skin had that almost translucent pallor that often came with Celtic blood, where Nathan had, or used to have, the colour of someone who spent a lot of time outdoors. 'I'm sorry,' she said, and her voice sounded edgy and cold. 'I wasn't concentrating.'

'No skin off my nose,' he said. 'You might need to apologize to the guy who's been typing up his thesis on that, mind.' He seemed to lose interest in the matter. 'You'll be the new research assistant,' he said.

And that had been the start of their friendship. Until . . . They'd been out together to a jazz evening in Leeds. They'd travelled there on Luke's bike. She could still remember the ride back, the road disappearing under the wheels, the bright moon, the speed, the silent intimacy of moving together to control the machine, the exhilaration of the cool night air rushing against her face. She remembered the car that had pulled out in front of them without warning, and the way Luke had laughed as the bike wove away from one disaster towards another, wove again, and again, and then the road was clear in front of them and he accelerated away as car horns dopplered into the distance behind them. The adrenaline was still singing through them when they got back to Roz's, and they had made love for the first time, tumbled together on the rug in front of the fire. The sex had been almost violent in its intensity, and she'd felt as though the blood was effervescing in her veins. 'I've wanted to do that since I first saw you,' he told her in the silence afterwards, before they'd had time to think about what they had done.

'Why did you wait six months to make your move?' she'd said, not really believing him. And they'd laughed, and just at that moment, anything had seemed possible.

But she was evading the issue. Did she believe that Luke could have killed Gemma? She remembered Luke's sudden anger as he slammed the filing-cabinet drawer shut. And she remembered the photographs with that disturbing overtone of violence. There was a darkness in Luke. It had seemed like a personal darkness, one she recognized, his tendency towards depressions, his drinking bouts and his wild behaviour – but what if it could also turn outwards? She remembered Nathan's fist slamming into the side of her head as she grabbed frantically and futilely at the banister to save herself from falling. She didn't think Luke had done it. But who was she to say what someone was capable of? How could she possibly tell?

Hull, Tuesday evening

A mist was rising from the river as Lynne let herself into the block of flats. The water had that slightly rotten sea tang that meant the tide was turning. She thought about the dark glittering water upriver, the towers of the Humber Bridge, the slender thread of the road vanishing into the distance, about Katya washed up on to a mud-bank and left there by the retreating tide.

She dumped her bags on the worktop, and checked quickly to see if she had everything she needed. She had invited Roy Farnham round, ostensibly to discuss the cases – and the possible link with the business of trafficking in people. He had left the restaurant last night as soon as she'd made her tentative identification of the Jemima picture, and must have put in a full night's work, because he'd phoned her that morning to tell her she was right – Gemma Wishart had been reported missing to South Yorkshire Police on Saturday. Wishart's mother had identified the watch that the Sleeping Beauty had been wearing, and a small, irregular birthmark high on her left thigh. 'We'll need to confirm from the dental records,' Farnham had said. 'But I don't think there's any doubt.' She'd wanted to discuss the case more, to look for links with Katya's death, but Farnham was tied up all day. That was when she had tentatively suggested an evening meeting, at her flat.

He wasn't directly her senior officer – anyway, not part of the same team – so social contact shouldn't be too much of a problem, but Lynne was wary. She had made the mistake once before of getting involved with someone from the job. She felt as though she still carried the scars from her few months with the austere and driven Steve McCarthy. It had been a turbulent relationship that had ended in bitterness and recrimination, and she had decided then that she would not let her work and her private life get entangled again.

But in that case, who could she have relationships with? Most of the men she met drew back when they realized what she did. Only fellow officers could understand the nature and the demands of the work. But a senior officer? People would say that she had earned her career on her back. A junior officer was impossible. Someone of the same rank? Then ambition and competition would step in, as she had found to her cost with Steve.

She checked the time. She had almost an hour before he was likely to arrive. She half expected him to call and cry off. She knew that Gemma Wishart's boyfriend had been brought in for questioning earlier in the day. She wondered if Farnham had anything more than the relationship, and the obvious ramifications of that, to point at this man. If he had known about her escort work, if he had been involved in any way, then there was a whole range of motives for Wishart's death there. Or if he hadn't known . . . There was no point in speculating. She should get the details from Farnham shortly.

She hadn't specifically mentioned eating, but he was coming straight from work. She put on some water for pasta and checked her supplies of tomato sauce, frozen at the height of last summer when the basil was fresh and fragrant. She'd bought bread on her way home, there was salad in the fridge and cheese and fruit. She could cover just about any eventuality. She had wine, if that seemed like the right thing. She took a quick shower, and was just pulling on a soft wool jersey when her entry phone rang. It was Farnham. 'Come on up,' she said, pressing the buzzer.

Sheffield, Tuesday evening

Roz planned to spend the evening working on her book. She needed to do something that would keep her mind occupied. But once she was sitting in front of her computer, she realized that she wouldn't be able to concentrate. She needed to do something a bit more active, and she thought about the software she'd brought home with her the other night, something that Luke had recommended and that Joanna had asked her to evaluate. That would be a distraction. The problem was, her own machine wouldn't run this particular program, so . . . suddenly she remembered.

She stood up and went through to the kitchen. She went to the locked cellar door and opened it. A puff of cold cellar air blew into her face. She looked up on to the top shelf and there, forgotten until now, was the laptop she'd brought back from the department on – when? – Friday night. The laptop that Gemma had been using until Thursday when she'd taken the less powerful machine with her to Manchester. And no one else knew that Roz had this. If the destruction of Gemma's data files had anything to do with her death, then this machine was priceless. She wanted to phone Luke to tell him what she'd found.

But he wouldn't be there. Her elation at her find had vanished. She needed to see what she had. There was no reason to assume that Gemma had left anything on this machine. She opened the carrying case and there, in one of the pockets, was a floppy disk and some sheets of paper. She looked at the paper – a few typed sheets with handwritten notes, symbols, scribbles – the transcript! Gemma's working copy! She turned the machine on, put the disk into the A-drive and looked to see what she had got. *Yes!* There was a folder marked 'Gemma'. She opened it and was disappointed to see just three files: *tapehull* – presumably a clean copy of the transcript of DI Jordan's tape. The second file was *draftreport hull*. Roz ran her fingers across the tight skin on her forehead. The hard copy of the report and the transcript had vanished from her desk. The other file was *mholbrook*. She opened it.

Dear Professor Holbrook
Re: Holbrook Archive

I contacted your assistant recently about access to the archive to do some tape comparisons. Apparently the collection is currently being catalogued and isn't available at the moment. You'll remember the tape I

The letter was unfinished.

Roz frowned. Was this anything to do with the tape and transcript? The Holbrook Archive? She racked her brains, but couldn't think of anything. She dug around on her bookshelves until she found her copy of the university directory, but there was no Holbrook in the 'current staff' section. She found him in the section for visiting academics and consultants. Marcus Laurence Holbrook. He seemed to have been doing some kind of consultancy work with the Department of European Studies. He was a specialist in the languages of the old USSR, which she should have guessed. That was Gemma's field. Had been Gemma's field. The Holbrook Archive must be a collection relating to these languages. Gemma's letter mentioned tapes.

Had Gemma wanted to check her analysis of DI Jordan's tape against another speaker from – she skimmed Gemma's report – from north-east Siberia? That seemed logical, and it might account for Gemma's remaining uncertainty about the tape. What was it she had said? 'It's just . . . There was something I wanted to . . .' Had Gemma managed to get access to the material she wanted? Roz read through the report. Gemma's conclusions seemed firm – there were very few 'possiblys' or 'maybes' in there. The report looked complete. But it wasn't. Gemma had said so. She frowned, thinking back. Gemma had come to her room to complain about being sent to Manchester at short notice, but more, to ask advice about the report. She'd said . . . *It's just . . . There was something I wanted to . . .* What?

She looked at the transcript and noticed that Gemma had written something across the top. First, in blue ink, the word 'cats', underlined and queried. *Cats??* This was surrounded by doodles, and scribbled dates and times as though Gemma had been making notes as she talked to someone. And then underneath, in different ink: *Check! 25, 127, 204.* And then a pencilled scrawl: *YO!! Check?* She looked at it for a while, thinking. The numbers referred to the lines that were marked with an asterisk – clearly the lines that were the source of the problem. But what that problem was . . . She shook her head. It meant nothing to her.

She made a copy of the transcript on her fax, copied the files on to a back-up disk, and made another copy to be on the safe side. Then she went to the phone and rang the number DS Anderson had given her to contact that morning. She assumed that they would be aware of the missing files by now. She needed to let them know that a few, at least, had turned up.

Hull, Tuesday evening
It was almost midnight and Roy Farnham was still at Lynne's flat. They had eaten early in the evening, shortly after he'd arrived, and sat at the table talking through the cases and the possible links. He was still trying to find the hotel cleaner, the woman who had, apparently, found the body then vanished. He wanted to know if Lynne had made any progress.

'Nothing yet,' she said. 'I'm looking. But these cases – do you still think they're linked?'

He frowned. 'I don't know. Gemma Wishart – whoever did it beat her half to death then strangled her. It's a bad business. John Gage – ' he caught Lynne's inquiring glance – 'the pathologist who worked this case, said that the ligature was tightened and released several times. He must have half strangled her and brought her round. Probably more than once.' Sexual sadism. Lynne thought about the kind of mind that would take pleasure in such a slow killing, such a slow death. Farnham hadn't finished. 'There were a lot of post-mortem injuries. He went on beating her after she was dead. That looks personal to me – real, lost-it rage. Which looks like the boyfriend.'

Lynne poured out more wine. 'Did he have sex with her?'

He nodded. 'Positives from all the swabs. He's a secretor, so we've got a blood group.'

'Rape?' If it had been an encounter between a prostitute and client, they might have had sex before the violence started, but if the post-mortem had found semen on oral, anal and vaginal swabs . . .

Farnham looked evasive. 'Gage thinks so.'

'And?' He hadn't told her everything. She hoped he wasn't holding out on her.

He shrugged in a you-asked-me way. 'Gage says it looks as though he had sex with her after he'd killed her, or while he was killing her. Something went on after she was dead.'

Lynne felt the contaminating touch of madness. Which kind of madness? That of someone who could kill a woman while he was having sex with her, maybe enjoy the process of fear, panic, and finally death with all its attendant . . . Or the madness of someone who would rape a dead woman. She needed to know, but she didn't want to know. She made a faint grimace of distaste. 'What do you make of the boyfriend?'

Farnham frowned. 'He's hard to read. Very cool. I cautioned him and he took it in his stride. Anderson said that he didn't seem surprised when they told him Wishart was dead – more resigned. He said he reported her missing because he didn't believe she'd sent the e-mail – which she hadn't – but then he thought she must have planned to go, after the letter arrived. He said she always intended to go back to . . . Some unpronounceable place in Russia. Claimed she had a boyfriend over there.'

'What about the escort work?' Hagan's story sounded unlikely to Lynne, and she could see that Farnham wasn't impressed.

'I showed him the photographs. That got him wound up.' Farnham paused for a moment, gathering his thoughts. 'He didn't like that. Tom Anderson gave him the "not bad if you like that sort of thing" treatment, and you could see it was getting to him. Then he kind of switched off, so I asked him about the escort work. I thought he was going to hit me.' He grinned. 'Pity he didn't, really. I'd have had something to hold him on. He admitted taking the photographs.'

They were sitting together on the settee at this stage, close enough to indicate that they were both interested in more than the case, but the discussion had irretrievably changed the mood. Lynne pushed the files away from her, stood up and stretched. He checked his watch. 'Probably time I was going.'

He paused at the door of her flat, leaning his arm against

the door jamb and looking down at her. She liked his face, which was ordinary but lit up attractively when he smiled. She liked his air of laid-back competence. 'Too much shop talk,' he said. He kissed her lightly on the mouth. 'Another time?'

'Another time,' she said, meaning it, as she let him out of the flat.

It was late, but her mind was too active for sleep. Roy Farnham thought it was likely that Hagan had killed Gemma Wishart. Lynne thought that he was probably right. When you looked at the case, the complexities vanished. Wishart's e-mail and letter were clumsy forgeries, the e-mail sent from an internet café close to the university where Hagan worked. Data had been removed from both of her computers. In one case this had just involved the removal of document files, but the other machine had been crudely wiped. This might have suggested that her death had something to do with her work, but Hagan could easily have wiped the machines himself. He had no alibi for Thursday night. He said he had stayed late at work setting up for a meeting the next day. He had been home to see if Wishart had left a message for him, then gone out on his bike.

Except . . . It was like looking at one of those pictures that could at one moment be an elegant woman, the next an old crone, but somehow never both. Gemma Wishart had been looking at evidence relating to Katya's death. And then she had died in a similar – not identical, Lynne reminded herself – in a similar way. Or in a way that had superficial simi-larities. If Hagan was the killer, he'd made clumsy attempts to conceal the death. He had sent an e-mail to assuage or delay concern. He had sent a letter, in the hope that the search for Gemma would end. And yet he worked in a group that specialized in identifying forgeries and faked documents. He had reported her missing to show them how concerned he was. He had wiped all the data off her computer to link everything to her work. He had been thrashing about in the deep waters of panic. That wasn't the mark of a planned killing.

On the other hand, the killer had muddied the waters very cleverly, linking Wishart's death with the obscure deaths of two women, deaths that weren't even officially identified as murders and might never be. How would he have known about those deaths? Press coverage had been minimal. He had taken the dead Gemma Wishart to a hotel room in Hull and posed her body in the bath. And if that killer was Hagan, all the time the ruined face of the woman he had been close to, made love to, cared about, would have watched him in mute accusation. That was the act of a psychopath.

9

Snake pass, Wednesday

The car had been reported on Sunday, apparently abandoned. A patrol car was sent to give it a brief check to see if there was any record of it. The missing number plates suggested that it might be more interesting than a vehicle abandoned by joyriders. Joyriders, anyway, preferred the city streets.

Police Constable Lee Taylor pulled his car off the road and looked the vehicle over. It had been driven well into the culvert, and was barely noticeable from the road. It interested him that someone had gone to such trouble to conceal the car from casual observation. His list of cars involved in recent crimes didn't include a red Fiesta, but he was reluctant to write the matter off on the strength of that. A walker had reported it late Sunday. It didn't look as though anyone had been near it since then. There had been rain the night before, but the ground around the car was undisturbed. He moved to the other side, noting the stains and splashes on the sill where the overhang protected it from the rain.

He kept away from the car as he moved round, peering in through the windows. The car was in the shadow of the rock, and he shone his torch through the windshield, trying to get a clearer view of the inside. It was empty. He gave himself a mental kick for being melodramatic, and wondered why he still wasn't happy. He went back to the other side of the car and checked the marks on the sill again. It didn't look to him as though the driver could have got out of the car at that side. The door was close up against the rock. And yet whatever had splashed on the sill looked as though it had splashed there when the door was open. He shone his torch through the windscreen again, and this time he thought he saw dark stains on the upholstery.

Someone could have been hurt in that car. He looked around him at the bleak landscape. It was a bad place to be injured and in need of help. The occasional car passed on the road, almost out of sight. The hills rose behind him, massive blocks of millstone grit, their harsh edges camouflaged by the sparse, thin grasses of the dark peaks. The wind was getting up, carrying an edge of ice as though it was blowing from the Siberian plains. The sky was ominous and dark. He looked across the valley to Kinder Scout, and behind him to Bleaklow. Who knew what the peat bogs and the heathers concealed? People came in their thousands in the summer to admire the beauty of these hills and moorlands, to walk, to tame the wilderness with cars and ice-cream vans and picnics. But Taylor thought that now, when the eyes of their public were turned away, when the trappings of summer were gone, the hills showed their true face, and that face was dark and threatening.

Sheffield, Wednesday morning
Roz walked along the corridor towards Joanna's room, trying to pretend that she had spent the morning doing something useful. For two hours she'd been sitting at her desk, trying to focus her mind on the next stage of the research program she had been working on, but she kept thinking about Luke. It had said on the news this morning that the police had released a man who had been 'helping them with their inquiries', but Luke hadn't been in to work, nor had he replied when she phoned. His answering machine took the call, and she left a brief message, but he hadn't made contact.

She couldn't concentrate. She was just marking time, and Joanna's summons, when it came, was a welcome distraction. Joanna was at her desk with spreadsheets, charts and work plans laid out in front of her. 'We've got to get these research proposals moving,' she greeted Roz. 'I know' – this was in response to Roz's half-articulated protest – 'it seems callous. But these have to be done.'

Roz nodded, turning over the forms that Joanna had pushed towards her. 'Have you heard anything?' she said. 'Is there any . . .'

Joanna cut her off firmly. 'It's in the hands of the police. I don't think there's anything more we can do. I've sent a letter to Gemma's mother.'

'I'm worried about Luke,' Roz said.

'I wouldn't be,' Joanna said frostily. 'He seemed fine this morning.'

This morning! 'Has he been in touch?'

'He was in when I got here,' Joanna said. Roz felt relieved and puzzled. He was back, and hadn't bothered to contact her. Joanna was talking again. 'I wasn't happy about . . . He's working from home at the moment.' She silenced Roz's attempt to ask questions. 'Not now, we've got some decisions to make. It's up to us to keep the group going – no one else is doing anything. I want you to find a good post-grad to take Gemma's classes for the rest of the semester. Can you deliver her lectures?' This was Joanna's way of coping, burying herself and everyone else under mountains of work that left no time for thought or reflection.

The two women spent the next hour going over research plans and figures that would direct the group through the next year. 'We'll need to get those advertisements out as soon as possible,' Joanna said. She checked her watch. 'I already have the go-ahead for the new research assistants. I'll hire them before any minds get changed.' That meant Peter Cauldwell. Roz wondered if their erstwhile Head of Department would try to close the group down before Joanna moved beyond his power base and beyond his control. 'We'll need to think of someone who can move in on the software side,' Joanna went on.

Roz wouldn't – couldn't – let that one past. She remembered the charming, and no doubt extremely talented, young man at Joanna's party. 'We have Luke for the software side,' she said.

'Well . . .' Joanna said after a pause, 'I was going to leave this for the moment. You've got enough to think about. But Luke's suspended as of this morning.'

Shock silenced Roz. Luke had always said that Joanna wouldn't miss a chance to get rid of him, but this . . . 'Why?' Her voice sounded sharp in her own ears. 'Luke hasn't been charged with anything,' she said, trying to keep her voice even. She didn't want to think about Luke being charged with anything. 'He wasn't arrested. They just wanted to talk to him.'

Joanna hesitated, looking down at the papers on the desk in front of her. 'I know,' she said. 'But that's not the problem.' She looked at Roz. 'I suspended Luke this morning because I found him downloading pornographic material from the internet. There'll be a disciplinary hearing. I'm sorry.'

Roz felt winded. Somehow, the idea of Luke trawling porn sites on the net seemed horribly linked with the photographs she'd seen forming on her screen, something that turned him into a stranger, someone she didn't know. And downloading stuff at work? Joanna must have got it wrong. But Luke hadn't denied it – he'd just gone without a word to Roz, without a bust-up with Joanna.

The silence stretched uncomfortably. Roz couldn't think of anything to say. She felt angry – angry with Joanna for suspending Luke, angry with Luke for leaving himself vulnerable, angry with the whole rigmarole of university politics. She wanted to dump the lot and go home. She couldn't be bothered. She couldn't, as Luke would have said, be *arsed*. She scooped up the papers from the desk in front of her. 'I'll take these to my room,' she said. 'I'll get back to you tomorrow.' Joanna raised her eyebrows but didn't say anything as Roz closed the door behind her.

Her own office seemed bleak and unwelcoming, so she went to the computer room to do some work on the program she and Luke were developing. She had research notes to write up. The room was empty and silent. There was no smell of coffee brewing, no gossip, none of Luke's speculative rambling about his current reading, which could range from popular physics to advanced maths, none of his barbed comments, no discussion of the work they were doing, Roz flying the ideas and Luke trying to shoot them down as they developed and refined the system. Luke's absence was as compelling as his presence, and she couldn't work with it. She picked up the phone and tried his number, but once again she got the machine. She was going to hang up, but then said on impulse, 'Luke, it's Roz. Please phone me. I've found some of Gemma's files, on the laptop.'

The thought of her discovery gave her an idea for something she could do, something she might be able to concentrate on. She could take another look at the report that Gemma had written for DI Jordan and see if she could find that final uncertainty, solve the puzzle that had been nagging away at her mind ever since she had found the transcript tucked away in the case with Gemma's laptop.

Hull, Wednesday afternoon

There was gunfire in the distance, the intermittent sound of automatic weapons. It had become a background to their day-to-day lives, far away, but getting closer in the way people looked at each other. People who had been neighbours, friends even, for years, suddenly had the dark eyes of suspicion and fear and hate. The gunfire began again, loud, close, just outside her door and she jerked upright, grabbing for her coat, looking round for Krisha, for her mother, the cold sweat of panic breaking out over her body.

The dim light of a winter afternoon filtered through the curtains that were pulled across the window. The settee felt lumpy, the cushions pushed out of alignment as she slept. The room was cold, the Calor Gas heater switched off. The sound of the typewriter started up again in the next room. Anna closed her eyes and waited for the thumping of her heart to slow down to its natural rhythm

She sat on the edge of the seat, clutching her coat round her against the cold. She picked up the blanket from where it had fallen on the floor, and wrapped it round her shoulders. She let the past few days trickle back into her mind, and for the first time she could think without the flood of panic pushing her onwards as though her only hope of safety lay in movement. She pushed the picture of the woman in the bath out of her mind. She had too many pictures of dead people in her mind. Angel had found her, that was what she had thought. He had left the dead woman to show her what was in store for her, and he had left the card to make sure she understood. But . . . what had seemed clear in the moment of panic didn't make sense any more. She wasn't important enough for that. If Angel had found her, she would be dead by now. He wouldn't bother with warnings.

Angel had been there, he had left his card. But maybe he didn't know that Anna had been there too. She had been right to run away. He could have come back at any time. She thought about him waiting for her in those narrow, empty corridors, and her stomach lurched. She had been right to stay away from her room as well. Someone had broken in and stolen her passport and her visa, someone had been waiting for her. It had to be Angel. Did Mrs Fry know him? Had she told him about Anna who had run away, and had Angel come looking for her?

She heard footsteps and the door opened behind her. She jumped up, spinning round, and Nasim was there, a reproving frown on her face, a steaming cup in her hand. 'Tea,' she said in her hard, abrupt voice, and pressed the warm cup into Anna's hands. 'Drink.'

It was another cup of the thick, milky tea, hot and sweet, and Anna felt it warming her, felt her energy start to return as she drank. She looked at the other woman who was watching her, unsmiling. Nasim nodded as Anna drained the cup, then she pushed a bundle into her hands. Anna looked. There was a towel, and there were blue jeans, socks, a T-shirt and a jersey, all worn and faded, but all clean. Nasim watched her for a moment then indicated that Anna should follow her. She led her down a corridor and out of a back door into a yard. The yard was dark, the high walls of the adjacent buildings blocking out the sky. The crumbling asphalt was spongy with moss and a fern grew out of the wall above her. Across the yard, there was a small outhouse and Nasim produced a key and unlocked it, gesturing to Anna to go in.

Inside, there was a toilet and a small basin. The walls were whitewashed brick and the floor concrete. It smelt faintly of disinfectant. Ignoring the cold, Anna stripped off her clothes and washed herself, using her T-shirt as a sponge. She couldn't do anything about her hair, but, as she pulled on the clothes Nasim had given her, she felt clean for the first time in days. The brief surge of energy from the sweet tea was fading now, and a lassitude and weariness was starting to weigh her down. She wanted to sleep again, to sleep and sleep and maybe not wake up but stay in the world of dreams – if the dreams could be about her mother, about Krisha, about her friends, about the farm . . .

The water dripped into the basin, the smell of smoke drifted into the air, *the translucence of a shower curtain with something behind it, and Krisha's doll on the floor, crushed by a passing foot.* A wave of giddiness and nausea washed over her and she clutched the edge of the basin, waiting for it to pass. The smell of disinfectant was stronger now, and she went back into the yard, leaning against the wall of the outhouse, breathing in the cold air until the sickness passed. She opened her eyes and saw Nasim gesturing abruptly to her from the door. She recognized the impatience. It reminded her of her mother: *Come in out of the cold! Come in out of the rain! Anna, you will make yourself ill!* Nasim looked at her, frowning, and touched a hand to her face. The hand felt cold. Nasim made a tutting noise, and led Anna back into the room where she had spent the night. The fire was lit, and there was a plate of triangular pastries on the arm of the settee.

Anna sat down and, under Nasim's dictatorial eye, began to eat the small, spicy parcels. Her stomach had been raven-ous for the sweet tea, but now her appetite seemed to have faded, and the nausea was coming back. She ate two of the pastries, sipping water to help them down. Nasim seemed to understand and her rather severe face relaxed after Anna had finished her second. 'Rest,' she said.

It was all Anna wanted to do, but she had to make some plans. She didn't know where to go, didn't know if the watcher had managed to follow her to the welfare centre, didn't know if Angel lurked in the streets outside, waiting for the darkness to come back. 'Matthew . . . ?' she said to Nasim. Matthew might know what to do.

Nasim shook her head and tapped her watch. 'Later,' she said. There was the *ting* of a bell, the sound of the front door opening. Nasim looked at Anna and put her fingers to her lips. 'Rest,' she mouthed, and disappeared through the door to the office. There was nothing that Anna could do. The waves of fatigue were overcoming her, and she wrapped herself in the blanket, cold still in spite of the fire, and lay down on the settee.

There were no customers at the Welfare Advice Centre when Lynne pushed open the door. She went straight round the counter and into the office at the back, where Nasim Rafiq was coming round the desk in response to the bell, an expression on her face that Lynne was unable to identify before it settled into a polite blank. The door at the back of the room that led to the small kitchen was open. Lynne could see a cup and a small pan on the worktop. In the office, the old manual typewriter was pulled out and had a sheet of paper wound into the carriage. There was a book open face-down on the desk. Lynne, who had become an expert at reading from just about any angle, read the title *Intermediate Business English, BEC 2*. She smiled at Rafiq. 'Quiet again,' she said.

Rafiq went over to the other door, and pulled it shut. 'Draught,' she explained. Lynne nodded. The office was cold. She didn't think that closing a door would make a lot of difference. Rafiq sat down in front of the typewriter. Lynne pulled a chair up to the desk and sat opposite her. After a moment, Rafiq said, 'Is mostly quiet, but sometimes is busy.'

Lynne wanted this woman's co-operation. She had a feeling that this place, ramshackle and unregulated as it seemed to be, would be a useful contact point for immigrants who

144

were in trouble and the people who might help them. The grapevine would spread the word. Katya had come here. The women she was looking for might come here. If that was the case, how much did Pearse and Rafiq know? Would they co-operate? She had to tread carefully. She wanted to break the ice, get under the woman's wary guard, but the impassive face watching her showed no signs of relaxing. Though Rafiq's spoken English was not very fluent, Lynne was pretty sure that her understanding was good. 'Could I talk to you?' she said.

Rafiq frowned slightly. Puzzlement. She gave a slight shrug. *What do you think we are doing?*

'Mrs Rafiq,' Lynne began again, 'I just need to check a few things with you.'

Rafiq's face remained impassive. She waited for Lynne to tell her what she wanted. Lynne picked up the book. It was exam preparation for various kinds of business English – letter-writing, memos, reports. 'Are you studying English?' she said.

Rafiq nodded at this obvious question. 'I . . . For here,' she explained. 'And later, maybe, work.'

Lynne wasn't sure of Rafiq's status. 'Where are you from, Mrs Rafiq?' She said. 'How long have you been here?'

In response, the other woman took her handbag out of the desk drawer and pulled her passport out. A card came out with it and fluttered to the floor. Lynne picked it up, and took the passport the other woman was holding out to her. This wasn't what Lynne had meant, but she was happy at the opportunity to get more information about this woman. She looked at it, noting that Rafiq had leave to stay as a visiting relative. She was travelling with her son, and Lynne looked at the photograph of the chubby-faced child. 'How old is your little boy?' she asked. She looked at the picture again and said, 'He's beautiful.'

Rafiq's blank face thawed for a moment into a smile of genuine warmth. 'Javid,' she said. 'He is six. He is . . . school, now.'

'Where does your husband work, Mrs Rafiq?' Lynne said.

'At university,' Rafiq said. 'Is engineer. Is teach.' She went on to explain in her limited English that her husband had been working in this country for a year, and had a contract for another three. She had been here for six months, having waited to make sure her husband was settled, and to get her paperwork sorted out.

Lynne looked at the card that had fallen out of Rafiq's bag. It was an appointment card for the local children's hospital, a private appointment made out for Javid Rafiq. Lynne gave it back to her and said, 'Is your son ill? I hope it's nothing serious.'

Rafiq looked at her in silence for a moment, as if she was weighing up her answer. She explained with some reluctance that her son had problems with his sight. Lynne couldn't be sure because of her limited English, but it sounded as though the child's optic nerve was affected, and without treatment he would go blind. That was the reason her husband had come to an English university to work. 'Treatment is better here,' Rafiq said. 'We pay,' she added defensively.

Lynne said, 'I'm sorry about your son. I hope his treatment is successful.' She smiled reassuringly at the other woman. There was silence for a moment, then Lynne moved on to the real reason for her visit. She took the photograph of Katya out of her bag, and put it on the desk in sight of both of them as she talked.

She explained about the women she was trying to contact, about the kinds of operations she was afraid were going on in the area, the dangers that the women were exposed to, isolated as they were from even the meagre protection the law gave to prostitutes. Rafiq listened impassively, and Lynne couldn't tell how much of what she was saying the other woman understood. At the end she picked up the photograph. 'This woman,' she said. 'She came to you. There may have been others. I can help them.'

Rafiq looked at the photograph for a moment, running her fingers over the paper as if she was touching the woman. She sighed. 'Is bad,' she said. She looked at Lynne for a long moment. 'Welfare,' she said. She reached to the shelf behind her and pulled out a handful of leaflets. 'For mother, baby.' She gestured at the list tacked to the wall behind her. 'Houses, doctors, clinic, benefit. Welfare. Not . . .' Her hand made circular motions over the photo. Lynne understood. Rafiq was telling her that this was a welfare centre, not a place where desperate prostitutes came for help. And if her son's future depended so much on her staying here at least for a while, why would she jeopardize it by doing something illegal, no matter how strongly she felt about the plight of the refugees? But in that case, what had made Katya come here?

She saw Rafiq look past her, at something behind her, and turned round to see Matthew Pearse standing there. His sudden presence made her jump. He was immediately apologetic, his confusion making the speech impediment she'd noticed before more pronounced. 'It's all right, Mr Pearse,' she said in the end. 'I was so busy talking to Mrs Rafiq I didn't hear you come in.'

'It's these shoes,' he said, his stammer abating. 'My land-lord persuaded me to buy some trainers. He's right. They're very comfortable, but no one can hear me coming.'

'Now you're here,' she said, 'I can ask you both. I'm look-ing for a woman who went missing just a few days ago. She's a possible witness to a serious crime.' She paused and looked at them. Nasim's face was expressionless. Pearse had a faint line between his brows. 'She's young, about twenty. Five foot two with dark hair.' They were still watching her. 'Her name's Krleza. Anna Krleza.'

Rafiq picked up the photo of Katya. 'Why?' she said. 'This woman, that woman. Why?' *Why are you asking us?*

Her face was hard to read. Lynne couldn't tell if she had reacted to the name or not. Pearse's face retained its faintly troubled expression. 'Mr Pearse?' Lynne said. He shook his head. She told him what she had told Rafiq and he heard her out in silence. 'They're in a double bind, these women, aren't they?' he said, when she had finished. His stammer made him sound diffident and uncertain, but his dark eyes were direct as he watched her. He had suspected that Katya

147

had been working as a prostitute, she remembered. She recalled the expression on his face when he said, 'I thought I'd persuaded her to come back' – a resigned sadness.

'How do you mean, Mr Pearse?'

'I mean that they are the victims of a crime – a very serious crime – but if they go to the police, they will be treated as criminals themselves.' His mouth moved silently for a moment. 'I mean,' he managed, seeing that Lynne was about to speak, 'they will be locked up. And deported. Eventually.'

It seemed more a request for information than a political statement, and Lynne responded to it as such. 'That's beyond my control, Mr Pearse,' she said. 'But they would be dealt with sympathetically.' She was aware of Rafiq watching her intently.

'Maybe for some of them, that's a worse option than what is happening to them now. But I heard what Nasim was saying to you . . .' Pearse's mouth reached for the words. He looked down at his hands and she could see him make a conscious effort to relax. After a moment, he could speak again. 'We are what we say we are. A welfare centre. Most of our clients – belong to immigrant groups – but not all. What they do have in common – is poverty and – an inability to understand – how the system works. I admit we don't question – the right of people to be here, but – if they are using the welfare system, the hospitals – the doctors, the schools, then I assume – that someone is doing that checking. We don't have the time – or the skills.' His speech sounded halting as he struggled to control his stammer.

'So why did she come to you? The woman you took to the hospital? What brought her here?'

'Maybe someone told her – that we don't ask questions,' he said. 'I don't know.'

It was a long shot, but Lynne showed him the photograph of Gemma Wishart. 'I don't recognize her,' he said. 'Is she one of these girls?'

'She's a murder victim, Mr Pearse.'

His hand hovered over the photograph for a moment, then

148

he touched his forehead and an expression of pain crossed his face. 'Poor child,' he said.

Sheffield, Wednesday afternoon

Roz spent the afternoon poring over Gemma's report and the transcript she had found in the laptop carrying case. Gemma had made a written version of the tape, underlining and highlighting the sections she wanted to look at closely. Next to those sections were phonetic symbols showing the pronunciation, with scribbled notes for the final report. Roz went through the report, matching the notes with Gemma's findings. Everything seemed to be accounted for, apart from the queried lines and that mysterious reference to cats.

The queried lines were all places where the woman's English failed and she spoke in Russian. Roz had very little Russian, but Gemma had supplied translations. The woman on the tape was answering questions, which Gemma had not bothered to transcribe, so Roz had to try and reconstruct the prompt to work out what the woman might be saying. She didn't have the tape – Gemma's copy had not turned up when she and Luke searched her room – and she didn't have a good reason to ask DI Jordan for another copy. She looked at line 204 of the transcript: *I . . . Ba-yi-n-sal . . . I stay . . . I . . . friend.* There was no translation next to the Russian phrase – maybe it just meant 'I stay' or 'I will stay'. The lines before and after suggested that someone was asking the woman what she planned to do: *I got place* and *I go*. Roz couldn't see any reason for Gemma's query. Line 127, Gemma had marked as indecipherable, but had written *jugun??* in the middle of the line. Line 25 Gemma had again marked as indecipherable with the queried word *di* at the end of the line.

She tapped her pen against her teeth as she thought. That was something that always infuriated Luke. 'Christ, Bishop!' he used to say. 'Are you trying to drive me insane or what?' She was thinking about Luke in the past tense. Her brief success at distracting herself was shattered as the events of yesterday came crowding back. She checked her watch. It was three o'clock. Maybe she should try and track down Marcus Holbrook, find out what this archive was, whether Gemma had managed to get access to it, and, if so, what she had been looking for. Maybe she could find someone who would translate the bits of the transcript Gemma had queried. She copied the lines out carefully then tucked the transcript in her briefcase.

The department she wanted was ten minutes' walk away from the Arts Tower, in one of the old red-brick houses that typified the area and that the university had slowly and inexorably overtaken. It was on what must once have been a quiet cul-de-sac, but was now choked up with parked cars and students walking three and four abreast, blocking the pavement and spilling out into the road.

The Department of European Studies was halfway up on her left. A group of students was on the steps outside, smoking. Despite the cold, they wore light tops, T-shirts, the garb of summer, their possessions slung in rucksacks on their backs, relaxed and confident. Roz remembered her own teenage insecurities and wondered if she had managed to project the same air of self-assurance in her student days. As she walked towards the door, the group shuffled round. Roz felt a stab of irritation, and walked square through the middle, rather than sidling through the narrow space they opened up. 'Excuse me,' she said. And then, mildly, 'Thank you,' as they closed ranks in silence behind her. She heard conversation and laughter start up again as she pushed through the door.

She was in a small entrance hall, stairs to her left, and a notice board facing her. She looked round. A door on her right said OFFICE, and to her left, almost obscured by the stairs, was a sign – INQUIRIES. She hesitated for a moment, then went to the office. She knocked and went in. The room was empty, apart from a young man who was leafing through some papers at one of the desks. He looked up at her and smiled guiltily. 'Oops,' he said, and moved hastily to the other side of the desk. 'Elizabeth just nipped out.' Then he looked at her again. 'Rosalind,' he said.

'Roz,' she said automatically. Only Nathan called her Rosalind. Then recognition dawned. It was the young man from Joanna's party, the high-flier, what was his name? Steve . . . ? *Sean.* 'Sean,' she said.

He looked pleased that she'd remembered. 'I didn't know . . .' he began, as Roz said, 'I thought you . . .'

They both laughed, breaking the ice, and he gestured to Roz to go on. 'I thought you were in Martin Lomax's department,' Roz said.

'Oh, I am. I'm just helping out here.' He came round the desk towards her. 'Elizabeth's gone to the copier,' he said. 'I'm just checking on some student marks. Which,' he added, 'I shouldn't be doing.' He gave her a conspiratorial smile. He had that easy confidence that Roz always associated with wealth and private education, which made him seem older that he probably was.

Roz remembered his attention in her at the party. It had been flattering then, but she didn't want to encourage it. 'I'm looking for Professor Holbrook,' she said briskly.

He looked at her. 'Marcus . . . he's around. I don't think he's in at the moment, though. He doesn't really . . .'

Holbrook was a consultant, Roz knew that. She also knew that he still kept up some research. She knew several people like that, unable to let go of the reins of academia, endlessly frequenting the Senior Common Room, occupying space in the libraries, agitating for rooms in the departments that had left them behind. 'Do you know where I can find him?'

'I might be able to help.' He was giving her his full attention now, half sitting on the secretary's desk, the bundle of papers forgotten beside him. 'I'm doing some work with Marcus. What was it you wanted?'

Roz didn't want to discuss it with him. She felt a bit hassled, and her words came out more sharply than she'd intended. 'I'd rather discuss it with Professor Holbrook.'

He looked put out for a moment, then seemed to remember something. 'You work with Gemma . . . Worked with Gemma.' He looked uncomfortable.

'Yes.' Roz looked at him. 'What do you know about Gemma?'

His embarrassment seemed genuine. He wasn't smiling now. 'I didn't make the connection at first. When I heard. She ... was just Gemma from Linguistics. Then ...' He scuffed the toe of his shoe along the carpet. 'She wanted to look at our archive. Marcus's archive.' He looked to see if she knew what he was talking about. 'Russian. We're putting together an archive of spoken Russian. It's Marcus's thing.'

The Holbrook Archive. That cleared up whether Gemma had contacted Holbrook or not. She remembered the unfinished letter on the laptop. According to the letter, the archive was being catalogued. 'You're writing the software?' she said.

He nodded. 'He asked my department for help. I was around, and I had these ideas, and Marcus thought they were cool so I decided, "Why not?"' He shrugged. 'You don't get really stretched here, you know.' Luke's voice supplied the subtext: *At a piss-poor hole like this.* Roz kept her face solemn. 'Now I've got into it, it's good – computers and language – it's something special.' He smiled at her. 'Your boss has been on to me about it. Says there might be a space with you.' He met her gaze. 'I'm beginning to think I might be persuaded.'

He was looking at her with a barely concealed interest. Roz felt irritated with Joanna, and her irritation extended towards Sean, which probably wasn't fair. But, anyway, she wasn't in the mood for flirtatious exchanges with young men. 'I really need to talk to Professor Holbrook,' she said.

He looked put out again. He seemed younger now than he had at Joanna's party. 'He might have gone for coffee,' he said after a moment's thought. He cheered up. 'I know where he might be. I'll walk across with you.'

'That's OK,' she said. 'Just tell me . . .'

'No. It's no problem. I need to see him anyway.' He seemed to have forgotten Elizabeth at the copier and his students' marks. She decided it would be simpler to let him walk her across than argue any more.

*   *   *

Sean took her to the Senior Common Room where he spent five minutes trying to persuade her to have coffee with him. 'Please?' he said. 'I'd really like to get to know you.' Roz pleaded pressure of work, and rather reluctantly he pointed Holbrook out to her. He was sitting over coffee by a window, browsing at the papers. Sean headed over with Roz behind him. 'Marcus, this is Rosalind . . . Roz Bishop. She was looking for you. And I need . . .'

Holbrook looked up from his paper, frowning. He had one of those small, thin faces that seemed designed to express discontent. 'Sean,' he said, 'I was *expecting* you this morning.'

'Got held up,' he said unrepentantly. 'I brought Roz over. She knows Gemma. Knew Gemma.' Holbrook kept his querying gaze on Sean, ignoring Roz, who stepped into the silence.

'Professor Holbrook,' she said, 'I worked with Gemma Wishart in the Law and Language Group. I wonder if I could have a word with you?'

He frowned slightly, and said, none too warmly, 'You seem to be doing that now. What exactly did you want?' He looked at his watch as he spoke.

Sean waited for a moment, then said. 'I need to talk to you about that new material, Marcus.'

Holbrook nodded. 'I'll be with you in half an hour.'

'OK. I'll be across in the department.' Sean looked at Roz. 'I'll see you,' he said. He paused for a minute as if he wanted to say something else to her, then went, leaving Roz with Holbrook.

'I can come and see you later, if you're in a hurry . . .' Roz said.

'No, no.' Holbrook was impatient. 'I'm far too busy for appointments. It will have to be my break. What can I do for you?'

Roz stepped firmly on her irritation. Holbrook was a respected man in his field. He probably was busy, and she was, effectively, jumping the queue for his time. 'Thank you, Professor.' She quickly ran through the problem in her mind. 'My colleague, Gemma Wishart . . .' She looked at him to see if he had picked up the reference, but he showed no reaction, just continued to watch her with an air of slightly exaggerated patience. 'I believe she consulted you about a tape she was working on. I just wondered – '

He raised his hand, stopping her. 'There's no need to go any further. I have already had to discuss this with the police today. Dr Wishart did not consult me. She merely wished to use my archive, and my assistant, whom you have met, told her in accordance with my instructions that it was unavailable as it was being catalogued.' He folded his napkin and dabbed his mouth. 'She then wrote to *me*, and I gave her access to it. She was interested in tapes from the eastern Siberian region. I had no knowledge at the time of what she was looking for, and I have none now.'

'Oh.' For a moment, Roz was silenced. She'd assumed that Gemma had discussed whatever her uncertainties about the tape were with this man. 'She didn't ask for any translations or anything?'

'As I told you, Miss Bishop . . .'

'*Doctor* Bishop.' There was only so much Roz was prepared to put up with from a touchy prima donna.

He bowed his head in acknowledgement. '*Doctor* Bishop, then. As I told you, she asked to consult my archive. I have collected a lot of material over the years and I am inundated with requests from researchers who . . .'

Roz listened with half an ear as she thought through what he was saying. Gemma's letter, unfinished, had said something about a tape. She risked annoying him further by interrupting him. 'Did Gemma give you any material for the archive?' she said.

He stopped in mid-flow and looked at her. 'Did Dr Wishart give me any material? I believe she offered me some. She had spent some time in . . .'

'Siberia,' Roz said.

'That is correct. I don't recall that there was anything she had that we needed for the archive. However, I could be wrong. You are welcome to look, if it will help you. Now, if you will excuse me . . .' He began to stand up.

'There is something else,' Roz said. The exaggerated expression of patience reappeared on his face and he sat back in his seat. 'I know that Russian is your particular field. I wonder if you could just look at these and tell me if they mean anything to you.' She showed him the lines from the transcript that she had copied down.

He looked at them in silence for a minute. 'It's hard to be exact in isolation,' he said.

'I'm sorry,' Roz said. 'But there was no more. Those were the full lines on the transcript.'

'I see.' He pursed his lips. 'Well, the first one is a colloquialism – it's something you say when you're irritated or frustrated. There is no exact translation.' Roz made a note. 'This one, *jugun*, is just a word for people. It's found in Siberia, it's a dialect word. And your third one seems to be a random syllable.'

Roz flushed. 'Yes, I'm sorry, it was just that Gemma queried it and I wondered what it meant.'

He shook his head. 'Is there anything else I can help you with, or may I return to my own work?'

'You said that Gemma wrote to you. What did she say exactly?'

'She said what I have told you. I gave her letter to the police.'

'Yes, I know, but if you could tell me exactly, I might be able to work out what Gemma was looking for.'

'What she was looking for was obviously comparison tapes for this –' he gestured at the piece of paper Roz had given him – 'whatever it is.'

'Yes.' He was almost certainly right, and Roz wondered why she kept persisting. 'I just want to know exactly.'

He sighed. 'I'm very careful with my correspondence. I gave Dr Wishart's letter to the police, but I kept a copy for my files. I can send one to you, if you want. Maybe that will satisfy you?'

'Thank you.' Roz smiled at him, trying to show that she did appreciate it, even if she couldn't warm to the man. She remembered the papers that had gone missing from her desk.

'Could you send it to my home address?' She wrote it down for him, and before he could get up to leave, added quickly, 'How would a Russian speaker pronounce "cat"?' She couldn't understand the reference to cats at the top of the transcript. And yet it had meant something to Gemma. *Cats*??

Holbrook sighed. 'In Russian? It's something like *korshka*. Or *kort*, for a tomcat. It doesn't sound a lot like the English.'

'I meant the English word.'

'Like the Russian word.' He looked at his watch. 'You'd get a pronunciation like *kort*. Something like that. Possibly. There are a lot of variations. Now, please . . .' He got up determinedly and left Roz sitting at the table.

Hull, Wednesday afternoon
The records for the Angel Escorts cell phone landed in Lynne's in-tray after lunch. With a sense of a legitimate reprieve, she abandoned the notes she was preparing for an impending meeting, and looked at what Farnham had sent through to her. He had scribbled a note: *Come and talk about this when you've looked at it.* She smiled at the addition: *Shop* ☺

The phone was new. It had been bought about a week before Wishart's death at a large retailer on the outskirts of Sheffield. It had been a cash transaction. The records showed just one outgoing call. On the night that Wishart had died, at seven forty-three p.m., someone had used the phone to call a Sheffield number. The call had lasted three minutes. Farnham had written next to the number: *Hagan.*

She checked when Farnham would be free, put together the stuff she had collected on Angel Escorts, and then went back to finishing the next section of her presentation. At four-thirty, she was in Farnham's office addressing him with the formality of the work place, which seemed strangely at odds with the cautious way they had been testing the boundaries of their relationship the previous night.

They relaxed once the door was shut and they were on their own. 'Bad briefing this morning,' he said. 'Forensics say she wasn't killed at the hotel, but the scene was so messed up we couldn't use it if he'd written his name on the wall in his own shit and left his calling card.' He rubbed his forehead with his fingers. 'One of the guests, the woman in the room next door, heard something.' He pushed a statement across his desk to Lynne. She looked at the place he was indicating:

Something woke me in the night. I heard someone moving around in the next room. It sounded as if someone was bumping into things. And there was laughing. Someone kept laughing. It was like when you've heard a really funny joke and can't stop.

She thought about someone in the hotel room with the dead Gemma, someone who killed, who had sex with a dead woman, who posed her in the bathtub. She thought about the laughter. Someone who killed women and destroyed their faces . . . Her eyes met Farnham's. 'It gives you a time,' she said after a moment.

'It hasn't got us much further. We still haven't tracked down the guy in the second room.'

'The room with the whisky bottle?' Lynne said. If the resident of the room had drunk that whisky, then it was unlikely he'd heard anything.

'We don't know for sure if the whisky bottle came from that room,' Farnham said. 'The Krleza woman had cleaned in there – and then all her stuff was mixed up. I've got the fingerprint people matching the bottle with the room. And a used condom.' He grinned. 'They love me.'

'So there was someone else there?' she said.

He nodded. 'Unless he was taking safe sex a bit further than most of us do. But no one saw anyone, of course. Only one person registered for that room. I've got the print people working on it.'

'What about the phone? Are you going after Hagan again?' If the choice were hers, Lynne would leave it for a while. She was interested to see what he had to say.

'It isn't enough. We put him through it, but his story holds together. He keeps appearing, does Hagan, but only in places where he has a legitimate reason to be. He's the boyfriend. He's been in the flat; he'll have been in her car, if we ever find it. He's got computer skills. He's got no alibi. And now there's this phone call, shortly before she was killed.' He looked at Lynne. 'How would a firm like Angel Escorts operate with the phones?'

'It varies. Most places, you'd phone a central number and then you'd either book the girl and she'd come round to wherever you'd arranged, or she might phone you and make her own arrangements. Sometimes the girls operate a bit more independently – they have their own number and the clients phone them directly and book, but the clients would usually register with the agency first.' She picked up the records Farnham had sent through. 'Have you got a location for this call?'

'Outside Glossop, to the east.' The route to the Snake Pass, the route Wishart had planned to take.

Lynne had been thinking about this since she had seen the records. 'So it could be Wishart's phone. It makes sense. The card looked like a personal card. So the number would be Wishart's business phone, for the escort work. If she'd just started out, that would explain why there's so little action on it.'

Farnham nodded. He'd thought of that as well. 'Hagan claims he didn't get back until eight. He stayed late at work. One of the caretakers says he saw Hagan leaving at around seven-thirty.' He tapped his pen on the desk. 'That "around" makes it possible. Hagan's got a fast bike. It's a bad road, but he could get from the university to his house in five minutes if the roads were clear.'

'OK. But if he wasn't there, Wishart – or whoever it was – must have left a message, or talked to someone. It's a three-minute call.'

'Hagan says there was no message.' Farnham shrugged. 'I can prove someone phoned him. There are a hundred good reasons why there's no message. I don't want to pull him in

158

and have him wriggle straight out. I want more to throw at him, and I want something he can't get out of. I've got someone watching for that phone. If anyone uses it, we'll be on to it like a shot. But in the meantime, I've got to wait.'

10

Sheffield, Wednesday evening

It was dark by the time Roz got home. The pavements shone damply in the light from the streetlamps and the breeze that was rattling the branches of the trees carried the threat of frost. It would be icy tomorrow. She picked her way carefully up the path, towards the stone lions that glimmered palely in the moonlight. She groped in her pockets for her key, and then impatiently in her bag where it had fallen to the bottom and was tangled up in a mess of old tissues, bus tickets, pens and loose change. She let herself into the house, and picked up the pile of letters that had landed on the mat. She flicked through them quickly, binning the junk mail before she could be tempted into looking at it. The rest looked tedious – bills, a bank statement that held no surprises, her credit-card statement – and a letter addressed in a familiar italic that she held for a few indecisive moments.

She had been anticipating it for days. The letters always arrived – one in the spring, for Nathan's birthday; one in early autumn, for her birthday; and one shortly into the New Year, their wedding anniversary. Nathan's mother had never reproached Roz for abandoning Nathan, had never taken for granted the financial contribution that Roz made to keep him in the residential home where he spent most of his time, never intruded her own grief into Roz's life. There were just the letters.

She put the rest of the post into the letter rack for dealing with, and went through to the kitchen, holding the envelope addressed in her mother-in-law's distinctive italic. She made coffee, and sat at the kitchen table turning the letter round and round in her hands. It was dark outside, and here at the back of the house where the walls and high trees shut out the sound of traffic, there was silence. She opened the letter.

It began with the usual salutations and hopes expressed for Roz's well-being. *I'm starting to get a bit stiff and creaky*, Jenny Bishop wrote, *but I suppose it's to be expected at my age.* At her age. How old would Nathan's mother be now? Only sixty, but the stresses of the past three years had taken their toll.

Jenny Bishop reported no change in her son's condition – none was expected. *He can't understand why I look so old*, she wrote. *He tells me to take things easy or I'll get ill. Why don't you come and see him, Roz, the next time he comes home? I keep hoping that something like that might just be the trigger he needs.*

There was always the plea in the letters, the hope that, somehow, Roz's presence might work the miracle that Jenny still lived for. Roz had long ago given up that hope. She put the letter to one side. She would answer it at the weekend.

She knew what she wanted to do this evening. She wanted to have another look at the files she had copied from Gemma's laptop. Her discussion with Holbrook hadn't been very helpful, but maybe when she looked again she would see – something. It was academic now, really. DI Jordan had the report and it gave her the information she needed. But the puzzle, and the sense of a job not done, nagged at Roz.

So, what had she got from Marcus Holbrook? He didn't seem to know much more than she did. Gemma had, apparently, consulted his archive. Tomorrow, she would try and find out which tapes Gemma had used, but for now, all she had were the letter, the report and the transcript. She read the report intently, but there was nothing there to help her. She couldn't see any place where Gemma might want to add information. She read through Gemma's discussion of the speech on the tape: *... confusion of the /v/ and /w/ phonemes ... devoicing of the final voiced consonants /b/ /d/ /g/ ... absence of auxiliary 'be' in present tense forms ...* and couldn't see why Gemma would want to expand the report. It wasn't an expert witness statement – she was simply being asked for an opinion and had given it, supported by pages of meticulous analysis.

She looked at the unfinished letter to Marcus Holbrook. Everything there was consistent with what Holbrook had said. Sean had told Gemma that the archive wasn't available. Gemma had appealed directly to Holbrook – on what grounds? Why would Gemma feel that Holbrook might be prepared to give her access to an archive that was in the process of being catalogued? Roz looked at Gemma's letter. *You'll remember the tape I* . . . The tape I . . . what? Gave you? Asked about? Offered? Whatever it was, Holbrook apparently didn't remember it.

Gemma had spent three years in Novosibirsk researching for her PhD. She must have collected hours of tapes. Maybe she had offered the whole collection to Holbrook, though it seemed unlikely, under the circumstances, that he would have forgotten that. Also, tapes of Russian speakers would hardly be unusual. Gemma had travelled from Arkhangelsk to Dudinka in the course of her research into – she racked her brains – Nenets, a language spoken in northernmost Russia, from the White Sea to the Yenisei River. There were about 25,000 people who spoke the language. Roz's geography of Russia was rudimentary, so she went to get her atlas to check on her locations. Novosibirsk was nearly a thousand miles south of the areas where Nenets was spoken. She looked at the map again, running her finger along the northern coastline. Gemma had enjoyed her time in Siberia, and she had travelled. Where was it, the place where they had given her the tapestry that glowed on the wall of her poky flat? There it was: Dudinka, on the mouth of the Yenisei River.

She felt a sense of achievement, which faded as she realized that it didn't get her any further. She racked her brains. *Something* in her conversation with Holbrook had rung bells and she couldn't think what it was. She tapped her pencil against her teeth as she thought. She looked at the letter again.

Dear Professor Holbrook
Holbrook Archive

I contacted your assistant recently about access to the archive to do some tape comparisons. Apparently the collection is currently being catalogued and isn't available at the moment. You'll remember the tape I

It looked as though Gemma was writing to someone she knew. There were assumptions of shared experience and knowledge – *You'll remember* . . . And the apparent assumption that Holbrook would do her a favour. The letter was obviously building up to a request for access to the archive, or part of the archive, presumably the tape that Holbrook would 'remember'. And yet Holbrook didn't remember. Nor had he said anything to Roz about Gemma. It had seemed odd at the time that he'd made no expression of regret, no reference to what had happened, just a rather querulous complaint that the police had talked to him. She had assumed it was just the way he was – the totally self-centred academic. But if he and Gemma had been friendly . . . Maybe he just hated any display of emotion. English male, stiff upper lip.

Hull, Wednesday evening
The post-mortem report had landed on Lynne's desk in the middle of the afternoon, but she hadn't had time to read it. It was after six before she managed to clear the backlog on her desk and start to look at the new tasks that had come in. Then she pulled the pathologist's report from her in-tray and looked at it. Once she knew how the woman she thought of as Katya had died, she would have a clearer idea of whether there was any link between her death and the murder of Gemma Wishart.

The report came down, in the end, to a conclusion of atypical drowning. There was evidence that the woman had been assaulted before she died, but those injuries – old and more recent bruises – had been documented at the hospital. There were in addition injuries to her hands that the hospital hadn't recorded. Her hands were bruised and one of the nails on her right hand was torn right down. The report noted that these injuries could have been sustained while she was in the water, but it was not possible to state definitively if the injuries were ante- or post-mortem. The toxicology study revealed nothing unexpected. There was a blood alcohol level consistent with a glass of wine or a double whisky, but no evidence of other drugs. The woman had eaten a few hours before she died, just some bread, nothing cooked or complicated.

There were few of the expected findings of drowning – no evidence of aspiration of water and no foam in the airways – but the report said that there were pinpoint petechial haemorrhages on the upper chest and neck. *These are not usually seen in drowning*, the report said, *but are found in cases of laryngeal spasm*. The pathologist noted that conditions around the time of Katya's death would make this a possibility and account for the lack of other signs of drowning. The sudden immersion in cold water would have chilled the neck and chest. If there had been immediate inhalation of water, the larynx would have gone into reflex spasm leading to rapid asphyxia. The report suggested that the body had been in the water for two to three days, but the low temperature made a more accurate assessment impossible.

Lynne frowned. She wanted something more conclusive. She went back over her notes. Katya had turned up at the Welfare Advice Centre on a Wednesday shortly after six. Nasim Rafiq and Matthew Pearse had spoken to her. Pearse had taken her to the hospital about an hour later. She was there for about an hour, then she had disappeared. Pearse had seen her near the car park, waving to someone. There was a final sighting near the Humber Bridge around midnight. Three days later, she had been found in the estuary mud. The pathologist's report fitted with the timings she had worked out. If Katya had jumped or fallen from the bridge shortly after the last sighting, then the two to three day immersion figure was about right.

But where had she eaten? And, more to the point, where

164

had she had a drink? There was still food in her stomach, so she must have eaten within four hours of her death. They might have given her food at the Welfare Advice Centre, but they wouldn't have given her alcohol. And anyway, that had been too early. She had arrived at the hospital at seven-thirty. She wouldn't have been given food there – in fact, she would have been told specifically not to eat until a doctor had seen her. So she must have eaten after she left the hospital, but where? Lynne thought. The security cameras recorded her leaving the hospital just after eight-thirty. It had been a cold night for wandering the streets. Attempts to track her between the hospital and the Humber Bridge had so far been unsuccessful. There was no record of a taxi picking her up, no one had seen her on the relevant buses, and no one, so far, had come forward to say they had seen her walking.

There would be an inquest and the verdict would almost certainly be accidental death. But Lynne wasn't ready to leave it yet. Now she had Gemma Wishart's report, she could send fingerprints and post-mortem dental records to Interpol. Katya had been young. She must have a family somewhere, and maybe that family was looking for her. East Siberia. She'd looked on the map. She imagined a cold, inhospitable place, flat plains and tundra, the icy Siberian wind cutting through a bleak, industrial landscape. She read the description of Katya –dark hair, high cheekbones, oriental eyes – and tried to picture the young woman going about her life, working, studying, or taking the first fatal steps into the sex industry that had brought her, finally, to the fading outpost of capitalism on the east coast of England where she had died.

Sheffield, Wednesday evening
Roz was reading in her study. She had lit the floor lamp behind the easy chair – old and tattered but so comfortable she couldn't bring herself to get rid of it – and lost herself in *Bleak House*. The rain was falling on Lincolnshire, on Chesney Wold. On the ghost's walk, the footsteps went back and forth, back and forth. A woman dressed in servant's black walked

towards the iron gate to look into the darkness of the burial ground.

Roz hadn't bothered to pull the curtains across the window – the hedge was high enough to give her privacy from the road, and she liked to look up and see the moon, and watch the branches of the trees swaying in the wind. There was the distant roar of traffic from the main road, but here, on the side streets, it was quiet. She ought to do this more often, sit and read, not for work or for research or for anything practical, but for enjoyment. Reading was a habit she had lost when she left Bristol. She and Nathan used to read to each other sometimes, each trying to enthuse the other with the books they particularly liked. Nathan tended to favour bleak, hi-tech science fiction, which she didn't like, but she had read all the Gormenghast books after he had started her on *Titus Groan*.

Bleak House had been one of her failures. It was probably her favourite book, but Nathan had greeted it with polite boredom. 'Dickens?' She could remember his look of dismay. 'What is this, Roz? School?' On *Bleak House* nights, they'd usually ended up at the pub, and eventually she'd given up. But the novel, with its dark web of corruption that spread from the centre to enmesh the highest and the lowest, still had the power to grip her, and she was surprised as she surfaced from its pages to find that it was nearly nine.

She let the book close over her index finger and sat for a while, staring at the moonlight reflected in the mirror. Her life had been on hold for too long. There were so many things she used to do that she never did now. She had lost touch with her university friends, now scattered around the country. She had made only a few friends in Sheffield – it was easier, sometimes, not to get close to people, not to run the risk of questions, explanations, talking about things she'd prefer not to think about. She had manufactured a life out of work and pretended that that was enough.

Maybe she should do what Jenny Bishop wanted her to do – go down to Lincoln and see Nathan. Maybe, after all this time, she would see him as he was and stop looking for the man he used to be. Then she would know that the man she married was gone, that it was over and that she had the right to move on. She could phone her mother-in-law now, and then the decision would be made. She went to the phone, and hesitated before dialling. Did she want to do this, or was it one of those impulsive decisions she would regret tomorrow? She . . .

There was someone outside. She could hear the sound of footsteps on the gravel of the drive. Someone was walking up the side of the house and round the back. She put the phone down and listened. The footsteps faded. Whoever it was, was in her back yard.

She hadn't turned the hall light on. Maybe a passer-by thought the house was empty. Most of the break-ins in the area were by opportunistic thieves who took advantage of empty houses. She didn't like the idea of someone creeping around the back. No one could see into the yard. The house next door was empty and derelict.

She knew the door was locked, but she wasn't sure about the garage or the kitchen window. Phone the police? How long would it take them to get here? It was probably kids. She picked up her mobile and walked quietly through to the kitchen. She tried to see out, but it was too dark. She could still hear those soft footsteps moving surreptitiously around the yard.

Dialling 999 seemed too dramatic, but she set her phone and kept her finger on the SOS button. Then she moved across the kitchen to the back door where the light switches were. She hesitated for a moment, then pressed the switch and light flooded the yard.

There was a clatter as she dropped the phone on to the tiled floor. She was looking through the window face to face with . . . The figure outside resolved itself into Luke, who had his hand raised to knock on the door. They stared at each other in shock for a moment, then Roz unlocked the door and pulled the bolts. 'Luke,' she said as she opened the door. Then, 'You frightened the daylights out of me. *Luke.*' She took his hand and after a moment's hesitation he came in and she put her arms round him. He felt stiff and awkward, then he relaxed and pulled her close to him, burying his face against her neck.

'Roz,' he said. 'Oh, Christ, I . . . *Roz!*'

For a few minutes, they just stood there in their clumsy embrace. Eventually, he freed himself and slumped down in a chair at the kitchen table. She closed the door behind him and looked at him. He was unshaven and pale. He looked as if he hadn't had much sleep, as if he'd been drinking or had taken something. His eyes had a hectic glitter. 'I'm not exactly feeling sociable,' he said as he sat down. 'I came to get the bike.'

She sat down opposite him. 'You look awful,' she said.

He gave a faint grin. 'Thanks, Roz,' he said. Then he shivered.

'Joanna told me . . .' she said.

'Oh, fuck Grey. I'll get it sorted.' He was so dismissive, she felt a flicker of relief. Whatever had happened, it sounded as though Joanna had got hold of the wrong end of the stick.

'Coffee?' She didn't want to offer him alcohol. He nodded. 'You're cold. I'll turn the heater on.'

She switched on the fan heater and opened a jar of coffee. The smell drifted into the room as she spooned it into the percolator. 'I've been phoning you all day,' she said.

'I know. I got your messages. I told you, I'm not feeling sociable.' He was hunched back in his chair, his hands on the table in front of him. He picked up a place-mat and began unravelling the woven threads. His eyes were narrowed with tension. She concentrated on what she was doing, aware of the silence in the room, of the faint drift of music from the road, the sound of a car pulling away, the night call of an owl. She poured milk into a pan. When he spoke, it made her jump. 'They said she was doing escort work.' His voice was flat. 'They think that's why she was killed.'

Roz turned round, the milk bottle in her hand. 'Gemma?' she said. 'What do you mean, escort work?'

'A prostitute, Roz. What do you think I meant? A call girl, a hooker, a tom. That's what they meant.'

'That's . . .' It was ridiculous. It was impossible. She remembered the photographs carefully stored on a disk that had fallen out of Gemma's bag. Bondage pictures. Porn on the net.

'They think I was her pimp. Or I didn't know and I found out. Either way, they think I killed her.'

Roz closed her eyes. 'But they've let you go,' she said.

'For now.' He discarded the destroyed place-mat and picked up a pen that was lying on the table. He began turning it round and round in his hands, watching the light catch it. 'They turned my flat over and they've talked to everyone I know . . .' Roz remembered the questions she'd been asked. 'They think I did it.' He shrugged and looked at her.

'Why do they say Gemma was a prostitute? What gave them that idea?' He didn't say anything. '*Was* she?'

'Oh, for fuck's sake, Roz! What do you think?'

'That they must have had a reason,' she said. There was silence as he sat and stared at the pen he was turning in his hands.

'Look, Roz, there's something . . .'

'I didn't know her that well . . .'

They both began speaking at once, and he shook his head when she gestured at him to go on. 'I just said I didn't know her that well. Not like you.'

He stared at the pen in his hands. 'I didn't know her that well.' His eyes met hers across the table. 'She was just passing through. I told you she planned to go back to Siberia, to Novosibirsk. There was someone over there, and she was going back to him. We didn't talk about it.'

No one talks about anything. Roz stood looking at him, wondering what to say next. She poured two cups of coffee and sat down. 'Why did they think that about Gemma?' she asked again.

She thought he wasn't going to answer, then he said, 'Those photographs. They showed them to me. They'd got them off a website – an escort site.'

That could be why Gemma had them on disk, so that someone could post them on a site. 'That disk . . . ?' she said.

He rubbed his face. 'I don't know. They were just photographs, for fuck's sake. She must have scanned them ... I don't know.' His hands were gripping his cup tightly. 'I don't know what to do.' His eyes were haunted.

But they weren't just photographs. The images were still vivid in her mind. The bright light made the kitchen seem stark; the red tiles on the floor, the black square of the window, the dishes lined up on the draining board. She didn't know what to say. She didn't know what he should do, either. 'Do you need to talk to a solicitor?' That seemed like such a clinical decision. Gemma was dead, and she was talking about solicitors. 'They want it to be you because you were having a ... relationship. That makes it easier for them. But they've let you go. They'll have to look somewhere else.'

Suddenly, he looked exhausted. 'It only takes one thing Roz. I've got no alibi. If they catch me in one thing ... They'll make a case, once they're convinced.' He put his face in his hands for a moment. 'The thing is ...' He stopped. 'I'm too tired for this, Bishop. I'll tell you in the morning. Can I use your sofa tonight?'

'Of course. You know that.' She held her cup in both hands and watched the reflection of the light. She shouldn't drink coffee this late. Then she thought of something. 'They know, do they? The police? About the photographs?'

He looked at her impatiently. 'I told you, Bishop. They showed me.'

'No, I mean, do they know you took them?'

He looked at her. 'Of course they do. I told them.'

She felt a tension she hadn't known was there vanish. The fact that she hadn't told the police about the photographs, about Luke, had been an undercurrent of unease ever since her interview. If they found out ... but they already knew. Luke had told them.

He was frowning slightly now. 'You didn't tell them?' She shook her head. He was watching her closely, his eyes narrowed. 'Why didn't you, Roz?' His voice was quiet, but his whole demeanour was alert as if the fatigue of a few minutes ago had left him.

'I don't know.' It sounded unconvincing in her own ears. She knew why she hadn't told them.

'Bloody Roz.' He was speaking slowly, but his fingers were white where he was gripping his cup. He looked at her, shaking his head. 'You thought I did it, didn't you?' His face was cold.

She didn't think that, but she could remember her moment of doubt and she felt herself going red. 'I thought . . . I didn't know what I . . .' *Nathan's fist, smacking into the side of her head, her hands scrabbling for the banister and missing . . .*

'Right.' He stood up. 'Well, Roz, I might just get a bit pissed off with you, and God knows what I'd be capable of then.' His voice was calm and reflective, but his face was set, white and angry. She knew from past experience that it would be useless trying to talk to him when he was like this.

'Wait,' she said. 'Wait.' She wasn't going to make excuses. He stopped at the door. She went back to her study and got one of the disks with the copies of Gemma's files. He was still waiting when she went back, his hand on the door, his face expressionless. She pushed the disk at him. 'Gemma's files,' she said. 'From the laptop.' He looked at her blankly, then nodded and put the disk in his pocket.

She wanted to stop him leaving, but she knew him well enough to know there was no point. She felt the swirl of cold air round her as he opened the door, heard it click quietly shut behind him. She heard the sound of the gate. She heard the engine burst into life, the asymmetrical beat of the idling V-twin, and then the sound of the engine rising to a scream before he changed up – a cry of rage in the silence. And she stayed at the table staring at her coffee as she heard him drive off into the night.

11

Hull, Thursday morning

Anna woke up with the sun in her eyes. It was shining on to her face from the skylight above her head. She could see the birds high up in the air, turning and wheeling in the pale morning light. The sky was blue, with a clarity that suggested frost. The couch she was lying on was lumpy, and the blanket smelt of dust, but the attic room was a haven with a door that locked and a high window that only the birds could see into. Matthew had been apologetic. 'It's not very comfortable,' he said. But it was safe and secret, and at last he had given her some hope.

She had spent the evening before in the dark back room of the Welfare Advice Centre, lying on the couch, drifting into a doze sometimes, but aware all the time that just beyond the door the work of the centre was going on. The banging of the typewriter, the sound of voices, the sound of filing cabinet drawers being opened and shut, made her realize that anyone, at any minute, could walk through that door and find her there. She had seen Nasim's look of anxiety when the door had announced an arrival earlier. She was not meant to be here, she knew that. She was putting Matthew and Nasim at risk. She was going to have to leave, and the thought filled her with dread.

As the light had faded and the rain began to fall, drumming against the window, splashing down from a broken gutter, Matthew had come back. Anna had been sitting in the dark in a half daze, her mind wandering around images of her childhood, images she retreated to more and more. There was a tree that grew in front of the house, a beech like the trees that grew in the forests high in the mountains. When she was a child, her father had looped a rope over one of the branches and made a swing where she could play. Later, she would sit Krisha on the seat and swing her while the little girl shrieked and giggled. She would do that when Krisha was refusing to wear the special shoes for her damaged foot, when she would throw herself on the ground and scream and kick her feet, and . . . *the bundle lying half in and half out of the door, tiny on the ground, with the sole of a shoe pointing towards the bushes where . . .*

Her eyes had snapped open. She was on the couch in the back room at the advice centre and Matthew was standing in the door looking at her. 'Anna,' he had said, 'I'm sorry. I woke you.'

She shook her head. She hadn't been sleeping and she was glad to have been pulled out of her waking dream. Matthew was looking serious, and she felt the tension of anxiety. She knew she couldn't stay here forever, but she dreaded the time of decisions.

'I do the night shift tonight. Nasim's gone,' he had said. 'Listen, Anna . . .' He had seemed to change his mind about what he was going to say. 'Are you hungry?' He was carrying a bag. 'I made sandwiches. Cheese. And I've got some apples. We can have some tea in a minute.'

Anna had moved along the settee to make space for him to sit down. 'Thank you,' she said. The sandwiches were made with the funny soft bread they had here. She had thought that she was hungry, but the sandwiches were tasteless and her hunger seemed to go after she had eaten one. It seemed an oddly unsatisfactory meal for someone who was working all night. 'This is all you are having?'

He had smiled and shaken his head. 'I had a proper tea earlier. When I went home. This is just extra.' He'd made them for her.

'Where is home?' She knew nothing about him except that he worked here, he'd helped her when she'd been in trouble, he'd understood without being told and he'd been kind. 'Your wife? Your children?'

He had looked down at the floor. 'I'm not married, Anna.' He was quiet for a few minutes then he said, 'I live on my own. I look after myself and I work here.' He had looked up at her and smiled again. His eyes were kind. 'That's enough for me.'

She thought about his twisted back and the awkward way he walked. Of course. He was like Krisha. Born with it. Women had not wanted him. 'You work here?'

He had nodded. 'It's voluntary work. I get a small pension because of . . .' He gestured at his back. 'So I've always done some kind of voluntary work. To put something back.'

He had looked down again, and then looked at her. 'That's something I want to talk about.' There was a brief silence, then he said slowly, as if he were choosing his words with care, 'Anna. Your parents were killed. You came here illegally, but you were very young. You might be able to stay. At least for a while. Will you let me find out?'

She stared at her hands. *Might be able to stay* . . . She had realized, after she ran away from Angel, that he had lied to her. But it must be too late. She was a prostitute, she was a thief. She had looked at Matthew. 'I have . . .' She didn't know how to say it.

'I know, Anna.' He did know. She remembered the sadness on his face the first time she talked to him. She hated him knowing. She wanted all that part of her life painted over, blotted out the way her father painted over the words that were written on the wall. 'Anna,' he had said, 'you are not to blame for what happened to you. Let me look into it for you.' He had seen the uncertainty in her face, and said quickly, 'It'll take a few days, but you can stay here. There's an attic – it isn't very nice, but it's dry and there's a couch up there. You can just rest and get your strength back.'

Staying. Working without looking over her shoulder. Getting far away from here and from Angel. Having papers and a passport that were hers, that she could keep. She felt a flicker of hope. If Matthew said that he could do it . . . Maybe it wasn't too late. 'Yes,' she said. 'Thank you.'

Roz was at her desk for eight-thirty. She planned to spend the day working on her interview research. The adaptations to the software she'd been testing the previous day seemed to work now. She could move on to the next stage by herself, and then come back to Luke to check the software again.

Luke. She wondered if she should phone, but what could she say? She didn't think that he had killed Gemma, but there had been that moment of doubt, and he might never forgive her for it. Maybe she could make him understand. Those pictures . . . they'd shown a side of Luke she had never seen before, never suspected. But then she'd never believed – despite the warnings from the doctors – that Nathan could have been violent. She had held that belief as firmly as an article of faith and it had cost her concussion, a broken ankle, and a realization that she could no longer trust her own judgement. And her own belief in herself – hadn't she wanted Nathan dead often enough in the immediate aftermath, because she couldn't cope with his terror and his despair? It had seemed almost as if death would be better than what was happening to him. And her own panic and fear when he had finally turned on her . . . If she had been strong enough, she could have done anything in that moment.

Her hand moved towards the phone, then drew back. She needed to give Luke time.

She switched on her computer and waited for it to boot up. She looked out of the window. It was a fine winter's day, the sky clear of cloud and the sun making the shadows sharp against the walls of her room.

Something on the monitor caught her eye. The screen was a deep blue, the deep blue that often meant trouble. The machine was telling her that the program she'd been running had not shut down properly and it was now going to run various tests to check for damage. Roz frowned as she watched it. She always shut the computer down properly. It was as automatic as breathing. She watched as the machine went through the processes, chided her for her carelessness, and then booted up. No damage, at any rate.

She dismissed it as one of those puzzles that seemed to be a feature of new technologies, and started work. Today, she found that she could concentrate. Her mind didn't wander into unwanted places and she was able to remain focused on what she was doing. She was distracted from her attempt to sort a tricky bit of the text into useful categories by the sound of her door opening and closing, and Joanna's voice. 'Roz!' Joanna, looking meeting-elegant was closing the door behind her. She looked pleased. 'Good news! I heard it from the vice-chancellor yesterday. The LLG is going to stay as an independent group, and we're keeping all our grants. And –' her eyes sparkled – 'I'm going to get funding for another appointment, *and* a couple of post-graduate students. We need a researcher on the software-development side.'

Roz tried to be pleased. She *was* pleased. It was good news for her as well as for Joanna. 'That's great.' Joanna seemed disappointed by her reaction, so she forced a smile and said again, 'That's great, really.'

Joanna looked at her for a moment. 'I haven't forgotten about Gemma, Roz. But I have to keep this thing going. If we let it go now, it will all go. It isn't just us, you know.'

Joanna was right. There was outstanding work, there were research contracts to fulfil – none of these had changed. 'We can't get very far without Luke,' she said.

'We can fund a research post now,' Joanna said. 'I've got someone in mind. And I had a brief word with Luke this morning.'

'How was he?'

Joanna clearly heard something in her voice, because she shot a sharp look at Roz.

'Singularly uncommunicative,' she said flatly. Roz looked back at her screen, not wanting Joanna to see her smile. She could imagine exactly how Luke had been with Joanna. At least he'd talked to her. 'But anyway, he plans to resign.'

'What?' Luke's unforgiving face flashed into her mind. That was typical of the angry impulse he was prone to. 'When?'

'I think it's the best thing.' Joanna evaded the subject. 'You left your door unlocked yesterday, Roz. I found it open when I came back to collect some files.'

'I didn't . . .' Roz began, then realized that she couldn't remember. Apparently she hadn't shut her computer down properly either. She sighed. 'I seem to have been all over the place recently. Sorry.' She needed to contact Luke urgently, stop him from throwing his job away on an impulse.

Joanna looked at her. 'I think we all have,' she said. 'But there's nothing else you can do, Roz. We'll just have to get on with it.'

'That's what I've been doing,' Roz said. 'And I did try and do some tracking down on Gemma's report.'

'That.' Joanna sighed. 'Gemma's report was complete, Roz. I had the woman from Hull on the phone about it. I checked it through and I can't see anything that should be there that isn't. If Gemma had speculations about it, then she was going beyond her brief, which was: Where does this woman come from? Gemma gave them a more precise location than they will have expected.' She looked at Roz to see if her message was getting through. 'You have to think commercially with these things. We were asked to do one thing, and we charged accordingly. There's always more you can find from a recording. You know that. You could go on analysing for years. But it isn't cost-effective. Gemma was still learning that. You, however, should know by now. Especially if we're starting up privately.'

'You're right.' Roz ran her fingers through her hair. It was important to separate the research and the commercial worlds. With research, you pursued the unexpected alleyways that opened up – there might be answers to questions you hadn't even thought of asking. With commercial work, you did what was requested. You did it well, but that was all you did. 'I suppose it's one of those things you feel you ought to do. Like sending flowers to a funeral.'

Joanna's efficient mask was replaced by a more human regret. 'I know. And it means nothing, really. When you think about what happened ... A few flowers, a report. Empty gestures.'

Roz rarely saw Joanna in reflective mood. 'What did happen? No one's told me.' The newspaper accounts had been brief.

'I know someone who knows someone,' Joanna said, 'but he didn't give me all the details. I didn't want them. Whoever it was beat her up and then strangled her.' Roz closed her eyes. She hadn't imagined a sustained attack. She'd imagined an impulsive blow. 'And then he posed her obscenely in a hotel bathroom. The police had to use dental records to identify her, I understand.' For a moment, the lines of tension showed on Joanna's face. 'The police are following up the queries on Gemma's report,' she added. 'We can't do it, for obvious reasons. They've sent the tape through to Bill Greenhough at York.' There was silence for a minute, and then Joanna's voice changed abruptly. 'There's work to be done. I've got the wording for the advertisements. I'd like you to have a look at them before I send them through.'

Roz nodded, keeping her eyes on the screen until Joanna had gone. Her hands were shaking. *Gemma!* No wonder Luke had been so angry. No wonder he didn't want to work with her any more. He must have thought that she believed ... She kept seeing things in her mind that she didn't want to see. Joanna's fastidious phrase, 'posed obscenely', made her think of the pictures that had formed on her monitor, photographs that had been sent out into the world on the web for everyone to look at ... But Luke wouldn't have – *couldn't* have done that.

She picked up her phone and dialled his number. She got the answering machine again. She hesitated, then said, 'Luke? It's Roz. Are you there?' Silence. Just the hiss of the tape. 'Listen, I just found out about – what happened to Gemma. I didn't know. When we talked, I didn't know. I'm sorry.' She waited again to see if he would pick up the phone, but nothing happened. According to Joanna, he'd been there not so long ago. He must have gone out. She put the phone down.

She felt restless and uncomfortable now. The need to sort things out with Luke was like an itch in her mind. The work that had been going so well had suddenly become a series of meaningless symbols on her screen. She saved it and shut the program down. Maybe she should go and get coffee, have a change of scene.

She went to the Students' Union in the end, to the coffee bar where they sold decent espresso and cappuccino. She isolated herself at one of the bar stools, and made a barrier of her newspaper as she stirred sugar into her cup. The news was depressing. The hospitals were in crisis because of the 'flu epidemic, the opposition parties were delighted. Roz thought about the anarchist slogan – *Don't vote: the government always gets in*. She turned to the science supplement. She was in the middle of an article about disappearing languages, when someone said, 'I don't usually see you here.'

Roz looked up. Sean Lewis was smiling down at her, a cup of coffee in his hand. Roz didn't feel like company, particularly not from the person who might be taking over Luke's work, but she couldn't think of a good reason not to be sociable. 'Oh, hello,' she said, with tepid welcome.

He didn't need any more encouragement. He pulled up a stool and sat down next to her. 'What are you reading?'

'A newspaper,' Roz said repressively, and then, deciding that she was being a bit too Luke-like, added, 'It's an article about dying languages.' She was glad it was such a minority topic – she didn't want to get into a long conversation with him. But to her surprise, he seemed interested.

'That was one of Gemma's things, wasn't it?' he said. 'Sorry. You won't want to talk about it.'

'That's OK.' Roz realized she had now more or less committed herself to a conversation. 'Yes. She did her research into one of the Russian languages.'

'She was telling me about her time in Russia,' he said. He looked into the distance, his cup held between his hands. 'She told me quite a bit about your section, the work you do,' he said. He seemed to be thinking something over. 'Can I talk to you?' he said. Roz shrugged, to indicate that that was what he was already doing. 'Joanna Grey said that there would be a research post coming up in your section – but I dunno . . . I kind of liked the things Gemma was doing . . . And I need a change of direction,' he said. 'I mean, MIT was something else . . .'

'But tough?' Roz said.

'As if! I can do this, that's the thing. It was too easy.'

Bright, but unfocused, Roz diagnosed. Extremely bright, if he'd found his PhD as easy as he said. She'd seen this problem before in particularly talented students who hadn't developed any particular interests and were often torn between the lucrative but restricting market and the more fulfilling but impoverished field of academia. She was think-ing about something else he had said. Gemma had talked to him about her work. Maybe they'd talked about the tape, about the queries Gemma was trying to sort out via Hol-brook's archive. 'What did Gemma tell you?' she said. 'About her work?'

'She was telling me about voice prints,' he said. 'That you're working on something that will produce voice prints, like fingerprints.'

'Well . . .' Roz was sceptical. This was the holy grail of forensic linguistics – to be able to draw up an acoustic profile of a voice that would say: This person, and only this person, could have spoken these words. But for the moment, the variability of the individual voice had defeated such attempts. Gemma and Luke had been interested in chasing up some money to pursue that line of research, but Roz thought that the possibility of producing anything that had the reliability of fingerprinting or DNA profiles was a long way off – if it were possible at all. 'It was one of her things,' she said. There was silence for a moment. 'Listen, Sean,' she said, 'you might be able to help me. I really need to know what Gemma was looking for in Professor Holbrook's archive. Did she talk about that at all?'

He thought for a moment. 'She just wanted access. That's all she said.'

Roz thought. If Gemma hadn't talked about it, then she'd

180

need to work it out for herself. She looked at Sean. 'Tell me about the archive.'

'What do you want to talk about that for?' For a moment, he looked put out. He wanted her to be interested in him. Then his face cleared. 'Listen, let me take you out for lunch. Then I'll tell you all about it.'

'I'm afraid I haven't got time,' Roz said quickly, then realized that had been a mistake. She should have refused point-blank.

'Tomorrow?' he said.

'Thanks, but I'm very busy just now. I need to get back. It would really help me, though, if you could tell me a bit more about the Holbrook Archive. If you can't, I can always go back and talk to Professor Holbrook himself.'

'And you'd rather talk to me.' He looked cheerful again. 'OK. But you've got to let me ask you something afterwards. Deal?' He smiled at her again, still leaning towards her, their arms almost touching.

'Deal,' said Roz. She moved her position slightly. She didn't mind being charmed by him, but she didn't want to send out the wrong signals. She listened as he told her about the system that Marcus Holbrook had been working on for several years. The Holbrook Archive was, in fact, a database. Holbrook was developing it into an electronic corpus that would allow researchers to answer in minutes questions about spoken Russian that would take years if the analysis were done by traditional techniques. 'But he didn't have the coding,' Sean said. 'It worked, but it was slow, clunky, full of bugs. It was, kind of, his baby. He didn't want anyone else near it, you know? But I'm sorting it for him.' Now that he was talking about his work, he forgot his earlier uncertainties and was explaining enthusiastically what plans he had for further developments.

She chose her moment and slipped back into the conversation. 'But Gemma never said what she was looking at?'

He looked disappointed, but said. 'Not to me. I can check. See if she left any records.'

'Thank you.' Roz finished her coffee. 'I'd really like to

know. Now, I think I'd better get back.' She slid off her stool and tucked her newspaper under her arm. Talking to the eager young man had been a pleasant interlude, but she could feel the pressure of the backlog that had built up over the past week.

'Wait.' He held up his hand. 'Our deal, remember?'

Roz laughed. 'OK. Go ahead.'

He stood up. Roz hadn't realized before how tall he was. 'I've got some tickets for the jazz festival at the Studio on Saturday night. Would you like to come with me?'

The show had been a sell-out for weeks, Roz knew. She'd tried to get tickets shortly after it was advertised, without success. But she also knew she didn't want to blur any boundaries by going to a social event with Sean. 'You're lucky to have tickets,' she said. 'Never mind a spare.'

He looked pleased. 'I've got contacts,' he said. 'You'll come, then?'

Roz shook her head. 'It's very nice to be asked – and thank you – but I'm busy . . .'

'Cancel it,' he said.

'I'm busy,' she repeated. 'And anyway, I'm married, so it really wouldn't be such a good idea.'

His face darkened. 'I don't fancy you, or anything,' he said.

That was so blatantly childish that Roz had to stop herself from laughing. 'Then you won't mind, will you?' she said.

He looked a bit ashamed. 'I do, actually,' he said. 'Sorry. Please come with me.'

To her surprise, she found herself considering it for a moment, but she knew it would be a bad idea. 'I'm sorry, I can't.' She picked up her coat, and stopped as a thought struck her. 'Can I access Holbrook's archive from the Law and Language Group? Or the main library?'

He was still looking put out about her refusal, but he managed a civil reply. 'No, it's not on the intranet yet. Marcus wants to issue it as a commercial piece of software. He might put a limited version out for students here. But we're putting together a pilot for detailed testing. You'll have to have a look at it. It'll be in the newsletter.'

'OK. I'll look out for it.' She gave him a smile as she turned to go. 'Thanks, Sean. That was useful.'

'Lot of good it did me,' he grumbled, but it sounded good-natured.

12

Sheffield, Thursday morning

Roz checked her voice mail when she got back to her desk after coffee. No message from Luke. Maybe he'd phoned her at home. The thought nagged at her like a jagged tooth, an irritation that would neither go away nor offer any immediate solution. If he'd wanted to contact her, why hadn't he phoned her here at work? Perhaps he didn't want to get Joanna. Perhaps he was still angry – Luke could bear grudges – and didn't want to talk to her. Yet.

She tried to concentrate on the work that had been going so well in the morning, but her mind kept drifting away from it, sometimes brooding about Luke's silence, sometimes worrying at the unsolved detail of Gemma's report. She forced herself to concentrate until she'd finished the section she was working on and could run the data through the program to see if it could recognize the tags she'd used to mark the different features of the interviews. As her mind became engaged with the problem, the worry of Luke, the irritation that was Gemma's unfinished report, retreated to the back of her mind. She keyed in the request and waited to see what would happen.

The program crashed. *Shit!* This was the problem of working on her own on a system that was incomplete. She needed Luke's input. She was stuck without it. Joanna would just have to stop this ludicrous suspension, or she, Roz, would spend the next few weeks sitting on her hands and . . . If Joanna's plans came to anything, she might find herself working with Sean. She wondered why she found that

184

prospect so depressing. Sean was bright, interesting . . . but he wasn't Luke. That was the problem.

She needed something to distract her. Gemma's report. It was all very well for Joanna to say that the report was complete, and to talk about commercial viability, but Roz wanted to know. She knew she could sort it out if she could just give herself the time. And she had some spare time right now. But what could she do that she hadn't already done? Sean had promised to check again to see what Gemma had been looking at, but Roz was pretty sure he wouldn't bother, now she had so firmly rebuffed him. Try Holbrook again? She tapped the pen against her teeth. Luke's voice spoke in her head: *Christ, Bishop, are you trying to drive me insane or what?* She put the pen down.

Joanna had said that someone else was looking at the tape. Bill Greenhough at York. Roz didn't know him all that well, but she'd met him at conferences. He seemed a pleasant enough man, approachable. A bit of digging around in academic directories gave her the number, and twenty minutes later, she was talking to him on the phone.

She explained who she was, and then said, 'I understand you're dealing with a tape for the Humberside Police.'

'Yes.' His voice was cautious.

'My colleague, Gemma Wishart, was working on that tape,' Roz explained. 'She . . .'

'She was killed, wasn't she? I'm sorry.' Brisk, professional sympathy. Then his voice changed. 'God, it wasn't anything to do with this, was it?'

'No.' Roz was quick to reassure him. 'No, nothing at all.' She thought about the police saying that Gemma had been working as a prostitute. 'It was just – Gemma asked me to help her complete the report and then, well . . . it happened. I suppose I don't like to think of her work left unfinished.'

'I can't really discuss it with you,' he said, but he sounded uncertain.

'I just wanted to know what you thought about the lines that Gemma queried. Did they tell you? It was . . .' She flipped through the pages in front of her.

'Yes, I've got those.' She could hear the sound of papers being moved. He must have the transcript in front of him.

'What's special about those bits? I've got translations, but it doesn't help.'

'You've got translations?' He sounded interested. 'I haven't managed to identify those. What do they mean?' Surprised, Roz gave him the translations she'd got from Marcus Holbrook. Greenhough should have been able to translate them himself. 'Where did you get those?' he said. 'What is it, anyway? I don't recognize it.'

'It's Russian,' she said. 'Someone over here gave me the translations. He said that *Ba-yi-n-sal –*' she spelt it out as she didn't know how to pronounce it – 'was a colloquialism for expressing annoyance, something like that.' Holbrook hadn't attempted to pronounce it either.

'Is Russian your field?' He sounded puzzled.

'No, not at all. I was just trying to sort out the last queries that Gemma left. That's why I went to someone else.' She didn't want him to think she was challenging his expertise.

'OK,' he said. 'Well, whatever you were told, that phrase is *not* Russian. And *jugun* is not a Russian word for people. It's not a Russian word at all. That "j" should tell you that. I'm trying to track it down, but I've had no luck so far.'

Roz was silent. Marcus Holbrook had been certain. She could remember his glance at the phrase and his instant identification. 'Are you sure?' she said after a moment.

'Absolutely.' His voice was cold.

'I'm sorry,' she said quickly. 'Of course you are. It's just that the person who told me – he seemed so certain.'

'Who was it?'

Roz hesitated for a moment. She didn't want to spread gossip about a colleague. On the other hand, Holbrook was a recognized expert. If Greenhough knew where the information came from, he might decide he'd been wrong. 'Marcus Holbrook,' she said.

There was silence at the other end of the phone, then Greenhough said, 'I think you must have got hold of the wrong end of the stick.'

Roz was annoyed and was about to deny that, when she realized that she could, possibly, have done just that. Possibly. She had scribbled some notes on her transcript, but she hadn't checked – had she? – that they were looking at the same things. She couldn't remember exactly. 'I'll check again,' she said.

'You do that. I didn't realize Marcus had seen these. I'll give him a ring.'

His voice indicated that he was about to end the conversation. Roz said quickly, on impulse, 'There's one more thing, Dr Greenhough . . .'

'Yes?'

'How would a Russian speaker pronounce the English word "cat"?'

'Cat?' he thought about it for a moment. 'You'd get something like an "e" sound, something like "cet".'

Holbrook had said something different. She couldn't understand. 'Thank you,' she said, 'for your time. If you find out what it is on the tape, will you let me know?'

'After I've submitted my report to the police,' he said. On that fairly friendly note, they rang off.

Roz was still short-tempered and irritable as she drove home. Everything seemed designed to annoy. The traffic was heavy in long stop-start queues. The car in front of her as she crept towards the Wicker Arches moved at a leisurely pace, even when a gap opened in the traffic in front of him. Roz wanted to put her foot down and close up each gap with a short, deceptive burst of speed. Prickles of tension and anger ran up and down her back, and she could feel her head starting to ache.

She finally escaped the main roads as she turned off towards the small recreation ground opposite her house. She found herself jerking the gear stick and slamming down the clutch in a stupid – and potentially dangerous – venting of her anger. She scraped the car as she turned into her driveway – something she hadn't done before even though the turn was tight. She let herself into the house and dumped her bags on the floor. The message light on the phone was blinking.

With a sense of relief, she pressed 'play', but it was only the bookshop telling her that the book she'd ordered was ready to collect. She tried 1471, but the bookshop was the last call that had been made.

Bloody Luke! He'd had time to think about her message. He'd know how she was feeling. He should have phoned. She kicked her bag out of the way, the childish gesture serving only to hurt her foot and make her feel both more angry and a bit foolish. She made a pot of tea and sat at the table letting the quiet of the house calm her down.

She would have to let Luke come round in his own time. She'd made the first gesture. Maybe he didn't want to talk to anyone. She'd have to stop thinking about this. She made herself get out her briefcase and find the notes that she'd made when she'd talked to Marcus Holbrook. There wasn't much – just the lines she'd copied down from the transcript and the translations he'd offered. But – there was no chance she'd made a mistake. No chance she'd got hold of 'the wrong end of the stick'. She remembered now. She hadn't shown Holbrook the whole transcript. She'd just copied out the lines Gemma had queried, and – she checked against her original – she'd copied them correctly. Marcus Holbrook had given her the wrong translations. Why?

She tapped her pen against her teeth as she thought. Holbrook was very touchy. Maybe he simply didn't want her to know he didn't understand something on the tape. That didn't convince her. She wondered if she should go and talk to him again. She realized she didn't know much about Holbrook's main research areas – just that he was some kind of expert in the Russian language. She went to her computer and logged on the university intranet. It was quiet in the evenings and worked quickly. She went to the library catalogues and did a search for Holbrook's name. It came back with a longish list of books and articles, plus some recent journal articles. The books had fairly opaque titles, and the journal articles seemed focused on the minutiae of changes in modern Russian. One recent title caught her eye: *Influence of bilingualism on Nenets-speaking children: a case study.*

Nenets – the language that Gemma had studied for her PhD. The article had been written by Holbrook himself, someone called Stefan Nowicki and – Gemma Wishart. She looked at the journal date. It had come out last summer, which meant the article itself must have been written some time before that – while Gemma was still in Siberia. Holbrook and Gemma had collaborated on a journal article, and yet Holbrook had behaved as if he hardly knew her.

Then the other name on the article struck her. Nowicki was the Russian academic who had helped supervise Gemma's research. That might explain it. The collaboration would have been between Holbrook and this man. They would have used some of Gemma's work and ideas, which was why her name was on the paper – she may even have written some of it – but Holbrook would probably not have concerned himself with a young researcher. Still, it didn't explain why he had misled her over the tape.

With the sense of frustration that always came from abandoning an unsolved puzzle, she put the stuff back in her briefcase. She'd gone as far as she could with it. She made herself something to eat, then spent an hour doing some much-needed clearing up, putting away books and journals that had crept off the shelves on to various surfaces, running the vacuum over the worst of the carpets, washing the dishes. As she cleared the kitchen table, she came across her mother-in-law's letter, left there to remind her she had a decision to make. She almost put the letter into the file where she kept all of Jenny's letters, but she picked it up and read it again. Jenny's suggestion, almost diffident in its wording: *Why don't you come and see him, Roz, the next time he comes home? I keep hoping that something like that might just be the trigger he needs.* Roz knew that Jenny's hopes were empty. Nathan was not going to make any recovery now, or not one that would restore his lost life. She could feel the decision firming in her mind, a decision she had pushed out of the way because it was one she didn't want to make. But she had to do it. She had to go and see Nathan because she had put off any decisions about her life for too long.

189

And if she was going to do it, it couldn't be postponed. She'd go at the weekend, on Saturday.

Hull, Thursday night
Lynne's day had been long, and not very useful. She was unenthusiastically getting up to date with her paperwork, which had suffered a bit these past few days, when her phone rang, breaking her concentration. It was Roy Farnham, cheerful, friendly, wanting to update her on the Sleeping Beauty investigation. 'What time are you leaving?' he said. 'I've got some stuff that might interest you.'

Lynne looked at the pile of work in front of her. 'About an hour.'

'OK. No point in hanging around. Let's go and get something to eat. I can tell you then. Shop,' he added. She laughed, and returned to her computer feeling more cheerful.

In the event, it was two hours before she and Roy were sitting at a table in the small Italian restaurant they'd been to before.

'All we know so far is that she comes from Siberia.' Roy Farnham poured more wine into Lynne's glass. 'And she ends up dead in the Humber. Anything else?'

'Not much, yet.' Lynne ran through the information she'd managed to get. 'But now I've got a better idea of where she comes from, there's more chance that I'll get a name.'

'And then what?' Roy said.

The waiter put a basket of bread on the table between them. 'Are you ready to order?' he said. They'd arrived at the restaurant much later than they'd intended. First, Lynne had got held up with a late query, then Roy had become entangled with a problem in his team. At least they both understood when this kind of thing happened.

Lynne looked at the menu. She'd spent the day making decisions. She didn't want to make any more. 'I'll just have pizza,' she said. Roy nodded agreement, and the waiter went away. Lynne was ravenous and buttered a bread roll. 'I don't know,' she said, her voice a bit muffled. 'It'll mean someone can tell her family. She was young – nineteen? Twenty? I know where she was on that last day up to the time she left the hospital.' She told him about the Welfare Advice Centre, about Nasim Rafiq and Matthew Pearse.

'What about them?' he said.

She went over Pearse's story about taking Katya to the hospital. 'He didn't see who she left with, but he got the impression she didn't leave alone,' she said. 'Then he went back to the centre. But there's something about the Rafiq woman. It might be that she doesn't like the police, it could be as simple as that. But she isn't happy when I'm there.'

Roy frowned. 'What do they do there? At this centre?' he said.

Lynne shrugged. 'They seem a fairly haphazard bit of voluntary support. Michael Balit – he's the Volunteer Co-ordinator – indicated that they were set up in a hurry when the dispersal scheme started. That place used to be a furniture store, and, to be honest, that's more or less what it looks like. I want to find out more. Something made Katya go there. It could be the kind of set-up that I'm looking for. But at the moment, they won't give me the time of day.'

Roy looked at her. 'That's something for Special Branch, Lynne, if they're involved in anything dodgy.'

Lynne was irritated. They were moving on to her territory now. 'I don't think that they are,' she said. 'But I think they might be a useful contact point. I'm not pulling Special Branch in on something as vague as that.' She wasn't pulling Special Branch in at all until she knew exactly what was going on there.

'Have you looked them up?' Roy topped Lynne's glass up again. He wasn't drinking much himself.

'I couldn't find anything. There's no record for Pearse, and Rafiq is legit. Her husband's here at the university. He's an engineer, and they've applied for a long-term stay. No reason why they shouldn't get it. But it's odd.' She told him about the Rafiqs' child, the little boy who was their main reason for coming here, the threat to his sight and the treatment.

'I can't see her putting her son at risk. Or her husband's work. And she must know the consequences of getting involved with anything dodgy.' Talking about it made her realize how much time she'd spent trying to track down Katya's last hours. 'Anything on Angel Escorts?'

He shook his head. 'The site's vanished. It was posted by an anonymous link – it's easy if you know what you're doing. We can't get a trace on it.'

'Luke Hagan knows what he's doing.' The site would be somewhere else now, under a different name. Among the multitude of escort sites, it was unlikely they would track it down. Their pizzas arrived then and they broke off their conversation as the waiter waved around pepper grinders and salad dressing. Then they were alone again. Lynne brought him up to date on her latest findings. 'The Siberian woman – Katya – the pathologist thinks she drowned. He's probably right. I'd just like it to be more conclusive. It's too much of a coincidence – Gemma Wishart doing that work and ending up dead herself.'

Roy wasn't convinced. 'I don't know,' he said. 'We've got some similarities – but I can't ignore the differences. The problem is, the first two bodies just don't give us the infor- mation – were they raped like Wishart? The evidence is gone. And Wishart was strangled.' Whereas no one knew for cer- tain – yet – how Katya and the Ravenscar woman had died. 'Is Wishart a copycat killing? What was there in her report to get her killed? What would be the point? You could just get someone else to do it.'

He was right. All Gemma Wishart had done was give them a closer estimate of where Katya came from. Put together with other things they had, it might lead to an identification. Killing Wishart wouldn't have stopped that. But someone had erased her files. 'The woman I've been talking to, Roz Bishop, says that Wishart still had work to do on the report.'

Roy Farnham nodded. 'I've talked to the people over there. Some of Wishart's files turned up. She was looking for something, but no one seems to know what. I've got

192

someone else checking the tape, but it's a long shot. His name's Greenhough, he's at York.' Lynne felt aware of her peripheral role, the fact that she was not part of the team working on this case. 'I've told him to copy you in,' he added, and she wondered if anything had shown on her face. 'There's very little to go on at the moment,' he said. 'The boyfriend had a motive, he had the opportunity – he's got no alibi – but there's nothing we've found that puts him there. Yet,' he added. 'We've got a murder scene now. And we've got a witness. That's what I wanted to tell you.'

He described the car half-hidden under the rocks in Derbyshire's Peak District.

'And that's where she was killed?' Lynne thought about the narrow, winding road over the Pennines, one she'd used often enough herself when she'd lived in Sheffield.

He shrugged. 'Looks like it. The blood is Wishart's. She was almost certainly killed in or near that car – she bled when she was inside it and she was still bleeding when she was dragged out. And the engine is dead. Something seems to have shorted the ignition, so it couldn't have been moved far.'

Lynne looked at him. 'What about the witness?'

'We've got someone in Glossop who saw Wishart's car – or a car just like hers. He says he saw it parked in the square at around seven-thirty. There are phone boxes there. He said he thought the driver was using the phone.'

Lynne thought about it. 'She stopped in Glossop to make a phone call?' And then a bit later made another from her mobile, ten minutes' drive outside Glossop.

Farnham shook his head. 'I don't know. The guy said he *thought* she was using the phone box, but he wasn't certain. What is interesting is that the records for the phone boxes show that someone called Luke Hagan's number at seven thirty-one.'

'So Wishart phoned Luke Hagan once from a Glossop call box and once from the top of the Snake?' Lynne thought about it.

'Assuming both those calls were made by Wishart,' Farnham said.

'What was the weather like?' Lynne was looking for a reason to use a phone box rather than stay in the security of a car and use a mobile.

'Pissing it down.' Farnham waited for a moment to see if she had anything else to say, then went on: 'We wondered if the battery was low on the phone, so she used the phone box on impulse – maybe just to give Hagan an ETA, or to let him know she wouldn't be back that night. Then the car breaks down – we know something went wrong with the ignition – so she phones Hagan for help.'

'Only there was no message. Or so he says.' It didn't make sense. 'If my phone was running out of juice and I broke down on the Snake in winter, I'd phone the AA before I started phoning my boyfriend. Especially if I knew he wasn't in.'

Farnham had clearly thought about that, because he nodded and went on, 'Someone made that call. Wishart might have done it – or someone else did.'

Someone else would almost certainly be the killer. 'Why phone Hagan?' Reporting in on a job well done, Lynne wondered. Gemma Wishart killed by her jealous boyfriend, or by her vengeful pimp.

Farnham guessed what she was thinking. 'Three dead prostitutes. Did they share a pimp? I need Angel Escorts, Lynne.' The heavily laden slice of pizza he was holding started sagging under its own weight, and he opted for the simple solution of cramming it into his mouth. 'Sorry,' he said, his voice muffled. After a moment, he went on, 'And there's still the missing cleaner from the hotel.'

'I'm looking,' Lynne said. 'But it takes time.' She rubbed her hand across her forehead. She was getting tired.

'OK,' he said. He picked up the wine bottle.

Lynne put her hand over her glass. 'I'm ahead of you,' she said.

'I'm driving,' he pointed out. Lynne had taken her car home first and they'd come in his. He smiled at her and his

194

eyes were warm. 'I'm not trying for drunk,' he said. 'Maybe just a bit incautious.' He put the bottle down and became business-like again. 'It might be worth having another go at the hotel, the manager. Her name's Fry.'

13

Hull, Friday morning
Lynne Jordan could sense pieces of the case fitting into place around her – but they still didn't give her enough of the pattern to form a picture. Lynne was sure that Nasim Rafiq knew more than she was saying. Angel Escorts. Selling women online. Could there conceivably be a link between the ramshackle advice centre and the escort agency? Pearse and Rafiq looked as unlikely a pair of traffickers as she had ever seen. She remembered Farnham's comment of the night before, and felt a moment of unease.

She had the feeling that she'd made a stupid mistake early on in an investigation, and had missed – and now lost – vital information. She'd found the Angel website, she'd found the dead woman there and she'd made the identification. But she had let herself get sidetracked by Farnham's investigation, and once it occurred to her to go back to the website, it was gone. All she had were the pictures of 'Jemima', Gemma Wishart. But the rest of the site would have yielded valuable information. Wishart may have been English, but some of the other women on the site were not, and these were women Lynne needed to track down. She'd let herself get distracted by the Wishart case – and neglected her own work.

She thought through what she might have missed. A route to the person who put the site online? Probably not. An anonymous posting was hard to trace. But the site existed to be contacted. A porn site was one thing, but an escort site was no use if men couldn't then contact the agency and hire one of their women. The phone numbers? Would those have been useful? Or would they have changed all the phones when they realized what had happened to Jemima? If she'd had the numbers, she could have got approximate locations on the phones – and if the phones were still being used . . . According to Farnham, the cell phone on the Angel Escorts card, the one that had been used to phone Luke Hagan's number, was resolutely silent.

All she had were the Jemima pictures, which were more use to Farnham than to her. She opened the file containing the pictures and looked at them again. The innocent, wind-blown picture of a young woman in jeans and T-shirt smiling at the camera. Then the other ones – the mischievous smile above the drawn-up knees: a revealing picture, but with an unexpected charm. Then the bondage photographs, one of Gemma Wishart standing with her wrists tied above her head, her body pulled tight, so that her pointed toes just touched the ground. Her eyes looked directly out of the screen, challenging and inviting. And the final photograph. To Lynne, it looked dark, the chiaroscuro obscuring rather than revealing, more sinister than enticing. Was that because she had seen the other picture: Gemma Wishart lying dead in the bath in an obscene parody of this photograph? She looked at the pictures and felt a sense of frustration. There was so much they could tell her if she just had a little more information. Luke Hagan had been the photographer, but Farnham didn't think he was involved with Angel Escorts. His life style and his activities didn't fit the profile of someone who was running a prostitution business. She looked at the pictures for any possible detail that had been missed, a piece of paper, a notebook, a letter on which Wishart would con-veniently have written *Luke Hagan killed me*. She ran her mouse pointer over the pictures as she thought, tracing the lines and curves of the figure.

It was like a crude joke. As the cursor moved across the dark shadow of pubic hair on the reclining figure, it became a pointing hand, and the words *Step inside and get to know me better* appeared on the screen. A link. There was a hyperlink on the page to something or somewhere else. Another website? Another page on this site? If it was another page, had she downloaded it when she downloaded the pictures? She held her breath as she clicked on the link, and breathed again as she watched more pictures form.

This was a series of small pictures that followed the standard system of soft porn in which a bit more was revealed with each picture until the images became crudely anatomical. Here, the lighting was harsh and Wishart was standing or using a chair to position herself. These photographs lacked the subtlety of the others and seemed more designed to expose and objectify. Lynne wondered if Luke Hagan had taken these. They showed no sense of personal involvement between the model and the photographer – which had been there, she could see, in the earlier pictures.

She was seeing Farnham later, that evening at her flat, but this couldn't wait. She picked up the phone, and five minutes later he was in her office looking at the pictures on the screen. He raised his eyebrows and checked it himself, running the mouse pointer across the photograph. *Step inside and get to know me better.*

'It's a bit sick,' he said, after a moment. He frowned and looked more closely at the pictures that appeared when the link was activated. He zoomed in on the face, and then on the torso, his eyes narrowed in thought. 'I'm not sure . . .' he said. He enlarged one of the photographs to fill the screen. It was a crudely anatomical shot with 'Jemima' lying back on a rug, touching herself and smiling in a detached way at the camera. 'Look,' he said. He took the screen back to the study in dark and light that was the linking picture, one of the pictures that Luke Hagan admitted to having taken. Lynne looked. He went back to the other picture. And back again.

She could see it now. 'It isn't the same woman,' she said. In both pictures, the woman was reclining. In the first one, even though her hands were pulled tight above her head, her breasts fell sideways under their own weight. In the smaller photograph, though her body changed slightly under the different pull of gravity, her breasts pointed upwards, as though they were in some way extra to her body, like an adolescent boy's drawing. Implants. Gemma Wishart had not had breast implants. The face in the smaller photographs was Gemma Wishart's, but the body was not.

They looked at each other. 'It doesn't make sense,' Farnham said.

'She wanted to get her pictures up quickly?' Lynne suggested. 'Used some that were available and had them doctored?'

'I'd be quicker and easier to take her own pictures,' he said. 'Anyway, why are they there? If they are there, why hide them?' That had puzzled Lynne as well. The crudely explicit photographs were not untypical of the many porn sites that proliferated on the web, but they didn't match the shots she remembered for the Angel website. Those were more glamour shots – plenty of tit and bum, she conceded, but more designed to whet the appetite of the browser: *You can only see so much. Some people can see everything, do everything. Just give us a call* . . . And she'd let that website vanish.

'What do you think?' she said.

'Anderson thinks this website's a fake,' he said. 'Or these pictures are. I'm beginning to come round to that idea. We've looked into Gemma Wishart's background and there's nothing, *nothing*, that supports this escort thing. No one knows anything, there's no money tucked away, no time unaccounted for – or not enough. There's just this.'

Lynne remembered that the Jemima pictures had struck her as anomalous from the word go. The first photograph wasn't a glamour shot at all. She remembered Des Stanwell's description: 'a posh student type'. The other shots were darker than the erotic glamour she remembered from the rest of the site. She wondered how easy it would be to tamper with an existing website. 'I think the site was genuine,' she said. 'One of my contacts, one of the prostitutes, seemed to recognize the name. And the rest of the site was different from the Jemima pages. I think Angel Escorts exists.'

His face was thoughtful. 'Maybe,' he said. 'We've got one or two lines to follow still.' They'd been to the address Celia

Fry had given them for Anna Krleza. 'No one there, of course,' he said. 'But someone had been – her stuff was packed. It looked as though she'd left in a hurry. We got this, though.' He showed her a photograph. Lynne looked at it. It was the head and shoulders of a young woman with a pale face, dark hair and dark eyes.

'It looks like a passport photo,' she said.

Farnham smiled without humour. 'It is,' he said. 'There was a young man in one of the rooms downstairs. He said that he'd been looking after her valuables, as she hadn't been back for a while. He said there'd been an intruder, Monday night. He'd been up the fire escape to have a look, frightened whoever it was away.'

But he hadn't called the police. 'Anna Krleza has a passport?'

'Made out in the name of Sheila Lovell. It would have rung bells the first time it was checked – whoever did it doctored a stolen passport.' Farnham shrugged. Someone was helping people to get fake passports, someone was helping them find jobs. 'OK.' He gave her his quick smile. 'I'll see you later.'

Sheffield, Friday morning

It was raining as Roz drove to work; heavy persistent rain from an unbroken grey sky. The air was cold, and the wind that always blew around the Arts Tower turned her umbrella inside out and whipped the rain against her face and hair. She shook the water off as she stood in the shelter of the entrance. Dave, the porter, greeted her with a grimace. 'Lovely day for it, isn't it?'

The paternoster was packed with students queuing to get to tutorials and seminars. Roz pushed through the crowds to the stairwell, aware again of the silence that surrounded her as soon as the doors swung shut. She climbed the stairs slowly, her feet dragging a bit. Her usual enthusiasm and sense of anticipation had gone. As she climbed the stairs, she tried to work out why she felt like this. Gemma's death? That had reached into the calm centre of her working life and touched it, contaminated it. But the work had remained. Now . . . it didn't seem to be enough.

The problem was still distracting her when she got to her office. She checked her in-tray quickly, but there was only some internal post, a tatty envelope, used and used again. She picked up the phone and rang the Department of European Studies. She got the secretary. Marcus Holbrook wasn't in. 'When would be a good time to catch him?' Roz said.

'I'm not expecting him in today,' the woman said. 'Just let me check.' There was the sound of papers being moved around. 'No, he's got nothing on today, so it looks as though he won't be in.'

'OK.' Roz felt that sense of frustration again. 'If he does come in, could you ask him to phone Roz Bishop?' She gave the woman her extension number.

There was a tap on her door and a cough behind her. A young man was standing in the corridor. She registered fair hair and an engaging smile before she recognized him as Sean. His hair was wet, his coat damp, but he was looking eager and pleased with himself. She felt depressed. She wasn't in the mood for Sean.

'Sean,' she said, keeping her voice to the cold side of tepid. 'Can I help you?'

'It's me that can help you.' He gave her a cheerful grin.

Roz wasn't playing any games. 'Did you want something?'

He was silent for a moment, looking at her as though he was mulling something over. Then he said, 'You asked me to look something up for you.'

Gemma's search! He'd said he'd check and see what, exactly, she'd been looking for. Roz had assumed he would forget. She felt her face going red. 'I'm sorry,' she said. 'I'd forgotten.'

He had that slightly petulant look now. 'You mean you don't need it any more?'

'No. No, of course not. I'd just forgotten that you said . . .' That was probably worse. She was saying she'd forgotten him. 'I didn't expect you to find anything,' she amended.

'Actually . . .' He looked rueful. 'Actually, I didn't. I know she had a look through the files, but if she found what she was looking for – there's no record.'

'And you came across in this weather to tell me?' Roz was amused and a bit touched. 'That's worth a cup of coffee.'

'There's a new place in Broomhill,' he said at once. 'We could . . .'

She shook her head. 'No, we've got coffee here. I'll get us some. Milk? Sugar?' Luke never minded Roz giving his coffee to visitors. She went along to his room, realizing that Sean was tagging along behind her. She got a shock when she opened the door. Some new equipment, still boxed, was stacked on Luke's desk as though this was surplus space. The room had been rearranged to create two new work stations for the post-graduate students Joanna had mentioned, Roz assumed.

Sean looked round the room as Roz turned on the coffee machine. 'You've got some good stuff here,' he said. He wandered round looking at the machines, fiddling with the knobs on the digital filters, looking at the software manuals. He looked like a child exploring new and interesting toys.

'It's all fairly standard,' she said. 'We aren't in the income bracket for real state-of-the-art.' She poured out two mugs of coffee.

'Is this where Luke Hagan works?' He was looking round as though he expected Luke to pop out of a cupboard any moment.

'Yes.' Roz wondered how he knew Luke.

'Gemma was seeing him, wasn't she?' He took the cup she passed to him. 'Thanks. Hey, serious coffee.'

'I've no idea.' Roz wasn't discussing personal things with him.

'Oh. Gemma talked about him,' he said, still looking round. 'She said he had a seriously cool bike.'

Roz said, 'Mm,' noncommittally.

'A Vincent Black Shadow. There aren't too many of those around. Gemma said he'd got it tuned up. She said it went like a rocket.' It would be a case of bike-geek meets bike-geek, Roz thought, if Luke were here. 'I'd like to see that,'

Sean went on. 'I'm into bikes,' he added, unnecessarily. 'Is he around?'

'He isn't in.' It was a pity, really. A bike conversation with Luke would have taken the pressure off Roz a bit. 'So. Have you made any decisions yet? About what to do next?' She was trying to make up for her earlier brusqueness, but she also wanted to find out more about Joanna's plans – if she was really serious about Sean taking a research post with the Law and Language Group.

'No,' he said after a moment. 'Still thinking. Why?' He smiled at her, that flirtatious gleam in his eyes again.

Roz moved quickly on to neutral ground. 'Are you seeing Professor Holbrook today? I tried to phone him, but he wasn't in.'

He shook his head. 'Not on Fridays. Do you want me to give him a message?'

'No, it'll keep.' Roz wasn't too sure how she'd word her query when she did see Holbrook. *Why did you lie to me?* seemed a bit . . . blunt.

He was holding his cup in front of him, looking down at it. 'I've still got those tickets,' he said, looking at her through his lashes. 'If you've changed your mind.'

'No,' Roz said firmly. 'I told you. I'm busy.'

That was a mistake. 'We could go out for a drink,' he said at once. 'Sometime when you're not busy.'

'Sean,' she said, 'I told you: I'm married.'

His looked put out again. 'You go out for a drink with Luke Hagan,' he said.

'*What* did you say?' She felt a stab of real anger.

'I'm sorry,' he said, unrepentantly. 'Gemma told me. She said that he liked you a lot. Well, so do I. I've brought you a present.'

Roz closed her eyes. This needed nipping in the bud right now. She should never have encouraged him. 'Sean, I don't want any presents and my private life is none of your business.'

'You'll want this,' he said. 'It isn't really a present. It's work. I just thought you'd be pleased.' He fished in his pockets and brought out a CD case. 'It's the pilot version of the archive. It isn't going to be available for ages. So I brought you a copy.'

She rubbed her hand over her forehead. 'Won't Professor Holbrook mind?'

He smiled. 'He won't, because he doesn't know. It's OK,' he added quickly, 'It's just that he wants to keep working on it. Here.'

She took it, against her better judgement. 'Thank you,' she said, uncertain what strings might be attached to this.

'Anyway, if you don't want to talk to me, I'd better go.' He waited for a moment to see if she would respond to that.

Roz ignored the hint in his words and said, 'Well, thank you for this.'

He waited for a moment longer, then said, 'OK. I'll see you around,' and left. She gave him a few minutes to get clear of the section, then went back to her room.

The archive. She turned the CD over and over in her hands. She'd have a look at it later. She wondered if Greenhough had a copy, and if he'd found anything. She debated whether to give him a ring again, but decided that there was no reason. She couldn't really justify the time she was spending on this. She'd look at the archive when she had an hour to spare, and see if anything jumped out at her. Other than that, there was nothing else she could do. She'd just have to forget it.

She checked the time. She had a lecture to give at twelve. She put her worries to the back of her mind and decided to spend the rest of the morning, what little remained, fiddling around with the program she had been devising with Luke. She made no progress. She just went over ground they'd already tested. She almost phoned him, but decided against it. She couldn't concentrate. Luke and Joanna's plans and her impending visit to Nathan warred for her attention. She'd phoned her mother-in-law the night before and told her of her plans, before she could change her mind. 'I'm so glad, Roz,' Jenny had said.

'Jenny,' Roz couldn't bear to see false hope, to see the renewal of disappointment and pain. 'I don't think it will make any difference. I don't think he'll remember me.'

'I know.' But Jenny's quick acceptance of Roz's doubts didn't ring true. 'Listen, Roz, let's give it a chance. And bring some of the photographs. Let's try.'

Roz closed her eyes as she thought about it. She'd prevaricated about the photographs. Maybe she could find some. Maybe she could take the ones from Clifton Downs, the ones they'd taken the day they'd borrowed a friend's dizzy young labrador and exhausted themselves playing chasing games, throwing Frisbees, having play fights on the grass. She remembered the dog – what was its name? – grabbing Nathan's foot in its mouth and dragging him across the field, growling with simulated fierceness. Roz had laughed so much she had barely been able to hold the camera.

It was a relief to go into the lecture theatre where her most pressing problem was likely to be inattentive students. She hadn't reviewed her lecture notes – something she almost always did – but the subject was at the front of her mind. She was talking to them about identifying a person's location from the way he or she spoke. She always started this lecture with the Yorkshire Ripper investigation, the tape that began with the dead voice saying – or reading, Roz always thought – the words 'I'm Jack . . .' She talked about the accent on the tape, and the subtle differences that located the speaker north or south of the Tyne. She saw a hand go up and nodded to the questioner. It was always encouraging when students spoke up in lectures – it showed they were listening and interested. 'Isn't it right,' the lad said, 'that they managed to pinpoint him to just a few streets.'

'That has been claimed,' Roz said carefully. 'I'd prefer to see some corroborative evidence – like the person who actually made these tapes. I'm not convinced that these days you can pinpoint someone as closely as that.'

'I thought they caught him?' Another student, female this time, from the front.

'Not the person who made the tapes,' Roz said. 'And it's

something to remember. You can be spot-on right, but it may do no good. These tapes actually held the investigation up – and the person who made them is still out there.'

When she got back to her office, her phone was ringing. She dropped her lecture notes and grabbed it. It was Marcus Holbrook. 'Elizabeth told me you were trying to contact me,' he said. He sounded querulous. She could see the thin, discontented face in her mind.

Roz thought quickly. She'd rather do this face to face, where it would be more difficult for him to refuse to talk to her. 'It's about Gemma Wishart's query,' she said. 'Thank you for the letter, by the way.'

'Which, as I told you, contained nothing you didn't already know.'

'Yes. Professor Holbrook, I need to talk to you. It's a bit complicated. I wonder if I could come across now?'

'I've only come in for a meeting,' he said. 'It was rescheduled at the last minute. Most inefficient. I have no time this afternoon.'

'I've got a copy of your archive,' Roz said. 'And I'd really like to go over it with you. Would you have any time after your meeting?'

There was silence for a moment, then she heard him sigh. 'I really do have better things to do than . . . Very well. I don't know what time the meeting will finish, but this department will certainly have closed by then. I have some business in the Arts Tower, so I'll come to your office, but don't expect me much before half past six.' And he rang off, leaving Roz with the prospect of some unplanned overtime.

Hull, Friday afternoon
It wasn't hard for Lynne to play good cop with Celia Fry. She had announced herself to the receptionist – *Inspector Jordan from Central* – and Mrs Fry had come scurrying out of her office looking tense and rattled. She relaxed a bit when she saw Lynne – she had probably been expecting Farnham, who had, if Lynne was reading correctly between the lines, given her a hard time. Fry was a small woman, a bit dumpy,

heavily made up. She clearly thought that Lynne would not be the problem to her that Farnham had been. She looked at Lynne with some calculation and said, 'Can I help you, Inspector . . . ?'

'Jordan,' Lynne held out her hand and smiled.

'Inspector Jordan. I'm really very busy and I don't think there's anything I can add to what I told your colleague.' She was looking Lynne unblinkingly in the eye.

Lynne smiled sympathetically. 'I'm sure,' she said. 'But there are some complications with this cleaner of yours, this Anna Krleza.'

Fry's face tightened with annoyance. 'I really can't help you any further with that, Inspector. Anna was here for less than a fortnight. We're short-staffed in the kitchen. I really don't have time . . .'

Lynne waited for the woman to run down, keeping her smile of conspiratorial sympathy in place. Fry subsided into silence, and Lynne said, 'I can quite see how these things happen, but we just need to make sure we've got all the paper in the right place now. Is there somewhere we can talk?'

Celia Fry took her into a cramped office behind the reception desk. She pushed the door shut and gestured Lynne to a chair. She lit a cigarette. She didn't offer one to Lynne but looked at her watch and said, 'I can give you five minutes. I'm sure all this paperwork can be dealt with at another time.'

Lynne had ignored the invitation to sit down. She took out her notebook and said, 'Can you give me an exact date when Anna Krleza was first employed by this hotel?'

The phone on the desk rang, and Fry picked it up. 'What *now*?' she snapped. Internal phone, Lynne surmised. 'Well, he'll just have to cope,' Fry said. She listened for a moment. 'Tell him he'll have to manage.' She put the phone down. 'Short-staffed,' she said, looking sour.

Lynne smiled politely. 'The date for Anne Krleza?' she said.

'I'll need to check the records.' Fry looked at Lynne and

added, with a sudden burst of aggression, 'Well, I can't remember everything!'

'Let me see,' Lynne said helpfully. 'She'd worked for you for, what, a couple of weeks? Now you found the body just . . .' she checked in her diary '. . . Friday. And that was the last day Anna Krleza worked. So we go back two weeks . . . Did she start work on a Monday?'

Celia Fry took a long pull at her cigarette. 'I can't remember,' she said again. 'I'll need to check the records. I told you.'

Lynne sighed. 'I have a problem here, Mrs Fry. I have information that tells me Anna Krleza has been working at this hotel for several months.'

Celia Fry picked a piece of cigarette paper off her lip with her nail. 'I can't imagine who told you that,' she said. She kept glancing at the phone. She seemed distracted.

'Maybe your receptionist will remember,' Lynne said.

'She doesn't have anything to do with the cleaners.' Fry was starting to look uncomfortable.

Lynne's voice was brisk. 'I have three separate identifications of Anna Krleza at this hotel on . . .' She flicked back through the pages of the notebook, saying as she did so, 'You see, Mrs Fry, there are two investigations underway now involving Ms Krleza. There's the investigation into the murder, of course, but there's also the investigation that the immigration authorities are carrying out in the light of . . .'

'Employing the cleaning staff isn't something I do, normally,' Celia Fry said, her assumed indifference becoming defensiveness.

'I'm sure.' Lynne waited to see where this was going.

'There's an agency we use, but the people they send aren't very reliable. Anyway, Anna turned up when I'd been let down badly and I just forgot to ask her for all her details.' Celia Fry looked at Lynne, read her expression and amended, 'It *seemed* like a couple of weeks. We're very busy. It just crept on for longer than I'd realized, and then suddenly there was all this.'

And so you lied in the middle of a murder investigation. And the woman was lying now. 'So it seemed easier to say that Anna hadn't been here very long.' Lynne needed the next bit of information now, so she smiled understandingly. 'I know how these things happen, but knowingly employing an illegal immigrant is a serious offence. Now, I'm sure that you were acting in good faith and if I can go to the immigration authorities and tell them that you co-operated fully as soon as we alerted you to the fact there was a problem, then I don't think they'll take it any further.'

Celia Fry watched her narrowly, waiting to see what she wanted. 'How did Anna know you needed a cleaner?' Lynne said. 'How did she know to come here?'

The other woman shrugged her shoulders. 'I don't know,' she said. 'Someone must have said something. I told you, I didn't ask. They know their way round, these people.' The phone rang again. Fry picked it up. 'Not now,' she snapped, and put it down. She seemed to have made her mind up about something. She picked up a diary from the desk and flicked through it. 'There,' she said, showing it to Lynne. 'Anna Krleza. She started in August. Second week in August.'

Lynne made a note. 'Thank you, Mrs Fry.'

'Is that everything?' Celia Fry stood up. 'I'll have to go and sort out this kitchen thing. This won't go any further?'

'Probably not.' Lynne followed the other woman out of the office. Fry, for all her anxiety about whatever was happening in the kitchen, saw her to the door of the hotel. She wanted her off the premises. Lynne waited until the other woman had vanished in the direction of the basement stairs, then went back in again and rang the bell on the reception desk. After a minute, a woman in an overall came along the corridor.

Lynne showed her identification, and the woman immediately looked wary. 'I'll get the manager,' she said at once.

Lynne shook her head. 'I want to talk to you,' she said. 'It's only a couple of things.' She smiled reassuringly.

'I wasn't here,' the woman said. 'I told them before. I was off that day.'

'That's OK,' Lynne said. 'There's just something I'd like to check with you.' She got the woman to confirm the details of the Mr Rafael booking, made an additional note in her book and thanked her. Then she added casually, 'You seem a bit short-staffed today.'

The woman raised her eyes to the ceiling. 'And doesn't she let us know,' she said, presumably in reference to Mrs Fry. 'I told her, I'm not doing kitchen work. It's her fault.'

'Why's that?' Lynne was fastening her coat.

'Well, she let them go, didn't she. Cook's going spare, but she wouldn't listen.'

Lynne picked up her bag. 'Maybe she wanted some that could speak English,' she said.

The other woman nodded emphatically. 'About time,' she said. 'Jabber, jabber, jabber. Couldn't understand a word. Like that Anna,' she said.

Lynne left the hotel for the second time. She was thinking. Celia Fry had employed more than one illegal immigrant, by the look of things. Farnham's threat to look closely at the hotel's employment practices had panicked Fry into getting rid of her off-the-books staff. Lynne could see the attraction of the immigrants for a low-budget hotel like the Blenheim. They'd be cheap labour, hard-working. And word would get round that there was work to be had.

Now she was thinking about the advice centre. Would they know about the Blenheim? Matthew Pearse seemed knowledgeable about the situations illegal immigrants found themselves in. Someone had sent Anna Krleza to the hotel. She thought back to her last visit, when she had asked Pearse and Rafiq if they knew Krleza. Nasim Rafiq had gone on the attack: 'This woman, that woman. Why?' But Pearse had never answered her question. He had moved obliquely into a discussion of the situation that such women found them- selves in – victims of crime who were unable to approach the authorities because they would be treated as perpetrators. Fair game for the pimps and traffickers.

Lynne had questioned enough people in her years as a police officer to have some ideas about the way people behaved when they were telling the truth and when they were lying. People tended to evade or hedge rather than tell a direct untruth. Neither Nasim Rafiq nor Matthew Pearse had denied knowing Anna. The question was, did they know her present whereabouts? Lynne was aware of a tension between her own work and the work she was doing for Farnham. Farnham needed any information that Pearse might have, and he needed it soon. Lynne needed an 'in' to the world of the illegal immigrants, she needed a way to reach the women and to make them see that she could help them. And that would take time and patience. She would work on Nasim Rafiq, use Farnham's interest as a means of putting pressure on the woman to talk to her. She checked her watch. She needed to pay another visit to the advice centre.

Sheffield, Friday evening

Roz was alone in the department. She'd become engrossed in disentangling some confusions in the system she and Luke had been working on, and it was after six before she realized. The cleaners had finished at six, the last people had left their rooms and silence had fallen on N Floor. She checked her watch. Six-fifteen. She could spend a bit of time having a look at Holbrook's archive. Maybe she could butter up the old curmudgeon by complimenting him on his achievement. After browsing through it for a while, she was none the wiser about Gemma, but she was impressed by the ease with which the data could be searched. Sean Lewis clearly knew his stuff. She wanted to show it to Luke, to see if it gave him any ideas about their interview database – though what they were trying to do was a lot more complicated than what Holbrook and Lewis had done. She shut down the machine, put the CD away and checked her watch again. Six forty-five. The time had gone quickly. What had Holbrook said? 'Don't expect me much before six-thirty.'

She was tired. It had been a difficult day and she wanted to go home. She was driving across to her mother-in-law's the following morning, and it was going to be another hard day. She did a quick calculation. She needed to leave her mail in the office before she went home. She'd go and do that, and by the time she got back, Holbrook would have arrived. If he wasn't here by seven, then she wasn't going to wait.

The corridor was dark. Only the emergency light was on. The caretakers must have thought the section was empty. She walked past the stairwell towards the lifts. The office was on the other side. She could hear the paternoster running on its endless belt. She unlocked the office door and left the small pile of envelopes for the caretakers to pick up and distribute through the internal post. She checked through the tray to see if anything had arrived after the clerical staff had left. There was nothing there.

She checked her bag to make sure she had her car keys and went back towards her room. In the dim light, the polished floor tiles reflected her movement, indistinct and wavering under her shadow. She looked along the corridor, past the lifts, back towards her own section. Something had caught her eye. She frowned, looking again. Holbrook? There was movement beyond the double doors, someone walking away from her down the corridor, a tall figure in a light-coloured garment, a coat or a mac. She felt a sense of déjà vu. What was it? She couldn't remember. Whoever it was, it didn't look like Holbrook. He was a small man.

But there shouldn't be anyone else wandering round the section at this time in the evening. She hesitated for a moment then moved towards the swing doors, trying to see the figure more clearly, but whoever it was had disappeared through the second set of doors. There was a lot of valuable equipment in the offices, and in Luke's room as well. Her room was just through the swing doors, the way the unknown visitor had gone. She turned back and walked quietly to the office and phoned campus security from there.

A cheerful voice greeted her and listened to what she had to say. 'It may be nothing,' Roz said doubtfully. She didn't want to raise the alarm unnecessarily. 'But we do have valuable equipment.'

'There'll be someone there in a minute, love,' the cheerful voice said. 'Don't you fret.'

'I'm not . . .' she began, but realized he had hung up. She took a deep breath and went back out into the corridor, locking the door behind her. She was assessing the risk to the equipment. All the rooms should be locked. Joanna never left her room open. No one had been in Luke's room apart from her, so that would be locked as well. The police had locked up Gemma's room, which was empty anyway. Had she locked her own door? She was pretty sure she had, but a doubt began to creep into her mind.

The corridor ahead was dark and silent. She tried to convince herself that there was no one there, that she'd been imagining things. It had just been movement in the dark and her mind had done the rest. She walked past the lift hall and to the swing doors that led back to her section. The corridor was quiet and empty in the dim glow of the security light. She hesitated for a moment, then pushed the door open and listened. Nothing. She could see the closed doors along the corridor – Joanna's room, her room: Joanna's executive corridor. And round the corner, Gemma's room, Luke's room, the meeting room. She let the swing door shut behind her, a slight whisper and a squeak of the closing mechanism. She listened again. Nothing. Silence, and the faint hum of the light. The door to the stairwell was on her right. She stopped, indecisive. The corner was ahead of her, dark and silent. It was irresistible.

She *knew* there was no one there, but there was a tingling feeling between her shoulders and she could feel the hairs on her arms standing up. She took a step. Then another. She was nearly at the corner. Her keys were in her hand. Then there was a *clunk* and a clanging sound as the lift started up. She jumped, the keys dropping from her fingers and landing with a clatter on the floor. Her heart hammered with shock and she had to stop and catch her breath. *Idiot!*

Then she thought she heard something moving on the corridor, moving away from her, towards the next 'L', towards the lifts – or was it just her imagination? She went round the corner and the empty corridor stretched away from her. Mechanically, she tested the doors. Joanna's door. Locked. Her door . . .

It swung open under her hand. She looked round. The room was empty, the stand-by light on the monitor glowing in the dark. She pressed the light switch. The desk was as she'd left it, tomorrow's work in a neat pile. The filing cabinet was closed and – she tested it – locked. She hesitated. Maybe she hadn't locked the door. It was one of those automatic things that didn't register. She must have left it, knowing she was coming back in a couple of minutes.

She heard the whisper of the double door, and footsteps in the corridor behind her. She spun round, and the cheerful voice of the caretaker said, 'Got an intruder, Dr Bishop?'

Roz let out the breath she didn't realize she'd been holding. 'I don't know,' she said. 'Probably not, but I'd like you to check these rooms.' She told him what she'd seen.

'Sounds like someone on their way to the stairs,' he said. 'I'll see to it. Don't you worry.'

Roz stood indecisively for a moment, then picked up her bag. 'I'll be off then. Thanks. Let me or Dr Grey know if you find anything.'

'I will,' he said.

'Night.' Roz headed for the paternoster. If the strange figure had gone down the stairs, then she was using the lifts. She stepped into the moving platform and sunk away from N floor. As she was carried down, there was a *thump* above her, as if someone had jumped into the following compartment. Someone else, coming down from N floor. But she hadn't seen anyone else. You could see the people waiting to get into the next compartment as yours descended. Unless the person kept out of sight round the corner and made a leap for it as the platform dropped below floor-level.

And there wasn't anyone else on N floor. There had been her, there had been the caretaker, and there had been . . . someone else. Someone else who was in the car above her, following her inexorably down to the empty entrance lobby and the deserted car park? She almost got out at the next floor, but the person above her would see her before she could move out of sight. She didn't want to be alone, high up in the Arts Tower, with someone who moved with that silent, gliding step, surreptitiously but quickly along dark corridors, someone whose intention was unknown.

She kept hoping on each floor that there would be someone waiting to ride down, but each landing she passed was empty . . . G floor, empty . . . F floor, empty . . . E floor . . . Friday night, people went home early, evening classes didn't run, the building was deserted. She took a deep breath and told herself to stop panicking. Whoever it was, he was leaving the building like she was. When she got to the ground floor, she would go straight to the porter's lodge. One of the caretakers might be there, and if not, whoever was on duty wouldn't be far away.

But she wanted to see the face of the person who was following her down. She didn't want to go home, alone, with the memory of that tall, anonymous figure walking away from her down the corridor. She wanted to see a familiar face and know that her imagination had been running wild. She was at the mezzanine now, with the ground floor coming up. She stepped out of the paternoster and looked round. No sign of the caretaker. She was frozen by indecision, and the next car glided down.

It was empty.

14

Hull, Friday night

The kitchen smelt of wine and warm bread. Lynne did a last check, and smoothed back her hair as the door bell rang. She glanced in the mirror as she went to the intercom, and pressed the entry button once she had confirmed that her visitor was Roy, commendably punctual. She could hear his feet on the stairs and she opened the door as he came up the last flight. He brought the smell of winter into the flat. He didn't say anything, just put his arms round her and lifted her off the ground as he kissed her. His jacket felt bulky against her. 'I've been thinking about that all day,' he said, when he released her. 'No shop tonight,' he added.

Lynne felt a bit breathless and light-headed. 'We've got things we need to discuss,' she said. He was looking down at her, a faint line appearing between his eyes. 'But we've got plenty of time.' She smiled and stepped back so that she was standing in the light from the open kitchen door. She saw his eyes widen slightly as she stretched her arms above her head, stood watching him with a half smile, letting him see what he had missed in the robustness of his first embrace. The way her dress clung to her and the translucence of the material in the light from the open kitchen door made it abundantly clear that she was wearing nothing underneath it. '"Been thinking about it all day," he says,' she taunted, 'and he doesn't even notice . . .'

He just looked at her, his face slightly flushed and his eyes getting darker, then he tossed his jacket on to a chair and came towards her. He put his hands round her waist, pushing

216

her back against the wall to kiss her. For better or for worse, she reflected, she'd committed herself now. She kept her hands on her head, enjoying the way he touched her, unimpeded by her arms. It was a symbolic submission, and she liked the eroticism of the implied dominance. He knew what he was doing. He could read her signals, listen to the quickening of her breathing and the words she whispered to him, and by the time he picked her up and carried her into the bedroom, her dress was on the floor and she had forgotten about her day, was as focused on the moment as he was. And for the next hour neither of them thought about anything else.

It was after nine when Lynne next checked the time. She had drifted into a light sleep with her head on Roy's shoulder, in that moment of absolute relaxation after good sex. She lay there for a while longer, enjoying the closeness. He had a solid, muscular body that she liked the feel of. She stretched, and he took it as a signal to stir, smiling easily at her. 'That was worth waiting for,' he said.

She met his eyes and smiled her agreement. It had been. 'Do you want to eat?' she said. She picked up her dressing gown that was draped over the back of a chair.

He grinned. 'I don't think I've got the strength for anything else.'

Lynne laughed and went to shower. Half an hour later, they were sitting close together at the table eating grilled tuna and drinking wine. 'This is good,' he said, topping up her glass.

He seemed to share her uncomplicated appreciation of the good things in life. Lynne could never understand why the food you ate should not be the best, why the place you lived should not be welcoming and comfortable, why the people you spent precious free time with should not be the people whose company you enjoyed. She thought about Steve McCarthy, who had seemed to see good food, good company, good wine – even good sex – not as the essentials that they were, but as things that took him away from the essentials, from the important things like work. And that reminded her of her hunt for Angel Escorts and for Anna Krleza, and the way her investigations into trafficked women and Roy's into the murders kept tripping over the same threads.

As if on cue, Roy finished his wine and said, 'OK then. What did you want to talk about?'

'I'll make coffee,' she said. She wanted to move the evening on before they started talking about work.

Ten minutes later, they were sitting on the settee with coffee on the table in front of them. Lynne wanted to find out what else Farnham hadn't told her. 'You said that you were coming round to the idea that the website was a fake, right?' He nodded, but didn't say anything, waiting to see where she was going. 'How long have you thought that?'

'It's come up at the briefings. The fact that there's no evidence to support this idea that Gemma Wishart was doing – or even planning to do – escort work.' He didn't seem aware that he hadn't kept her up to date with this.

'You didn't mention it,' she said. 'When we've discussed the case.'

He shrugged. 'A lot of ideas get thrown around at a briefing, Lynne. You know that. I wasn't convinced until you showed me that link.'

'And that makes the card a deliberate plant.'

He nodded again. 'Along with the most fucked-up crime scene I've ever had to deal with. Yes. That's our thinking. Someone's playing games. Angel Escorts. Mr Rafael. Business cards dropped on the floor. Someone's telling us something, and he's making sure we listen.'

'What about the phone calls?'

'It's hard to tell. I've got a watch on that number. If anyone uses that cell phone, we'll know.' He still wasn't giving her much.

Someone had interfered with the scene. Someone had pointed a great big arrow at Angel Escorts – the name, the card. They had followed that arrow and found their dead woman, Jemima the call girl. Anyone would know that once they got that far, they would find out who "Jemima" really was, though maybe not quite as quickly as they had actually done. Unless . . . Lynne began to feel the prickling sensation she felt when she was on surveillance, that two-o'clock-in-the-morning unease that suggested unseen eyes, malicious eyes, watching you. Unless the person who'd so helpfully pointed the way knew that she had seen Gemma Wishart and would make the connection.

Women with their faces smashed, women who were working as prostitutes, patterns that made a picture neither of them wanted to see. 'Why the faces?' she said.

'That could be his thing, or it could be to make it difficult to identify them.' He'd thought about it. 'Copycat or the same person? We don't even know if the first two were murdered.' Unanswered questions.

'Have you followed up on the Blenheim?' She'd phoned him with the information she'd got from Celia Fry. If he wasn't going to tell her, she would have to ask.

'We're looking at it,' he said. 'Anything new about the advice centre?'

Lynne was aware of a feeling of reluctance as she shared her doubts about Nasim Rafiq. She could remember his sharp advice about passing the information on to Special Branch. 'I don't see that she'd put her son at risk,' she said in the end. 'She's starting to listen to me, I think.'

'You aren't a social worker, Lynne.' He was frowning slightly as he listened.

'I'm not being a social worker.' She could hear the annoyance in her voice and saw him register it. 'But she can help me – I can help her. Quid pro quo.'

She couldn't tell from his face what he was thinking. He had his arm along the back of the settee, his fingers resting lightly on her shoulder. 'When are you going back?'

'Tomorrow,' she said.

There was silence. They looked at each other, and each read the message in the other's face. The mood of easy, relaxed pleasure was gone. They both needed to be alone. She looked at her watch and he was quick to pick up the cue. 'I'd better go,' he said. 'It'll be an early start tomorrow.' He looked down at her, more uncertain than she'd seen him.

'It's been good tonight,' he said after a moment. 'I'll see you soon, OK?'

'OK.' Lynne waited until his feet had clattered down the first flight, then she shut the door. She double-locked it and fastened the security chain, then she checked the windows to make sure that they were all bolted. *Paranoia*, she chided herself. But sometimes a little paranoia was a healthy thing.

15

Sheffield, Saturday morning

The forecast had promised a clear day, fine but cold with snow on high ground. By nine, the clouds had rolled in and the bright sun of early morning became a sullen, frozen grey.

Roz's journey got off to a bad start. She had left the car out in the road the night before. She'd just parked, grabbed her bag, locked up and left it. And now she had a flat tyre, and her spare was flat as well. She'd changed the wheel a few weeks ago and had meant to get the spare fixed, but she hadn't. *Idiot!* She looked closely at the wheel. It looked as though someone had driven a nail into it. Probably the lads from three doors up – amiable, loutish goons who would find a piece of minor vandalism like this the height of wit.

She looked at her watch. It would take forever to get someone out here to fix it. She needed to take the spare in, get it repaired, bring it back, change the wheel . . . She had the perfect excuse not to go. All she had to do was pick up the phone. Jenny would be disappointed, but she would understand. Her mother-in-law's face formed in her mind, the time she'd first come to see Nathan after his illness. She and Nathan's father had been on holiday when Nathan first went into hospital. Roz had spent a week trying to find out where they were staying, and then Jenny and Ed had spent a frantic three days trying to get a flight home. By the time they got back, Nathan's life was no longer in danger, but the son they had loved and been so proud of had changed beyond retrieval. Roz sometimes thought that Jenny blamed herself, believed that if she had been there for those crucial days,

221

she might have held on to the unravelling skeins of Nathan's mind.

And then Nathan's father, an apparently fit man of sixty-two had died the following year. He had had a sudden and massive heart attack. Jenny Bishop had changed then. The bright, witty woman that Roz had met on her first nervous visit, became old. If her son had lost his past, Jenny had lost her future. All she had left was the faint hope – because nothing unknown is impossible – that Nathan might, one day, come back as he used to be. It was that unyielding hope that had driven Roz away.

Now, she stopped as her hand was reaching for the phone. She had to go. It wasn't just the response to Jenny's appeal. She needed to make her own decisions, finally to let go of her marriage, to start her life again. She remembered Luke's voice in the evening dimness: 'People get ill, they grow old, they die. In the end, you have to move on.'

She checked the train times. There was one she could catch that would get her there before midday. Depressed at the prospect of the journey, and dreading the day ahead, she set off for the bus stop, wondering if there might be something, a bus strike, a train strike, *something* that would give her a way out.

She got to the station with minutes to spare. She pushed to the front of the queue, apologizing to the waiting line, and bought her ticket. Cash, she was short of cash. She paid with her Switch card and ran into the station, thankful that the train was leaving from the nearest platform and she didn't have to run across the bridge. The train was waiting, a rickety two-carriage affair with hard bench seats. It was crowded, and Roz had to squash on to the end of a row of three people. The metal bar along the back of the seat dug into her. More people piled on. They were standing now.

The train set off with a lurch, and Roz tried to switch her mind off. She was stuck on this vehicle for over an hour. She didn't want to think about the day ahead, so she let her mind wander back to the evening before, to the figure she had seen briefly through the glass doors, and the belief she'd had that there was someone following her down on the paternoster. And Marcus Holbrook. She'd forgotten about him in all the panic. Why hadn't he turned up?

She closed her eyes as the train shook and rattled its way through the countryside, stopping at all the small stations between Sheffield and Lincoln. As they pulled into her station, she picked up her coat, reflecting that she hadn't really dressed for the weather. She'd been planning to drive, and her lightweight shoes and shower-proof jacket had been chosen more with comfort in mind than protection from the weather.

She checked her watch. Just gone twelve. The train was on time. She felt a growing reluctance to move, a temptation that was getting stronger and stronger to turn around and take the next train back. She had managed to cope for the past two years without any contact with Nathan. She might have felt guilty, but it was a guilt she could cope with. So why was she planning to put herself through what could only be the worst kind of ordeal?

Because her unresolved attachment to Nathan had ruined whatever she might have had with Luke. It didn't matter if that was a friendship – about the best friendship she had ever had – or if it could have been something more. Because of Nathan, because of her fear of any more involvement, she had backed off, pushed him away for reasons that, then, he hadn't been able to understand. Now they were barely friends, just colleagues. Not even that any more, and she missed him.

She knew Lincoln. She had come here often enough with Nathan in the days when they had no chance of affording a car. She could catch a bus at the top of the main road. It would take about twenty minutes to get to Jenny Bishop's. That would give her enough time to think, to decide what she wanted to do, what she wanted the outcome of today's visit to be.

As the bus meandered through the town, she was reminded of how attractive it was. It was quiet, old, lacking the frenetic bustle of Sheffield. The bus dropped her at the corner of Garden Road, the street where Nathan had been born and had grown up. 'I'm so grateful that Ed and I didn't sell it when Nathan left home,' Jenny had said more than once in her phone calls to Roz, in the earlier days when she had thought that Roz might come back. 'It's somewhere Nathan can recognize.'

And now she could see the house. She remembered her first visit to this neat semi with its small front garden, a lawn surrounded by narrow beds. The wall round the garden was low, with a wrought-iron gate. It had been spring when Nathan had brought her here for the first time. 'Stop looking so nervous,' he'd said as they walked up the road together.

'What if they don't like me?' To Roz, the road reminded her of the places where some of her school friends lived, the friends whose mothers had careful voices and who watched with narrow-eyed judgement for Roz to display signs of ill-breeding.

'What if they don't?' Nathan had said cheerfully, dismissing her fears.

The house looked smaller than it had been in her memory, and shabbier as though it had been left just a bit too long without paint and filler, without the gutters renewed, without the constant work and attention of maintaining a house. There was someone standing by the door, as there had been in her mind picture, standing looking – not down the road, but at something in the garden. She watched him as she walked up the road, intrigued by the intensity of his concentration. He was tall, heavy. His face was puffy, his hair thinning on top. He didn't notice her until she arrived at the gate. The sound of the hinges made him look up.

He smiled at her then, and as the laughter lines round his eyes creased, past and present came together and this rather overweight, rather unkempt stranger became Nathan. She felt as though someone had punched her in the stomach. She stopped and stared, waiting for a moment for recognition to dawn on his face.

'Nathan,' she said.

He looked puzzled. 'Are you looking for Mum? She's around.'

'How are you, Nathan?' He looked uneasy, a young man trying to think of a polite way to tell one of his mother's friends he had no idea who she was. Roz said quickly, 'Don't worry. We've . . . you don't know me.' And that was true. In his mind, he was about eighteen. He'd never met Roz, and now, he never would. That future had gone forever. His body looked older – there was a heaviness about him and a clumsiness to his movements that had been there since his illness. But his face looked oddly young, despite the thinning hair and the deepening of the lines round his eyes.

His face cleared. 'I'll call Mum,' he said. 'Come in.' He turned to lead the way into the house, and his eyes became transfixed on what he had been watching before. Roz looked over his shoulder. A spider was spinning a web between the shrub and the wall, and his eyes were focused and intent.

They watched it in silence for a while. 'It's beautiful,' Roz said.

He looked round. 'Sorry,' he said, his smile friendly. 'I didn't see you. Are you looking for Mum? She's around.'

Roz's smile felt frozen on her face. 'It's OK,' she said. 'She's expecting me. I'll find her. Don't let me disturb you.'

He gave her his cheerful grin, and just for a moment, her husband looked out of a stranger's eyes at her. 'It's no trouble,' he said.

As they stepped through the door, she heard feet on the stairs and Jenny Bishop came hurrying down. Her face was tense with hope. 'Roz! I'd almost given you up!'

'I'm sorry,' Roz said. 'The car broke down. I came on the train.'

Nathan was staring at his mother. 'Mum, are you all right? You look . . .'

She forced a smile. 'I'm fine, Nathan.' Her eyes went to Roz, who shook her head gently. Jenny Bishop's face collapsed. 'Come and sit down. I'll make tea.' Her voice was flat.

Roz found herself alone with Nathan. She didn't know what to say to him. She looked round the room, noticing what she'd been vaguely aware of in the hallway. There were no mirrors. She remembered a mirror over the mantelpiece, but it had been replaced by a picture. Feeling as though she was talking to a stranger, an adolescent son of a friend, she heard herself saying in tones of bright encouragement, 'What are you doing these days, Nathan?' She wanted to stop this pointless attempt at social chitchat, but the words just came out of her mouth in a nervous flood.

He looked puzzled. 'I don't know,' he said. 'I don't know.' And for a moment his face looked sad.

Hull, Saturday

For the first time, the advice centre had clients. There were three people, two men and a woman standing at the counter. Nasim Rafiq was at the counter talking quickly in a language that Lynne didn't recognize, and jotting information down as one of the men spoke to her. Lynne caught her eye as she came through the door. Rafiq looked quickly at the door, then nodded at one of the chairs. *Wait.*

Lynne was aware of eyes on her, but as she looked, the eyes were directed down to the floor. The discussion at the counter went on, rapid and staccato in Lynne's ears. Then the group left, unsmiling, clutching leaflets and some papers that Rafiq had been writing on. They didn't look at Lynne, but kept their eyes down as they went past. Lynne was alone with Nasim Rafiq. 'You're busy this afternoon, Mrs Rafiq,' she said.

'Small bit busy.' Rafiq made a dismissive gesture and indicated to Lynne that they should go through to the other room. Lynne followed her behind the counter, and Rafiq retreated behind the fortress of her cramped desk.

Lynne had gone over the questions she wanted to ask in her mind, and had decided that Rafiq was more likely to respond to a direct approach. She smiled and said, 'Mrs Rafiq,

226

I hope I won't have to keep you long, but I need some more information.' The other woman said nothing, just waited. 'When I was here the other day, I asked you about a young woman, Anna Krleza. I wanted to know if you had seen her. You never answered my question.'

Rafiq sat quietly, a faint line between her eyebrows. 'Many people,' she said after a moment's thought. 'Sometimes, they come once, twice? Names . . . ?' She spread her hands in a gesture of helplessness. *How can I remember them all?* But she still hadn't answered the question.

'Mrs Rafiq, do you remember Anna Krleza?'

'I do not remember.' The words were spoken with leaden certainty.

Lynne had had a strong feeling that the woman might prevaricate, but that she would not actually lie. That firm response had surprised her. Maybe Rafiq didn't know Krleza. Maybe it had been Pearse who had had all the contact, Pearse who used his contacts with the hotels for the homeless to find work for people without papers. As she thought about it, her eyes took in the room again, the desk, the shelves with boxes of leaflets, the phone, the list of addresses and numbers on the wall.

She stood up and moved closer to the list. It was typed under headings: Doctors, Clinics, Landlords, Support Groups, Benefits. But there were numbers written on the list as well, just scribbled at the edges, under no specific headings. And there was a number there she recognized, written in a scribbled italic script, unlike the neat, careful writing of Nasim Rafiq. She checked it in her notebook to confirm. It was the number of the Blenheim Hotel.

She turned to Rafiq, who was watching her with puzzled incomprehension. Lynne thought. Rafiq hadn't written that number, and probably did very little phoning, given her limited English. 'Whose writing is this?' she said.

Rafiq looked worried. 'Matthew Pearse,' she said after a moment. 'He write numbers. Sometime.'

Pearse. The sooner they talked to Matthew Pearse again, the better. 'When is he here again, Mrs Rafiq?' she said.

227

Rafiq twisted her hands in the fringe of her scarf. 'Tonight,' she said. 'Late.'

'And where is he now?' Lynne wondered if it would be worth Farnham's while putting out a call.

Rafiq shook her head. She didn't know. Lynne decided to up the pressure. 'Mrs Rafiq, I recognize that you are doing important work here.' She gestured to the door to indicate that she had seen the people waiting, and had seen the signs of poverty and need. 'But you have to operate within the law.' Rafiq made no response. 'I think Anna Krleza came to this centre, Mrs Rafiq. It would have been about six months ago. I want to know if she has been here since then, if she has been here recently.' The other woman maintained her silence, but she was listening to what Lynne had to say. 'Mrs Rafiq –' Lynne made eye contact to make sure she had Rafiq's undivided attention – 'I'm investigating a murder.' She let the word hang there in the silence. 'I don't know what's going on here. But if there is something you aren't telling me, you could end up in serious trouble.' She could see the tension in the other woman and pushed a bit more. 'That could affect your son, Mrs Rafiq.'

'It . . .' Rafiq began, then stopped. Lynne thought she saw fear in her eyes.

'I can help you,' Lynne said. 'If you help me, I can help you.' She watched the uncertainty flicker across the other woman's face as she weighed up Lynne's words.

'Six month . . .' Rafiq gestured. 'I am not here.' I wasn't here six months ago. Lynne thought fast. Rafiq knew something, she was sure of that. Lynne could bring major pressure to bear, take her in, subject her to a formal interview, but if Rafiq was on the fringes of anything dubious, then the consequences for her would be catastrophic. If Lynne could persuade the woman to trust her, then she would get the information she needed, and protect Rafiq from the consequences. And Rafiq would make a useful contact. She gambled. 'Think about it, Mrs Rafiq. If you tell me what you know – it may be very little – but if you tell me, I will help you, I promise. Think about it.' She looked into Rafiq's eyes and let the silence build. 'You can contact me here.' She gave Rafiq her card and stood up. 'If I don't hear from you, I'll be back. I need to talk to Anna Krleza.'

She phoned Farnham on her way back to the car. He needed to know about Matthew Pearse.

Lincoln, Saturday afternoon
Roz spent the afternoon with Nathan and his mother. Nathan wandered restlessly, everything he started to do forgotten almost before he had conceived the intention. Each time he came back into the room, he asked who Roz was, what she was doing there. Each time his eyes fell on his mother, he expressed anxiety at her appearance. To him, Jenny Bishop had aged ten years or more overnight. Once, Jenny tried showing him the photographs that Roz had brought. He recognized himself – those pictures represented the way he thought he still looked – but he was unhappy and frightened by them. 'I don't remember,' he said. 'I didn't do that.' *If there is truth in sight* . . . And his eyes looked lost and afraid, for a moment, until the thread was broken again.

Then Jenny put a tape in the cassette player, Beethoven's violin concerto. The music filled the room. And as she watched, something happened. Nathan's rather aimless wandering stopped. His attention focused on the music. As the violin climbed away from the orchestra and tumbled down a melody line, he caught Roz's eye and smiled in shared appreciation. For a moment, she thought she had seen recognition. He was caught in the music, in its past, its now and its developing patterns. It was like the way he had watched the spider, rapt and attentive. She looked at Jenny. The tension in her mother-in-law's face increased.

Jenny was hoping that under the influence of the music, with whatever stimulation it was giving to Nathan's damaged brain, he would remember. Roz sat quietly as the music poured out its complexities in a multi-layered pattern she could only follow in part. As it wound to a close, she watched Nathan. His eyes were calm, concentrating on the sound. He seemed in contact with the two women in the room, looking at them occasionally, aware of their presence. As the music ended, he seemed to withdraw, but the air of quiet contemplation stayed. And she realized then that Nathan was still there, that the man she had loved and married still existed in a place where she could no longer reach him, and he could no longer reach her.

Then, slowly, the restless movement began again, the frown of bewilderment as he looked at Roz, the repeated questions, the sense of actions begun with intent but aborted before they were realized. Jenny sat motionless in her chair. Then she took Nathan's hand and drew him out of the room with her. 'Go and check the garden, Nathan,' she said. She looked at Roz. 'He's calmer in the garden.' Roz remembered the quiet figure watching the spider spin its web. She couldn't speak.

Jenny looked at Roz. 'I have to take him back to the home tomorrow. I dread it. He doesn't know why I'm taking him there – he doesn't recognize it. To him, I'm taking him to a place he's never been before and leaving him with people he's never seen. And I'll bring him home next weekend, and he'll forget he's ever been away.'

'I wish . . .' Roz didn't know how to finish her sentence. She didn't know what she wished for.

'There's nothing you can do,' Jenny said, 'that you aren't doing now. Even if you looked after him sometimes it wouldn't be any better. He doesn't know you and he never will.'

'I could come here sometimes. Look after him here.' Roz wasn't sure if she meant this.

Jenny shook her head. 'It's easier for him in familiar surroundings, but he'd keep finding a stranger in his house. It could be dangerous. He seems calm now, but he panics. You know what happened before.' *The fist lashing out at her, the frantic grabbing at the banister, the stairs as she tumbled . . .* 'Thank you for coming, Roz,' Jenny said. 'We've tried. I had to try. You do understand that?' Roz nodded, not trusting her voice. 'You don't have to come back again,' Jenny went on calmly. 'You'll be welcome, of course you will, but it's probably better if you don't.'

Roz took a deep breath. 'You know I'll always take responsibility if . . .'

'If I die?' Jenny grimaced. 'They understand Nathan at the home. As long as he can stay there . . .'

It was so little, in the end, that Jenny Bishop was asking her to do to fulfil the promise she'd made to Nathan. *For richer, for poorer, for better for worse, in sickness and in health* . . . I will pay the fees of your nursing home. *I'm sorry*, she said in her mind, to the memory of Nathan on the day they married. *That's not how I meant it, not then.*

It was late by the time she left, almost nine. She declined the offer of a lift. It would have meant subjecting Nathan to the confusion of the car. When she got to the station, she found she had just missed a train and had a three-quarter of an hour wait. She bought herself some coffee from the vending machine, remembering that she was short of cash. She debated walking back into the town centre to look for a cash machine, but the rain had started in earnest now, and she had her ticket. She could get some money from the machines at Sheffield station. She had enough to get her home anyway, as long as she used the bus.

She walked up and down the empty platform, the minutes crawling slowly by, almost welcoming the discomfort of the cold. Her mind was detached, in a kind of limbo, and she wanted it to stay there. She didn't want to think about the day. She wondered what to do when she got back. She couldn't bear the thought of going back to her house, to its empty silence. It would be too late by the time she got back to go out in search of friends, of company, and anyway, there was only one person in the world she wanted to talk to. Luke.

Hull, Saturday evening

Anna, sitting in the dark. She had been daydreaming and the voices pulled her back. For a moment she was confused, then the smell of dust from the blanket reminded her that she was in the attic of the welfare centre. She looked at her wrist, instinctively, but she had lost her watch somewhere

231

in the past few days. She couldn't remember. What day was it? The recent past swirled round her in a confusion of images.

She felt cold. Her mind seemed to have a sharp clarity that felt strangely detached, as though her head was floating above her. The voices were on the landing below, indistinct. She listened. One voice was a staccato *jab, jab, jab*. The other was lower, a murmur that responded to the *jab, jab* of urgency in the other voice.

'. . . must go.' *Jab*

'We can't . . . on the street.' *Murmur*

'Police . . . trouble . . . ask questions . . .' *Jab*

'. . . a place. Tomorrow . . . more day . . .' *Murmur*

She could only get words here and there. It was Nasim and Matthew. They were talking about her. The police. Trouble. She thought about the dark streets and the eyes watching her and . . . Angel, waiting, somewhere, out there in the night. She felt the tightness of panic in her chest.

'A few days,' Matthew had promised. *A few days.* But Nasim was talking about the police. The police. The police had looked away when the men came. The men had told Anna's father to leave and he wouldn't. His friends, his neighbours, he said. This was just bar talk and politics. The trouble wouldn't come there. It would all blow over like it had in the past. Then the men had taken him while the police looked away.

'They won't just send you back, Anna,' Angel told her. 'You know what they'll do, young girl like you. Then they'll lock you up – you shouldn't be here and you shouldn't be doing what you're doing. You're lucky you've got me, sugar. I'll look after you.'

But he hadn't. And she had hurt, maybe killed, Angel's friend. She hadn't told Matthew about that. Angel was looking for her. She had come here and they had helped her. They hadn't asked questions, they'd given her food and clothes, they'd given her shelter.

And someone was looking for her now. The police were looking for her too. The image of a shower curtain, shadowy, bulging slightly, formed in her mind. She felt the worm of panic inside her and made herself be calm. The strange detachment helped. Her mind seemed to drift away. She needed some money. If she could get some money, quickly, then she could get away. She could go to . . . She thought about the places she had heard people talking about. She could go to London – she could find work in London easily. All those hotels, pubs, bars, cafés – they would need people. She could find the ones that wouldn't ask questions. Or she could go to one of the other cities – Manchester, Edinburgh, Glasgow. All places where one person could vanish below the surface and scratch out a living. But Matthew had said, 'A few days . . . You could stay . . .'

She switched on the light, its heavily shaded bulb casting a dim light round the room. She heard feet on the stairs and then a knock at the door. 'Yes?' she said.

Matthew put his head round the door. 'Anna?' His voice was a whisper. 'Can I come in?'

'Yes.' She looked beyond him but there was no one there.

'Did we wake you? I'm sorry. Nasim's gone home. She's a bit worried. We've had a visitor.'

'The police?' she said.

He sighed and nodded. 'You heard us. Yes. They're looking for someone.' She made an inquiring noise, her throat dry. 'There's been a serious crime committed. A killing. I don't know exactly . . .' He was watching her face as he spoke.

Cold. It was cold. 'Now?' she said. 'Killing today?'

He shook his head. 'Some time ago. I don't know.' A killing. A murder. The woman in the bath. Now the shower curtain was pulled back and she could see the broken face and the bruises on the grey flesh. She shivered. 'Are you all right?' He was concerned. 'I'll get you another blanket.'

He waited to see if she would say something, then said, 'You need to talk to someone, Anna. I know some people who won't let you down. I've been looking into your case. I know someone who might help you, but you've got to talk to him.'

Staying, with a job and papers and a place to live. It had

been a good dream, but it was too late. Murder. It didn't matter if it was Angel's friend or if it was the woman in the hotel room. The police thought she had done it. She was a prostitute, she was a thief and she was a killer. It was too late. 'Yes,' she whispered. 'Thank you.'

A phone rang downstairs. 'I'd better get that,' he said. 'It could be urgent. Get some more rest. We'll talk in the morning.'

She lay down again. He hadn't closed the door properly and it swung open. She could hear his voice drifting up the stairs as he spoke to the person on the phone. She couldn't make out the words, but his voice sounded calm, as though he was soothing someone's worries in the middle of the night. She waited after the call had finished. He didn't come back. She waited until everything was silent again, then slipped off the couch. Her things, what bits she had, were in a carrier bag by the door. She pulled on the clothes Nasim had given her, the jeans, the T-shirt, the socks and shoes. Her jacket was still damp and dirty from her nights on the streets, but it was better than nothing. She bundled it under her arm and listened at the door. Silence.

She crept down the stairs, pausing, listening. The stairs creaked as she reached the bottom and she froze for a moment, but no one came. The door to the downstairs back room was ajar. She edged up to it and peered in. It was empty, but there was a bag on the table. She slipped in and looked inside the bag. Sandwiches. Cheese sandwiches like the other evening. She put the bag into the carrier. One day should be all it would take. She needed a bus ticket to London, but she had to be realistic. She would need a bit of money for food, for shelter. Once she was there, she could survive. No one would find her there.

She slipped out through the door that led to the yard. She remembered Nasim's face as she watched Anna from the window. *Come in out of the cold!* She was letting them down, Nasim, Matthew, they wouldn't understand when they found that she had gone, and she couldn't explain to them. The yard was pitch-black. The ground felt spongy under her feet as she picked her way cautiously across to the wooden gate she remembered seeing in the wall. Her hands touched the damp brick of the outhouse and she felt her way round it until she was at the wall, then the gate. There were bolts, one at the top and one at the bottom. She had to run her hands across the surface to find them, recoiling a bit from the cobwebs and the flakes of old paint that stuck to her fingers. The bolts themselves were well oiled and moved easily. She pulled the gate firmly shut behind her.

The night was cold, but she felt warm, a sheen of damp breaking out over her skin as she ran down the gennel and into the city night.

Sheffield, Saturday night
Roz's journey back was bleak and cold and comfortless. The train rattled and shook, the heating wasn't working and the temperature dropped and dropped. There was no refreshment trolley, so she couldn't warm herself with a hot drink or console herself with a beer. Her day played itself through and through her mind, mixed with memories of the past that couldn't bring her anything but pain. If Nathan had died, she might be able to look at these memories now, and be glad of the happiness they'd had, but with Nathan stuck like a fly in amber, pinned to his eternal present, the memories were bitter.

There was just one thing she wanted to do. She wanted to see Luke, she wanted to tell him what had happened today, she wanted him to put his arms round her and talk lightly about penance and guilt, and about astronomy and maths and time and eternity. He would tell her she didn't need to feel guilty, and he would mean it. He would say things like: 'What are you planning to do next, Bishop? Walk on water?' She wasn't really planning to trail all the way out there when she got back – it was more of a daydream to get her through the nightmare journey – but when she got into Sheffield and started looking for a taxi, she saw the bus to Luke's pulling in at the stop outside the station. Signs and portents. She ran through the driving rain, her feet splashing in the puddles, and made it on to the bus just as the driver showed signs of preparing to leave. He sat there with exaggerated patience as she dug in her bag for her purse and counted through her change to make up the fare.

Luke lived in one of the suburbs on the edge of the moors, a high and bleak place where the snow tended to drift in the winter and the buses were liable to stop their journey before the last climb. Roz had to press her face against the window as the bus ploughed through the bad weather, trying to spot the landmarks that would tell her where to get off. They were nearly at the terminus now, but she recognized the end of Luke's road as they went past it, a crescent of older houses set back from the road.

The rain had stopped now, and she hurried down the hill from the bus stop, past the stone walls with dark evergreen shrubs pushing over them and brushing their wet leaves against her face. She reached the corner of Luke's road, realizing with a hollow feeling that she hadn't thought this through. It was Saturday night. Luke might be out. Or he might have someone with him. Or . . . There was no point in wondering. She was here now. The house, which had been converted into four studio flats, was just across the road. Luke's was on the ground floor to the left of the door.

His window was dark, but the lock-up where he parked his bike was padlocked, so he might be in. She pressed his bell, then, realizing that it probably didn't work, tapped on his window with her fingers. She didn't know what she was going to do if he wasn't there. She hadn't made any plans. She'd just stepped on the bus outside the station like an automaton. She banged on the door again.

'OK, OK.' The light came on, on the other side of the glass and she felt her tension dissolve in relief as she heard his voice. 'For Christ's sake, it's after . . .' He flung the door open impatiently. There was a moment's silence. 'Roz.'

'Hello, Luke.' They looked at each other. 'Can I come in?' she said. 'I know it's late. I'm sorry.'

He stood back and she stepped into the hallway. The house felt warm after the cold outside. He pushed open the door

236

to his flat and shut the front door behind him. He was wearing jeans and a black jersey, but his feet were bare. She
thought she might have woken him up, but there was music
playing quietly, a distinctive herbal smell that suggested he'd
been smoking, and his computer was switched on – the
screen was turned away, but she could see a dark background
and pulsing letters. Heavy curtains were drawn across the
window, stopping any light from showing outside.

He went over to the machine now and logged off. The
screen went dark. Then he leant his hand against the wall
and looked at her. 'So, Roz. What can I do for you?' He
spoke with the bland politeness he used when he was talking
to Joanna.

She didn't know what to say to him. She hadn't thought.
She'd just needed to see him, needed that easy rapport she
was used to sharing with him, a tuning into each other's
moods. 'I just . . .' She didn't know what to say. She had
always been able to talk to Luke, but now the words just dried
up in her head. She found herself saying, 'I . . . wondered if
you'd looked at those files – Gemma's files. If you'd found
anything.'

He looked at his watch. 'It's commendable enthusiasm,
Roz, coming round so late with queries about work. *No*, is
the answer. I didn't find anything. And the reason I didn't
find anything? There wasn't anything to find.'

She had forgotten, after the events of the day, how angry
he'd been. She wanted to explain, but the expression of polite
inquiry on his face made talking, real talking, difficult. She
groped around for a subject. She needed to break the ice.
'Joanna . . .' she began.

'Look, Roz, I've had it up to here with Grey. One of the
big plusses of my life at the moment is that I don't have to
have anything to do with her. This flat is a Grey-free zone,
right? So whatever it is, tell someone else, OK?'

'OK. I thought you might want to know what's happening.
If you don't, well, fine . . .' Her voice tailed off into his silence.
'What are you doing?' She nodded at the computer that he'd
switched off.

He gave her a long look. 'Well, Roz, I hadn't quite decided. I thought I might set up a string of call girls. Or, on the other hand, I thought I might beat someone to death, truss them up like a prize turkey and dump them in a bath somewhere. What do you think?'

'Oh for Christ's sake, Luke, stop it!' She had seen him often enough before switching between coolness and hostility when someone had aroused his anger or his contempt. He would usually rage to her afterwards about the person who had offended him. 'Christ, Roz, what was it with that arsewipe?' He just kept looking at her, the hostility more overt now. She thought about the polite incomprehension that had masked the shell of Nathan, about the tears in Jenny's eyes when she talked about taking him back to the home. She thought about Nathan saying, 'I don't know . . .' and the flash of terror in his eyes that dissolved into blankness. *I'm too tired to play games, Luke!*

'I wanted to say I was sorry.' She looked at him, trying to gauge his reaction. He didn't say anything, just stayed where he was, watching her with that look of polite inquiry. 'I told you, I didn't know . . . what had happened to Gemma. I never really believed . . . But if I had known, I'd have known that you couldn't . . . That's all. If you'd thought about it, you would have realized.' She felt angry with him now, and the anger made his hostility easier to cope with.

He shrugged. 'OK. You've asked your question about the files. You've said you're sorry. Anything else?'

'Luke . . .' She didn't want to leave it like this.

He moved across the room to the door and opened it. 'What did I say that sounded like "I want to talk to you," Roz?'

OK, if that was the way he wanted it. 'I'll go, then.'

She couldn't resist slamming the front door behind her. She was halfway down the path before she realized it was raining again. The wet leaves of the shrubs overgrowing the path brushed against her legs. Her jacket wasn't waterproof and she hadn't brought her umbrella. Well, that was all right. She'd get wet. She headed down the road towards the bus stop, feeling the rain start to soak through her hair and drip down her neck. *Fuck him!* Luke, with his stiff-necked pride and his arrogance and his moodiness, just . . . *fuck him!*

16

Hull, Friday night

And now Anna just had to keep moving. The city streets raced past, cars and lights on the main roads, silent pavements and pools of darkness on the back streets. Anna, with nowhere to go, no plan, no place, no friend. She kept her eyes on the ground; her mind was a blank that refused to think. *Keep moving.* She had walked this way before, maybe an hour ago. She was coming to the road that divided the city centre from the docks. Across the road were the car parks and shops of the docks area. Somewhere she could find a quiet place, somewhere to sit down and think.

She was in quieter streets. She hadn't been this far before. There were people around now. A woman in a short skirt and cut-off top walked slowly by, close to the edge of the pavement. Her shoes had very high heels, looking heavy and out of proportion at the end of her long, thin legs. Her hair was fair in the streetlight. She stood on the corner for a moment, then turned and sauntered slowly back. She didn't seem to notice the cold that was chilling Anna through her coat. Anna retreated into a doorway. She knew what the woman was doing.

The woman was like a child's drawing, bright in the darkness. A woman behind a drawing, like the mechanical doll that had lain on the bed with Angel's . . . *friends? Clients?* You could do what you wanted with it, the doll. It would do all the things that you wanted it to do, and it didn't matter because the doll wasn't real. *Krisha's doll, its face smashed on the floor behind the translucent curtain of the shower smiling smil-*

ing . . . The woman who was like a drawing with her bright hair and her bright face, the features all drawn in bright colours, turned again in her saunter and a car drifted past, slow, silent, just the sticky noise of its tyres on the road. The woman stopped, looked, but the car passed and disappeared down the street. Anna shrank back in the doorway. But the driver had been – just a man, hunched down over the wheel, timid, nondescript.

Angel wouldn't be on the streets looking for her, not here, not at this time. The car was coming back now. The drawing woman had been expecting it. She had been watching out. She knew how they worked. Anna watched her make eye contact, watched her dip and smile, watched her move over as the car slowed, stopped, watched her lean into the open window and begin the negotiations. Then the door opened and she was in. The car drove off.

Anna moved out of the doorway and hurried down the road. Some of the streetlights weren't working, and the unevenness in the pavement made her stumble. A car went past her on the road and turned left ahead of her. She could hear the sound of another car behind her, and looked over her shoulder. The car was moving slowly. It was sleek and black. She turned round and kept walking, kept her head down inside her collar. *Go away, go away.*

The car drifted past her, slowing. The interior was dark and impenetrable. She hesitated. Turn back or walk past it? She couldn't stop now. She speeded up her steps; not quite a run but fast, purposeful, trying not to look at the car, her eyes pulled sideways as she drew abreast. A low hum. The car stopped, and the window began to slide down.

'Anna!' A hand circled her wrist as she leapt back, her heart hammering, her breath stopped in her throat. Her legs turned to paper, to water, as the car pulled away with a screech of rubber, leaving Anna gasping by the side of the road, seeing the edges of her vision start to darken and cloud at the edges. 'Anna!' And hands held her arms as the darkness retreated and her breathing slowed and Matthew was there, his face twisted with alarm and concern. 'I didn't mean

241

to frighten you, Anna. I've been looking for you. Why did you go? What are you doing?'

She knew what he thought. She tried to explain. 'I need . . . get away.' Her voice was catching in her throat, which felt dry and gritty. Matthew looked at her and touched her forehead with his hand, shaking his head. He carefully asked her no more questions. She kept looking at his face to see if there was reproach or disgust, but he was just frowning slightly, looking concerned as he helped her.

'Come back, Anna,' he said. 'Whatever this is, we can sort it out.'

She let him lead her back through the streets. 'I've got my car,' he said. 'That's how I saw you.' She remembered the car that had gone past a few minutes earlier. 'I didn't realize it was you at first.'

She shook her head. 'The police,' she said. 'The trouble.'

'I know,' he said. He looked worried. 'There's somewhere else I can take you. Listen, Anna, I'm going to see someone tomorrow. I told you.' They'd reached his car now and he opened the back door, looking round nervously. She thought about Angel, about the way he'd looked at her, about Matthew's smallness and his frailty, and was frightened for him.

She huddled down in the car, curled up on the back seat, keeping her head low. 'Keep out of sight,' he cautioned her. 'In case the police are looking for you.' He didn't say any more, but kept driving. She could hear the note of the engine change as he switched gear, felt herself pulled in different directions as he negotiated the corners. She could see the streetlights moving and turning above her head. It felt as though he was driving them through the back streets, keeping off the main roads. Then the car lurched and bumped as if they were driving over a badly rutted surface. 'It's all right,' he said in a low voice. 'I'm taking you back to the advice centre, but we're going by the back lane.'

She could remember it now, the uneven path she had run along in her earlier flight. She had done no good by that. She should have stayed, told him everything and let him help her if he could. Anna was tired of running. 'I am sorry,' she said.

'Anna . . .' His voice sounded tired. 'You're not to blame for what happened to you.' The car slowed and stopped. There were no lights here, and the darkness filled the car. His voice was low. 'I couldn't see anyone at the front when I went past. There's no one here. Listen, Anna, I daren't take you back in, not where you were. There's a place next door. It isn't very nice – I'm sorry – but I've used it before.'

He tucked the car in by the wall behind the centre, and helped her out. The moonlight made the wall gleam faintly in the night, but the car was in deep shadow. He pushed open the yard gate, and led her across to the high wall of the abandoned warehouse. She could remember rather than see boarded-up windows and broken glass. She heard muffled sounds, something being lifted, a slight grunt of effort, his breathing getting heavier. 'Matthew,' she whispered.

'It's all right,' he said. He was panting. 'It's just a bit heavy. The boarding over the door here – you can take it off.' He was silent for a moment and she could hear him catching his breath.

She thought about his twisted back and his awkward walk. 'Let me help,' she said.

'It's done, Anna.' His breathing was easier. 'Come on.'

She was aware of cold air in her face as he took her through the black hole that was the entrance. There were steps leading downwards. He held her arm to guide her. She heard a door open and close, the sound of a match and the sudden, sharp smell as it ignited. She saw his head turned away from her, narrow tiles, and then the light went. 'Got it,' he said. And then there was a brighter, steady light. He looked at her in the light of the storm lantern, smiling.

She was in a small room under the stairs, almost a cupboard. The walls were tiled in narrow white lines and the floor was flagged. There was a bench across one wall with a mattress on it. There was a small cubbyhole adjoining it with a deep sink low down on the wall, a tap and a bucket. The corridor went past the room and ended in a door. He put his hand over the lantern to dim the light, and tugged at the door. It opened into darkness. She felt a sense of space. 'Where . . . ?'

'It's the basement of the warehouse,' he said. 'It runs along underneath it. But be careful if you go through there. The lane runs along the back. Someone might hear you if you made a noise. Safer to stay in here.'

They sat together in the small room, and he gave her an anxious smile. 'Tell me what happened, Anna,' he said.

And she told him then, sitting quietly in the dark, and he listened to her story about Angel's friend, about the way she had hit him, about the stolen money. She told him about the woman in the bath, about how she'd run away. She heard his slight intake of breath then. 'You said – police. Looking for me,' she said. 'For a murder. I . . .' *I had to run!*

He sat there in silence when she'd finished, his hands clasped between his knees, his head hanging down. 'I wish you'd told me this at the beginning, Anna,' he said. She nodded. She should have done. She had let him help her again, before he had known what she had done. But his voice, when he spoke, was gentle. 'You did what you had to, Anna,' he said. 'Listen, this murder – it wasn't the man . . .' Here, the distaste in his voice was clear. 'This – man who hurt you. You're a witness, Anna, that's all. You found the woman in the hotel.' She felt a slow relief flowing through her.

He took her hand. 'Listen, Anna, you'll have to go to the police. No, don't panic. You've done nothing wrong. But there's your immigration status . . . I'll go and see this person who can help you. He'll know what to do.' He was looking worried again and she felt the anxiety start to gnaw. 'It's the weekend. I need to go to . . . It'll take a bit of time. And I'll have to find him. Anna, you might be in for a long wait. I may be gone overnight. Here –' he pointed to a carrier bag he'd dumped on the makeshift bed. 'There's some food in there: chocolate, some peanuts. And there's water in the tap. I'm afraid the plumbing's a bit . . .' She could see that his face looked uncomfortable. 'There isn't a . . . just a . . .'

She realized what he was trying to say and felt a wave of affection for him, to be embarrassed for her, after everything that had happened. She smiled at him. 'There is bucket,' she said.

He blushed and nodded. 'You'll be all right, Anna,' he said. 'I've used this place before.' And then he left her.

Roz fought her way through the storm to the bus stop, which was on the most exposed corner on the top of the hill. The wind cut through her. She could feel the damp start to seep through her clothes. She began to shiver. She'd forgotten to pick up her gloves in her sudden exit from Luke's and now her fingers were starting to ache with the cold. She shoved her hands deep into her pockets. The rain was getting heavier now, and she had to choose between standing in the inadequate shelter of the bus stop and peering through the obscured glass, or getting a clear view of any approaching bus but getting soaked in the process.

She could feel the loose change in her pocket. She pulled it out and checked it quickly. It was enough to get her back into town. Then she could go to the cashpoint and get money for a taxi. Maybe she could find a phone and get a taxi from here. They could stop at a cash machine. It would cost her a fortune but it would be worth it to get out of this cold. She looked round to see if she could see a call box. There was nothing in sight, but further down the hill on the corner where a cypress, its branches heavy with water, overhung the road, there was someone standing. She could see the glimmer of a light-coloured coat. Someone else waiting for the bus? That might mean a bus was due. She checked her watch and her heart sank. She hadn't realized how late it was. It was after midnight. There wouldn't be a bus at this time. She'd just leapt on to the bus outside the station on impulse. She hadn't thought about what she was doing, and now she was stranded in this godforsaken part of Sheffield in the freezing cold and wet with no idea about how or when she was going to get home.

The reflections of the streetlights danced as the rain

splashed up from the ground and the road stretched away in front of her, wavering and obscured in the shattered light. Headlamps appeared in the distance. A bus? No, a van that swept past sending a spray of water up from the gutter that splashed into the shelter and soaked her calves and feet.

She could feel the tears of self-pity begin to prick behind her eyes. She concentrated on the anger she felt at Luke and the tears retreated, but she could feel a bleak hollowness inside her that wouldn't go away. She had to make a decision. She couldn't spend the night standing in the bus stop. She looked behind her, towards the corner where the man had been waiting but now there seemed to be no one there. Or was there? The bushes around the tree moved in the wind making a shape like a man standing close in against the trunk . . . no, it was just the tree . . . she couldn't tell. She wrapped her damp jacket round her for the illusion of warmth, and set off down the road. There had to be a phone box somewhere on this route. And if there wasn't? Then she'd walk back into town. That was better than standing freezing at the bus stop.

Her shoes weren't waterproof and the rain had soaked through them. She could feel the wet cloth of her trousers clinging to her legs. *You should have thought this through, Bishop.* It was almost Luke's voice in her mind, the way he talked to her when they were disagreeing about the solution to a problem, or when they hit a snag in a project. *What makes you the authority, Hagan?* She was so tired and cold, it was hard to concentrate. There were no mirrors on the walls. Nathan looked at her and said, *I don't seem to do much.* She was falling asleep on her feet.

The storm abated for a minute, and in the new silence she thought she could hear someone walking in the road behind her. She remembered the figure waiting under the tree and glanced quickly over her shoulder. The road was empty. She told herself not to imagine things, but she was alone and it was dark and lonely. The houses were set back and the cars were few and far between.

She couldn't stop shivering now. A car swished past, sending up an arc of spray, and vanished into the darkness. There was someone on the road ahead of her now, walking quickly away from her down the hill, hunched into a light-coloured mac. She was walking into the wind, and it blew the sleet into her face and through the gaps in her jacket, wetting her, chilling her to the bone. Her face was starting to feel stiff and numb, and she put her head down and pulled the wet collar of her jacket round her.

When she looked up, the road was empty. Whoever had been walking ahead must have turned off at one of the side roads. She was approaching the end of Luke's road now. She could go back, ask to use his phone, but she wasn't sure if she could face his hostility again. A car was pulling out from a side road further down the hill. It was coming up the hill towards her, slowly, as though the driver wasn't sure where he was. It was illuminated briefly as it passed under the streetlight, a dark, expensive-looking car, and she felt a stab of envy for the person who was safe behind its wheel. She wondered why the driver was going so slowly. Looking for an address?

Then she wondered if she might be the target of the driver's attention. A single woman walking alone after midnight – he could be an opportunist . . . someone who'd driven past earlier and seen her on her own, vainly waiting for a bus that wouldn't come. The empty road and the silent houses told her that there was no one out here to help her. Without thinking about it, she turned the corner towards Luke's and speeded up her pace. His house was just across the road now. Through the sleet, she heard the note of the car engine change and she began to run. Car lights illuminated the road, and she heard the deeper engine note of acceleration. The shadows in the moving light disorientated her for a moment. She tripped, feeling the sting of gravel on her knee, and the car lights overwhelmed her, then she was scrambling to her feet and through the gate, hammering on his window, not bothering with the front door. 'Luke!' she shouted. 'Luke!' Silence, and the swish of car tyres on the road. She hammered on the door. Where was he?

Then the light went on and the door opened. The car swept by and into the darkness. She pushed past Luke and slammed the door shut behind her, leant against it breathing hard, feeling her legs start to shake as the shock took her. 'Roz?' Luke was looking at her in bewilderment. 'What . . . ?' He stared at her. 'For fuck's sake, look at you! What have you been doing?'

She looked down at herself. Her jacket was wet and her trousers were soaked. One trouser leg was ripped and her knee was bleeding. Water dripped from her hair and from her clothes on to the floor. Her face was numb with cold. 'I missed the bus,' she said. 'I just need to use your phone.' She heard her voice sounding so matter of fact and conversational that she started to laugh, then she was shivering so hard she could barely stand up.

He grabbed her wrist and pulled her through the door of his flat. 'Where's your car? What are you doing running round the streets at this time? Shit, Roz, sometimes you shouldn't be let out off a lead.' His face was tight with exasperation and concern.

'I came on the bus from the station.' He helped her peel off her wet jacket and draped it over the radiator. Her shoes, which were sodden, were leaving marks on the carpet. She pulled them off. Her socks were soaked, so she tugged at them, her fingers clumsy with the cold. 'I'd been to see Nathan. I just wanted . . .' What had she wanted? She bit her lip and the shivering overwhelmed her.

There was a look of regret on his face now. 'Of course you did,' he said. 'Come here.' He put his arms round her and held her close against him, pressing her face into the roughness of his jersey. 'I'm sorry I was a bastard. Oh, Christ, look at the state of you. Let's get you dried off.' She remembered him arriving at her house just five days ago, drenched in a sudden rainstorm, the night before the police came and took him away.

'I'm not the only one who doesn't know enough to come in out of the rain,' she managed through chattering teeth.

She felt him laugh as he steered her across the room. He

kept his arms round her as he picked up a towel from the bed and rubbed her hair. She tried to blot the worst of the wet from her clothes. 'You need to get out of these,' he said. He was right. The wet clothes were chilling her more and more. She fumbled with the cord at her waistband. The knot was damp and she couldn't untie it. Her fingers were too cold to undo the buttons of her cardigan.

He looked at her for a moment. 'Here,' he said. He untied the wet cord holding her trousers, frowning slightly as he concentrated on the knot, then he unbuttoned her cardigan. Her legs didn't want to hold her up. He kept one arm round her, supporting her as he pulled off her cardigan and her wet trousers. She leant against him and let him undress her, just moving enough to accommodate him. He pulled her shirt over her head, then reached behind her and unfastened her bra. She felt her breasts fall free as he slipped it down her arms.

Then he reached to the bed and pulled the quilt back. 'Lie down,' he said. He tucked the quilt round her. She felt like ice to her core, as if she would be cold forever. 'I seem to spend all my time putting you to bed these days, Bishop,' he said. 'Let's get you warm.' His voice was light, but his face was serious and intent. He pulled the jersey over his head, unfastened his jeans and slipped them off. He wasn't wearing anything else. He got into the bed beside her and pulled her against him. His skin felt fiery hot against hers. 'Ice maiden,' he said. He tucked her hands under his arms and wrapped his legs round hers. Then he just held her as he ran his hand gently up and down her back and talked to her about nonsense things, about the anomalies of the universe, about the mysteries of numbers; Luke-rambling, familiar, comforting, safe.

Slowly, the cold released its grip and the shivering stopped. The mattress felt like a cloud of cotton wool underneath her, and she was cocooned in his warmth. He ran his fingers through her damp hair. 'Is that better?' he whispered.

She looked up at him. 'Luke, I'm sorry I . . .'

Her touched her face. 'Ssh. Not now.' He kissed her and

she put her arms round him, tasted the smoky cannabis taste of his mouth, breathed in his closeness that felt so familiar, so right and yet so new. He ran his hands down her back, cupping her buttocks, stroking the inside of her thighs, touching her and teasing her with his fingers. He kissed her neck and her breasts and she arched her back pressing close to him. He put his hands on either side of her face and looked at her. 'Do you want this?' he said. 'Are you sure this is what you want?'

'Yes,' she said. 'Luke. Yes.' And she did. And he was whispering her name, *Roz*, and she could feel his erection hard against her stomach. He pushed her thighs apart and she guided him into her and he moved slow and gentle and deep and his warmth was all around her.

She could hear the wind driving the rain against the window. In her mind she could still see an empty road and a dark car moving silently towards her. She held him tighter and he said it again, *Roz*, as he moved and it was like a question, over and over, *Roz? Roz?* And the night and the fear dissolved and dispersed in her answer and her quickening delight. She had known Luke as careless and reckless, had known him as a loyal friend and as an exciting lover, had known his volatility, his sometimes cruel tongue and his restless anger. She had known his kindness too, but she had never experienced before his capacity for tenderness. If she had known it, she would never have walked away from him or have let him walk away from her.

17

Sheffield, Sunday morning

Between the university and the hospital, the houses are stone, with heavy gateposts and big gardens. Mature trees grow between the houses, shading them with their dense foliage in the summer, in winter, twisting their skeletal arms to the sky. The roads are a mixture, straight lines, crescents, cul-de-sacs. They look like residential streets, the houses with their gardens and their high-ceilinged spaces. At weekends the side roads are quiet enough for children to play, to run from house to house, to ride their bikes or skate or play football. But at the weekend, these roads are deserted.

During the week, the streets are thronged with students, the cars are parked up close to the garden walls, making it difficult for anyone trying to negotiate the pavement. Each house is an office, a department of the university, a discreet sign on each wall: University of Sheffield, Department of Cultural Studies. University of Sheffield, Department of European Studies. One cobbled cul-de-sac runs between the old church that has been converted into a drama studio, and an uncompromising square of terrace. During the week, drivers take a risk if they bring their cars up this road looking for parking space. The cars are sometimes double-parked, and there is no space to turn, leaving the driver with no option but to reverse into the busy main road. But at weekends, and on Sundays in particular, these streets are abandoned and devoid of life, the houses shut up tight against intruders, the pavements empty of cars and people.

The old gardens are mazed with paths and walkways to

facilitate travel from one department to another. A high-walled gennel forms part of this system, running along the back of a red-brick building, behind the road that forms a T with the top of the cul-de-sac.

The storm from the night before had not blown out. A thin wind cut through anyone out on the streets that morning, and flurries of rain spattered against pavements and windows. It was a day to look out of the window and go back to bed. The woman who was walking up the cul-de-sac wrapped her coat around herself and thought of the warm bed she had left half an hour before. She wouldn't have dreamed of using the gennel at night, but in daylight it was a convenient shortcut from her flat to her department. She was a researcher who worked in one of the old stone houses, and to her, Sunday was another useful working day. It seemed a crime to drive a car for such a short distance, just ten minutes' walk if she used the short-cut, but as yet another spatter of rain blew into her face, she wondered if she shouldn't have compromised on her principles for once.

The ground was sodden, and the rain had turned the footing into a treacherous mass of mud and dead leaves. The cul-de-sac was neglected, and the surface was a patchwork of new repairs and old cobbles that were slippery under her shoes. As she entered the gennel, the air, shut in by the high walls, smelt of wet decay and the grey light of the winter morning dimmed. She wrapped her scarf more closely round her neck, and picked her way carefully along the narrow alley.

It was silent down there in the grey shadows. The walls shut off the sound of the city, the distant roar of traffic, the drone of planes, the church bells, the sounds you didn't notice until they were no longer there. The sudden silence made her aware of how alone she was, and she looked back to the entrance to the gennel, and ahead to the brighter light at its end. Her pace quickened.

There was a heap of something half blocking the path. It looked like a pile of dead leaves and rubbish, and she edged her way round it, trying to stop her coat from brushing against the crumbling wall. Her foot caught against the leaves, disturbing the pile so that it shifted, the wet clamminess touching against her shin. She moved her foot backwards to free it from the leaves, grimacing with distaste. Something cold gripped her round the ankle.

She jumped back instinctively, slipping on the wet ground, falling as the hand that the dislodged leaves had revealed kept its hold on her. She heard the scream stifle in her throat as she saw the hand, blue and claw-like, touching her, gripping her, and she couldn't get free. She scrabbled backwards on the ground, her breath coming in panicky gasps, struggling to release herself as the whole leaf pile began to move as she pulled away.

Then she was free and she was clawing in the mud, trying to push herself into the wall, trying to regain her feet before the thing in the leaves came after her and pulled her into the darkness, and she was making mewing sounds in her throat and she couldn't get away, and . . . The hand was still. Now her leg was free, the hand was still. Almost weeping with terror, she staggered to her feet. She could see it now, the shape in the leaves, the rigid claw of the hand protruding, and as she looked, the lineaments of a face began to form in the shadows of the leaf pile, the mouth gaping, the eyes staring upwards.

It was the smell of coffee that woke Roz. As she surfaced from sleep, she was aware of a dim light on her closed eyes, the warmth of a quilt tucked closely round her, the smell of coffee and toast. She stretched and turned over, opening her eyes. The curtains had been opened slightly to let in the daylight. The sky looked grey and cold. The clock by the side of the bed said eight-thirty. She could hear the sudden gusting of the wind and the rattle of rain against the glass, and she snuggled down under the covers, feeling a moment of almost childlike comfort and warmth. She lay with her eyes shut, listening to the sounds. A door closing nearby, the sound of water running, the clatter of pots. Then Luke was sitting on the edge of the bed, putting a tray down between them, with cups of coffee, toast and orange juice. His hair was wet from the shower. He looked unshaven and heavy-eyed, but his smile was warm. 'Breakfast,' he said, and leant across to kiss her.

To her surprise, she was hungry. She realized that she'd eaten very little the day before, and the hot buttered toast, the rich coffee and the sweetness of the orange seemed like the best things she had ever tasted. Luke didn't have much, just drank coffee while he watched her. 'You're starving,' he said after a while. 'I'm a lousy host. You come round at midnight in the freezing cold and I sling you out into the rain. Once you're good and wet I drag you back in here and shag you senseless.'

Roz finished the last piece of toast and looked at him. 'That bit was all right,' she said, licking butter off her fingers. 'That bit was fine. I could have done without the rain.' She put her cup down and stretched. 'The bed's full of crumbs.'

He poured himself another cup of coffee. 'Go and grab a shower. I'll sort it.'

The hot water of the shower felt luxurious after the remembered cold of the night before. It seemed OK to borrow Luke's toothbrush. She wrapped herself in a towel and went back to where he was leaning back on the pillows watching the winter weather. She curled up next to him and he put his arm round her. She rested her head on his shoulder, looking at the bleak winter landscape. She felt warm and relaxed. 'I haven't got any clothes,' she said. 'Mine got soaked.'

'You don't need them.' He smiled at her and pushed her gently back on to the bed. 'Got anything better to do today, Bishop?'

They spent the morning in bed, making love, talking, watching the rain that fell with a relentless persistence, drenching torrents when the wind dropped, wild spray as the storm blew up again. They talked about a lot of things, catching up on the months of estrangement, talked about things that had seemed off limit before. She told him about her visit to her mother-in-law's to see Nathan, she told him

254

about the eighteen months after Nathan's illness when she had tried to look after him, the eighteen months of increasing chaos that had culminated in the attack that had sent her down the precipitous staircase. 'I gave up after that,' she said. 'I knew I couldn't do it any more. He had to go into a nursing home. I couldn't manage. I don't think Jenny will ever forgive me.'

'Has it ever crossed your so-called mind that maybe she understands? If he doesn't know you from Adam, if he gets so scared he attacks you, what can you do?' The exasperation in his voice was the old, familiar Luke.

'Why didn't you phone me?' she said. 'When I left those messages? I kept waiting for you to phone and you didn't.'

He looked down at her. 'What messages?'

'I left them on your answering machine. Just saying that I didn't think . . . you know.'

He shook his head. 'I didn't get any messages. That's why I was so pissed off with you. One minute you're telling me that you think I killed . . .'

'I never did,' she protested. 'I never said that.'

'Shut up and listen. One minute you're calling me a killer and the next minute you're banging on my door at midnight and babbling about files, and Grey, and being sorry. I never got any messages.' Talking brought the reality back and he frowned, uneasy, reminded of something he didn't want to think about. 'Roz, what made you think – even for a moment – that I'd hurt Gemma? I haven't lifted a finger to anyone, not since I was a kid.'

'Nathan never lifted a finger to anyone,' she said. 'And then he knocked me out and broke my ankle. I never thought . . . And suddenly you were different. And there were the pictures. I felt as though I didn't know you any more.'

'The pictures.' He gave a half laugh that sounded angry. 'I was going to tell you that night, and then I lost my rag.'

She remembered the night in her kitchen when he had come back from his interview with the Hull Police. 'Tell me what?'

'I don't know where to start,' he said. 'I think I've been a complete arse and I don't know what to do.' He lay back on the pillow. 'Oh, shit. It's all a mess. I told them some of it, but they didn't believe me. I don't think they did.'

'Told them what?' Roz shook him. 'Luke, what is it?'

'OK.' He propped himself up on his elbow and looked down at her, running his hand up and down her arm. Then he looked out of the window. 'It was never a big thing, you know, me and Gemma. I was so pissed off with you, Roz. What the fuck did you want from me? I couldn't work it out. And she was missing her guy in Novosibirsk. She wasn't going to see him for ages, unless she could pull off another grant from somewhere.' He pulled a face. 'I'm such an arse-hole. I thought you needed to know that I wasn't on tap just for when you wanted me. And her guy was in the middle of a divorce, so it was all a mess.'

'Stefan Nowicki,' Roz said.

He looked surprised. 'How did you know? Did Gemma tell you?'

Roz shook her head. 'It was a guess. He was her supervisor.'

Luke gave a faint grin. 'Christ. I'm glad I didn't have to shag my supervisor. OK, yes, that's who it was. So we'd get pissed together, do pills, drown our sorrows . . .'

'You mean you weren't . . . You didn't . . . It wasn't a sex thing?' as he spoke, she'd felt the bitter twist of jealousy. She wanted to believe that he and Gemma had not been lovers.

'Don't be stupid, Roz. Of course it was. Best way to drown your sorrows that I know of. But she was off in a few months – sooner, if she could get the go-ahead.' He closed his eyes. 'I liked her a lot. Don't get me wrong. She was all right, was Gemma.'

Roz was angry with herself. She wondered why she had never understood, at the time, what Luke was feeling. None of this should have happened. But there had to be more. What Luke had just told her didn't account for the deep unease she sensed in him.

After a few minutes, he began talking again. 'Those photo-graphs.'

Roz tensed. She still found the photographs disturbing – not just the fact that Luke had taken them, but the overtones of dark violence that she sensed in the pictures. 'I hate those photographs,' she said.

'I didn't take them. What do I know about photography? It was her Russian guy, this Stefan. She showed them to me – that was what started . . . OK? But then she had that break-in, and the photos went along with all the other stuff.' He sighed. 'That was when the stupid bit began. Gemma was worried the photos might reappear, get Nowicki into trouble. His wife didn't know about Gemma, right, and the divorce was all getting sorted – so she asked me to say I'd taken them if they ever turned up somewhere embarrassing.'

'So you let me think . . .' That hurt. He hadn't trusted her enough to tell her the truth about the photographs.

'Yes. I'm sorry, Roz. But you were all management-speak and Grey this and Grey that. You weren't like yourself any more.' He looked at her. 'I thought you were rubbing my nose in it. I told you. I've been a complete arse.' He lay back on the pillows staring at the ceiling. 'There's something else. That morning, the morning of the meeting, the pictures turned up.' His face was pale, tense. 'I'd been helping Gemma set up a website, private work – she wanted to get some money behind her. We were coming in early and working on it. She wasn't online at her flat.' He looked at her. 'OK, I know. Misuse of university property.' Roz didn't care about that. 'It was all on Gemma's machine. I went to check it out when she didn't come in – after you told me about the e-mail. I thought she might have left a message. I went up on the site, and they were there, the pictures.'

'On the website?'

He nodded. 'I thought she must have found them and put them there herself – a kind of joke to let me know. I took them off – you know, OK, I've seen them, kind of thing. And then she didn't come back.' He took a deep breath. 'But the really, really stupid thing was what I told the police. They showed me the pictures and started going on about Gem being a prostitute. I thought they must have got it from the website – kinky pictures and stuff about discreet document vetting. I thought I must have done something stupid when I took them off, left them up there somehow. So I told them I'd taken the pictures. I knew she wasn't a prostitute, that the pictures didn't mean . . . And I'd promised her. It seemed like just one thing I could do. The police said she'd phoned this number. If I'd been here – maybe she was in trouble then. I keep thinking that. If I'd been here, then maybe I could have done something.' He frowned as though he'd thought of something. 'If she'd phoned, she'd've left a message. I think my answering machine must be fucked. It was OK before, though.' Roz remembered that he'd got the message about Gemma's laptop. 'So I told the police, and then later I find out that the pictures had turned up on this porn site. And I was stuck with what I'd told them.'

'And you haven't . . . Luke, you've got to tell them now. Listen, those photos were on a disk in my office. How did Gemma get them if they'd been stolen?' And she hadn't told the police.

'I don't know. Think about it, Roz. They're not going to knock themselves out looking around. I'm the perfect ready-made suspect. And the photos only make it worse. I lied to them. There's no proof those photos were stolen. Gemma never reported *that*.'

Roz closed her eyes. Luke was right. It was all a mess. 'I still don't understand about the disk,' she said. 'The one with the photographs on. Why did Gemma scan them on to a disk?'

'I don't think she did,' he said. 'She behaved as though they were the only copies she had, when they were stolen.' Luke disentangled himself and stood up, pulling on the jeans he'd discarded on the floor the night before. He was pulling away from her, as though the things he was telling her were putting the distance back between them.

'And you haven't told . . .'

'Anyone, until now.' He looked at her, anticipating what

258

she was going to say. 'I can't tell the police, Roz. Not now. Gemma's machine was wiped, remember? There's nothing left.' He ran his fingers through his hair.

'So where did the police get them? The pictures?' Roz was trying to sort out what he'd told her.

'That's what I've been trying to find out. They said they got them off an escort site – you know, a rent-a-shag site. I've been trying to find it. I've written a program that will do a picture search – look for a particular image on the net.' He shook his head before she could speak. 'All I've found so far have been some pretty amazing porn sites.' He looked at her and there was a glint of humour in his eyes.

'That was what you were doing when . . .' She felt a sudden surge of relief.

'Oh, yeah, Grey.' He dismissed it. He looked defeated. 'I've given up, more or less. Someone was messing around with that website, but what would finding the pictures prove? I don't know if it's worth it.'

Roz thought about what he'd told her. She thought about Friday night when she had stayed late for the meeting that Marcus Holbrook had set up. She thought about the tall figure moving away from her, just through the swing doors. *Whoever it was beat her up and then strangled her. And then he posed her obscenely in a hotel bathroom.* She reached for Luke's hand as the cold of the night before washed over her.

Attendance at Mass had been as poor as it always was these days. The priest walked down the central aisle, his head bowed in recognition of the Presence on the altar before him. The sanctuary lamp burned in the darkness, the gilding of the altar shining faintly in the shadows. He walked slowly across to the side aisle, suddenly uneasy, suddenly unwilling to look. He read the inscription at the base of the statue. *Requiem eternam dona eis, Domine: et lux perpetua luceat eis.* 'Eternal rest grant unto them, O Lord: and may perpetual light shine upon them.'

He wasn't surprised when he saw that the candles were there again. He had begun watching out, not knowing if this was an act of hope – the candles proclaiming a faith that the life of the soul would continue after death – or a cry of despair, a plea that one day the visitor would be reunited with some lost loved one, and that they would share the eternal bliss of Paradise. Today was Septuagesima Sunday, the day on which to consider the consequences of sin – physical and spiritual death. Maybe the mysterious visitor, the person who lit the candles, had gained some comfort from the words of the Mass.

Then he noticed that another candle had been lit. There were four candles, not three, and one of the cards where requests for prayers could be written had been slipped into the box. With a sense of quickening unease, he looked at it, but it was not illuminating.

Lamb of God, who takest away the sins of the world, grant her rest.

Hull, Sunday morning

The cold spell had passed, taking away the bright clarity of the frosty air, and leaving behind a grey dampness. A fog came down over the city, trapping the pollution from the cars, from the chemical plants, so that the wet air stung and burned against the skin.

Lynne Jordan lingered over breakfast – fruit, yoghurt, coffee and toast. She preferred to get up an hour earlier and have her day get off to a leisurely start, than have the extra time in bed and a stress-inducing scramble. She sat in the window, watching the estuary appear and vanish through the mist. In summer, she would be able to sit on the small balcony and watch the sea birds and smell the salt water – even on tainted water like the Humber, a tainted sea like the North Sea, it was worth living so close. She remembered Friday night, with Roy, and smiled, stretching. She felt good.

The memory of the sea stayed with her through the drive in to work, and made the routine of paperwork more bearable as she went through her in-tray at eight-thirty. 'Christ,' she grumbled to her assistant, 'Who thinks up all this stuff?' Farnham had sent through a box of papers that had been collected from Gemma Wishart's flat with a note to say that his team had found nothing relevant but that she might like to have a look. The report was in from York as well, from the expert Farnham had asked to look again at the Katya tapes. She opened the report with a sense of anticipation – she was curious about the reservations that Gemma Wishart had expressed to her colleagues. But it wasn't illuminating. His findings supported the original ones – Katya was a Russian speaker, probably from Eastern Siberia. There were items on the tape that he couldn't account for – brief sections, words and phrases that he didn't recognize. He proposed that the speaker might be bilingual, and might speak one of the many languages that co-existed with Russian in that vast area, but which one he was unable to say.

She looked at the pile of papers in front of her: letters, diaries, research notebooks, articles – the miscellany of someone who collected paper she thought was important.

OK, discard the diaries from the period before Wishart's trip to Russia. The letters had been sorted by date and sender. Lynne put all the letters dated '97, '98 and '99 to one side. The research notebooks related to Wishart's travels in Russia, and they were carefully labelled: *April 1998, Novosibirsk; July 1999, Dudinka*. There were four notebooks. Maybe the diaries or the letters would help her to narrow her search down.

The diaries were purely a business record of appointments, deadlines, meetings – no personal notes or comments. They reminded Lynne of her own diaries, which told a story, but only to someone who knew the significance of particular names, particular places. Lynne spread out the map and pored over the areas where Gemma Wishart had worked. She checked the written notes on the transcript. *YO*. Could that be a place? There was a city or a town to the east of Gorky called Yoshkar Ola, but that was hundreds of miles away from anywhere that Gemma had travelled. She made a note to check, and went back to the map. Gemma had spent time in Novosibirsk and in Dudinka. Dudinka was on the Yenisei River – but that didn't give her 'YO'.

Was it worth trawling through the books of research

notes? Lynne certainly wasn't up to that task at this stage. She looked at the contents pages. Gemma Wishart had listed, roughly, the contents of each book. Inside, there were more detailed notes about the backgrounds of the people she had recorded, and, in some cases, transcripts of the tapes she had made. She looked at the contents page of the notebook marked *Dudinka*:

1. *Male, 63. Fisherman. Russian, Nenets*
2. *Female, 19, Factory worker, Russian, Nenets, English (some)*
3. *Female, 31, Surveyor, Russian, English*
4. *Male, 16, Student, Russian, Ostyak, German (some)*
5. *Female, 18, Student, Russian, Ket, English (some)*
6. *Female, 25, Teacher, Russian, Selkup*

There were two notebooks for Novosibirsk, one for Dudinka and one for Igarka. She photocopied the contents pages. Perhaps she ought to get Greenhough looking over these books, see if he could track down what Gemma Wishart had been looking for. She sent the contents pages to him as a starting point.

She went back to Gemma Wishart's report and her transcript of Katya's tape. Something wasn't fitting together, and she didn't know where to look. Greenhough said that Katya was probably bilingual – not unusual, apparently, in that part of Russia. Gemma Wishart seemed to think it was important to get a translation of those words – she had been searching and consulting. But what could four words tell her? Wishart's search had taken her to someone called Marcus Holbrook, some kind of authority in the Russian language. Farnham's men had talked to him, but he hadn't been able to shed any light on what she had been looking for. Lynne's mind felt like porridge. She wasn't finding any way through this.

She had Greenhough's home number. He was defensive at first, thinking she was criticizing his report, but once he realized she was simply seeking information, he thawed. *Aca-*

demics. 'I'm not an expert in the languages of Russia,' he said. 'It's not my field at all.'

'Who would you suggest?' Lynne said. For Christ's sake, he was an expert in Russian, wasn't he? How hard could it be?

He laughed. 'Good question. Look, Inspector Jordan, I don't even know how many languages we're talking about here. I can think of six without even trying – Ossetian, Yiddish, Mordvin, Tatar, Chechen, Georgian. There could be fifty, sixty, even more. I'm not sure anyone could give you an exact number. And it's not something that's researched much over here. You'd need to go to a Russian university, and even then you'd have trouble.' Lynne was quiet as the implications of this sank in. 'Inspector Jordan?' he said.

'Sorry. I was thinking it over. I was led to believe that Dr Wishart might have identified the language.'

'Well,' his voice was sceptical. 'I spoke to one of her colleagues, Rosalind Bishop. She had been told, quite erroneously, that the problem sections were colloquial Russian. Which they most certainly were not.'

Lynne felt her mind start to focus. 'Who told her that?'

Greenhough was silent for a moment. When he spoke, he sounded reluctant. 'I think she'd misunderstood something she'd been told,' he said.

'By who, Dr Greenhough?' Lynne tried to keep the asperity out of her voice.

'He's a well thought of expert in the Russian language. In this country. So he certainly wouldn't have made that mistake.' Lynne waited. 'He's based at Sheffield now, but he's retired. Marcus Holbrook, Professor Holbrook.'

Holbrook. 'He retired through ill health,' Greenhough said. 'He had a heart attack a few years ago.'

'So what does he do now?' Lynne wasn't sure why she was pursuing this, but someone, possibly this Holbrook character, seemed to have been pulling the wool over someone's eyes about this tape, and she wanted to know why.

'Academics never stop researching,' Greenhough said indulgently. 'And he's involved in student exchanges. Students come from Russian schools and universities into this country, we send ours over there, it all sets up links. Marcus has lots of contacts over there, so he set up privately once he retired.'

I bet he did, Lynne thought as she put down the phone. *I just bet he did.*

When she went to Roy Farnham's office she found him poring over an atlas, a file of papers fanned out on the desk in front of him. He frowned when he saw her, but then gave her a quick smile and said, 'I'm a bit pushed, Lynne. Can it wait?'

'I don't think so.' She told him about her conversation with Greenhough, about Holbrook's business interests.

It took him a moment to take on board what she was saying, and then the slightly distracted air he'd had as she came through the door vanished. 'How the fuck did we miss that?' he said.

How the fuck did I miss it, Lynne thought. She appreciated the fact that he'd said 'we', but she was the one who had been trying to identify Katya. She should have found it. 'Right,' he went on. 'It gives us another link. This Holbrook character is bringing students over from Russia, Wishart is looking at a tape from a Russian woman . . . OK. We haven't quite got it. We need the connection. I want Holbrook's operation under the microscope. Let's see if there's anything dodgy about it. I want him interviewed. I want any link between him and Hagan.' He frowned. 'Christ, I need those new people yesterday.'

He had turned back to his desk, and was tapping his finger on the atlas, his eyes screwed up with thought. 'What is it?' she said.

'Look.' She leaned over the map with him. 'Wishart spent three years in Russia. In Siberia. Your Katya was Russian – from Siberia. And now we've got this Holbrook character. Gemma Wishart came back to work in this country and came to Sheffield – where Holbrook has his business. There are too many connections. I don't like coincidences.' His finger traced a line across the page. 'She travelled all across this part – from the Yenisei River, here, Dudinka, right?' Lynne looked. Dudinka was a port on the mouth of the river. 'Across to here, Beloye More, the White Sea. That's over fifteen hundred miles.'

'When did she do that?' Lynne tried to relate the flat colours on the page to the reality that Farnham was describing.

'Ninety-eight, according to her mother. She showed me some of the letters Gemma sent.' Lynne kept her face towards the map, but glanced sideways at his face and was surprised to see lines of tension by his mouth, the downward turn of sadness and regret.

Gemma Wishart would have been just twenty-three when she went wandering that vast expanse, from the ice-bound port of Arkhangelsk to the Kara Sea. She'd travelled in a country that was undergoing turmoil and upheaval. A woman with a taste for adventure. Lynne remembered the glint of amusement in her eyes as she spoke at the meeting where they had met. She remembered the same glint in the eyes of the woman in the photographs. A woman who would pose for bondage photographs with that gleam of challenge on her face. A woman with a taste for risk? A woman who had died violently.

But Farnham was pulling her attention back to the map again. 'Coincidences,' he said. He waited to see if Lynne would see the connection that he had.

'Arkhangelsk,' Lynne said. 'Archangel. Angel Escorts. Mr Rafael.' She looked at him. 'If someone is bringing women into the country, from Russia . . . Was Wishart involved?'

'She'd have had the contacts,' Farnham said. 'But – it doesn't feel right. She was only twenty-three when she was over there. And we've been over her personal stuff already. I told you, she wasn't making any extra money – not that we've been able to find. If escort work would have been lucrative, what would trafficking be worth?'

'But she would have had the contacts. Was someone else using her?'

He nodded. 'That's where I want to look. I was looking at

Luke Hagan. Now there's this Marcus Holbrook. This has to go to Immigration. I'll contact Special Branch. Holbrook's operation needs to go under the microscope.'

There was a knock on the door. DS Anderson came into the room. 'Mrs Rafiq's in Interview 3, sir,' he said.

Farnham glanced quickly at Lynne and said, 'OK, I'll be along. Five minutes, Tom.' The door closed. He looked at her in silence for a moment then said, 'She's my best line to Anna Krleza.'

Lynne felt winded. She hadn't expected this, not without her involvement, not without consultation. 'I thought we'd agreed about Rafiq,' she protested.

'We discussed it,' he said. 'But I want information. And I need it quickly. I know you want Rafiq to help you with the trafficking thing, Lynne, but this is murder. It has priority.'

Nasim Rafiq would know where Farnham's information had come from. The fragile trust that Lynne had begun to establish would be shattered by the force that Farnham could bring to bear in his search for the killer of Gemma Wishart. And the ammunition he was going to use was the ammunition that Lynne had given him. Her careful work was about to be steam-rollered into the ground, and Nasim Rafiq would be the casualty. She stepped firmly on her anger – it wouldn't help her here – and thought quickly. 'If I'd known you were going to move so fast, I'd have put the pressure on, got her some guarantees.'

'I know. You told me.' He was looking down at her, his voice careful, professional.

Lynne had a sudden flashback to Friday night and felt herself flush. This was why she was wary of mixing work and her personal life. But it had been her decision and she had to take the consequences. 'I want to sit in on the interview,' she said. Rafiq was her witness.

'I was going to ask you anyway,' he said. 'Once we'd got her here. But I want this fast and certain. Matthew Pearse seems to have vanished.'

Lynne felt anxiety tighten her stomach as she thought

266

about the gently spoken man with the compelling eyes. 'Since when?'

'Just since last night,' Farnham said. 'He was supposed to be at the advice centre, but he wasn't there when we went to look for him. He hasn't been home, either. No one's seen him.' His voice was matter of fact, but the implications of what he was saying were clear in his voice.

She could understand the reason for his urgency. She couldn't argue any more. He was looking impatient now. He wanted to get on. 'And the advice centre?' she said.

'I've got search warrants.'

Thanks a bunch, Farnham! She was silent for a moment as she got her anger under control. 'I thought you were keeping me informed,' she said.

'I'm telling you now, Lynne, that's why we're having this conversation. We're searching Pearse's place and the advice centre. Are you in on this?'

She took a deep breath. 'I'm in, of course.' Whatever was going on at the advice centre would disappear now. She'd played her cards too close to her chest, waiting for something more definite, and now she had no ammunition to stop him.

Matthew Pearse's face stayed in her mind as she followed Farnham down the corridor. She remembered his suppressed anger when he had spoken about the plight of the trafficked women – on the wrong side of crime and on the wrong side of the law – and the compassion in his voice. But if he had been helping them to escape, and helping other illegal immigrants to escape the debt bonds of the people who smuggled them in, then he had made some dangerous enemies. She thought about Katya and her lonely death. It didn't matter what the post-mortem results were, or what an inquest might say. Katya had been murdered – everything in her experience told her that. But Katya, an unknown prostitute, was expendable. Matthew Pearse hadn't thought that. She wondered if the gentle man with the twisted back and the determined eyes had any inkling of how dangerous the people he opposed could be.

But when she had talked to him, he had treated her as if she was the dangerous one.

Sheffield, Sunday

N Floor was deserted, the corridor lights turned low. Roz had a queasy flashback to Friday night as she stepped out of the lift. Luke was looking round him with a frown, as though he was revisiting a place that didn't quite match his memories of it. Roz went to her room. The CD that Sean had given her just the other day, the archive, was in her desk drawer. 'Computer room,' Luke said.

He barely reacted to the newly arranged furniture and the boxes of equipment that were in there awaiting Joanna's new organization. 'She doesn't waste time,' was all he said. He loaded the archive on to his computer, and began playing around with the program. 'It's not bad,' he said after a few minutes, which was about as near as he ever came to praise of something he hadn't written himself.

Roz pulled up a chair and sat next to him, looking at the screen. 'Gemma wanted something from that,' Roz said, 'and I don't think Holbrook wanted her to have it.' She'd told him about Holbrook, his abrupt unfriendliness, the way he'd tried to mislead her. 'He was supposed to meet me here,' she said. 'He fixed this late meeting time and then he never turned up. There was someone here, though, in the section. It was odd . . .'

'You're being paranoid.' But he took her hand. 'I'll ride shotgun for you, Bishop. If there's anything here, we'll get it sorted. Don't worry.' He kissed her palm and closed her fingers. Then he turned back to the screen. 'Now, what are we looking for?'

They searched the archive first for the items that Gemma had queried on the transcript. *Jugun*, the word that Holbrook had said was Russian and that Greenhough had said was not. There was nothing there. Then they tried the odd phrase *Ba-yi-n-sal*. A Russian colloquialism, according to Holbrook. Nothing of the sort, according to Greenhough. Again, there was nothing. In desperation, Roz tried *cat* and *cats*. Nothing.

'If he didn't want her to find it, he probably removed it,' Luke said.

'Can you check? Do your deleted data thing?' Roz hadn't really expected to find what they were looking for so quickly, but she felt frustrated anyway.

Luke was jumping through the systems now, getting a grip on the way the archive worked. 'It looks quite simple,' he said. 'It won't do as much as the one we're developing.' He thought about her question. 'Didn't what's-his-face tell you this was a new version or something?'

'Sean. Well, he said it was a pilot version. He said Holbrook was still working on it.' She tried to remember if Sean had said anything else.

'OK,' Luke said. 'But that means if anything was deleted, it might have been deleted before this was put together. There's no trace of any major changes on here.'

'Couldn't you look at the programming?' she said.

'Not without the source code. Anyway, that would take . . . Let's see what it'll do and what it won't do. We might find something there.'

They worked for an hour. Holbrook's program was designed to give the researcher as much information as possible about the way in which Russian speakers used their language. It allowed you to ask questions about different pronunciations, about variations in dialects of Russian, about the drift of Americanisms into the language. But it gave them no indications of what Gemma might have been looking for. After an hour, they came to a stop. They'd tried the queried phrases from the transcript. Nothing. They'd tried looking for evidence of recent deletions from the archive. Nothing. They'd tried to look for anomalies in the way the program worked. Nothing.

Luke rubbed his face. They were both tired. 'What do you want to do?' he said.

Roz shook her head. She felt both apprehensive and weary. After what Luke had told her, she had a sense of time running out. How long would it be before the police found *something* they could use to connect Luke to Gemma's death?

She knew as well as anybody the fallibility of the justice system, the difficulty with which the errors of the law could be redressed. She had a sudden, almost farcical picture of a future, her husband trapped in the cage of his illness and her lover behind the physical bars of the prison gate. She realized that Luke had said something. 'What?'

'Coffee,' he said. 'I'll sort us out some coffee. We'll have to have it black, OK?' She nodded absent-mindedly, staring at the monitor. Whatever Gemma had wanted was in there somewhere. There had to be a way to find it. She closed her eyes and let her mind drift. *Jugun. Ba-yi-n-sal.* What was it and what did it mean? What was the woman saying that was so important? One of their problems was that the program was designed to look for pronunciation. They didn't know how the words or phrases were spoken. She was having to rely on Gemma's transcript. If they didn't know what the language was, they couldn't work out how to pronounce it. If they couldn't get the pronunciation right, they wouldn't be able to find it on the archive.

Her mind began to focus. Gemma must have known what it was to have written it down the way she did. *Jugun* might have been a guess – a shot at representing the pronunciation, though Gemma usually used phonetic script for words she didn't recognize. They all did. But *Ba-yi-n-sal.* She *had* to have known what that was to have written it so precisely. So if she knew what it was, what language it was, what had she been looking for in Holbrook's archive? That wouldn't have given her a translation. Something was nagging in her mind now, something that was going to come clear, was going to . . .

'Gemma wasn't looking for a translation,' she said. 'And she knew what it was.'

He stopped what he was doing and came across to her. 'OK,' he said slowly. 'How do you work that out?'

She explained her thinking. 'And listen, Holbrook said that Gemma didn't give him anything for his archive, but he's been lying about everything else. So he's probably lying about that. What if Gemma . . .' Then she saw the flaw in her argument. 'No, that wouldn't work.'

'Come on, Roz, I'm not a mind reader. What wouldn't work?' Luke pulled out a chair and sat down opposite her, listening.

'I thought maybe she was looking for the tape she'd donated, but she could just go to her own originals. It'd be easier to find from there, anyway.' But she still had the feeling it was on the tip of her tongue, the thing they were looking for.

Luke shook his head. 'You didn't pay too much attention to what Gemma was doing,' he said. 'The break-in, remember? Someone helped themselves to her cassette player and all her music. They just scooped up the case with all her tapes in – including her old research tapes.'

'No back-ups?' Roz said.

He shook his head. 'She started backing everything up after that. That was why I knew there should have been back-ups in the department when her computer was wiped. That was why I went after Grey for a proper back-up system. No, she lost all her tapes. The stupid thing was, they wouldn't even have wanted a load of tapes of Russian.' Luke looked at her speculatively. 'Or would they?'

'So that must have been it. She wanted to check one of her tapes.' Roz felt a moment of triumph, and then a sense of letdown as she realized that, without Gemma's originals, this didn't get them much further. She tapped her pen against her teeth as she thought.

'Shit, Bishop.' Luke took the pen out of her hand. 'Drive me round the bend, why don't you?' He tossed the pen on to the desk. 'So, where does it get us?'

'If we can find out what it was,' Roz said, 'we might be able to work out why Gemma thought it was important.' She rubbed her eyes. 'I wish my Russian was better,' she said. 'It's like driving blindfolded.'

She racked her memory. She reached past Luke and typed in 'Kat'. The program barely paused. *Search item not found.* 'Shit.' Luke looked at her in mild surprise. Roz rarely swore. 'I though it might be the spelling,' she said. 'Whatever Gemma meant when she wrote "*Cats??*" on the transcript. I don't

271

know how the other things are pronounced, but . . .' She remembered her conversation with Holbrook:

How would a Russian speaker pronounce 'cat'?

In Russian? It's something like korshka. *Or* kort, *for a tomcat. It doesn't sound a lot like the English.'*

I meant the English word.

You'd get a pronunciation like kort, *something like that . . .*

But Holbrook had told her lies. Greenhough hadn't said that: *You'd get something like an 'e' sound, something like 'cet'.*

Now it was clear. 'It's been under our noses all the time,' she said. 'It's on the transcript.' She reached past him again, and typed in 'Ket'. She pressed the 'find' button. And the program immediately responded, jumping to a page of information about minority languages in Russia. It was a short section halfway down a page:

Ket *or Yenisei-Ostyak is one of two surviving members of the Yeniseian family of languages, spoken by the Kets, a people indigenous to central Siberia. In the twentieth century, the Kets have come under the influence of the Russians, among others. Most Kets today speak Russian . . .*

The word 'Ket' had a link marked which Luke clicked and then on 'play'. A woman's voice began speaking, soft, young-sounding; and interspersed with this voice, in the role of interviewer, a second voice, Gemma's voice, speaking quick, fluent Russian, far beyond the halting understanding that Roz had. She touched Luke's hand. It felt cold. The interview became a conversation, the voices overlapping, moving from serious and reflective to quick, giggling exchanges. Two friends, chatting. The language spoken switched between Russian and English as the two competed to practise their language skills. They were talking, part of the time, about Ket, and the accent and the intonation of the second speaker changed as she switched into this third language. The English that the Russian woman spoke was rudimentary and halting, and most of the exchange seemed to be in Russian. It wasn't a professional tape, nor part of Gemma's research, but a rarity that Holbrook would not have been able to resist. A dying language, and Gemma had found

272

a young woman who spoke the language and had interviewed her.

'Ket,' Roz said. 'That was what Gemma gave to Holbrook.
A tape of a bilingual Russian–Ket speaker. I still don't understand what this has to do with it, but we've got to get it to
the police.' Luke looked at her for a moment, then nodded
a quick, reluctant assent.

Hull, Sunday
Matthew Pearse rented a bedsit on the east side of the city,
not far from the docks. The house was a small yellow-brick
terrace next to a row of shops, a fish-and-chip shop, a dry
cleaners, a pub. According to the landlord, Pearse had lived
there for several years. 'He's a good tenant,' the landlord
said. 'Pays his rent on time, keeps the place tidy, doesn't give
any trouble.' He didn't know anything about Pearse's life.

The room showed minimal signs of occupancy. It was
sparsely furnished. The single bed was against the wall, away
from the window. There was a small table next to it with a
table lamp, one of those made from an empty bottle. Under the
window was a gate-leg table and next to the door, a melamine
wardrobe. Next to the wardrobe was a cupboard that looked
as though it came from a set of kitchen units. Everything was
clean and neat. The bed was made with nylon sheets and a grey
blanket. There were no pictures, no ornaments, no personal
touches, apart from a book on the bedside table.

Pearse seemed to own very little. The wardrobe contained
a clean shirt and trousers, ironed, on a hanger. There were
socks and underpants in one drawer, one pair of each. The
socks were darned. There was also a vest. *One to wear and
one in the wash*, Lynne thought. The kitchen unit contained
a cup, plate and bowl, and there was one set of cutlery in
the drawer, along with a tin opener. There were some tins
– beans, spaghetti, rice pudding, and a small sliced loaf, open,
the wrapping carefully twisted to keep the remainder fresh.
There was a half-used carton of milk. Farnham sniffed it and
pulled a face. 'It's gone off,' he said.

The book by the bed, closed around a bookmark was

Teilhard de Chardin's *The Phenomenon of Man*. Tucked away between the pages at the back of the book was a photograph, a bit faded with white cracks running across the corner, as though someone held it often. It showed a girl dressed in white, with a white veil. She was holding a basket of flowers up at the camera and smiling. A wedding photograph? No, she was too young – fourteen, fifteen?

Lynne went downstairs to the hallway leading to the front door. There was a table there where post was dumped for residents to collect. She looked through it. There were more names than there were rooms, and some of the letters looked as though they had been there for some time. In the pile were a couple of letters for Pearse – recent post, unopened and unread.

It should have been evidence of a bleak life, this room with its almost complete absence of any personal record, of any personal life, but to Lynne it looked more like the room of someone whose personal life existed elsewhere, for whom the routines of eating and sleeping were tedious distractions from the things that were important. But from the point of view of an investigation, it told them nothing. Farnham left the search team with instructions to strip the place to the boards, and headed off for the advice centre that, they hoped, would reveal more.

The advice centre, when they arrived, was closed, locked and silent. It was as Lynne remembered it from her quick exploration on her first visit. The boxes of leaflets stood on the shelves in the small office. The typewriter had a sheet of paper wound into it. Lynne pulled it out and looked at it. It was blank. The desk drawers were empty, apart from Nasim's book: *Intermediate Business English, BEC2*. Lynne flicked through the pages, which were heavily annotated in Nasim's ornate Arabic script, but there was nothing there. She went out into the yard, which was dank and sunless, sunk below the mass of the abandoned warehouse with its boarded-up doors and windows. She'd missed the entrance to the attic, which was half concealed behind a pile of boxes, on her earlier visit. Lynne knew that she hadn't been conducting a search, but she was also aware that she'd allowed Nasim Rafiq's apparent willingness to let her look round blunt her powers of observation. She'd been careless.

The attic contained a small bed under a peeling skylight. The bed was made up and had been used recently. A dark, wavy hair lay on the pillow, which was indented where a head had lain. Lynne could guess who the recent occupant had been. She closed her eyes, trying to get a sense of Anna Krleza, but there was nothing, just the dry smell of old wall-paper, the sound of the sea birds that she heard from her own window, and the distant murmur of city traffic.

Hull, Sunday morning
Nasim Rafiq was a study in silence, her dark eyes watching Farnham as he explained the interview procedure to her, then moving to Lynne as her presence was explained. Lynne tried to read her expression, tried to send a message: *Enough of the truth to help us, not enough to incriminate yourself!* Rafiq seemed to have no problems understanding what Farnham was saying, cutting off his move towards the interpreter with an authoritative gesture. 'Is no need,' she said.

Farnham took her through the early stages of the interview with routine questions he knew the answer to. How long she had been in the country, what her husband did, how long the family planned to stay. She was a teacher, she told them in a sudden burst of loquacity, and was planning to take the necessary qualifications to allow her to teach at an English school, but her English was not as good as it should be. She relied on the interpreter to explain parts of this to them. Then she fell silent. Lynne remembered the textbook on the desk, when she had talked to Rafiq at the centre, when Anna Krleza was almost certainly hidden away somewhere. She remembered the open door at the back of the office, and Rafiq walking over to close it, commenting on the non-existent draught. She wondered why the woman had taken the risks she had.

'Tell me about the Welfare Advice Centre,' Farnham said. 'How long have you been working there?'

She explained, again through the interpreter, that she worked as a volunteer and had been there for about five months. 'It help my English,' she added. 'And . . .' She stopped and spoke to the interpreter.

'The plan is to develop an advice, counselling and training centre there, for the asylum seekers they move up here,' the interpreter said. 'She speaks Pushtu – that's what they speak in Afghanistan. That's why they asked her to get involved.'

Languages, Lynne thought. Katya's stumbling English, Gemma Wishart's expertise, the queries on Katya's tape. And Nasim Rafiq, pulled into the complex web around this case by the language she spoke. Was it as simple as that? Farnham pushed the photograph of Anna Krleza across the table. Rafiq's eyes turned away. He kept his hand on the photograph, not looking at it, looking at Rafiq in silence as though he was thinking something through. 'Matthew Pearse,' he said after a while. She didn't react, but waited for him to ask his question. 'You've worked with him for five months?' She nodded. 'Do you know where he is?' He shot the question at her.

'He . . .' She began confidently, then frowned. 'At centre?' Farnham shook his head. 'I do not know,' she said. Farnham let the silence build for a minute before he spoke again. 'Matthew Pearse – he's a good man?' She looked blankly at him. 'He does a lot of good work?'

She hadn't expected this. She blinked. 'He is very good man,' she said. 'He . . .' She spread her hands out. Her English wasn't up to explaining what she meant.

Farnham didn't turn to the interpreter. He pushed the photograph across the table to her. She didn't look at it. She was watching him. 'Good men,' Farnham said. 'It's easy to be good, to stand on your principles . . .' He looked at the interpreter and waited as she talked to Rafiq in rapid syllables. Then he went on, 'To stand on your principles when there's nothing you have to lose.' Farnham absently pushed the photograph around on the table. 'Do you have children, Mrs Rafiq?'

The abrupt change of subject threw her. She looked at

276

him, at Lynne who kept her face neutral, back at Farnham. She looked uncertain. 'One. Boy.'

'How old is your boy?' Farnham's voice was detached.

Rafiq looked at him, and then at Lynne. Her calm now seemed the calm of resignation. 'Six year,' she said.

He nodded, to show her he already knew that. 'It's important to your son, isn't it, Mrs Rafiq, that you stay here? You and your family?' She looked at him in silence. 'Isn't it?' His question was sudden and sharp, and she flinched.

'Yes. Is very important.' Her voice was shaking slightly.

He pushed the photograph towards her. She watched him with an intense concentration. 'Mrs Rafiq,' he said, 'I'm going to ask you this question just once, so think very carefully about your answer.' His tone was matter-of-fact, devoid of sympathy. 'Do you know this woman?' Rafiq looked at him, looked at Lynne. She looked down at the photograph. She closed her eyes. Swallowed. She began to shake her head. 'Mrs Rafiq,' Farnham said.

Her eyes met his. 'I know her,' she said.

Nasim Rafiq came from the north-west of Pakistan. She had started doing voluntary work for the reason she said: to help her with her English, which she needed to work on if she planned to teach. Asian people in Hull were at a disadvantage, she explained. There was no real community like there was in comparable cities where people could support each other. Asians in Hull were mostly people like her – isolated individuals who were recent arrivals, here for work or family reasons.

The refugee dispersal programme had plans to send some Afghan refugees to Hull, so her arrival as a speaker of Pushtu was very welcome. The advice centre was in the process of being set up – no referrals were expected or intended until some basic work had been done on the building, and she had been surprised to find that a few people were already coming through its doors. Matthew Pearse, who seemed to have been running the storage depot there, had explained that, in need, people came and he didn't want to turn them away. She set to work translating the local welfare advice leaflets into Pushtu and, under Matthew's unobtrusive guidance, had paid little attention to the other comings and goings at the centre. She had enjoyed what she was doing and was looking forward to the centre beginning its proper work. She had been lonely sitting at home while her husband was at work and her son was at school, and she was a conspicuous oddity when she stepped outside her front door.

But then . . . she became aware of another, hidden stream, a trickle of desperate people. After dark, after the centre closed, after the hours when she should have left and Matthew was there alone, that was when they came. She had seen people escaping from hunger and disease and violence, people in deep and terrible debt. She had seen families who had been torn apart, parents from their children, brothers from their sisters, wives from their husbands. She knew what the law said, but she listened when Matthew said, 'If you don't ask, then you don't know. Just go home and let me handle it. Don't worry.' These were the ones that seemed to come in the night – hollow-eyed young men, haunted young women. There would be a silent presence in the building for a day or two, and then they would be gone and Matthew would smile gently if she asked him a question.

Then the woman had arrived. Rafiq had looked at Lynne at this point. 'The woman you say . . . die,' she said. *Katya.* She had arrived one evening, injured and bewildered. Nasim had wanted to get the police, a doctor. Matthew had said no: 'You don't know what you're doing!' He'd been angry for the first and only time. He'd taken the woman to the hospital, then he'd talked hard and long to Nasim. 'They all need our help. We can't let the police come to her here. It'll be all right. I won't involve you again.' He'd promised, but then Anna Krleza had arrived, alone and terrified.

'Very young . . .' Rafiq said, her voice flat and sad as she told them about Krleza's short stay at the centre, her sudden departure. Pearse had phoned her late on Saturday to tell her that Anna had gone. 'He say he go find,' Rafiq said. She hadn't been back to the centre since.

'What now?' Lynne said to Farnham as they returned to his office.

'It's in the hands of Immigration as far as she's concerned,' he said. He picked up the phone and began to key in a number.

Lynne stopped him. 'She trusted me,' she said. 'She told me about her son.'

His face was serious. 'I didn't make any deals,' he said. He picked up the phone again. 'She may have been an unwitting observer at the beginning, Lynne, but she let it go on. She withheld information. I can't ignore that.'

'I let her think a deal was a possibility,' Lynne said. 'I was with you. She must have thought it was on the table.'

He looked at her. 'Why did you think I wanted you there?' he said.

18

Sheffield, Sunday afternoon

Roz had tried the number she had for Inspector Jordan without success. She looked at Luke who was pacing the computer room, fuelling his tension with black coffee. 'She isn't there,' Roz said.

'Oh for Christ's sake, Roz,' he said irritably, 'what difference does it make? So we've found what Gemma was looking for – one of her pet languages. So?'

'So, nothing. We don't know. The police might.' The handset started emitting a two-tone hum and she put it back on the base. 'There has to be something. Why else did Holbrook try and stop me finding it?'

'You *think* that's what he did, Roz. You don't know.' He ran his fingers through his hair. 'Look, he gave you some bum information when you interrupted his break. Do you know how often I do that when some student comes over and starts yada, yada, yada?'

'Since when do students ask you about murder inquiries?'

'Come on, Roz, he gave Gemma access to the fucking thing when she asked. And he gave it to you. That's not hiding it.' They had fallen into the familiar pattern of work, the pattern they used when a problem was proving intractable. Luke, the voice of impatient scepticism, Roz the voice of reason, setting the arguments out into logical strands until they could see their way through.

'He didn't,' she said. 'He didn't give it to me. It was his assistant. His student, Sean.'

'OK, so why does this Sean give you Holbrook's archive

when his boss has spent all his time trying to stop you getting to it? That really makes sense.'

'He tried to chat me up,' Roz said. 'He knew I was interested in the archive. I don't think he knew Holbrook had been stonewalling. I think he brought it over as an excuse to have another go, that's all.'

Luke gave her a long look. 'OK,' he said after a bit. 'So you've got the archive and Holbrook doesn't know . . .'

'He does,' Roz said. 'I told him. And he set up a late meeting, here.'

'And you thought you saw an intruder and phoned security, and Holbrook never showed . . .' He was still now, looking down at the floor, thoughtful. 'Roz, if Gemma found something, it's got to be more than this language, this "Ket".'

'So I need to get this through to them.'

He nodded a reluctant assent. 'There wasn't any Inspector Jordan. There was a guy called Farnham. He was the one they were kow-towing to. But listen, Roz. I still don't see where this gets us.'

She shook her head. She didn't know either. 'I've been dealing with DI Jordan. I'll contact her,' she said. 'If I don't get her this time, I'll leave a message.'

Hull, Sunday evening

Lynne sat down at her desk and rubbed her eyes. She felt weary beyond belief. She should have left two hours ago, but the backlog of work caused by the arrest of Nasim Rafiq had kept her pinned to her desk. And she didn't want to go home leaving the unfinished threads of her investigation unravelling in her hands.

She finished typing her report on her interview the day before with Rafiq. She read through it, dissatisfied. There was nothing there that would cover Rafiq's back. It made it clear that she had been concealing something, that she had made no attempt to assist Lynne. It gave the facts, but not the context, and the report system allowed little scope for context, not anything that could be weighed on the loaded scales operated by the immigration department.

She ran her hands through her hair and sighed. She'd done what she could. Rafiq had taken risks – she would have to take the consequences. But Lynne could leave the report for now. Farnham wanted it, but he wouldn't look at it tonight. He had all the information that Lynne could give him. She could leave it until the morning. She grimaced. *Postponing the inevitable.*

It was her day off tomorrow. That would give her a bit of time to think. If there was anything she could do to help Rafiq, she would find it. She saved the report, but didn't print it out. She was tired, and she couldn't make decisions when she was tired. That was when you made mistakes. She noticed, as she stood up, that the message light on her phone was blinking. She went to pick up the handset, then stopped. Whatever it was, it would have to wait. She needed to get home.

Hull, Sunday

The room smelt of damp, a sour, mildewy smell. For a moment Anna lay there in confusion, the patterns of her recent days and nights swirling round in her head as she tried to locate herself. Then she remembered the storm lantern, and reached her hand out to switch it on. She found the carrier bag that Matthew had left and ate some chocolate. Her head was aching and her throat felt dry and scratchy. She kept feeling hot, and then she was shivering with cold. It was hard not to cough. She needed to get more of the flat, tepid water. Matthew hadn't been certain when he would be able to come back. 'As soon as I can,' he'd said. 'As soon as I can.'

She'd drifted in and out of sleep as the day drew on. Once, she woke up drenched with sweat from some dream that left her gasping with terror but was gone from her memory before she was properly awake. There was just the lingering sense of horror. Her throat was so painful now it was hard to swallow. She made herself drink some more water and her throat eased a bit. Her arms and legs were aching, and she stretched to try and ease them. She rolled off the mattress

282

and stood up. Maybe if she walked around a bit the aching would ease.

She pushed open the door at the end of the corridor, and moved into the larger room she'd sensed rather than seen the night before. The flagstones felt cold and gritty under her feet. The soles of her shoes made a whispering sound against the stone that echoed in the silence. Her eyes were becoming accustomed to the gloom now. There was a sense of space, as though the room was higher and vaster than she had first thought. The room opened up in the dim light, a stone floor stretching away into dark corners, walls of uneven, crumbling brick, the flagstones of the floor disappearing into the shadows, the low ceiling supported by pillars of brick. There were windows along the upper edges of the walls, narrow horizontal slits that were barred on the outside, and encrusted with dirt. Under the windows where the light shone faintly through, the wall gleamed as though water was seeping down.

Her imagination was creating sound and movement around her. She thought she could hear something in the further reaches of the cellar, the sound of breathing in the cold blackness. There was a shape in the darkness, at the far end of the aisle created by the pillars. She moved closer, wary of obstacles hidden in the shadows.

It was a stone table of the kind used to provide a cold surface for storing perishable goods. She could remember such tables from the outhouses at home. Above the table, in the ceiling, was a wooden frame, the kind of frame her mother used to hang the cured hams from. It was strange, seeing these familiar objects in this cold silence. Behind the table, there was a door that stood out slightly from the wall, a narrow door, heavy metal that was pitted and peeling. It looked like an old cold store, a walk-in refrigerator. This cellar must have been used for food storage at some time. She tried the handle, and the door sighed open, moving with a silent smoothness that took her unawares, and she staggered slightly. Then the smell of decay hit her nostrils. Something had gone rotten in the sealed atmosphere. She caught a glimpse of the inside as she slammed the door shut, the heavily lined interior leaving no more than a coffin-like space encrusted with filth. She wondered what could have been stored in there. The stench lingered.

Something moved across the windows above her head, sending darker shadows across the aisle. She froze as the shadows paused, but then they moved on again. She watched intently but there was no further sign of movement. Even if there was someone, who would know she was here? As long as she kept quiet, she was safe. Just a few more hours, just until Matthew came back. Her throat felt dry and sore again, and the ache in her arms and legs was getting worse. She went back to the small room and lay down, letting the slow hours drift past her. He would be back soon. He had said so.

He had promised.

Sheffield, Sunday night
It was after sunset and the streetlights were lit, shining on the wet roads, the pavements glistening with past rain when Luke and Roz went back to Pitsmoor. The rain had kept people indoors, and the streets around her house were mostly empty. A few teenagers were hanging around the small park, a woman was pushing a pram, a neighbour was working under the bonnet of his battered car. Luke parked his bike by the side of the house. She looked up at the windows of the derelict house next door as she felt in her bag for her key. They were black and empty in the darkness.

The house felt strange as she opened the front door, as though she'd been away for longer than the day and a half she had. The chaos of her hurried departure was still there to clear up: the bag with its contents dumped on the stairs where she'd tried to find her spare keys, the Yellow Pages lying open by the phone, the Saturday post scattered on the kitchen table next to her breakfast plate – the sense of life suspended.

Luke headed for the kitchen to make coffee as she scooped up the clutter from the stairs. She was aware of him straightening up the post and dumping the dishes into the sink, as he waited for the kettle to boil. 'That's a bit more civilized,' he said. He was quiet for a moment, then he looked at her. 'Do you want me to stay?' he said.

She was surprised that he'd asked. She'd just assumed that he would be staying. She wondered if he wanted to go back to his place. They'd spent the previous night and all of the day together. He'd become irritable and short-tempered as the afternoon drew on. He needed some space. She was surprised that she didn't feel that need herself. She was so used to being alone that she found the company of other people became intrusive after a while. 'Do you want to stay?' she said.

'Christ, Bishop, let's not get into "After you." "No, after you." Sling me out if you don't want me, and I'll come back tomorrow.'

'I want you to stay. But not if you don't want to.'

'Of course I fucking want to!' They glared at each other and then he started laughing. 'OK,' he said. 'I'll stay.' He ran his eyes over her. 'You're a mess, Bishop. You look as if you spent last night on the tiles.'

'I did,' she said. But he was right. Her clothes had dried out over the cylinder at Luke's, but they were crumpled and mud-splashed and she wanted to get out of them. 'I'll go and change, have a shower.'

'I'd join you,' he said. 'I've got some plans . . . But I'll make us something to eat, OK?'

She nodded. 'I need an early night,' she said. 'I . . .'

He gave her a half smile. 'You're ahead of me. That comes into the plans.'

She felt herself smiling back. She couldn't stop it. Everything was wrong, everything was chaos, but she felt happy. 'I've got to get up early and get the car fixed. I'm going across to Manchester tomorrow, remember.'

He frowned. 'You never told me. Can't you tell Grey to stuff it?'

'No, it's important. I don't have to be there until twelve, so there's plenty of time. It's just the car.'

'I'll get the tyre fixed for you in the morning,' he said. He looked as though he was thinking something over. 'How long are you going to be over there?'

'It's just a meeting. I'll be back by about seven.'

He was still looking a bit thoughtful. Then he pulled himself back to the present. 'I'll get us some food. Go and get yourself out of that lot. Half an hour, OK?'

When she came down again, he'd made a risotto and was just putting it out on to plates. He'd opened a bottle of wine and had dug out some salad from the bottom of the fridge. 'Short on food, plenty of wine – my kind of kitchen,' he said. She'd forgotten that Luke was a good cook when he took the trouble. It was one of the things he used to do, before events had pushed them apart: cook for the two of them before they did whatever they had planned for an evening. It was after nine when they'd finished eating, and Luke picked up the half-full wine bottle and their glasses. 'We'll finish this in bed,' he said.

Despite Roz's intentions to catch up on her sleep and be prepared for the meeting the next day, she was still awake at one o'clock. Luke had fallen asleep, his head heavy against her shoulder, his arms round her waist. Music was playing quietly on the radio. She couldn't be bothered to switch it off. She lay there for a while, watching the dark window of the derelict house, watching the moonlight fade and brighten as the wind chased the clouds across and away, watching the patterns of dark and light on his face.

Detective Inspector Jordan didn't contact them.

Hull, Monday morning

Lynne had spent Sunday night trying to control her anger: anger with Farnham – pointless – and anger at herself for losing control of an important aspect of her work. She had been so sure that Farnham would be willing to play it her way – he had treated her as the expert in her field, had discussed his moves as they affected her, had treated her with professional respect. Or so she had thought. But in fact he had held out on her all the way. After she had invited him into her work and into her bed, he'd shafted her. *Nice one, Lynne.*

It should have been her day off, but she couldn't relax. Days off were her days for shopping, for reading, for catching up with friends, for walks along the low mud cliffs of the east coast. But she couldn't think of anything she wanted to do. She felt too restless, and her mind was turning the problems over and over in her mind: Nasim Rafiq, Katya, Anna Krleza. She switched her computer on in the end, and began another search for the lost website – a futile task, but one that gave her the illusion of action. But the faces of the women looking back at her became one face, Gemma Wishart's ruined face; the bodies became the slim figure of Katya leaving the hospital, a small, anonymous figure walking into the night and to her death. She saw Nasim's dark eyes look into hers with accusation and betrayal, and behind Nasim, a small boy watched her, the unknown Javid.

She saw Roy Farnham's face as he listened to her, quiet, absorbed, nodding as he took in what she was saying, absorbing, absorbing and giving nothing back. *Farnham, you bastard, you didn't have to do it like that*! Another site appeared on the screen, another black page with red lettering, another naked body and the warning 'Adult Site'. She couldn't face looking at any more. She had to do something. She pressed her fists against her eyes and tried to force her mind out of its restless loop and into a more constructive mould.

There was no point in being angry. Farnham had done the right thing. There was a witness who was missing, there was someone who might know where that witness was, who might have been hiding her, there was evidence of a crime. She was the one who was at fault. She should have pressured Nasim into revealing what she knew as soon as her suspicions were aroused. Farnham had warned her: 'You're not a social worker.' She'd resented that as patronizing. He'd been right, though. She'd wanted Nasim as an informer, and she'd been sympathetic towards the woman's situation. So she'd left her like a tethered lamb as Farnham closed in.

But Nasim was still her witness to Katya's last movements, Nasim and Matthew Pearse. Matthew Pearse. He had gone looking for Anna Krleza over twenty-four hours ago and he still wasn't back. He was playing a game with some very dangerous people, and so was Krleza. They might have gone to ground. They might have somewhere they could hide.

And Nasim would co-operate with her now. She could talk to her as part of her ongoing investigation, suggest to her that the concealment of Anna Krleza was done out of ignorance or fear. That she, Lynne, would support that interpretation if there was anything else that Nasim could tell her. If Nasim could produce Pearse and Krleza, Farnham might be prepared to treat her just as a witness, not someone who had been obstructing his case.

OK, she needed to move quickly. Farnham was still holding Rafiq, presumably on charges relating to her concealment of an illegal immigrant. Lynne was pretty sure that Nasim didn't know where Matthew Pearse might be, but she might have picked up some pointers as she worked with the man. Lynne needed to talk to her.

19

Sheffield, Monday morning
It was just after eight when Roz woke up. Luke was still asleep beside her. Despite the chaos of the last two days, she felt relaxed and rested. The radio was playing quietly. She stretched and he began to stir, reaching for her and pulling her on top of him as though sleep had been the briefest interlude in their encounter of the night before.

Later, she yawned over the kettle as she looked out of the kitchen window. Low pressure had settled over the city and the sky had returned to leaden dullness. She made coffee and put toast under the grill, looking out at the grey blanket that seemed to be covering the sky. The clouds would be low over the tops. She wasn't looking forward to the drive. Luke came into the room and stood behind her, putting his arms round her waist as he looked out at the cheerless day. 'Who wants to go out in that?' he said. He whispered into her hair. 'We could go back to bed.' They stood there together for a moment, then he said, 'I'll take the car to that garage down the road. Get you a new wheel.'

'The tyre's down,' she said.

'It'll pump up enough to get it there,' he said easily. 'What time do you need to be off?'

She thought. The meeting started at twelve. It was a fairly informal affair, so it wouldn't be a serious problem if she was a bit late. 'About half ten,' she said. 'I've got some stuff to put together. I meant to read through it last night.'

'OK.' He was pouring coffee. 'I'd better get started.'

'Aren't you having anything to eat?' she said.

'At this time? You're joking, Bishop.' He picked up her car keys and headed for the door. 'I'll be back in a bit,' he said.

It took her longer than she'd planned to get her stuff together and get herself ready for the meeting, but even so, she was starting to feel anxious about her deadlines by the time he returned. 'Queues,' he said succinctly, giving her an approving once-over. 'You'll turn into Grey yet,' he said, in reference to her suit which, OK, she had bought because she admired Joanna's tailored elegance. 'Listen,' he said, 'give me a ring when you're coming back, OK? Phone me from Glossop, give me an ETA.'

He was watching her with apparent insouciance, but she could see the underlying tension. 'OK,' she agreed. 'I've got some catching up to do with people – it won't be before seven. Could be later.'

'OK,' he said. 'And come straight across to mine,' he said. 'Don't bother with coming back here.' His concern wasn't rational, but she could understand it. She was beginning to feel it herself.

'I'll be fine, Luke,' she said.

He smiled. 'I know,' he said. 'I know.'

He'd got the wheel replaced, fixed her up with a new spare and filled the tank. She was going over on the Woodhead Pass, the straighter, faster road across the Pennines that was more easily accessible from the Pitsmoor side of the city, but if she was coming back to Luke's then she'd make the return journey on the Snake, come in on his side of Sheffield. He walked to the car with her. 'Phone me,' he said again. 'When you're on your way back.'

'I'll phone,' she said. 'I'll phone.' He watched her as she drove off, and she thought about how good it felt to have someone to come home to.

Hull, *Monday morning*

Farnham was waiting for Lynne when she arrived in her office. 'I've arranged for Holbrook to be picked up,' he said. 'I don't want him doing a bolt. Do you want to be in on the interview?'

Lynne had heard from Immigration who had sent through information about Holbrook's student exchange business. It was apparently above board. Immigration were aware of it, the few students he brought across were accounted for, and there had never been any problems associated with the enterprise. 'Have you got enough on him?'

Farnham looked into the distance, calculating. 'I'd be happier with a bit more. Let's have him in and put him through it.'

'I need to talk to Roz Bishop,' Lynne said. 'Gemma Wishart's colleague,' she added, in response to Farnham's querying glance. 'She left a message on the answering machine. She must have left it on Sunday. It was a bit garbled, but the gist is, she and Hagan have found out what the mystery words on the tape were.'

'Any use?' Farnham was alert.

Lynne shook her head. 'I don't know. Like Greenhough said, it's one of the other languages you find in Russia. It might help us get an identification. I don't know. There's something . . . Anyway, Bishop isn't there today. She's in Manchester. And there was no reply from Hagan.'

'OK,' he said. 'Let me know.'

'And I want to talk to Nasim Rafiq,' she said, holding his gaze.

He looked away as he thought. 'OK. But later. Immigration are coming in this morning.' He headed back for the incident room, muttering, 'Bishops, angels, give me strength,' as he went.

Lynne had to be satisfied with that. At least the pressure of an ongoing investigation would keep Nasim there for the moment. Immigration wouldn't be able to take her to one of their detention centres. There was something she needed to do, anyway. When she had listened to Roz Bishop's message, something had started nagging in her mind, something she'd seen but not noticed that was now trying to catch her attention. She went through the morning's post again, but there was nothing there that seemed fit the sense of *something missed* that she was getting.

She needed an expert to talk her through this. Roz Bishop wasn't available, but there was someone else who might be. She had better luck with Bill Greenhough. He was immediately interested. 'Ket? That explains why I couldn't identify it. *Ket!* And Gemma Wishart spotted it? I'm impressed.' Lynne could hear the sound of paper being moved around, pages being turned. 'Right. Got it. It's also called Yenisei-Ostyak. That name isn't much used now.' Yenisei-Ostyak. *YO.* The notes on the transcript were coming clear. But why had Gemma Wishart been so excited? Was it just the linguistic rarity? She'd written *check!* on the notes, and had then gone to Holbrook's archive. *You remember the tape I . . .* Was she checking the fragments of this language against another speaker . . . ? Lynne remembered the research notebooks.

'Did you get the stuff I sent you from Gemma's research?' she said.

'Yes, I'm just looking. Right. It's there. In Dudinka, she's got a record of . . . let me see . . .' He read it out. '"Female, eighteen, Russian, Ket, English (some)." She had a bilingual Russian–Ket eighteen-year-old with some English.'

'Is that unusual?' Lynne said.

'Most Ket speakers will be bilingual. But the point is, there are so few of them left – between five hundred and a thousand at the most. It's a real oddity, Ket. A language isolate – it isn't related to any other languages – except, possibly, one of the Native American languages. A Ket speaker. And to find one who speaks English as well . . . Just about unique, I would have thought.'

Just about unique. But Katya apparently spoke Russian, Ket and had some English. Enough to make herself understood. The pathologist had estimated Katya's age at late teens, early twenties. Gemma Wishart said that Katya came from north-eastern Siberia. The research notebook referred to Gemma's work in Dudinka, the port near the mouth of the Yenisei River where it flowed into the Kara Sea. 'Thank you, Dr Greenhough,' Lynne said. 'I'll get back to you if I need anything else.'

She hung up on his, 'I'd really like . . .' and went back to the incident room where Gemma Wishart's research note-books were kept. She went through them until she found the one relating to Dudinka. Then she went through the pages, checking. *There!* In July of 1999, Gemma Wishart had interviewed Oksana Ilbekov, an eighteen-year-old student at Novosibirsk Institute of Pedagogy. She was studying linguistics. Gemma's notes were careful and detailed. Oksana had an interesting background. Her mother was a Ket from the Yenisei River basin in central Siberia. Her father was a fisherman, a Russian, from Dudinka. Her mother had died when she was a child. When she was in her early teens, her father had been killed in an accident at sea, and she had gone to live with her mother's family. She was learning English as part of her course, and had plans to spend some time in Britain to improve her skills in the language.

Suppose . . . Lynne knew how dangerous supposition could be, but her source of information dried up here, and she was due to bring Holbrook in this afternoon. She had to have enough to arrest him or to eliminate him by the time her interview with him was finished. Gemma Wishart had known Marcus Holbrook. Holbrook brought students into the country. Suppose she had passed on Oksana's details to him . . . A friend's recommendation, someone she could trust.

And then, Katya's body had been found in the Humber Estuary, a young woman who had escaped from prostitution, who had wanted to talk to the police, who had been panicked and incoherent, who had not known who she could and who she could not trust. And the tape of her voice had gone to the expert at the Forensic Linguistics laboratory that the Hull Police customarily used, and on to the desk of the one person who might – just – recognize the voice. And Gemma had. Or at least she had recognized phrases from the language she had encountered when she met Oksana. And she had wanted to check what must have seemed to be an impossibility against her original tape. Which, according to Roz Bishop, had been stolen. No wonder Marcus Holbrook had not wanted her to have access to his archive. He couldn't bear to destroy the tape. He had to include it. He must have assumed that the recording would never be heard by anyone who could make the link. And then Gemma had died. But now Lynne had a possible name for Katya.

Hull, Monday afternoon
Nasim Rafiq looked tired and stressed. She listened to what Lynne had to say. 'I do not know,' she said wearily.

Lynne suppressed her impatience. 'I'm trying to help you, Nasim,' she said. Couldn't Rafiq understand that? 'If you'd told me what you told DCI Farnham, I could have done something. I still can. But I need your co-operation.'

Rafiq looked down at her hands, then back at Lynne. 'You promise . . .' she said. *You promised me!*

'You didn't give me anything I could use,' Lynne said.

She saw the desperation in the other woman's eyes. 'You *promise*!' she said again.

'I said I could help you if you helped me. You didn't.' There was no point in wrapping it up. She watched Rafiq take in this confirmation of her fears. 'I can't promise anything now,' she said. 'I will try to help you, but you've got to give me something I can work with.'

Rafiq was silent for a long time. Lynne could see her struggling with her doubts. She had probably seen a lot that told her not to trust any representatives of the authorities. But she had no choice. 'I want . . .' she said eventually. 'If I know, I tell you.'

This was what Lynne had feared. Nasim now had nothing else to tell. Her involvement had been as peripheral as she had told Farnham. Enough to incriminate her, not enough to help her. 'Think,' she said. 'Anything. You told us that Matthew Pearse helped several people while you were there. Where did they come from, who sent them, where did they go, who were they – you must know something.'

Her face was tense with concentration. 'At first,' she said, 'I think it . . . work, advice. I am trying to learn. But he say, "No."' Her hands pleated the edges of her scarf, which had slipped off her hair. 'So I work on English, I work on leaflet,

I . . .' She made a gesture to indicate that she couldn't find the words. Lynne waited, giving her time to think. Nasim Rafiq's eyes were dark, and Lynne felt an impatient anger with Matthew Pearse for putting her at so much risk. 'Many weeks now,' Nasim said. 'I do not remember.' Lynne felt her own responsibility. If she had come down hard before Farnham had, she could have got this woman some kind of deal, interpreted her behaviour by its spirit rather than by its act.

'Why didn't you leave,' she said, 'once you realized what was going on?'

'Matthew,' Rafiq said. 'He say . . .' After Katya, he had told her the thing that had come between her and her sleep ever since; 'You're involved now. If they find out, you will be in trouble as well.' Trouble would revoke her leave to stay. It might revoke her family's right to stay. It would cost her son his sight and her husband his work that paid for their son's treatment. She *had* wanted to leave the centre then, but Matthew had said he needed her to be there, 'Just for a few more weeks.' He'd promised to find someone else who wouldn't be as vulnerable as she was.

But now Rafiq had something else to tell her. 'Dead woman . . .' she began.

Lynne looked at her. 'The woman who came to the centre?'

'Matthew say that we do not want police. So I say he comes back from hospital, takes me home. But later.' She looked at Lynne apprehensively.

Lynne was frozen for a moment. Had she understood Rafiq? 'He came back late?' she said. Rafiq nodded. 'What time?'

'Late,' Rafiq said. 'He take me home, but the car . . . it stop. It won't . . .' She made a gesture of trying to start a car. The car had broken down. 'I get home, maybe midnight?' Lynne closed her eyes. Matthew Pearse had come back from the hospital later than he said, the night that Katya had vanished. In that case, he had no alibi, and they only had his word about the car collecting her from the hospital. Rafiq had sat on that information. Lynne had known she wasn't telling everything and had played it softly, softly, and now Anna Krleza had vanished. A weight of responsibility dropped on to her shoulders.

'You can help?' Rafiq's voice was tentative. She had offered that piece of information in the hope that it would give Lynne something to work with, not realizing the significance of what she had withheld.

'I'll do what I can,' Lynne said, the flatness in her voice concealing the anger she felt – towards herself as much as towards Rafiq.

Nasim's mouth tightened as she kept her emotions under control. Then she looked at Lynne, and now there was a glimmer of something in her eyes. 'I write down,' she said. 'I am trying to learn. I write down, little bit.'

'You wrote something down?' Lynne leaned forward. 'What? What did you write?'

Nasim stumbled through her explanation. When she had first worked at the advice centre, she had made some notes about what to do if people came. 'He tells me, do not write it, so I do it secret, after. Or I am forgetting.'

'What did you write?' Lynne asked again. This could be something or nothing.

Rafiq shook her head. 'I not . . .' She couldn't remember. 'Where?' Notes on paper. If Pearse hadn't wanted things recording, he would have thrown the notes away. 'Did you take them home?'

'At centre,' Rafiq said. Lynne's heart sank. They hadn't found any notes at the centre. They'd found very little. Rafiq's voice was urgent now. 'In book,' she said. 'After he say no, I write in book.'

The textbook. The book Rafiq had been using to improve her English. Lynne could remember it now in the desk drawer with notes in the margin. It had been there when they had searched the place. Lynne breathed out hard to release the tension. Had Farnham's team brought it in? 'OK,' she said. 'I'll look for it and I'll take it from there.'

Anna woke suddenly. She could feel the sweat running down her back and the chill it left behind it. She couldn't clear her head properly. She had to do something and she couldn't remember what it was. She needed to stand up and start moving, and the effort seemed too great and then she was standing up and her head felt light and she needed a drink. That was it. She needed to get up so that she could drink, only the trees were in her way and she was creeping through the bushes and the smell was in the air, sweet and rotten, and she woke up again to find she was still lying on the mattress shivering with the cold, and damp with the sweat that had broken out all over her body.

She sat up and wrapped the blanket round her shoulders like a shawl. She couldn't remember exactly when he'd gone. Her head ached and her mind was confused. She struggled to her feet. The room felt claustrophobic. What time was it? Was Matthew back? Her legs felt weak and trembling, and she knew the fever was going to return. She walked down the short passage and opened the door, carefully, quietly. It should have been dark. The little daylight there was had gone, but there was a pale, flickering light diffusing the cathedral spaces of the room, illuminating the pathway between the pillars. She walked down the aisle of light, towards the stone table that gleamed dully in the darkness. And there were more lights now, flickering points along the aisle and in the recesses on either side of the pitted door, but beyond the lights, the shadows held their secrets.

She walked down the aisle, slowly, towards the table. Her feet were strangely reluctant now, heavy, as though the whispering darkness was pulling her back. The stone surface still glittered, the wooden frame above it sent its shadow across the floor like a cross under her feet. But on the table, among the shadows moving in the dancing light, stood a long-stemmed cup and, in front of it, a silver plate.

Anna moved closer. Her feet brushed against the flags. The cup was filled to the brim. The lights gleamed in its surface. Another step. Now she was standing in front of the table. She put out her hand and ran her fingers over it. Bread. She hadn't eaten since the night before, but she felt a strange reluctance to touch the bread that had appeared so silently on the table. She lifted the cup and found she was breathing in the smell of it. Wine. He'd brought her wine.

'Where are you?' Her voice whispered around the emptiness. She turned, looking behind her and the shadows looked back. And the room breathed in the silence, like a sigh from a carious mouth, a waft of decay, and she was creeping through the woods listening to the drip, drip of the water and breathing in the old smoke and that smell, that abattoir smell in the spring among the flowers and the trees and the sunlight glinting through the branches.

'Matthew,' she said, her voice dry in her throat. And like an answer to a prayer, he was there, and he was speaking, and she knew she was in the throes of another fever dream because the words he spoke had no meaning.

Introibo ad altare Dei . . .

It was almost six by the time Lynne had finished her interview with Nasim Rafiq. She tried to contact Farnham with the information about Pearse's alibi, but he wasn't in his office and he wasn't answering his mobile. She left a message in the end, and began her search for Rafiq's book. She needed to find it. The stuff from the centre, the stuff that had been taken away, was with Immigration, but Farnham had an inventory. She looked through it carefully. There was no mention of the book she could remember finding in the desk drawer. It must still be at the centre. She checked the time. She could go to the advice centre now, get it, have it safe.

She went back to her office, noticing the pile of papers that had accumulated in her in-tray. As she collected the stuff she wanted from her desk, the phone rang. She hesitated for a moment, then picked it up. It was Michael Balit from the volunteer group. 'Inspector Jordan,' he said cheerfully, 'I thought you might be dedicatedly plugging away when I got your answering service at home.'

'Mr Balit,' she said coolly. 'What can I do for you?'

'Ah, well, I've had some rather disturbing reports,' he said. He didn't sound particularly disturbed. She didn't respond to this, but waited for him to get to the point. 'One of my volunteers, Mrs Rafiq, seems to have been arrested, and I've had the family on my back.'

'That's not my investigation,' Lynne said. Let Farnham deal with this. 'But Mrs Rafiq is helping with inquiries, yes.' She let him absorb that, then said, 'While we're talking, maybe you can help me with a query I have.'

There was silence on the other end of the line. He was obviously thinking fast. 'All right, Inspector Jordan. What do you want to know?'

'Who put Matthew Pearse in charge of the advice centre?' She needed all the information she could get, now.

'Ah, well, it wasn't quite like that,' Balit said. 'He came to me. He'd found the property and knew it wasn't being used. He suggested it as a furniture store.' Lynne waited to see if he was going to add anything. 'He knew they were short of storage.'

'Who?' Lynne wanted to know who had moved to get the premises.

'Oh, the local churches. They co-operate quite a lot when they aren't doing battle for souls,' Balit said. 'Pearse thought that surplus donations could be stored there.'

'He works for the local churches?' Lynne said.

Balit laughed again. 'I don't know if you'd call it work,' he said. 'He's a priest. RC. He's been – what-you-call-it? de-bagged? – defrocked. Got involved with one of his parishioners, I believe.'

Matthew Pearse, a priest.

'Lord, I am not worthy that Thou shouldst come under my roof . . . Say but the word and my soul shall be healed.'

Domine non sum dignus, ut intres sub tectum meum . . . And her fever must be worse, because he was standing there and the open door was behind him like a frame, a blackness beyond the aisle of light, and deep in the blackness something red glowed with a steady flame. He was dressed in the robes of a priest that gleamed dully as the candles guttered, sending threads of black smoke through the air. As he lifted the cup in front of him she could see its glitter in the flickering light. And he was there in front of the table, and she took the bread from his hand, and swallowed the wine as he held the cup against her mouth. He was there, and it was Matthew, but the stench was in her nose and the blackness was behind him. 'Matthew,' she said. His eyes looked into the darkness beyond her.

'May almighty God have mercy on you, forgive you your sins and bring you to life everlasting.'

Misereatur vestri omnipotens Deus . . . And she was walking towards the door, the walls were blackened and the roof had fallen in and the small foot lying so still across the threshold, and the shower curtain bulged, its pink translucence revealing and concealing the shape behind it and she didn't want to look behind that curtain, she didn't want to step across that threshold, but the fever pulled her away to a high and distant place and the wine swum in her head.

And his hands on her arms were inexorable and she stumbled as she crossed the small step and he released her so she fell forward into the narrow space. And the stench was all around her and the fear made her retch. It was the smell of decay and human waste and her hands were against a soft, seamless wall and she turned to the side to escape and the softness was pressing against her and at the other side the room sighed again and the air grew heavy round her chest as the glimmer of candlelight was cut off by the closing door.

The moon was starting to rise by the time Lynne reached the advice centre. The day had reminded her of an anxiety dream, one where she knew she had an urgent appointment but kept getting held back and distracted by irrelevancies that pulled her away from the places she knew she ought to be or the things she knew she ought to be doing.

The sense of urgency must come from the impending

decision about Nasim Rafiq by the immigration authorities. But that wouldn't be until tomorrow. If the book contained the kind of information Rafiq claimed, it might be enough to keep the authorities at bay. So why did she have this sense of time running out, this feeling that she was doing one thing when she should be doing something else?

She unlocked the door and let herself into the now familiar room, the old shop front with the high counter, and went through to the office. Nasim's desk was there among the shelves and filing cabinets. She pulled open the desk drawer, and felt the slight tension inside her relax as she saw the book. She picked it up and flicked through the pages. It was as she remembered it, annotated in an unfamiliar script, but there were also numbers and the occasional reference in the Roman alphabet, references that looked like names and addresses. *Yes!* This could be gold. She slipped it into a cover and tucked it under her arm.

She checked the other drawers to see if there was anything else that had been overlooked, but they were empty. She sat down at Nasim's desk and thought. She'd missed things here twice. She'd missed the attic room when she'd first looked round, though it seemed unlikely that Anna Krleza had been there at the time – Nasim would hardly have been so relaxed about her visit. She'd missed the significance of the notes in the book that she was now holding. What else might she have missed?

She thought about Matthew Pearse talking to her, his voice halting but his eyes steady and serious. A priest, Michael Balit had said. A priest who had blotted his copybook. That might explain why he seemed to devote his time to community work – substituting the needy in the community for the parishioners who would have been in his care before. It might also explain the conviction that would lead him to break the law when he saw people in need, that combination of faith and of being an outcast.

She got up and went through to the back room, remembering Nasim watching her as she came down the stairs. She crossed to the small off-shot with the sink and two-ring hob.

She still had that feeling of something missed, something she hadn't noticed and should have done.

The window off the off-shot looked out on to the yard. The rising moon was large in the sky, shining into the yard, casting its faint light across the moss-encrusted ground. She looked at the bricks of the warehouse wall, blank except for openings running in a narrow line at ground level, barred and dark. She didn't know why she was still here. She had lost count of the number of hours of unpaid overtime she must have put in. She needed to go home. *Something you've missed, something you've missed . . .*

She let her mind free-associate. *Katya.* Katya coming to the advice centre. A prostitute. 'I thought at the time she had been working as a prostitute . . .' Matthew Pearse's voice. Escort agencies. Gemma Wishart. Angel Escorts. Mr Rafael. *Now with angels and archangels . . .*

Now her mind was moving fast, making the connections, seeing its goal before her conscious mind could perceive it. *Religion. Priests. Holy Communion, the body and the blood. . . .* She remembered the post-mortem reports on Katya, on the Ravenscar death: 'small amount of alcohol in the blood-stream . . . eaten shortly before . . . bread . . .' Bread. Alcohol. Body and blood. Bread and wine.

The chamber had closed around her with the sigh of an air-tight seal. She was pushed against the back and the door pressed against her like a second skin, She turned her head to one side, trying to free her mouth to breathe. Her fingers scrabbled to insert themselves into that narrowing gap, but she heard the click of the lock engaging. She tried to find some leverage, something to grip, to pull on, to force the door open, but the soft sides of the chamber pressed her arms against her sides. She couldn't push her hands up to her face, to free her mouth to breathe. She tried to struggle, but the closeness of the chamber held her. She forced her head back, gasping at the small pocket of air above her head. Now she could see the red light that glowed above her, giving a faint illumination. It was a candle, so close she could feel the warmth of its flame, but as far out of her reach as if it had been a hundred feet away. There was a text under the candle, and now she could see it, now that the red light was burning. *Out of the depths I have cried to thee, O Lord, Lord, hear my voice.* She was in a box with a sealed door. Matthew had imprisoned her in a box and she couldn't move, she couldn't breathe. The need to move freely, the need to move beyond the confines of the space, was so compelling that she struggled, trying to fight her way through the impervious door and walls, the muffled silence making it seem like a dream, as though nothing that happened in this place impinged on the world and she was reduced to the impotence of, *Let me out! Let me out! Let me out!*

The air around her face was hot and heavy. Her chest felt tight and though she was breathing her lungs felt starved. The red light was flickering now. It was going to go out and leave her in the dark in the box. It was a flame. A candle in red glass. A flame that was burning up the oxygen, but she didn't want to snuff it out, to be alone in the smothering dark.

Lynne spoke urgently to Roy Farnham, the cell phone infuriatingly indistinct as the surrounding buildings interfered with the signal. 'Pearse?' he said. '. . . Matthew Pearse is . . .' His voice cut out then came back, suddenly clear. 'Where are you, Lynne?' The signal broke off in a buzz of interference. She moved through into the off-shot, and the signal came clear again. '. . . Lynne?'

'I'm at the advice centre.'

'What? Where? Lynne, listen . . .' His voice faded.

'The advice centre,' she said, moving closer to the window to get the signal back.

'. . . in . . .'

'What? This is hopeless. I'm coming in.' Her foot caught on the uneven boards. It was hazardous moving around in the dark. The phone faded in again. 'I said I'm . . .'

She stopped. There was something out there, across the yard. A light. The faintest glimmer, across the black square of the yard, low down, close to the ground. A light in the shadow of the warehouse wall? Something metallic, gleaming in . . . in what? The clouds were covering the moon now. She moved round carefully, trying to get a better view, but the yard was in darkness. There was just that faint glimmer, no . . . *yes*, there it was again. 'Roy,' she said. 'Roy?'

'. . . Lynne?'

The phone, the fucking phone! She was off duty and she hadn't brought the radio. She kept her eye on the light, a faint flickering that she kept losing and finding again. She went on talking into the phone, saying it over and over again so that Roy would pick up the message in its garbled bits. 'There's someone, something in the yard. Of the advice centre. In the yard. There's someone there. In the yard. The advice centre.'

'. . . hear you, Lynne. In the . . .'

She wasn't sure how far the bad reception area stretched. She had to make a decision. She could get back to her car, drive off until she could communicate clearly, give whoever or whatever it was a chance to get away. And if she was right, if Matthew Pearse had killed Gemma Wishart, Katya and the Ravenscar woman, then Anna Krleza was in deadly danger. If she wasn't dead already. 'Lynne . . . me?'

The light vanished. She made her decision. 'I'm going across there,' she said. 'In the yard. At the advice centre. The yard. The advice centre.'

'. . . don't . . . way.' She couldn't tell if he'd understood or not. She switched her phone off. She didn't want it ringing and alerting whoever it was out there. She sent up a quick prayer of thanks that the lights at the back of the centre hadn't been working, and turned the handle of the back door, slowly, carefully, pulling it open as quietly as she could. It stuck for a moment, then made a small sound as it pulled away from the paintwork. She put her bag on the floor, pulled out the tiny pencil torch she always carried, and slipped into the yard, keeping her eyes focused on the place where that point of light had been. She felt with her feet, cautiously moving across the uneven surface. The high wall of the warehouse cut off the city lights, and the clouds were thick and heavy. She felt rather than saw the wall, aware of it as a solidity, a change of pressure in the air in front of her. Her hands brushed against it.

Here. It had been here, whatever it was. She felt around, low down the wall, and her hands touched bars, the sticky feel of cobwebs. The clouds drifted and the moon shone into the empty yard, and she remembered then the spaces along the bottom of the wall, a light source for whatever was underneath the deserted warehouse. The light she had seen, it must have been shining through a gap in the boarding or a clear patch in the grime. The night darkened and went black as the moon went in. She moved along the wall, trying to catch the angle again to see if the light was still there, but there was nothing. She needed to get into that warehouse.

She put the torch in her pocket and took her phone out, listening through the night sounds for the sound of anyone closer, anyone in the warehouse, the advice centre, the yard. Her imagination was creating noises around her: breathing in the night, surreptitious footsteps, the stealthy opening of a door. She clamped down on her imagination and made herself listen. The yard was silent. She switched the phone on, muffling its electronic beep under her coat. She was about to key in the number, when she heard the sound.

A muffled scraping ahead of her, in the blackness where the walls of the two buildings formed a right angle. She pressed the SOS button on the phone, her fingers fumbling in her pocket for her torch. Then a light stabbed through the night, shining into her eyes and dazzling her. It was just light and dazzle and blackness and she was falling sideways as something came whistling out of the darkness and crashed against her shoulder, against the place where her head had been a second before. She heard a grunt, and a voice, oddly gentle, said, 'Anna.' She rolled sideways into the shadow, gripping her torch, her only weapon, not able to silence the hiss of pain as she rolled on to her injured shoulder. The circle of light swung round, and she rolled away again, knowing that she couldn't hold him off for long, not injured, not

305

in the dark with her eyes dazzled by his light. Her hand groped across the ground, feeling for the phone that had fallen when he hit her. She heard his voice again, 'Anna!' And she threw herself towards him and felt the impact as she knocked his legs out from under him, the crash of the light hitting the ground, the sound of glass, and then there was darkness.

She was on her feet, one arm dangling uselessly, trying to orient herself and get back to the centre, her only route to the safety of the road. And then the moon came out, and he was kneeling on the ground, frozen in the moment, his hands feeling at a bag that had burst open in his fall. He didn't look up as the thin light illuminated the yard but reached around him, his hands drifting above, but not touching, the shattered bottle, the long-stemmed goblet that rolled to stillness as she watched, the dark stain soaking into the moss. She heard his whisper, 'No!' as the sound of sirens blotted everything out and cars screeched to a halt in the lane and figures came running through the door of the advice centre and she knew that Farnham had heard and had understood.

20

Hull, Monday evening

Matthew Pearse didn't look at the officers teeming round him. He crouched protectively over the broken glass and the dark liquid seeping into the moss, over the long-stemmed metal cup that gleamed in the torchlight. One of the officers attempting to get him to his feet kicked it, and Pearse screamed as if the foot had landed on him, 'Consecrated!' Farnham pulled Lynne away from the melee into the relative seclusion of the off-shot. 'Are you hurt? Are you OK?' Then, seeing that she seemed undamaged apart from the stains on her jeans where she had fallen, he said, 'What the fuck did you think you were doing?'

She flexed her fingers and found the feeling was starting to come back in her injured arm. 'I'm OK. There was something going on in the basement,' she said. 'Anna Krleza . . .' They were going to be too late, because she had not asked the right questions, because she had let herself get distracted between the needs of two investigations.

'They're getting in there, Lynne. What the fuck were you doing?' She had never seen him angry before.

'This,' she said, showing him Nasim's book that was still lying by the side of the sink. 'Nasim Rafiq wrote a lot of it down – names, addresses . . . I don't know. I came to get it.'

He started to say something, but a shout from across the yard pulled him back. Lynne followed him. The boarding that had apparently covered the passage leading from the

307

street to the yard was being pulled away. Lynne recognized the scraping sound she'd heard before Pearse attacked her. 'He came through there,' she said.

It wasn't a passage, it was an entrance into the warehouse, steps leading downwards into the darkness. At the bottom of the steps was a right-angled turn, and a short passage ending in a door. There was another door to the right, leading to the space under the stairs. Farnham shone his torch through. The tiny, tiled room had recently been used – there was a mattress that had been slept on, a cardigan thrown across the blanket. A small cubbyhole contained a tap, a drain and a bucket. There was no one there. Farnham pushed open the door at the end of the short passage, and the basement opened out in front of them.

It was a church, Lynne thought, looking at the line of candles that guttered with the disturbance of their entry, then steadied. A line of candles led between brick pillars towards a stone table on which a three-branch candelabra had burned low. Two of Farnham's team turned on their flashlights, and the candle flame paled as the shadows retreated and the room became a dusty brick basement. Lynne turned and turned again, expecting at any moment to see the huddled shape of a body, to see Anna Krleza at last, her face a secret behind the blood and shattered bone. She had felt the weight of the mallet, the strength of his arm. Her shoulder was a dull ache, but the movement was coming back. Maybe it wasn't broken.

Someone called out from the far side of the room. Lynne looked across and saw a metal door, pitted, heavy. One of Farnham's officers was trying to open it. He wrestled with the handle and looked at Farnham. 'It's locked.' She recognized the young constable, Des Stanwell, and for a minute, the picture of Gemma Wishart floated in front of her face. *Some kind of posh student type* . . . She felt a cold clarity and a sense of distance as if she was watching everything from a long way away. Farnham's voice was urgent: 'Get that door open!' Someone pulled a loose bar from one of the windows and made an improvised crowbar.

The door resisted, then swung open. They fell back instinctively from the wash of foul air carrying the stench of old corruption and sharper, more recent smells, vomit, urine. Just for a moment, they were frozen around the figure that had slumped out of the space as the door opened, the figure who must have been pressed against the door as the air went. Anna Krleza. She was so small. Lynne registered the bruised hands and the torn nails, and knew that she was in the place where Katya had died; that Katya, too, had struggled in that confined crypt in the muffled dark as the air was used up and her cries and shouts couldn't breach the air-tight seal on the door.

But Anna Krleza was still alive – just.

Matthew Pearse sat at the table with his face in his hands. He had said nothing since Farnham had cautioned him, but now he looked up towards Lynne and said, 'Anna?'

Lynne looked at Farnham. He nodded. 'Anna's alive,' Lynne said. 'I don't know any more than that.'

'Too late,' Pearse said. 'I was too late. I should have . . . yesterday. But I was weak. She'd tried so hard.'

'What do you mean, Mr Pearse?' Lynne said. 'You were "too late"?'

'To save her,' he said. 'To save her.' His hands moved restlessly. 'It's hard for them,' he said. 'They don't know, they don't understand. *Judge not*, Inspector, *that you be not judged*. If they are not fully aware of their sin, how can they be condemned?' He sighed. 'But sometimes – there is full awareness and the intention to continue with the sin. If you have repented and then knowingly sin again, can your repentance ever have been true? Or are you condemned eternally to the pit of Hell? Anna tried so hard, but she was going back to her old ways. I had to save her.'

Farnham leant forward. 'And the other three?' he said. Pearse looked at him. 'The woman we found at Ravenscar?' Pearse bowed his head in assent. 'Who was she?' Farnham said.

'I never knew their names.' Pearse was rubbing one hand

309

restlessly round the other as though he was trying to relieve cramp or stiffness.

'The woman who came to you for help?' Farnham went on. 'The one you took to the hospital?'

'Oksana,' he said. 'That's her name. She told me that.'

'And was she going back to her old ways?' Farnham said. 'Did you have to save her too?'

'She wanted an abortion,' Pearse said. 'She told me when we got to the hospital. Then she cried. She knew it was wrong. She hadn't cried before.'

Lynne felt her breath tight in her throat. She thought about Katya/Oksana, young, frightened, crying the tears of relief that she had, at last, found somewhere safe. How had Pearse got her to leave?

He seemed to see the question in her face. 'I told her that the men were looking for her and she wasn't safe,' he said. 'She was very frightened of them. Of one of them. I told her I could take her somewhere safer.' He had met her at the car park entrance. 'She knew she could trust me,' he said.

Lynne wanted to close her eyes. She was aware of Farnham shifting in his chair beside her. 'And the other one?' he said. 'Gemma Wishart?' Lynne could read his unspoken question. *You raped and tortured her. Are you going to tell us you were saving her?*

'I didn't know her name,' Pearse said. 'I told you. *Gemma.*' His voice was soft. 'That's a pretty name. She showed me the way. I didn't mean for her to die, but I left her, and when I came back, she was dead.' His face twisted slightly at the memory. 'She must have fought so hard to escape. She was . . . Her face was . . . But that was when I understood. That was when I realized what I had to do. It was stormy that night,' he said. 'When I put her in the sea. It was the spring tide.' He smiled at them. 'Nearly a year ago. I'm glad you found her,' he said.

There was silence in the interview room. Nearly a year ago. Pearse had started killing nearly a year ago. Lynne could hear the electronic tick of the wall clock, suddenly loud. It seemed to pulse with the words in her head: *How many? How many? How many?* She looked at Farnham, whose face was tense with the shock of realization. He leant towards Pearse, forcing the man to look at him. 'And the woman in the hotel? At the Blenheim?' Pearse's look of blank incomprehension was more convincing than any denial.

Then there was a knock at the door. It was Anderson. 'There's something come through, sir,' he said. Farnham paused the interview and gestured Lynne to come with him. Anderson started talking as soon as the door was shut. It was a moment before Lynne could take on board what he was saying 'It's the communications people,' he said. 'They've only just contacted us. The cell phone, the Angel Escorts cell phone. Someone used it this afternoon. I've got a location on it. It's over in Sheffield. A place called Lodge Moor.'

Farnham looked at Lynne. 'That's where Luke Hagan lives.'

Glossop, Monday evening

The light was starting to fade by the time the meeting finished, and by the time Roz left Manchester, it was dark. She'd had to negotiate the city centre in the rush hour, feeling an irritated impatience with drivers who seemed to assume that telepathy or second sight was an attribute all drivers had. Didn't they ever have to negotiate unfamiliar city centres? A four-wheel drive took advantage of a slight hesitation to cut in front of her, forcing her into the wrong lane. Ignoring the bad-tempered horns, she slowed and held up the traffic as she eased left, making them make way for her. She thought about the manoeuvrability of Luke's bike, the way he could always weave in and out of fast-moving traffic queues, leave the hot and angry cars behind him as he accelerated into the distance.

It was after half-past six by the time she was beyond the urban sprawl of Manchester, and the roads were quieter. The rush hour was over, and she lost some of the heavy traffic when she turned off towards Glossop. She was running later than she'd said. Perhaps she should have phoned Luke sooner, let him know she was held up. She was approaching the viaduct now, the high bridge that carried the railway line across the road, winding through the small patch of countryside that had not yet been swallowed up by the creeping cities.

Glossop was an attractive town of dark stone, with the high hills and moorlands to the north and to the east. But to her, tonight, it was a long main road that was always longer than she remembered, a featureless drive past garages, supermarkets, and an old church that had been converted into a warehouse. She was approaching the square now, where there would be a place to pull in and make her promised phone call. She was late, and Luke would be getting worried. She should have phoned sooner. She saw a parking space and pulled in rather abruptly, prompting an irritated beep from the car that had been crowding her since she had turned towards Glossop.

She rang Luke's number, doing a quick estimate for the rest of her journey. She should be there in half an hour. She looked at the sky as the phone was connecting, and saw the clouds low on the hills, heavy with rain. Three-quarters of an hour, play safe. If the clouds were down she'd have to go slowly. The phone was ringing now, then it clicked. Luke's voice: 'Leave a message and I might get back to you.' She felt a stab of disappointment. 'It's me,' she said. The perfect message. *This is me, is that you? Meet me here in five minutes.* 'It's Roz. I'm running late. It's seven-fifteen and I'm just leaving Glossop now. There's cloud on the hills. Give me three-quarters of an hour.' She kept hoping he'd pick up the phone. He often ignored his calls, let the machine take them. But he didn't. *Up yours, Hagan.*

She was tired. She wondered what the chances were of getting some coffee in Glossop. She decided she couldn't be bothered, couldn't be *arsed* to get out of the car and go in search. Luke would fill her up with one of his caffeine infusions as soon as she got back. It wouldn't be long now. Then she remembered that he was going to tell the police today about the photographs. She remembered his half-joking, 'You'll find me in custody when you get back,' and felt a twinge of anxiety.

She drove on, and the lights of Glossop thinned, became the lights of individual houses and then she was driving in the dark as the road began to climb in front of her, falling away to empty land on her right. There was the last house ahead of her as the road curved to the right. Its windows were dark. The rocks were higher now, with the thin grass of the peat moors that rattled as the wind shook them. The first wisps of cloud were drifting in the air in front of her, and she slowed down, slowed again as the mist became thicker and the road reduced to just a few feet ahead as her lights reflected off the fog.

Her phone rang, and she groped across the seat to pick it up. It would be Luke, responding to her message. She didn't dare take her eyes off the road, but picked the phone up and pressed the answer key. 'Hello? Luke?' It buzzed and crackled in her ear, and she thought she could hear someone laughing but it was hard to be sure, then the signal cut off.

21

Snake Pass

The fog was getting thicker as the car climbed. Roz was crawling now, peering through the windscreen, trying to see the road ahead. Once, a car loomed out of the mist, dangerously close, swerved and disappeared down the hill. Now she felt as though she was isolated on an empty track that vanished invisibly behind her and in front of her, the mist luminous against the dark of the night. The road was still climbing. She wasn't at the top yet. There was something in the road ahead of her. She strained her eyes trying to see it, and then it moved, revealing itself as a sheep as it hurried away from her light.

Then she was out of the cloud and the road curved away in front of her, winding round the rocky edges towards the summit. She accelerated, trying to get as much distance as she could before the mist came down again. As she reached the top, the wind was blowing, whipping away the last of the cloud and making the car judder. She was on the top now, the road straight and narrow in her headlights, running across the winter-dead moor with its dark peat pools that gleamed as her lights caught them.

Once she was across this bit, she would be heading off the tops, down towards Doctor's Gate. Then there was the long run off the foothills of the Pennines, through the conifer forest and past the dams. Then, finally, back, to coffee and comfort, and Luke. She felt a jump of optimism, and then the anxiety she'd felt in Glossop. *Don't anticipate trouble. He'd have let you know.* She was nearly at the stones marking the start of the long and winding descent. She could see a light in the mirror behind her.

Then her engine cut out. Just like that, without warning, it was dead and the car was rolling to a halt. The wind whipped across the moors and the car rocked. She slammed the gears into neutral and turned the ignition key again and again. Nothing. What . . . ? Luke had filled the tank that morning. The car was running fine. But the cold feeling that was coming over her had nothing to do with the cold outside or the sound of the wind. *Gemma vanished. Gemma came back across the Snake . . . beat her up and then strangled her . . . and then he posed her obscenely in a hotel bathroom . . . and what else? What else? What else?* She was reaching for her phone as the sound of an engine reached her. It was the irregular beat of a V-twin, and relief flooded through her as she saw the unmistakable shape of Luke's Black Shadow as it pulled into the side of the road in front of her.

'Luke!' She opened the door and got out as he leapt off the bike and ran towards her. He'd come to meet her. He was worried enough to come to meet her. But something in her mind was saying *No!* and she hesitated. Then he was there, and he grabbed her arm, pulling her towards him. And his fist slammed into the side of her head.

Everything stopped. She fell back against the car, her head cracking against the door as it whipped back, and she couldn't move. Her hands, her feet, wouldn't obey the instructions her mind was sending to them. She slumped on to the wet ground and she could see his feet, his boots, as he walked towards her.

Hull, 7.30 p.m.
Lynne felt the frozen impotence of inaction. Farnham had been on the phone to Sheffield within seconds of getting the information from Anderson, and a team had left at once for Luke Hagan's. And the cell phone was silent again. Lynne tried to picture the scene. She knew Lodge Moor, the high road and the houses exposed to the wind that blew from the bleak emptiness of Redmire Moor. She heard the click of a

315

lighter behind her, and for the first time in ages she felt the deep need to inhale nicotine into her lungs, as the sharp smell of the smoke drifted across her face.

A phone rang, and she jumped. Farnham swore under his breath. It wasn't the phone they were keeping free for the Sheffield team. She could hear the sound of conversation behind her, and someone came across and spoke briefly, quickly, to Farnham. He looked at the waiting group. 'That was Sheffield,' he said. There was a puzzled murmur. 'Another query. They've only just tied this in with our investigation. They found the body of a man on Sunday morning, near the university. He'd been strangled, with a ligature.' He looked at Lynne. 'It's Marcus Holbrook,' he said.

Holbrook. Lynne's mind was jumping around trying to connect the threads. Holbrook, who brought students into the country. Holbrook who had, apparently, tried to mislead Roz Bishop about Gemma's search. Holbrook, who was implicated in some way, she was sure, in Oksana's presence in this country, if not in her death. She could hear Matthew Pearse's uninflected voice: *She was very frightened of them. Of one of them.* She remembered that Pearse had gone missing, briefly, at the weekend. She remembered the anger in his voice as he talked about the plight of the trafficked women.

The phone on Farnham's desk rang and he picked it up. He listened for a moment, then pressed the loudspeaker button. 'They're in,' he said.

Lynne listened to the voice speaking at the other end, indistinct and slightly distorted. The flat was empty. There was no sign of Hagan, and no indication of where he might be. 'He's left his computer on,' the voice said.

'What's on it? What was he doing?' Farnham's voice was urgent.

'Just a . . . There's a picture, a woman . . .' Lynne wanted to be there, to check the files that Hagan had been using, to see this for herself. She looked at the computer on Farnham's desk, and clicked to check the programs it would run. Farnham was watching her as he listened, and he nodded at her as he realized what she was doing.

316

'Ask him if Hagan's got NetMeeting installed on that machine,' she said. A program that would allow computers to share files, one that was often bundled into a general package. There was a quick exchange of instructions, and then, like a window opening into a dark distance, or, Lynne thought, like a window opening into a diseased mind, the picture that was displayed on Luke Hagan's machine formed on the screen in front of her. It was the picture of Gemma Wishart reclining on the bed, the one that had been parodied when her body was positioned in the bath.

With a sense of inevitability she moved the mouse pointer across to the pubic area, and the message appeared. *Step inside and get to know me better.* Lynne clicked on the link, and the picture began to form. But instead of the pornographic sequence she had been expecting, she found herself staring at the body positioned in the bath, the hands pulled above the head and tied, the knees pushed apart, and the bloody ruin that had been Gemma Wishart's face. She felt the sick touch of madness, and she remembered the statement from the hotel guest: *And there was laughing. Someone kept laughing.*

The phone crackled into life again. 'Hang on. There's a call . . . No there isn't. That's odd. That's really odd. It didn't ring. There's no sound but the answering machine's moving. The tape's running.'

Lynne looked at Farnham. 'Remote dialling,' he said. 'My machine does that. You key in the code and collect your messages.' The phone calls to Luke Hagan's number! The first one would have been Gemma, phoning from the call box in Glossop, leaving a message as Hagan wasn't in. He was out because he was riding to meet her on the dark tops. And the second call was Hagan phoning in to collect and erase any incriminating evidence that might be on the machine.

A terrible sense of familiarity was flooding over her. Gemma Wishart had expressed doubts about some unspecified aspect of the Katya tape and had vanished on her way back from Manchester. And now Roz Bishop had found something out, and had left an unintentionally cryptic

317

message for Lynne. She was driving back from Manchester, and she was late. She looked at Farnham. 'Roz Bishop,' she said.

'It's OK,' he said. 'They've sent a car across to meet her. They did that as soon as we alerted them.'

'Do you know which way she was coming back?'

Farnham spoke quickly into the phone. 'They've checked,' he said. 'She uses the Woodhead road.'

So it was just wait. She wanted to be over there, she wanted to be doing something. She could see the same gleam of frustration in Farnham's eyes. He was about to end the call, reluctant to cut them off, even briefly, from what was happening so suddenly outside his sphere of influence, when the voice started talking again over a sudden babble of sound, doors banging, voices shouting, all distanced and distorted by the phone. 'It's . . .' the voice became indecipherable. 'In the lock-up, he's . . .' It was indecipherable again, and Farnham's face expressed anger and exasperation as he snapped a demand for clarification. 'Sorry, sir.' The voice was calmer now. 'We've found someone, in the lock-up where Hagan keeps his bike. The bike's gone, but . . .' Lynne listened as he told them what they had found among the debris of tools and the detritus of mechanical work, dark smears on the floor suggesting that something had been pushed or rolled into the concealing shadow. A man lay on the floor, his head a mess of blood, his face swollen and battered. But he was still recognizable, the officer said, still identifiable. Luke Hagan lay on the floor of the lock-up, his head a bloody ruin.

And then someone was shouting behind her, a voice that was sharp with a sudden urgency. 'The cell phone is active and it's moved. Its last location was Glossop.'

The Snake Pass.

Snake Pass

There was bumping and jolting. Her head was rocking from side to side. Her arms were pulled above her head, making it impossible to support her neck. She didn't know where she was. She tried to move her arms but they were tied somehow – she could feel the tug and abrasion of a rope. She felt sick and her head ached.

It was beginning to come back to her. Her car had stopped, and Luke had come to find her. Luke? Someone had hit her, and she had memories of the ground dragging past her face, of being pulled to her feet, of being able to stand but not able to control her movements, of a voice saying, 'Use your legs, bitch. Don't you know what they're for?' And her brain was saying *Run*, but her legs were like rubber that bent and sagged out of control, and all the time the voice was whispering, accusing as he manoeuvred her into the car. 'Like that, bitch, on your back.' She was lying on the reclined passenger seat with her hands pulled above her head, tied to something – the head-rest? The voice had become more confident, gloating, giggling. 'You spend too much time on your back.' He ran his hand up and down her legs. 'You know how to spread them though, don't you?'

And the car was moving. He must have pushed it to start it rolling, and now he was steering it off the road again, where the ground was uneven and rutted and the car lurched, wrenching her unsupported neck. She twisted her head to look out of the window. Darker shadows loomed in the darkness above her. He was steering the car into one of the old quarries or water cuttings, off the road, away from the slightest chance that anyone might come, might realize what was happening.

And her head was clearing. It was going, that feeling of her body not responding to the signals her mind was sending it. Now, now that it was too late, she could move again. He hadn't tied her legs. She wasn't completely helpless. She tried to focus her mind on that to quiet the terror that was beginning to overwhelm her. He'd taken his helmet off now, but it was too dark in the car for her to see. Should she try not to look? If she didn't know who it was, might he let her go?

She knew it wasn't Luke. That knowledge gave her a bleak comfort. She'd known from the moment he came running towards her, his speed that of threat, not of support. Her subconscious mind had tried to warn her, but she had reacted too slowly, stunned by bewilderment and a terrifying sense of déjà vu.

The car lurched to a halt. 'That'll do,' he said. He turned round and looked at her. His face was in darkness. She saw his hand reaching up to the light, and closed her eyes. She felt his hand on her neck, squeezing just a bit, but she could feel the pressure starting to build up in her head. 'Open them,' he said. His breath had the sour smell of excitement. Then he giggled. She opened her eyes. He was leaning over from the driving seat, his face close to hers. He waited until she had reacted, then he smiled. 'Surprise!' he said.

A young face, fair hair, a slightly petulant expression. She could see it in her mind looking at her with self-conscious guilt from the other side of a desk, looking sulkily at her as she turned down his invitation, looking pleased as he arrived at her office door. Sean Lewis.

'Sean . . .' she said. And then there was nothing else to say. Her mind seemed to shut down.

'This is so cool,' he said. 'You wouldn't come on a date with me. I could have shown you a good time. And now you've got in the way and you've got to go. Like Wishart.' He shuddered slightly, and giggled again. 'It was *so-o-o* cool.' He pushed his face closer. 'She turned me down as well.'

His grip on her throat was tighter. She tried to swallow. He relaxed his grip, and she coughed and retched. She knew she had to keep him talking, try to distract him, play for time, but her voice shook. 'It wasn't because I didn't like you,' she said.

'You don't think this is because you turned me down?' he said. 'Don't flatter yourself. This is business. You got in the way.' He put his hand on her breast and squeezed it hard. '"Oh, Sean, I'm sorry, I'm married."' His mimicry was a cruel parody. '"Oh, Sean, don't talk to me like that!" You spread your legs for Luke Hagan, didn't you? You and the Wishart bitch both. Was it three in a bed? Well, you got in the way and now you're in trouble.'

320

He pulled her jacket open, the force of it ripping off the buttons. He pushed her blouse up. The thought of his hands on her made her stomach heave. *Keep him talking!* 'I don't understand. How did I get in the way?' She tried to conceal her revulsion. 'I didn't mean to get in the way.'

His eyes narrowed. 'You had to go after that fucking archive!'

'You gave it to me!' She said that before she could think, and it made him angry.

He pinched her nipple hard, making her gasp. 'Do you like that? You like that, don't you?'

'I don't understand how I got in the way.' He was hurting her and the pain made her want to cry out, to beg him to stop, but she knew that would just make him worse. She could plead for information, give him the sense of power that way.

He moved across on to the passenger seat, straddling her, pinning her legs down with his knees. 'I've got to kill you. But first, we're going to do it. I'm going to fuck you. You'll enjoy it. I know what you like. I watched you with Hagan. You didn't know that, did you? You'd have liked it, though, wouldn't you? You liked it when he . . .' And he told her what she and Luke had done, and she knew he'd been watching them, listening to them. His obscene litany was fuelling his excitement and his rage. She tried to shut out his voice. She could feel anger under the terror, an anger that she tried to hold on to. Her legs were pinned under his weight. If she tried to move them, he would feel her struggling and he would get more excited, more sadistic, more violent. 'You're a dirty cunt, aren't you?'

'Sean,' she said, fighting to keep her voice level, 'you still haven't told me. You still haven't said how I got in your way.'

'Don't you know?' His voice was jeering. 'Wouldn't you like to know!' He had a piece of cord in his hands and he was threading it carefully behind her head, round the back of her neck. 'Shall I tell you? I'll give you a clue. A party game. Gem recognized the voice, only she didn't know she'd recognized the voice. So she had to go. Now it's your turn. Guess.'

The cord encircled her neck. 'It just pulls through the loop here, see?' He pulled and the cord bit into her neck. The air cut off and the pressure began to build up intolerably. She could feel her head pounding and her mouth gaped as she reached for air and she started to struggle. He giggled and released the cord. 'Not too much,' he said. 'It can get a bit messy. We don't want to spoil the party. No one can see us from the road, here, and no one's going to look for you.'

She choked and gagged. *Luke.* Luke would know she was late, Luke would know the way she was coming. He had her message. She just had to keep him talking.

He seemed to be able to read her thoughts on her face. 'Hagan won't come,' he said. He giggled. 'Not any more.' He could see the tension in her face and smiled, enjoying her suspense. 'I thought I'd better not bring the car. I thought you might recognize it. I was watching Hagan that night. I knew he was looking for things I didn't want him to find. I wanted to keep an eye on him. And then you turned up.' He giggled again. 'Gagging for it, weren't you? But he threw you out. I followed you up the road and saw you at the bus stop. So I thought I'd give you a lift. Take you somewhere and give you what you wanted. But you went running back to Hagan, didn't you?' He gripped her hair and forced her head back. 'Didn't you?'

She remembered the car, the dark car pulling out of the side road near Luke's. 'I didn't know it was you,' she said, her voice choking with the pain of speaking. 'I didn't . . .'

He let go of her. 'But never mind. There was Hagan's bike, all ready to go.' He looked petulant. 'I hit him, but he wouldn't go down. He kept fighting. Thick Paddy shit. Skull like iron. But he went down in the end. Bye-bye, Hagan.' He was pulling the cord tight again as he spoke, excited by the memory. He smiled and ran a caressing hand over her. 'So it all worked out for the best.' He released the cord slightly and said, 'I'll take the bike back. It's only a loan. And they'll find Hagan's blood under your fingernails when they find you, and they'll find the bike smashed into the back of the lock-up. They won't look too hard.'

Luke. She could feel the tears running down her face. She knew it was the worst thing she could do, but she couldn't stop herself as the fear combined with the grief and somewhere the will to fight drained out of her. He jerked the cord tighter and lights were flashing in front of her eyes as the pressure built up. He was going to tighten and release it, tighten and release it as he'd done before. He was going to play with her, take her through the experience of death several times while he had his party. He must have done this to Gemma. She tried to pull back against the pressure of the cord. Make him apply more pressure than he realized, strangle her quickly, let him have his party on his own.

There was a blackness closing in round the edges of her vision and her lungs were screaming for air. She couldn't stop herself from struggling and the pressure in her head and in her chest was more than she could bear. She felt a sudden flood of warmth as her bladder let go, and heard him laughing, a distant, echoing sound. Then the lights were stronger, a flashing, pulsing blue and the pressure on her neck released, suddenly, and she was gagging, retching, and she threw up, her body convulsing as the car door opened and he vanished into the darkness. And there were voices and shouting. Everything seemed far away and distant and all that mattered was trying to breathe as she choked on her own vomit, twisting her body round to cough and clear her throat and lungs.

And someone was saying, 'Roz. It's all right, it's all right, we're police officers. You're safe,' and her hands were free and she was falling out of the car into the arms of the woman who had spoken. The blue lights were still flashing, and in the noise and the chaos, Sean's face loomed out of the darkness for a moment and she thought

323

she was going to wake up in the car again and hear his voice in her ear, but the face disappeared and the woman who was supporting her, who was struggling one-handed out of her jacket to wrap it round Roz, was saying, 'You're safe, we've got him, it's OK, he can't hurt you any more.'

And then she thought, *Luke*. And it all went dark.

22

The man they pulled out of Roz Bishop's car fought for a minute, then gave up the struggle. He said nothing after the obscenities he shouted at the arresting officers, but his wallet contained bank cards and a driver's licence in the name of Sean Lewis. He agreed by means of a single nod of the head that this was his name. He said nothing else until, two hours later in the interview room in Hull Police HQ, Farnham charged him with the attempted rape and murder of Roz Bishop. Then he told them that it had been consensual sex. 'It was her idea, playing a rape fantasy game,' he said. 'She likes that.' Then he said, 'I want my solicitor.'

Lynne Jordan kept in contact with the hospital in Sheffield where Roz Bishop was being treated for shock and minor injuries. 'They're keeping her in overnight,' the police officer who had been assigned to the case told her.

'Did she say anything?' Lynne said.

'She kept asking about Luke Hagan. It sounds like Lewis told her what he'd done to Hagan. But she said – hang on, I wrote it down – she said about Lewis . . .' He began reading: '"Lewis said that Gemma recognized the voice, only she didn't know she'd recognized the voice. That was why she needed the archive. He said it was a game." Then she got in a state and the paramedic shut me up.'

Gemma had recognized the voice. It wasn't Oksana's identity that had to be concealed – Gemma, presumably, could link Oksana with Holbrook. Gemma had been very dangerous to Lewis. 'What's the news on Luke Hagan?'

'Nothing yet. He's still in surgery.'

'Is he going to make it?' Lynne wondered how many deaths would lie at Lewis's door.

'Touch and go,' the man said, and Lynne left it at that.

Sheffield, Monday night, Tuesday morning
Roz woke up. She was in a small, bare room with a high window. The bed she was lying on felt both clean and uncomfortable. A hospital bed. A ceiling bulb cast a flat light. *I don't want to wake up in the dark!* She could remember saying that to the nurse who had administered an injection. 'To help you relax,' she'd said over Roz's queries. She felt strangely alert, slightly distanced from her surroundings. The dim light reminded her of the light in the car, and her mind began to form the voice and her throat began to ache where he had pulled the cord tight.

But there was something else. She'd asked and asked before she would let them treat her, pushing them away until they told her. Luke had been 'hurt' they said. They didn't know, they said. They couldn't tell her. But in the end, the police officer who had held her as she fell out of the car had said, 'Roz, listen. Luke's alive, but he's badly hurt. He's in theatre, and it'll be a few hours before they have anything to tell you. That's the truth.' *Now let them get on with it,* was the unspoken addition, and Roz had stopped fighting.

A few hours. That would be now. No one had come to tell her. The call button had been clipped on to the pillow close to her hand. She didn't need that – she wasn't seriously hurt. She sat up and picked up the dressing gown that was lying across the bottom of the bed. It was white towelling, thick and soft. And she was wearing a silky nightshirt. These weren't hers. Roz didn't wear expensive nightclothes. She didn't usually wear anything. A T-shirt if it was cold. And she had an old, faded dressing gown that was at least two weeks on the wrong side of a wash. Joanna. Joanna must have brought them in for her.

She went along to the nurse's station. She felt the drag of dread in her stomach and part of her wanted to go back to bed, ask for a pill, sleep a bit longer. Until she asked, Luke was alive. Hurt, damaged – but still alive. Once she asked, she might have to accept, to start accepting, that she would never see him again, never talk with him again, never touch him again, never lie beside him in the night. The pain in her throat was so bad it was difficult to speak, to get the question out as the nurse stood up, alarmed by Roz's sudden appearance in the small hours of the night. 'Luke?' Roz said. 'Luke Hagan?'

She expected to have to explain and wait while phone calls went back and forth. If the news was good, they would have come and told her. They would leave her sleeping if the news were bad, give her a few hours less grief to bear. The nurse had to repeat what she was saying before Roz could take it in. 'He's back from theatre,' the nurse said. 'He's stable.'

Luke had never been stable in his life. 'Where is he?' she said. There was no point in asking about the future. No one could give her an answer now. 'Where is he?' she said again. The nurse told her he was in the high-dependency unit, was expected to stay there at least until the morning. 'I have to go and see him,' Roz said.

The nurse demurred, but eventually she phoned through, and Roz found herself being wheeled through corridors and into a lift.

'I can walk,' she said.

'Second-class ride's better than a first-class walk, love,' the porter said cheerfully. 'Don't knock it.' The corridors were long and dark, the walls and the floor scuffed with the passage of many people, people who were not apparent now, in the small hours, the time when babies were born and sick people died.

The lights in the high-dependency unit were dim. Each bed contained an immobile figure, each bed was surrounded by equipment, lights, drip-stands, the paraphernalia of the hospital front line. She could hear the hiss of ventilators, and for a moment she was back beside Nathan's bed, listening to the ventilator breathe for him, and she wanted to run away.

327

Luke was on a bed to one side of the unit. He was breathing by himself. 'That's good,' the nurse said. The green line of the monitor ran its monotonous course across the screen. Part of his head was covered by a dressing. They hadn't shaved off all his hair. She could see dark curls, matted with blood and dirt, to one side of the bandage. One eye was swollen shut. One side of his face was an almost featureless mass of bruises, the black swelling running into and distorting his mouth.

'He looks bad,' the nurse went on, 'but most of that is superficial swelling and bruising.' She'd introduced herself as Liz, and was apparently caring for Luke tonight. She looked very young to Roz, but also very calm and very efficient. 'He's doing as well as can be expected,' she said in response to Roz's query. In her mouth it didn't seem like a cliché, but a genuine assessment of the situation.

'Luke,' she said. Her throat felt thick and she had to swallow hard.

'He can probably hear you,' Liz said. 'But he won't be able to respond. Talk to him. It'll help.' She pulled up a padded chair by the bed. 'Use this,' she said. 'I don't think Luke will be using it tonight.'

Roz took his hand and leant over the bed, resting her arms on the pillow beside his head. She began to talk. She said very little about the night. She just said, 'I'm safe. He didn't hurt me.' Which was true enough. She told him about Joanna's nightshirt and dressing gown. 'They've got seriously expensive labels in,' she told him. 'I'm wearing a designer dressing gown.' She talked to him about her ideas for a holiday, a place some friends had told her about in the Pyrenees that had been her promised treat to herself when the next stage in the project was over. 'We could go together,' she said. 'If you could face two weeks of seclusion. Good wine, good food, wonderful walks . . .' If he would ever be able to walk again. She told him about Joanna's executive corridor, a joke she'd never shared with him before. The monitor's *beep . . . beep* was the only thing that told her he was still alive.

Liz leant over and shone her torch into his eyes, quick and away, quick and away, checking his vital signs. *Déjà vu*. Roz could remember when they did that for Nathan, when they said, 'The coma's lifting, he's coming round,' and the sudden relief in their tones had made her realize, then, how ominous his continued lack of consciousness had been. But Nathan had never come back from that dark place, not the Nathan she knew. *Luke!*

The airless atmosphere made her head ache and her throat felt dry and sore. She was so tired, and she felt cold and tingling and remote with the shock. It was replaying in her head like a video on an endless loop, over and over: the road disappearing under her wheels as she headed back to Sheffield, but now there was a sense of dread as the car went relentlessly on through the mist, then the engine cutting out, the bike pulling to a halt, the relief that Luke had come to meet her, the blow in the night and the hands and the voice. She shuddered and Luke stirred and made a sound.

She jerked awake, and the nurse was there again, checking. She gave Roz a reassuring smile, and then looked more closely. 'You should go back to your bed,' she said.

'I'm not leaving him,' Roz said. 'Not yet.' She drank some water, and then she talked to him about the things they used to do – would do again. 'Do you remember,' she said, 'those trips to Leeds? That time we went to the jazz festival?' That memory was painful, because though they had shared a night she didn't want to forget, it had also marked the beginning of their estrangement. 'I didn't understand, then,' she said. He lay still on the bed, his face white around the bruising, his eyes sunken in his head. She thought she could see a bluish tinge round his lips, and felt cold deep inside, in a place the warmth of the hospital couldn't reach. She told him about her plans for her next book. 'It's so boring,' she said. 'Maybe you'll wake up just to shut me up.' She ran her hand lightly over his hair, barely touching him for fear of hurting him, then she told him that she loved him because she realized that she did. She must have fallen asleep, because she woke up suddenly and it was daylight outside and Luke's good eye was half open, looking at her. 'What the fuck was I drinking last night?' he muttered, and closed it again.

Hull, Tuesday morning
The records faxed through from various universities gave Farnham more information about Sean Lewis. He was twenty-five with a PhD in Informatics. He was on a temporary contract, and his current professor expressed some puzzlement as to why he'd taken a fairly low-key research post. Up to this point, his profile didn't look too remarkable – an able and talented young man who lacked direction. But with further digging, the picture looked a bit different. He had a small flat in an expensive block, way beyond the reach of a research assistant, and his bank account and financial records suggested that until a few months ago, he had been deeply in debt.

Though he'd been academically successful, graduating with a first from Oxford, his history rang alarm bells to anyone who could see the whole picture. He had had an indecent assault complaint made against him while he was still an undergraduate. The charge had been dismissed when the woman, an itinerant with convictions for soliciting, failed to appear in court. For reasons that were unclear in the records, he had not been offered a post-graduate research place at the university, though he had gone to MIT with excellent academic references.

He'd left MIT under a similar cloud. A fellow student had accused him of date rape, and though the charge was dismissed, the Institute did not offer him further employment when he had completed his doctorate.

An examination of Roz Bishop's car showed that the ignition had been simply but cleverly sabotaged. An electronic circuit consisting of a timer and a switch had been hooked on to a wire in the ignition. When the ignition was switched on, the timer started. After a delay, the timer operated the switch, short-circuited the ignition and killed the engine. 'Look,' the engineer explained to Farnham. 'You just attach it to the wire. Next time the ignition is turned on, the timer starts, and after a set time, bam, the engine cuts out. Take the whole lot off after, and no one's going to notice a thing. You don't even have to strip the insulation with these connectors.'

'So how long has she been driving round with this in her system?' Farnham said.

'It must have been put in today, before she started driving back. You wouldn't want to leave it for long. It's very simple. Once the timer starts, it won't reset,' the engineer said. 'The car'll break down somewhere on the way. If you time it right, it'll be somewhere quiet.'

And with the run back over the Snake Pass, the chances of that happening were high, Farnham reflected. Lewis had taken very few risks. He'd followed her back from Manchester, and erased the message she'd left for Luke Hagan, just in case anyone found Hagan sooner than he'd expected. Farnham wondered what they would have made of it if Hagan's bike had been back in the lock-up with forensic evidence linking it to Roz Bishop's death, and Hagan dead on the floor beside it. Hypothetical. He made a note to ask the forensic team to look at Gemma Wishart's car again, to see if the ignition wires showed evidence of anything having been attached to them.

Interpol had responded to Lynne's query about Oksana Ilbekov. She had told her friends that she had been offered a place at Manchester University for a term's study and had left Novosibirsk in December. She took the train to Ekaterinburg, a twenty-four hour journey, and had caught the train to Moscow the following evening to pick up her flight to London. She never boarded the plane, and there was no record of her arrival in Moscow.

Manchester University had no record of her. She had, apparently, never applied there and never been offered a place, though the university did, like all UK universities, take exchange students. The search for Oksana had centred on Moscow, but the assumption among the authorities had been that hers was a voluntary disappearance.

The extent of Marcus Holbrook's involvement was hard to ascertain. Lynne spent time on Tuesday in Sheffield tracking down Holbrook's connections. He had lived in a small house close to the Mayfield Valley on the west side of Sheffield. It was an expensive residential area, but not beyond the reach of a retired professor, and Holbrook had bought the house some years ago. It had the slightly shabby look of a place that was lived in but not noticed, as though Holbrook's real life went on somewhere else. A search of his finances revealed money in several UK bank accounts, and documents for offshore accounts as well.

Lynne looked through some of the statements. For the past five years, there had been regular deposits that looked like a salary or a pension, with occasional, irregular additions. There was nothing there that looked out of place. Then, just under a year ago, shortly after Sean Lewis had come to the university, he started paying in larger amounts. There was travel documentation, letters, letterheads – all stuff that someone in Holbrook's line might be expected to have – but useful, very useful, for someone who wanted to start bringing people into the country illegally.

His desk contained lists of contacts at universities in England and in Europe. One of those contacts was Stefan Nowicki at Novosibirsk, but the two men had a known academic link. The records of Holbrook's phone calls revealed that he had made several phone calls around the time of Oksana's death to a private number in Novosibirsk, which proved to be Nowicki's when Lynne traced it.

Matthew Pearse had spent Tuesday night in custody, but he seemed calm and unruffled when Lynne and Farnham faced him again in the interview room. Lynne thought about the comfortless bedsit they had searched, and wondered how much worse a cell would have seemed.

The warehouse basement had already provided some useful findings, and the forensic experts were still working. The chamber where Anna Krleza had been imprisoned was an old cold store built into the wall. It had been modified by the addition of thick insulation and padding until its capacity was reduced to a coffin-sized space, an air-tight trap to anyone who was shut inside. Anna Krleza was not the first person to have been shut in there.

The pathologist had supported this conclusion when Farnham went back to him about 'Katya's' death. 'It's not an easy thing to identify with certainty,' he said. 'Asphyxial deaths where there is no physical trauma are notoriously difficult – the circumstances of the recovery of the body are a major factor in making that diagnosis.'

The story Pearse told them was slightly different from the one that Lynne had got from Michael Balit. He had had a relationship in his teens with a girl who lived locally and she had become pregnant. 'I wanted her to marry me,' he said, 'but she . . . I could understand it. Even then, I was . . .' He gestured at himself. 'She left her daughter, our daughter, with her parents. They didn't know I was the father, but I kept up contact, all the time I was training, and after, as much as I could.'

Years later, Pearse had got the chance and had come back to the area as a priest. His daughter was now sixteen. 'A member of my flock. I was responsible for her, and she had no idea who I was. Lisa.' He looked sad as he spoke the name. He had been shocked by what he found. The home his daughter lived in with her grandparents was strict and unloving, and she was mixing with the wrong crowd, getting involved in drugs, promiscuous sex, all the baggage of troubled adolescence. 'I tried to help her,' he said. And she had been drawn to the man who had befriended her. 'Her grandparents gave her a home,' he said, 'but they never really gave her any love. I loved her.' He realized then how much he had missed her, and how much he had damaged her by leaving. 'It was unforgivable,' he said. 'I have never forgiven myself.' Lynne remembered the photograph in his room, the young girl dressed in white.

'You have a picture of her,' she said, and he smiled, but his face was sad.

'Her Confirmation,' he said. 'That was before . . .' Lisa had killed herself. She had been in the early stages of pregnancy. The father was unknown. 'The coroner said it was an accidental overdose,' Pearse said. 'They do say that. If they can. To spare the family. But I knew.' His face was white. 'The sin of despair. The unforgivable sin. She died in despair, and I have read the scriptures and my books and I can't find one thing that offers me the comfort that she found forgiveness. She will suffer that despair for all eternity.' He sighed. 'That was when I left the priesthood. That was when I knew my ministry was on the streets.'

'And then . . . I met her down on the old docks. A year ago. She can't have been more than seventeen,' he said. She had been a street prostitute. 'I used to see her. I would talk to her sometimes. Her English was poor. She thought she was coming over here to work as a dancer, she told me.' He shook his head. 'The people who brought her here, they threw her out when the heroin took hold. It's hard for those girls once the drugs have got them. They can't go to hospitals or rehabilitation. And she was terrified of going back. She told me she wanted to change, wanted to leave the streets, get off drugs. But she went back. She wasn't strong enough.' He looked at Lynne. He barely seemed aware of Farnham. 'I shut her in. I thought I was saving her from the drugs. She was dead when I came back. And I knew then that I *had* saved her. *Gemma.*' He said it softly.

'She wasn't called Gemma,' Lynne said. 'We don't know her name.' *We don't know her at all.* She thought about the girl, young and alone on the streets of a strange country, then killed, her body dumped and swept away with the flotsam, unknown and forgotten. And the girl found on the beach at Ravenscar, the only record of her existence a cadaver in the morgue, no name, no face – just a number. And the question that had haunted Lynne ever since Pearse had begun his confession: Were there others, lost in the sea somewhere? And then there was Oksana.

'Oksana,' she said. Pearse nodded. 'She was seen near the bridge that night.'

'I took Nasim home that way,' he said. 'I pretended that

the car had broken down. It was a cold night. She walked to the phone box to call the AA.' He grimaced. 'I told her my back was too bad to walk far. I had the coat I'd lent to Oksana in the car. Nasim didn't know about that. So I gave her the coat to wear while she walked to and from the phone.' Lynne remembered the witness statements: a woman in a red coat walking by the side of the road. And the extra detail in the other statement: the woman's dark hair and the heavy metal buttons on the coat. Of course. One had seen Nasim walking towards the phone box, the other would have seen her walking back.

Pearse was talking again. 'I couldn't risk anyone coming and checking at the centre. Too many people depend on us. After I had left Nasim, I went on to the bridge and left the coat there. Were you thinking of ghosts, Inspector? Of the unhappy departed? That's all superstition, I'm afraid.'

'Why the faces?' Lynne asked suddenly. 'Why did you destroy their faces?'

He looked surprised. 'For their families,' he said. 'Their families wouldn't want to know. It was best if their families never knew.'

Sean Lewis was implicated in Gemma Wishart's death by both the evidence of his own words to Roz Bishop, the circumstances of his arrest, and the forensic evidence that lined up, damningly, against him. His fingerprints matched those that had been taken from Gemma Wishart's flat after the break-in. He was a secretor whose blood group matched that of the man who had raped her. DNA tests would confirm or exclude his involvement. Farnham wasn't offering odds. A search of his flat revealed newspaper cuttings, one about the Ravenscar woman, one about 'Katya', small, unimportant news stories about unknown dead women, taken from the local press, and a collection of pornography devoted to bondage and sado-masochism.

Lewis indicated that he was prepared to talk to them. He insisted that he had been in Roz Bishop's car at her invitation, that she had instigated their liaison and that she had introduced him to violent sex-and-bondage games. 'It was a rapist-in-the-car fantasy,' he said. The idea had been that he would come to meet her and they would play out the game before coming back to Sheffield. 'She wanted it,' he kept saying. 'She was loving it right until you lot came along.' It may have got a bit out of hand, he conceded eventually. He wasn't familiar with this kind of thing. He'd tried to follow her guidance. That was why he had the pornography, he added, to try and please this older woman with the exotic tastes.

He admitted that he had had sex with Gemma Wishart the night she disappeared. It had been consensual sex. It may have been a bit rough – but that was the way she liked it. Those photographs proved that. They'd met up in Manchester by agreement, and then she'd left to drive, as far as he knew, back to Sheffield. He didn't know anything about her death. He'd heard rumours that she'd been working as a prostitute, and he'd assumed that was how she had met her end. It was nothing to do with him.

As Farnham laid the evidence in front of him, he began to show signs of tension for the first time. 'You're supposed to stop this!' he burst out at his solicitor at one point.

Wearily, the solicitor asked for a break, but Lewis interrupted him. 'I don't want a fucking break!' he shouted. 'I want to go home!' He looked at Farnham. 'You're treating me like some kind of pervert, some kind of rapist!'

He claimed to know nothing about trafficking. Holbrook might have cut a few corners bringing people over. 'The law makes a market,' he said. 'It's like drugs. If you make a market, someone will use it.' He confirmed that Gemma had approached Holbrook about Oksana Ilbekov. 'She gave him the tape and asked him if he could help this woman come across on one of his exchange schemes. Her parents were dead, she was some kind of Eskimo or something – up to her neck in reindeer shit. If Marcus was involved in anything dodgy, then she would have been perfect.'

He looked at Farnham. 'If she wanted to work as a prostitute, it was nothing to do with me! Gemma Wishart told him

336

about her and gave him the tape. Silly sod went ape about it. And he kept the tape. Stupid shit.' When Farnham showed him the cutting about Katya's death, the cutting that had been found among his possessions, he looked unsure for a moment, then shrugged. 'She ran away. Holbrook was worried people might think . . . you know.' When she had been found dead in the Humber Estuary, it had been a relief, until Gemma turned up asking questions. 'I told Holbrook he ought to destroy that tape,' Lewis told them. 'Or Gemma could do her forensic linguistic thing – match the voices. I thought he'd got rid of it. Holbrook said he'd got it covered. But he needed some help.'

He'd broken into Gemma's flat and stolen her tapes along with her sound system to make it look as though the tapes were just a random casualty. He'd broken into Luke Hagan's as well. He wasn't able to account for that so easily. 'It seemed right at the time,' he said. He'd got the code for the answering machine in case it came in useful. It had seemed like a good idea to plant evidence that Gemma was working as an escort. 'I put it everywhere I could think of,' he said. 'Just in case she tried to get Holbrook into trouble. Then no one would listen to her,' he said.

'Why plant evidence,' Farnham said, 'if she was working as a prostitute anyway? You just said she was,' he added.

Lewis looked sullen for a moment. 'I wanted to make sure people would know,' he said. 'They don't understand what women like Gemma are all about. I just wanted to make sure.'

It would all have worked, he suggested, if Holbrook hadn't kept the tape on the archive. He hadn't known that, he said, until Roz Bishop had found it. 'I was keeping an eye on things,' he said. 'But I didn't plan for Holbrook being such a stupid shit. So that was that,' he said. 'It was business, pure and simple.'

Farnham asked him about Angel Escorts. Lewis shook his head. 'I made them up,' he said. For the first time, he looked nervous, uncertain. 'I just needed a name, you know? There's no Angel Escorts.' He looked round the room. 'It was all business,' he insisted.

Hull, March

It hadn't been business for Sean Lewis, Lynne thought just over three weeks later, as she put together the paperwork to complete the final link between Katya, dead in the Humber Estuary, and Oksana, the young student gone missing in Ekaterinburg. It hadn't been business at all. Gemma had certainly represented a danger to him. But if all he had wanted was Gemma dead, Lynne was certain he could have arranged it so that no police investigation, or no murder investigation, was ever involved. Suppose Gemma had simply vanished? Suppose she had died in a car accident, an unwitnessed hit and run? Suppose she had died of a drugs overdose? Lynne often wondered how many of the deaths that happened every day were unrecognized murders.

The computer taken from his flat contained some interesting files, concealed from a casual observer. There was hard-core pornography, photographs devoted to the extremes of bondage and the infliction of humiliation and pain. There were also a series of doctored pictures of Gemma, put together in a narrative sequence, starting with the bondage picture of her on the bed with her arms pulled above her head, moving through the sequences of calculated sadism that the other images showed, and ending with the image of her body sprawled in the bath. There was the start of a similar sequence for Roz Bishop that began with a photograph of her sleeping – lying on a bed with her arms flung out, the sheet pulled away from her breasts – and moved on to a series of pictures of her on the same bed with Luke Hagan. Lynne wondered what Lewis had planned for the final picture.

Matthew Pearse remained pleasant and co-operative. He was a model inmate at the remand centre, using his out-of-cell time to counsel other inmates and, on some occasions, staff. He told Farnham what he knew about Anna, about her fear of a man called 'Angel'. Pearse told them about Anna's belief that she had killed Angel's friend, her flight to the advice centre and the help he'd given her. Someone else had come looking for Anna, he told them, a couple of weeks after he'd found her a place to live and work at the hotel. A young man, twenty-ish, fair. 'He had a cut on his face,' Pearse said. 'Here.' He gestured towards his eyebrow. 'I didn't know then about Anna's troubles, but I didn't tell him anything.'

He had been concerned, he told them, when he had seen the man near the Blenheim a couple of weeks later. Pearse had kept a discreet eye on Anna, but as time went on and nothing happened, he decided that the man meant no harm and left it. 'It was safer if I had no contact with Anna,' he said. Farnham showed him a photograph of Sean Lewis. Pearse nodded. 'That is the man,' he said.

Lynne remembered the dedication with which Sean Lewis had pointed the investigation towards the name Angel Escorts. He now claimed that the name was fictitious, but according to Pearse, Anna had run away from a man called Angel. If that had, somehow, been known to Lewis, then leaving Gemma's body in the hotel where Anna worked, leaving the business card . . . perhaps calculating that Anna would recognize the name at once, and tell the police as soon as the body was reported. She might have been able to take them to Angel Escorts, and the police would break up an operation that, presumably, was in strong competition with the business that Holbrook and Lewis – no matter how much Lewis might deny it – were setting up together. But Anna's terror of either Angel or the police had made her destroy the scene and run. Like so many of Lewis' plans, it was over-clever, over-complicated and it had gone wrong.

There was one thing that puzzled Lynne. Lewis had come looking for Anna months before Oksana died, long before Gemma would have been digging round in Holbrook's archive, dangerously near to identifying Oksana Ilbekov, and, therefore, the people who had kidnapped her. Why had he been looking for Anna? A puzzle. Lynne shelved it for later thought.

Anna Krleza was a silent figure in the detention facility for illegal immigrants. Her status as a refugee was ambiguous. Her family had been traced to a village in Kosovo. Her father was Albanian and her mother was Roma. The family had vanished during the turbulence of the NATO action. No one knew, or no one would say, what had happened to them, but the house was a burnt-out ruin and the walls were daubed with graffiti about gypsies and witches. An argument was being conducted around her. The immigration authorities and the Home Office said she was exaggerating her condition so that she would be allowed to stay in a country she had, after all, entered illegally. She was Roma, and there was a massive surge in bogus asylum claims from gypsies who said they were being persecuted. Her family were probably fine – these people didn't stay in one place. Anna Krleza should be repatriated.

The Refugee Council said that Anna was a victim of crime, not a perpetrator, and as a result of the crimes committed against her needed treatment that would not be available to her if she was sent back.

Farnham had gone to see Anna her while she was still in the main hospital, undergoing tests to see if there was any unidentified damage that was causing her continuing silence. He had, with a doctor in attendance, showed her a photograph of Sean Lewis. For a moment, the pale, withdrawn face had flashed into terror, then the blank closeness had come back and she had not reacted again. Anna would go wherever she was told do go, do whatever she was asked to do, but her eyes were blank and dead. When Lynne looked at her mute face, she felt again the responsibility of the hours she had lost.

Angel Escorts, now Lynne's first priority, had vanished as if it had never existed.

There was a knock on her door, and Roy Farnham came in looking a bit wary. Their contacts had been strictly professional since the Sunday he had pulled Nasim Rafiq in for questioning. 'I've got some news,' he said after a moment. Lynne waited. 'Rafiq,' he said. 'They're going to let it go, Immigration.'

Lynne was surprised. 'They aren't going to charge her?'

He shook his head. 'She was acting under duress. She

co-operated with the investigation in the end. She collected evidence and passed it on. The notes in the textbook,' he added. 'They found the guy who's been doing the passports.'

'But she'd been concealing evidence,' Lynne said. 'I didn't think they'd budge.'

Farnham shrugged. 'Let's say it's politically expedient to show a human face just at the moment.' He was referring to the backlash from the recent wave of racist attacks on the Afghan asylum seekers. 'Pearse's brief is going for unfit to plead. He'll probably get it. And we're no nearer clearing up Holbrook's death. No forensics. *One* of them did it, and my money's on Lewis, but pinning it on him . . .' He looked discouraged.

Lynne was inclined to believe Pearse's denial. He had admitted the other killings without hesitation – though maybe Holbrook's murder didn't fit so easily into his philosophy of death and redemption. Lewis had seemed genuinely shocked when he heard about Holbrook's death, and had asked for a break in the interview. He was being remanded in custody and, after that day, he had asked to be isolated from the other prisoners. 'You're treating me like a rapist,' he said. 'They might do something.'

Farnham was looking uncharacteristically hesitant. 'I know . . .' he said. Then he stopped and began again. 'Do you want to go for a drink tonight?' he said. 'Or sometime?'

Lynne didn't trust Farnham. He'd used her professionally, become her lover privately, and had ruthlessly kept those worlds completely separate. It was all ambivalences. Clearly, for him, the job came first. As it did for her. It was difficult. It was impossible. She didn't trust him. But the sex had been amazing.

'I can't stand the town pubs,' she said. 'You owe me dinner.'

'OK,' he said. He smiled. 'There's a decent place just down the road from me. I'll pick you up – eight?'

'OK,' she said. She met his eyes. 'This time – definitely – no shop.'

Hull, March

Anna sat very still, very quiet. It was gone now, the pain in her hands and the ache and stiffness of bruises, the cold, light-headedness of her fever. And now, she found that she could sleep. Or if not sleep, at least not wake up, just let in a peripheral awareness of her surroundings, a chair, a bed, footsteps and voices – things that she didn't have to worry about any more. She was walking in the forest. The trees were autumnal now. The leaves were a deep gold in the late summer sun. Anna knew these woods well, the paths that wound through the deep glades, the place where the stream trickled down over the rocks, the water spraying into a rainbow in the diffused light, the paths where she used to walk with her father, the paths where she used to take Krisha to play among the trees.

There were paths in the forest she was learning to avoid, paths that led to the smell of burning, paths that led to the sound of water dripping in the silence. Sometimes the voices spoke to her, over and over again. *Anna? Anna? I need you to tell me . . .*

Ms Krleza, you are not helping yourself by . . . Ms Krleza . . . ? Again and again.

But Anna had found a safe place, the only safe place, a place that no one could take her away from. She wasn't coming back.

23

Shetland Islands, September

It was a long journey, but Lynne had ten days and took it easy. The case was effectively over. Matthew Pearse's plea of insanity had been accepted by the DPP. Sean Lewis was dead. He had hanged himself in his cell. He had given no indication of suicidal intent, and had left no note, but the circumstances seemed unequivocal. He had been found one morning hanging from his bedframe. The cell door had been locked. Lynne had shared Farnham's sense of frustration, of things unaccounted for, but the coroner's verdict was clear.

Lynne took the train to Aberdeen and the overnight ferry to Lerwick. In the morning, she was on the Shetland Islands, driving north to Toft to pick up the ferry to Yell. Yell was bleak, the centre desolate moorland, the shore rocky and barren. She pushed north and further north to Gutcher. There, she caught the ferry to Unst, her destination. She looked at the package on the seat beside her.

It was incongruous, a carrier bag and a large plastic container – an urn, the undertaker had called it. It was industrial green with a black screw lid; a utilitarian receptacle for what came out of the crematorium furnace. Oksana's people were poor. Her parents were dead. She had no close family. She had been, as Sean Lewis had said, *perfect*. Her ashes were to be disposed of where she had died.

Lynne had undertaken to fulfil that request. Oksana had died in an underground tomb. She wouldn't have wanted her ashes scattered in Matthew Pearse's 'church' to mingle with the dust and the damp until the demolition squads

343

moved in. Her body had been found in the Humber Estuary. Those polluted waters seemed a sad place to lie. But the North Sea – that was different. Lynne had looked at the map. If she went to the most northerly of the Shetland Islands, Unst, she could scatter Oksana's ashes there. She had traced the seas beyond Shetland, the seas beyond the north. To the east was the Barents Sea, and east again was the Kara Sea. She was being quixotic, but she had a vision of Oksana's ashes carried on the currents and drifting until they met the place where the waters of the Yenisei River joined the icy wastes of the Kara Sea, and Oksana's journey would be over.

She left the main road now, following the B road to the wide Voe of Burrafirth. She parked the car and lifted the heavy bag. She would have to walk from here. Ahead of her, she could see the cliff edge, and beyond it, the sea. The land was empty, and though the sky was blue and cloudless, the air was cold. There was a small building by the path ahead of her, low and stone-built, surrounded by a drystone wall. She wondered if it was an outbuilding, the remains of a croft, or maybe a warden's cottage for the nature reserve of Herma Ness. But it looked too small, too bleak to be inhabited. As she got nearer, adjusting the awkward weight in her arms, she saw that there was someone standing in the doorway watching her.

It was a woman. Something about her dress and her stance said *old woman*. Her head was covered in a heavy black shawl. Her face was brown and weathered, and her dark eyes watched Lynne impassively. Lynne took a breath to say, 'Good afternoon,' but before she could speak, a dog raced out of the door behind the woman and barked, its teeth bared, its ears laid back. Lynne looked at the dog. It was large, black, of indeterminate breed. It stood in the gateway on guard, barking and threatening to advance. She nodded politely to the woman, and walked past, keeping her pace steady, avoiding the eyes of the vigilant dog, but she was aware of the two of them watching her as she crossed the green heathland towards the clifftop and the distant sea.

The cliffs of Herma Ness were sheer, and Lynne looked at

the rocks hundreds of feet below, the sea blue and crumpled, flecks of white dancing across the surface as the water surged and fell against the cliff face. She knelt on the edge with the wind behind her and unscrewed the black lid of the urn. She tipped it slowly, and the fine grey ash fell in a stream. The wind caught it and scattered it through the air as it fell, dispersing it into a grey cloud and then invisibility. Lynne sat on the clifftop for a while, looking north at the endless sea where it merged with the sky in the misty distance.

Night came later here, but the land was already in shadow as she walked back along the path towards her car. She must have missed her way somehow, because she didn't pass the stone building again, with the old woman and the dog. Her car was a silhouette on the road when she reached it. She put the empty urn on the seat and turned back for a last look at the sea. Then she drove south towards the light, leaving the shadowlands behind her.